Shield of the Rising Sun

PATH OF NEMESIS BOOK III

# SHIELD
## OF THE
# RISING
# SUN

## ADAM LOFTHOUSE

LUME BOOKS

LUME BOOKS

First published in 2020 by Lume Books
30 Great Guildford Street,
Borough, SE1 0HS

ISBN 978-1-83901-197-9

Typeset using Atomik ePublisher from Easypress Technologies

www.lumebooks.co.uk

# Other books by Adam Lofthouse

*Path of Nemesis:*
*The Centurion's Son*
*War in the Wilderness*

*Oathbreaker*

*For Ralph*
*With all my love*

# PROLOGUE

**Spring, 172 AD**
**Egypt**

Senator Avidius Cassius sweated profusely under the high sun. It was not yet April, but already the heat was so intense, his toga was drenched in sweat. He cursed, once more adjusting his robes, trying in vain to prevent the wet patch on his back from rubbing his skin. 'Gods above,' he muttered under his breath, not wanting to let his discomfort show in front of the marching legionaries, all cased in armour. Four slaves trotted alongside his horse, each holding a wooden post attached to a giant sheet of fabric which formed a makeshift shade for the senator and his bald head. He had allowed himself that one small comfort, at least.

'Legate, how much further to Alexandria?' Cassius asked in a voice he hoped did not carry a whining tone.

'No more than four hours, Senator. Would you like to call a halt? We could all do with a rest, sir,' Legate Marcus Aquilla replied. Aquilla was Cassius' man through and through. He commanded the Twenty-Sixth Flavia Firma, a legion originally formed by the emperor Vespasian one hundred years or more before. He had served Cassius for over eight years, fighting under him in the Parthian Wars, where we had won himself great acclaim as a tribune for his steadfast leadership. Cassius had sent for him and his men from Samosata, where they had been based, after he had been given the extraordinary title of *Rector Orientis,* giving him complete power over the eastern provinces and their armies.

The reason for that complete power was about to become apparent.

Cassius made to reply to the legate when a piercing scream stopped him in his tracks. They were travelling west, and to their front was a small settlement that spread to either side of the cobbled road. Aquilla had sent scouts into the settlement, but they had reported it to be deserted, nothing but derelict one-room houses made of mud and clay. The cry came from the north and was quickly followed by a cacophony of noise as hundreds of scantily dressed men, armed with nothing but spears, streamed from between the buildings.

'Jupiter, have mercy!' Cassius exclaimed as a fresh wave of sweat cascaded down his face. He stared in panic as the mass of armed men moved closer to the column of legionaries who were looking anxiously to their centurions for orders.

Aquilla saw the shock and indecision on his commander's face and moved quickly to form his men. 'First century, get into line! Shields up, men! Shields up! Second century to their right and the third to their left. Varo, you're in charge here, get the rest of your cohort formed up behind them and repel that attack!'

Varo, the *primus pilus,* or first spear centurion, nodded before issuing a string of orders himself in a gravel-filled voice that had dominated many a battlefield.

'Razin, on me now!' Aquilla barked to the commander of the cavalry auxiliary *vexillation* that accompanied the Twenty-Sixth. 'Split your men into two wings, and get on our flanks. I want you to box those bastards in, leave them nowhere to go but onto the point of our swords. No heroics – do not, under any circumstances, get yourself killed, understood?' The Moorish cavalry commander nodded and swivelled his mount away, off to relay his orders to his men.

Aquilla cursed under his breath. He had just 120 cavalrymen under his command; he had a feeling he would have great need of them in the months to come, and he did not want to lose them all here.

'Sir,' he said, turning to Cassius, who was still looking, open-mouthed, at the charging Egyptians. 'Sir, I suggest you move back down the column, it's going to get a little hot up here.'

Cassius took two deep breaths as he struggled to regain his composure. He had led armies to victory against the Parthians, had won himself much honour and advancement in those wars. By all the gods, he was a pro-consul of Rome! He was not going to let a bunch of barbarian farmers be the end of him.

'Absolutely not, Legate. I am the supreme commander of all Rome's armies in the east. I am the man that took Artaxata from the Parthians, I shall stay where I am.' He nodded to Aquilla, giving conviction to his words.

'Very well, sir,' Aquilla nodded, musing that such an answer was to be expected from a man of Cassius' stature. The legate stayed beside the proconsul as the Egyptian rebels hit the shields of the first century with an almighty thud. Varo had not had time to order his men to throw their *pila,* and now, they used the long-weighted javelins as spears to devastating effect. Not one rebel in their front rank survived the headlong charge onto the *scutums,* the legionaries' large rectangular shields doing their jobs well.

Aquilla pushed his mount forward so he was just four ranks from the front. He jumped in both surprise and fear as a spear flew past his face, so close, he felt the rush of breeze, even if he did not see the fearsome iron point. He hefted his shield from the left side of his saddle and drew his sword, steering the mount with his knees. He forced himself deeper into the ranks of the Twenty-Sixth, eager to wet his blade. He was almost amongst the men at the front when a firm hand grabbed his bridle and steered the horse from its path. 'Without being rude, sir,' centurion Varo said, 'your bleedin' horse is right in my men's way, and I think we could all do without losing our legate today, don't you, sir?'

Aquilla smiled at the man's words. He was yet to fight an engagement as a Legate of Rome; it would have been perfectly acceptable to join the fighting as a tribune, but a legate should stay away, always be in control of the battle.

He backed away, his eyes never leaving the maelstrom to his front. He saw, with satisfaction, that Razin had formed up his cavalry to either side of the Roman line and was, even now, charging into the fray. The Moorish cavalry wore very little armour and carried small, round shields. Their main weapon was a lance, similar to the *pila* used by the legions but longer and heavier. Aquilla himself had tried to wield one from horseback just a few months before, when he had first met Razin and his men on the road to Egypt. He had been unable to ride and hold the heavy lance in just one hand; he marvelled at the strength the auxiliaries possessed.

Even as he watched, Razin led his men from the front, and with the first lunge of his lance, he ran one man straight through the chest, the point exploding from the rebel's back to hit the man behind him in the side. One thrust, two kills.

On the left wing, the second cavalry squadron had also charged, and Aquilla noted with envy that his young senior tribune, Valerius Sulla, was leading them deep into the ranks of the rebels.

Aquilla shrugged his jealousy aside and tried to slow his breathing. He counted to thirty and felt his racing heartbeat subside to a normal rhythm. His men were doing more than hold their own, he noted, they were advancing now at a steady pace. Varo's booming voice could be heard over the tumult of battle; 'Step, push, step, push!' Step by bloody step, the rebels were being forced back. Aquilla craned his head and looked into the small town. More and more men were appearing from between the buildings, but they had nowhere to go.

Turning, Aquilla looked back down the road where the rest of his legion was standing, impudent in the scorching sun. He scanned the ground to his column's left and saw a small path that snaked through dense woodland. He paused a moment, stewing on his decision. They were at the western edge of the Nile Delta now. For the last two days, they had been travelling through land that was rich and fertile, fed by the numerous branches of the great Nile that funnelled through Egypt to the Mediterranean Sea. The river was, though, unpredictable. Solid ground could be flooded in a heartbeat; they had almost been cut off from the rear four cohorts of the legion just the day before, as the river rose like a demon from the underworld coming to swallow its prey.

He looked back to the front. As he turned his horse, the smell of combat invaded his senses, and the tang of blood in the air burnt the hairs of his nostrils. Looking into the town, he saw a man with wild grey hair, standing atop a house, urging the rebels into battle. Decision made, he turned back and rode a short distance down the column to the second cohort, passing Cassius without so much as a glance.

'Centurion Decanus, well met,' he said. 'Get your men down that track, follow it and see if it loops around into the town. If it does, do not hesitate, take them in the flank.'

Decanus saluted and turned to his men without a word. He had been in the legions for nearly twenty years, a centurion for over ten. He had commanded the second cohort since just after Aquilla had taken over the legion, and he thought the man sensible and reliable.

Aquilla watched as the second cohort marched off at the double, men loosening swords from their scabbards and fitting helmets even as they ran. He rode back down the column. The waiting men from the rear centuries of the first cohort were drinking water and readying *pila*, preparing for the signal that would initiate the order to rotate, where they would then replace their comrades at the front.

'Where are they going, Legate?' Cassius asked as he came within earshot. He was pointing back down the column at the gap left by the second cohort.

'There is a track that leads into the Delta, looks as though it loops back around somewhere either in the town or on the other side. If we can outflank them or hit them in the rear, then it's over, sir,' he said, knowing full well what was coming next.

'I should have been consulted before you made a decision like that, *Legate!* I am the supreme commander of all the emperor's forces in the east! You cannot just send my men off into some swamp without consulting *me* first!'

Aquilla bit his tongue and tried to keep the annoyance from his face. *In case you hadn't noticed 'Supreme Commander', we are under attack by thousands of blood-crazed rebels, and if I hadn't taken the initiative whilst you were busy shitting your breeches, then we would most likely be dead already!* 'Yes, sir, sorry, sir, it will not happen again, sir.' He left his commander without another word, not trusting himself to hold his tongue.

The Twenty-Sixth had already pushed the rebels back into the town and were holding their line at the edge of the first buildings. Varo quickly told him he had been wary of entering the town for fear of being flanked and his men being lost in the honeycomb alleyways that were shadowed by every house. Aquilla agreed and was about to issue fresh orders when the second cohort streamed from the alleys to the south. The legions left and hit the flank of the rebels with the force of a tidal wave. *Pila* whistled through the air, and the wet crunch and spray of blood, when they found their targets, made Aquilla squirm even as he rejoiced.

'Push on into the town!' he ordered Varo before letting his impatience get the better of him. He forced his mount through the throng of legionaries and gave her his heels as they freed themselves from the press. Hauling his sword from its scabbard, he whooped with joy as he galloped amongst the terrified rebels. The first sweep of his blade took off the top of a man's head; with his second lunge, he bit deep into the shoulder of another. The rebels were in full flight now, their resolve dissipating like a spring thaw once they realised they had been outflanked.

Razin sped past him at the gallop, he too whooping with joy as he left his lance in one rebel's chest and drew his sword and sliced it across another's back in one fluid motion. The rest of the Moorish cavalry raced after their commander. Aquilla noted with relief that Tribune Sulla was still with them. He was good friends with the boy's father, and the father was also a prominent member of the senate; it would do Aquilla's advancement no good if the lad were to be killed whilst under his command.

Aquilla slowed his mount to a walk, the sudden adrenalin rush of battle now receding. More and more legionaries filed past him, Varo desperately trying to keep them in order. Aquilla had seen first-hand in the east what happened when a legion was allowed to run riot – it wasn't pretty. Even after eight years, the scenes after the capture of Artaxata still haunted his dreams. 'Varo, form the men back into column and bring me a report of the losses as soon as you can,' he ordered as he dismounted.

Cassius pulled up beside him and struggled down from his horse. Aquilla noticed with amusement that he had left his four slaves and his shade behind. 'Gods below,' the proconsul muttered as he fiddled with his robes, 'how hard it is indeed to maintain some level of decorum when out in the field.'

'Indeed, sir,' Aquilla said with a tight smile. He turned from his commander to hide his amusement, wiping his sword clean on the hem of his tunic. 'Varo will bring us the butcher's bill shortly. What are your orders?'

But Cassius was already walking off. The dead and dying littered the streets of the abandoned, nameless town. The stench was horrific, and he used the sleeve of his toga to cover his nose. He stepped over the body of a man who had died cradling the remains of his severed intestines. Black blood welled from the deep gash in the rebel's stomach, and yet again Cassius cursed the dogged heat. He had walked many a battlefield in the moments after victory had been won; summer always made the vile stink richer. He did not think he would ever get used to it.

Overhead, carrion birds squawked to each other, already eager to begin their feast. He pondered that he had seen no birds on their two-day journey through the Nile Delta, and he wondered how they had managed to locate the field of battle so quickly. Aquilla marched up behind him and reported the legion had lost thirty men, another fifty injured. The Moorish cavalry had suffered six casualties, and a further four men were likely to succumb to their wounds, but Cassius barely listened.

He thought of the job ahead and of the wild old man that had been haranguing the rebels from atop the very building he now stood next to. Isidorus was his name, if Cassius was not mistaken, and he was the man who had driven these peasants to rebellion. Fed up with rising taxes and more and more of the vast quantities of Egyptian grain being shipped off to Rome to feed the plebs, he had whipped his people into action. In one bold move, they had defeated the Second Traiana legion in open battle, presumably swarming them with their superior numbers. The Second, Cassius knew, had been grossly undermanned, as was every other legion across the empire. The great plague that had cursed the lands around the Mediterranean showed no sign of slowing down. Many men, he knew, even went as far as to blame him for the thousands and thousands of deaths since he had taken the city of Seleucia, a conquest which had proved to be the last of that great campaign.

First, his men had complained of a high temperature, then the sweating and vomiting had begun. In each case, it was followed swiftly by large puss-filled boils sprouting without warning all over their fever-racked bodies. At the end, blood poured from swollen ears, oozed from noses and mouths, and the victims died in silent agony. The smell of death had lingered long in his nostrils, the taste to this day still fouled his tongue. Instructions from the emperor himself had reached even as far as the eastern provinces: all bodies were to be burnt. The emperor's personal physician, Galen, claimed that the remains of the deceased could still infect the living, even from ten feet under the ground. The pyres had been both awe-inspiring and awful.

Cassius, of course, knew it to be no fault of his own. How, in the name of all the gods, could he have brought this great plague on Rome and her people? It had not been the curse from some priest at the high temple of Apollo, as he knew full well was whispered in taverns across the breadth of the empire. It was nothing more than rotten luck. He had been lucky his reputation had survived it. It was not the emperor he had to thank for that or even the recently deceased caesar, Lucius Verus, who had been the commander of that doomed strike into the far deserts of the east. It had been the empress Faustina who had saved him.

It must be ten years, almost to the month, that Faustina had taken Cassius to her bed. By all accounts, her husband, the Divine Marcus Aurelius, was not much of a lover. Too reserved, too *stoic*. His imperial majesty would much rather spend his nights at his desk, studying the many documents of imperial correspondence that were thrust his way by his clerks, or setting stylus to tablet and recording the many *philosophical* thoughts that whirled around his complex mind.

*His loss is my gain,* Cassius thought with a wry grin as he allowed himself to think of her curves, the pale skin that was soft to touch. He felt his loins stir and quickly shook his head free of lurid thoughts. *Get yourself together, man, you have a campaign to run!*

But once more, his thoughts turned back to his lover. She had sent him a letter. It had arrived with his official appointment as supreme commander of the east and his orders to travel to Egypt with all haste and put down the rebellion. The letter had read that the health of the Divine Augustus was ailing and that his wife feared he was not long for this world. Their only surviving son, Commodus, was just a child. Who would take the throne if Aurelius died? And what would become of her?

Fear, Cassius knew, would be rife among those of the imperial family.

Just the previous winter, a coup to topple the emperor had been uncovered in Pannonia. A soothsayer, by the name of Alexander of Abonoteichos, had plotted to kill the stoic fool and drape himself in the purple. Aurelius, true to nature, had seized all of his personal correspondence and burnt it before it could be read. Cassius was very thankful that he had.

He had been a staunch supporter of Alexander from the first, winning him support in the senate as well as securing the allegiance of the eastern legions. Well, nearly all of them. There were two in Cappadocia that had refused the bribes he had offered, but plans had been in place to have them dealt with. Indeed, Alexander's own father-in-law had been a governor in the east. He had been exiled, the only man of senatorial rank to suffer any kind of punishment. Long had it been the policy of the Divine Marcus to completely rule out men of senatorial standing to suffer the ignominy of death, nor would he order them to take their own lives. *One of the man's policies I can actually support.*

Cassius had never intended to follow through with his support for the soothsayer. Alexander had just been a pawn in a bigger game. Cassius wanted the old conman to rid the emperor from his path. With that accomplished, he would march on Rome with *his* eastern legions, men who had fought the Parthians with *him,* and men that would be loyal to only *him.* But Alexander had allowed himself to be discovered by the dreaded *frumentarii.* He had grown sloppy, too confident, and paid for it with his life. Cassius would not make the same mistakes.

Aurelius would die soon, that was certain. When he did, Cassius would march on Rome at the head of an army and claim the throne by force. Commodus was too young, and only once in Rome's illustrious history had a father been succeeded by his son. It would not happen now, not if he had anything to do with it. Commodus would have to die, of course, along with the rest of the imperial family, Faustina included.

*But first, to crush this rebellion.* Becoming the man that pacified Egypt and ensured the grain ships kept flowing to Rome would win him favour with both the senate and the plebs. Aurelius had done him great honour in giving him this task, this responsibility. *If only the old fool knew he was signing his son's death warrant.* He smiled once more, looking up into the deep, blue sky. One day, he would rule the greatest empire that the sky had ever seen. What more could a man want from life?

'Orders, sir?' Aquilla asked.

Cassius had no notion of how long the legate had been lingering at his side. Trying not to appear flustered, he forced himself to think. 'These rebels have already beaten one legion in open battle. By all accounts, the Second Traiana is down to fewer than a thousand men and will not leave their fortress in Alexandria. We cannot allow the same to happen to us.'

'So, what do we do?' Aquilla said with a raised eyebrow.

'What we do, my dear legate, is take their greatest strength and make it their weakness,' Cassius said. He gestured with his arms to the vast swathes of marshland south of the town. He sighed at Aquilla's frown. 'The land, dear man, the land! We use it to our advantage. The river cuts through in so many places that the islands that have formed in between its flowing waters are small, and one never knows how long that land will stay above the waterline from one day to the next. They cannot keep all their numbers in one place, there simply isn't enough dry ground.

'So, we use that to our advantage. We commandeer as many river craft as we can, pack them full of our men and take down this Isidorus and his band of followers one small group at a time. It will not be quick and at times, will be frustrating. But that, my dear man, is the way to do it.'

Cassius allowed himself a satisfied smile. He breathed deeply, careless of the stink of drying blood and open bowels. 'Come, Aquilla. We have work to do, and all for the glory of Rome.'

# PART I

# BATTLE ON THE ICE

# CHAPTER I

**Twenty-one years later, January, 193 AD**
**Carnuntum, Pannonia**

'The emperor is dead!.'

It is shouted from every street corner, from every vendor in the forum and by all the drunks in the tavern across the street. The emperor is dead. Four words that change so much for him.

He sits in the shadow of the open window. The wind carries tiny particles of ice in its gale and when he breathes in deeply through his mouth, he feels those particles stinging the base of his throat. He pays it no heed.

The emperor is dead. War will come. That's what the vendors are shouting from their stalls in the forum. They brave the snow and hailstorms every day, hustling their wares to the unsuspecting people of the city, each man desperate to earn enough coin to keep their family warm and fed through this darkest of seasons.

He looks from the window of the second-storey apartment that has been such a comfort to him and yet remains so unfamiliar. It was his first home, his mother's apartment when she had carried him through childhood, twenty-one years ago now. *Twenty-one. What do I have to show for it?*

On the small straw cot that serves as his bed is an off-white tunic waiting to be worn. Military issue ox-hide boots sit next to the cot. He knows if he reaches down and picks them up, the leather will be rough and coarse, the hobnails on the sole still sharp, and the iron will glimmer in the winter's grey light. He doesn't. He can't.

Twenty-one. Most men his age are already proven in their profession. They have their own small home and a wife and children to warm it. He has neither. The legions were where he was supposed to find his home, his place in the world, or so everyone had told him.

How could he not be immediately at home in armour, after all? Was he not the son of a legend, who was, in turn, the son of the most famous centurion the Fourteenth Gemina Martia Victrix Legion had ever produced? He would walk through the great wooden gates of the fortress just to the east of Carnuntum, the smell of dusty leather, horse sweat and excrement wafting through his nostrils, and at once, he would know that this is where he was destined to be, this is where he belonged.

Except it hadn't quite worked out that way. Five years previously, he had walked through those very gates, had sniffed the putrid air, looked into the eyes of the hard-bitten soldiers who practised their craft with wooden swords on practice posts and seen no warmth there, no sense of belonging or even any desire to belong.

His father had been a soldier, his grandfather had before him. But nowhere is it written that the son has to tread the father's path.

'Are you brooding again?' He has not heard the old man shuffle into the apartment. He turns, a rueful grin fixing his thin lips. It seems age has done nothing to dampen the man's skill set.

'Brooding? Me? Now when have I ever been known to do that? How are you, Uncle? You should be wearing a thicker cloak, it is freezing.' He stands and moves across the creaking floorboards. They have not been changed in his lifetime, those floorboards. They bend and curve as the weather slowly rots them, but he will keep them till they grow so weak he falls straight through. He has a strange attachment to them; they are one of the few things left in the world that link him to his parents. On the back of the apartment's crooked old front door hangs a thick blue cloak that he bought a few days previously with the last of his coin. He wraps it around the old man's shoulders.

'I have no need for that,' the old man wheezes in a voice that is growing more and more to resemble a crow's squawk. 'Shutter that window and light some candles, that will soon get some heat into these old bones.'

Calvus has been old for as long as he can remember. He has vague memories of the old Briton from when he was just a toddler, scampering across these very floorboards. It hurts him, as they always do, the memories. What hurts him more is the continued affection the old man still gives him, all Calvus still does for him, despite what happened. Despite the heart-wrenching agony he has caused him. *It was all my fault. Meredith, Marcus. All my fault.*

He lights the candles, four of them, dotted around the one-room apartment. The light they give off is weak, but no worse than that provided by the slate-grey sky. They glow as the flames strengthen, and a warm light basks the room.

'Got any food?' Calvus asks as he lowers himself awkwardly onto the straw cot.

'No,' he replies. 'I spent the last of my coin on that cloak.'

Calvus grunts and pulls the cloak tighter around him. 'Nice cloak,' he says, admiring the fur-trimmed collar. 'But you need to eat, lad.'

'I'll eat, Uncle. You don't need to worry about me.'

'So you keep saying, young Faustus. But I do worry about you. You are all I have now on this godforsaken earth. I shall worry about you until the day I rise to heaven and meet our Lord himself.'

'*Your* Lord, Uncle,' Faustus says with a petulant pout. 'I shall never understand your obsession with your god or his supposed son who died on the cross.'

'Watch your blasphemy around me, boy. Do not take our Lord's name in vain.'

Faustus smiles. Despite his bitter feelings towards the old man's religion, the smile is full of warmth and love. 'Sorry, Uncle. I do hope you do not expect *me* to die for my sins,' he adds with a wink.

'I fear you are destined for the fires of hell, dear boy. But I hope not for many years yet.'

'War is coming, have you heard?'

Calvus nods. He studies his hands for a moment as he composes his next words. 'What are you planning to do?'

'Me? Nothing.'

Calvus sighs. Faustus sees the disappointment in the Briton's eyes. He feels the familiar guilt rising in his torso, trying to drown him in self-pity.

'You know, of course, what it is I believe you should do.' This is not a question, merely a statement. There has been many a talk in the last six years about what it is Faustus should do. He is not prepared for another. Not now.

'I am no soldier, Uncle. We've been through this a thousand times already.'

'It is in your blood.'

'It is not! I think that was made perfectly clear to everyone the night I did nothing to prevent two murde—'

He tries to cut off, to shut down his voice before he says it. He fails. 'I'm sorry,' he says with a sigh. 'I should not have mentioned that.'

'It was not your fault then, Faustus, and it is not your fault now. There was nothing you could have done to save them, nothing anyone could have done. Do not let that one bad event form the basis of your life, haunt your every dream.'

'My father would have saved them,' Faustus says. Tears cloud his crystal-blue eyes so they shimmer in the dim glow of the candles' light. *My father was the best of men. A hero of Rome. How can I ever emerge from his shadow?*

Calvus laughs. It is a dry wheeze, and he erupts into a coughing fit which causes him to double over. Faustus steps across the room and leans out an arm in support. Calvus brushes him away. 'You know not of what you speak, dear boy. When I first met your father, he would have run away at the first sight of men with bared knives. You stood your ground; no man can ask for more than that.'

Faustus studies his feet to hide his blush. He sits once more on the window ledge, his back against the wooden shutter. As it always does when he thinks of that dark night, the scar just above his left hip burns. He closes his eyes and relives the moment the knife tore through his flesh. He remembers screaming before the pain hit, then collapsing in a heap when it did. After that, there is nothing but blackness.

'Tell me of him,' Faustus says.

'Huh?' the old Briton replies. He looks tired, Faustus thinks, and wonders if he should be walking him back to his own house instead. But despite his reservations, he asks again.

'You know your father,' Calvus says. 'Why do you need me to speak of him?'

'I want to know what he was like back then. Back when he was new to the legions.'

He watches Calvus, sees once more the tiredness in his eyes, the pain behind them. *What must those eyes have seen in his time in the army? Let alone what they witnessed in the years after.* Faustus knows of Calvus' past. He knows he was a legionary in the Fourteenth Legion. He knows he served with his father and even under his grandfather. He knows also that after the Briton lost the fingers on his left hand, he was discharged from the army and employed as an agent of the *frumentarii.* They are feared, the *frumentarii,* perhaps more by men inside the empire than out of it. They are spies, snitches, seekers of truth, and they will stop at nothing to get it.

'We have spoken of this before. You know of the war with the Germani tribes, the victories, the defeats, the friends lost along the way. I have no wish to retell such stories.' Faustus hears the quiver in the old man's voice. It is faint, disguised by his gruff Latin. He was brought up to speak the tongue of the Britons; he did not begin to learn Latin until he was a man grown. He sees, too, as Calvus raises the stump of his left hand: it is fingerless, nothing but the thumb remains.

'I know, too, the tale of how you cut those fingers off. It was my favourite story when I was a boy,' Faustus says with a forlorn smile.

'To this day, I cannot believe I had the balls to do it! But, it was a unique situation.'

'Stuck halfway up a mountain in the middle of winter, somewhere in Germani territory with just seven men for company? It doesn't *sound* that unique, Uncle,' Faustus says, unable to keep the smile from his voice.

Calvus cackles another dry laugh, and this one does not end in a coughing fit. 'I was there when you were born, you know. Your mother squeezed this very stump as she pushed you out, just down the street there, in the basilica.'

The smile drops from Faustus' face at the mention of his mother. He has never had the opportunity to hug her, to breathe in her scent, to look upon the golden fire of her hair that Calvus can describe so vividly. She is dead, gone from this world. Faustus has never asked Calvus how or why, but he knows the old man has the answers, believes he may have even been with her when it happened, though he has not yet put together all the pieces of the puzzle. If only he could muster the courage to ask.

'You were searching for my mother when you lost your fingers,' Faustus says instead.

'We were. She had been taken, as you know, from the veteran's settlement to the east. She was a slave of the Marcomanni for a while, but she escaped and fled north. She went to lands that even Rome has no names for. Lands where in the summer, the sun doesn't set and in the winter, doesn't rise. Lands dominated by ice and snow. A truly godforsaken place.'

'And yet she came back. You found her.'

'Of a sort. We had some help, a… mutual friend. But yes, she came back, for a time.'

Faustus arches his eyebrows at Calvus' pause, and his words: *mutual friend?*

Before she had died, Calvus' daughter, Meredith, had filled in a lot of the blanks that Calvus left out of his stories. Growing up, Meredith had been the closest he'd had to a mother. Her and her own son, Marcus, had been his family. They had even lived in this very apartment for a time.

'Tell me of what happened after she left,' Faustus says. He thinks he has worked out a way to glean more information from Calvus without having to ask the direct question that is on his mind. If he had asked *why* his mother had suddenly fled Carnuntum just weeks after bearing a son, he knew he would get no answer.

'What do you want to know?' Calvus asks.

Faustus frowns, thinking. *What do I want to know? Everything!* 'What did my father do?'

'Your father? There was not much Albinus could do. He had no notion of where your mother could have gone, and he was a soldier, just promoted to the rank of centurion. He could not just desert the army; they could have crucified him.'

Faustus knows this already, he wants more. 'So, what did he *do*?'

'Well, he fought the Germani, of course. Him and every other soldier on the frontier! I have told you of the battle against the Quadi, have I not? God saved the Fourteenth that day, of that, I have no doubt.'

Faustus laughs. 'The rain miracle? I did not know that was the work of God! Surely, Jupiter invigorated his soldiers with water? Spurring them to victory against the barbarians, no?' He says this only to wind the old man up, who does not take the bait.

'It is one of those battles I wish I had been a part of. There really is nothing like walking from a battlefield with your brothers in arms, tired to the bone, covered in other men's blood but alive and victorious. You would find out yourself if only yo—'

'No games, Uncle! I tire of your badgering. Tell me the story of the "miracle from God" and the battle on the ice! I want to hear about that, too.'

'Ha! So, finally, the boy wants to hear of war, eh? Okay, okay. But let's go out, find a street vendor and get some food. Come, come, I have coin. Let us eat and talk. Well, I shall do the talking, and you can do the listening.'

They leave the small apartment and make their way down the rickety wooden staircase. Outside, the wind is strong, and the ice particles have turned to hail. Faustus has no cloak, so he just squints as he is assaulted by the vicious pieces of ice. He lifts the hood of his new cloak above Calvus' head, and they shuffle quickly down the deserted street. They turn right at the end and can see the forum up ahead. The smell of hot food wafts up their nostrils, and they quicken their pace.

Hunched under the poor shelter offered by the awning of the street vendor's stall, they eat in silence, devouring the nameless stew Calvus has bought. When their bones are warmed and their bellies full, Calvus begins.

# CHAPTER II

**August, 172 AD**
**Somewhere north of the Danube, Germania**

Centurion Albinus Silus braced against his shield as another Germani warrior thumped his body against it. Sweat stung his eyes, the metallic taste of blood was rank on his tongue, and all he could smell was sweat and shit.

He had lost all semblance of time; they could have been fighting for an hour or a day, he knew not. He knew only thrust and step, thrust and step. The sun was baking, his mouth as dry as a desert floor. He stepped forward again, thrust out with his shield and plunged his sword into the guts of a barbarian. 'Forward, forward!' His voice was nothing but a rasp. It hurt to speak, to shout was unbearable, but he was a leader of men, he had to keep encouraging his century.

By his most recent calculation, they had already lost twenty men, and that was taken a while ago now, when he had last rotated out of the line. He could hear Fullo, his *optio*, at the rear of his century, barking orders, heaving men into line. For a brief moment he wondered if his friend was as tired as he, then reasoned that every man in the field must be exhausted. They had been fighting since dawn.

They were attacking the Quadi, one of the largest and most powerful tribes in the south of Germania. Their former allies, the Marcomanni and their king, Balomar, had surrendered the previous winter, handing over thousands of captured Roman soldiers as well as all their weapons and cartloads of provisions. Their king was said to have confined himself to his private quarters in his hall, such was the weight of failure. It had been Balomar that had initiated this war, six years ago now. He had organised a raid on a small Roman veteran settlement a few miles east of Carnuntum. That settlement had been the home of Albinus and his father and Licina, his lover.

Licina had been captured in the raid, taken north into Goridorgis, the capital of the Marcomanni, where she had been kept as a slave until she escaped. Fleeing north, she had then fallen into the custody of Albinus' father's greatest enemy: Alaric Hengistson. Alaric had sent her off in a ship to distant lands in the frozen north. He had thought he would never see her again.

But in a desperate bid to find her, Albinus had led seven of his comrades north, through Germania's harsh winter, to the shingle beaches that faced the North Sea. He had not found Licina, but he had found Alaric. One to one, Albinus had fought the man responsible for his father's death, and killed him. They had left the barbarian's body where it lay and were just returning home when they had encountered Julius Decanus, who, unbeknown to Albinus, had become Licina's lover in their journey north through Germania.

Julius had travelled back across the North Sea and brought Licina back to Albinus, who married her. They lived in a small one-room apartment in Carnuntum and had been happy, so happy, for a time. Albinus had been away with the army for large swathes of those precious months, fighting Balomar and his fellow barbarian chieftains. Licina had been all alone in Carnuntum, pregnant with his child. She had been caught up in a plot by a man named Cocconas, who was the very man who had first taken her from her home in that winter raid. Isolated, friendless, Licina had no choice but to submit to his rule.

It was all within a matter of days that Albinus had discovered first he was a father and that his wife was a traitor to the empire. Cocconas has been involved in a coup to kill the emperor, but it had been snuffed out before they could strike. A man named Alexander of Abonoteichos had been behind the coup. He was an easterner, a soothsayer, and it had been he who had advised the Divine Marcus Aurelius to sacrifice two live lions by throwing them into the River Danube from the wooden bridge at Carnuntum. Albinus had seen, first-hand, how catastrophic that had been.

So, Licina had fled without a word to Albinus. She had left their newborn son, Faustus, in the care of Meredith, who was the daughter of an old comrade of both Albinus and his father. Calvus, it had turned out, had been busy after his discharge from the army. He had been appointed into the *frumentarii,* and it had been he who had discovered the plot to kill the emperor, he who uncovered Licina's role in it. Albinus could still remember the pain in his friend's eyes as he was forced to recount the crimes his wife had committed.

That had been in December of the previous year. The last six months of Albinus' life had been the worst. Worse than the pain of losing his father, worse than the pain of losing his brother soldiers, Libo and Longus. He did not think he could survive without his beautiful bride, still didn't.

His son, Faustus, was still in the care of Meredith in Carnuntum. She had promised to look after him as if he were her own. She was a good woman, and Albinus trusted her implicitly. But it did not make the pain of being away from Faustus any easier to bear.

In January of that year, Albinus had been officially promoted to the rank of centurion. Tenth cohort, sixth century. He was the most junior centurion in the whole legion, but he knew his father would be beaming down at him from Elysium with pride. He had moved quickly to secure his friend, Fullo, as his *optio* – the second in command of the century. He had also requested a friend from his old century be allowed to transfer with him. Taurus, the first spear centurion of the Fourteenth Legion, had allowed the request, and so Bucco stood now at his shoulder, as he had done many a time with both Albinus and his father over the years. Rullus, the last surviving member of their previous *contubernium*, was the standard-bearer for the first cohort, so had not been able to move with them.

So now, Albinus was once again back on campaign, back fighting the barbarians. He stepped forward again and slashed wildly at an approaching Germani warrior. The slash hit nothing but air. In his tiredness, Albinus was slow to recover his position. The warrior aimed a lunge with his spear at Albinus' groin, and only Bucco's quick reactions saved him. Albinus did nothing but watch on in horror as the spear sped towards his unprotected right side, but in the last moment, Bucco brought his shield across, and the spear clanged off the bronze boss in its centre.

Still frozen, still panting, Albinus watched on as the legionary on his left stepped forward and hacked the barbarian in the neck. Blood spurted from the gaping wound, dark against the brightness of the sun. The warrior slumped to his knees and was quickly trampled by his comrades behind him as they pushed forward into the fray.

'Sound the rotate, sound the rotate!' Bucco bellowed in a voice hardened by war. He had already served his twenty-five years when Albinus had enlisted, desperate to avenge his father and fight the barbarians. Bucco said he had sworn an oath to Silus, Albinus' father, never to leave his side. In keeping with that oath, he had signed himself back up. He was in the last of the three years he had been required to serve, and Albinus dreaded the day the veteran would leave the Fourteenth for the last time.

The horn-blower stood in the fourth rank of the sixth century. Close enough to hear orders from his officer at the front, far away enough from the fighting to stay alive. He looked at Albinus even as Bucco repeated the order. Legionaries were not allowed to give orders on the field of battle, it had been known to have been the death of some who had dared. Albinus just nodded, too tired to speak. The horn-blower breathed in deeply and blew on his bronze instrument till his cheeks glowed red. In an instant, the men in the front rank turned side-on, keeping their shields to the enemy. In the small gaps that appeared in between, the second rank surged forward, smashing their shields into the enemy before lunging at any exposed skin. Groin or neck, groin or neck. The months of training on the drill field paid off; scores fell from their first attack.

Fullo pressed past Albinus and slapped his friend on the shoulder. There were no words, for none were needed. Albinus retreated to the back of his men and slumped down on the hard ground. He looked up, and to his dismay, saw the sun had not yet reached its zenith. It was not yet midday, and already, his water skin was empty and he boiled in his armour.

'You there,' he said, pointing to the nearest legionary, 'go back to the base of the hill and find water, as much as you can carry. You and you go with him, hurry now.'

The three legionaries ran off, as eager to quench their thirst as their centurion. Albinus tried to distract himself and stood to gauge how the battle was faring. The Quadi held their position atop a steep ridge. Albinus thought the incline to be roughly two hundred paces. Large rocks and tree stumps dotted the approach, making it hard to keep the men in line as they advanced. They were facing to the east and had charged up into the face of the rising sun that morning. That had been a mistake. The first hour of the battle had been inconclusive, simply because the Romans were unable to see their foe clearly. The Quadi warriors had had th+eir backs to the sun, with the benefit of the high ground and their deadly ash spears giving them an advantage in reach. But the large rectangular *scutums* of the legionaries had paid dividends then, and the losses had been minimal.

But they had lost any momentum that initial charge would have given them, and all morning the fighting had been hard, each step forward paid for in blood. The sixth century of the Fourteenth Legion was on the far right of the Roman line. The ridge was so wide and the Quadi numbers so great that the entire legion was deployed. It was normal for four cohorts to be in the first wave of attack, the rest kept in reserve so they could rotate in and out throughout the duration of the battle. There would be no such luxuries today. Legate Marcus Valerius Maximianus had no reserves to call upon, save a two hundred-odd-strong auxiliary cavalry that was as good as useless on this kind of terrain. They sat by their horses in the shade at the bottom of the ridge, guarding the supply train. Albinus was no coward, but right then, he envied them.

'Jupiter's cock, it's fucking hot!' Bucco exclaimed with his usual bravado as he slumped to the dirt and tore his helmet free from his bald head. Albinus thought he looked old. Crows' feet winged his eyes, the smile lines around his mouth had grown deep, and his tanned skin looked like old ox-hide. He wore standard-issue mail over an off-white tunic. Until recently, he had worn the old segmented cuirass that the legions had sported for so long. He had broken his in battle against the Naristae, another of the Germanic tribes, the previous year and had been unable to get it repaired. As it wasn't made anymore, he'd had to resort to the new armour. He still, though, carried the old-style *gladius*. Whereas the modern short swords were slightly longer and forged of a straight piece of iron ending in a triangular point, his curved in and out, like a river, before it reached its tip. Bucco thought this an advantage over the newer blades, as the wider edge behind the tip forced a bigger wound, and therefore, was more likely to yield a killing blow.

'I don't suppose you have any water?' Albinus asked, more in hope than expectation. Bucco shook his head.

'Ain't known a summer this hot in twenty years,' he said. Albinus watched in disgust as he licked the free-flowing sweat from the corners of his mouth. 'Salty,' he said and grimaced.

Albinus turned from his friend and walked among the rest of his men. Six months he had been their commander, and still he could name just a handful. He had been told that in his day, his father could name every man in his century and most in the first cohort. Remembering eighty names was proving to be a challenge too much for Albinus, let alone commanding a century in the first cohort where the five centuries were all double strength.

He walked through the men, slapping shoulders and sharing the odd joke. A man he knew named Pavo was pissing in his helmet, four other men surrounding him, all eagerly eyeing the headgear's contents. 'What in Jupiter's name are you whoresons doing?' Albinus barked as he approached. 'Stand to attention when I address you,' he snapped at one poor man who still only had eyes for the piss-filled helmet. 'Pavo, explain yourself.'

Pavo was an experienced soldier who had served well over half his time. He had short dark hair and a squashed nose from being broken too many times. He just shrugged at his officer's question. 'We're thirsty, sir. Ain't no one got any water?'

'Juno's tits,' Albinus muttered through clenched teeth. His throat was as dry as anyone's, but he was not about to resort to this. He debated whether to take the matter further then decided it wasn't worth the effort. 'Carry on, Pavo,' he said with an air of disbelief before turning away.

He looked back up the hill where just thirty paces away, Fullo was fighting in the front rank. The battle had slowed, he could sense it. The Quadi would be just as tired and thirsty as them, he reasoned. The men of the Sixth were leaning on their shields, putting no more into their supposed advance up the hill than their weight. The Germani, too, seemed content to do no more than hold their own. At the battle's start, they had been forming small wedges and trying to force an opening in the Roman line. There was no such enthusiasm on display now.

Albinus heard hoofbeats to his rear and turned to see Legate Marcus Valerius Maximianus approach him at a canter. As one, the men of his century not engaged in the battle stood and saluted, Albinus removed his helmet and stood to attention. 'Sir,' he said as the legate dismounted.

'Good to see you, Centurion. How are your men faring?'

'Not made much progress up the slope, as you can see, sir, but we're holding our own.'

The legate nodded. His hair had now lost the last of its colour and was the dull silver of iron. His grey-green eyes were slits as he squinted against the sun's light. 'We have to take this hill, Centurion. The emperor commands we strike deeper into Quadi lands; we have to make it happen. Do you have any water left?' Albinus shook his head. 'Apollo be damned, none of us have.'

'Is there no more with the baggage train, sir?'

'None. The last of it was sent to the first cohort an hour or so ago. The Quadi tried to flank them from the treeline to the north, but they managed to repel it.' That news caused a stir of emotion from Albinus. Twice he had served in the first cohort in his short time with the Fourteenth, once as a legionary and then again as an *optio* in the first century. Both had been fairly short-lived, but he had come to love the men that fought under centurion Taurus, and the centurion himself.

'You have fresh orders, sir?' It would be unusual for a legate to bring orders directly to his centurions, but then Maximianus had not always behaved like a standard legate.

34

'No. Actually, I was rather hoping you might have a bright idea or two. You have proven yourself to be very resourceful in the past.'

Albinus gawped in surprise. Resourceful? There were just over fifty centurions in the legion, and each one had considerably more experience in warfare than he. To have been noted as a good commander in an army full of them was a real compliment.

'Thank you, sir... I... err...'

He turned away and once more looked at the battlefield, this time, with fresh eyes. From his vantage point, halfway down the slope, he could see very little apart from the backs of his men and the ninth century, which fought at their shoulders. Looking left, that scene replicated itself as far as the eye could see. To the right was just bare rock where the ridge gave way to a fairly short but sharp cliff. The Quadi had chosen their ground exceptionally well: the only place to assault them was directly up the ridge or risk facing the perils of the cliff face. His eyes narrowed as he studied it more closely. Was it his extreme lack of hydration playing tricks on him, or was there a narrow track that led off into the rocks? An animal trail perhaps? Where did it lead?

'Do you see that, sir?' he said, pointing to the track. 'If I can have the auxiliaries, without their mounts, of course, I could perhaps lead them through that path. The rocks give way to a cliff, which appears to bend around this ridge, but the path must lead somewhere or else it wouldn't be there.'

He watched in tense silence as his legate followed his chain of thoughts. 'Follow the path, get in behind the bastards and cause some disruption. Reinforce this flank with another eighty men, and we can have this battle sewn up in an hour. Mars have mercy on your enemies, young Silus,' he exclaimed through a dry chuckle. 'I will send the cavalry up to you now, though I know full well how much they will hate it. I shall also skim the rear ranks of ten of the centuries in the centre and send them here. Where is your *optio*? Can he command whilst you are gone?'

'He is, right now, sir,' Albinus said, motioning to Fullo in the front line of his century. 'Fullo is more than capable, you'll get no problems from the sixth.'

A short time later, Albinus was leading two hundred men of the Ala Noricorum through the narrow path and into the cliff face. They were not, as Maximianus had predicted, especially happy about leaving their mounts and fighting on foot, let alone at the potential prospect of having to climb a bare cliff. They were commanded by Decurion Flavius Bassus, who Albinus judged to be of Italian stock by his pure and unaccented Latin. His men appeared to be mainly from Noricum, or at least along the Danube frontier. Their Latin was heavily accented and to an Italian would be, at times, incomprehensible. But to Bassus, it was the norm.

'You have a plan, I'm assuming?' Bassus asked as he trudged along behind Albinus.

*No, not at all.* 'Of course, of sorts. We follow the path, flank the fuckers and cause as much disruption as we can. When our attack begins, the men on our right flank will push forward, and together, we will fold up their line and win the day.' He spoke with a confidence that he did not feel.

'So, how exactly are we going to get in position to flank them? Have you scouted this path? You do *know* where it leads?'

*Oh, just shut up.* 'No. I merely saw an opportunity, and the legate agreed it was worth a shot. If we can't get up, we will simply have to turn around and go back. Any more questions?'

'No. I have established you are leading us into a deadly attack without any real idea of how we are going to get into position or how many men we will be facing when we arrive, which I had assumed you were. Just wanted to see for myself if you were as nuts as everyone says you are.'

'Who says?' Albinus said, stopping in his tracks and resting a hand on his pommel.

'Everyone in the legion. You are quite famous, you know.'

Albinus scoffed. 'Hardly. I am the most junior centurion in the entire legion. I would wager none of the men outside my century even recognise my face, let alone know my name.'

'Oh, everyone knows your name. You are Albinus Silus, son of *the* Silus. And as for your face, those eyes and that scar make you instantly recognisable. We had never met until earlier today, but I knew who you were before the legate even introduced us.'

*My face?* Albinus had piercing blue eyes, inherited from his father, and a small button nose atop a thin-lipped mouth. He was pale-skinned with hair the colour of wet sand. On the left side of his jaw, there was a jagged scar where he had taken a spear in the Fourteenth's defeat to Balomar and his tribal army six years before. It had been his first battle and a complete disaster for the Fourteenth.

'So, what else do men say of me?' he asked as he began his light jog again. His armour jingled as he ran, the tight links of his mail clawing at his skin through the rough fabric of his tunic.

'They say your shoulder popped out of its joint in your first battle. You let a surgeon reset it before rejoining the fight where you then stopped a spear with your face. You went on to engage in a fighting retreat for the rest of the day, in the front line of your legion's defensive square. I have also heard you fought your way into the ranks of the Naristae, leaving your century behind, armed with nothing more than your *optio's* staff. Any of this actually true?'

Albinus hid a grin as he ran. It was true, all of it. His first battle had been a bit of a catastrophe for both him and the Fourteenth Legion. He had popped his right shoulder from its joint after wedging his sword in a barbarian's spine. After a Greek surgeon had reset the joint whilst the battle still raged, he had put his armour back on and returned to the fray, only to catch a spear through his left cheek. He had felt the deadly iron point brush his tongue as it licked in and out of his mouth. The scar still itched him now. It was also true that whilst fighting the Naristae, he had advanced from the shields of the Fourteenth's first century and beat a bloody path through the massed tribesmen, armed with nothing but his long wooden staff. It had been that act of heroism that had earned him both a harsh dressing down from the legion's first spear centurion, Taurus, and promotion to the rank of centurion.

He had of course, also in the last few years, duelled with the king of the Marcomanni in battle and fought his way to the northern shores of Germania, but he thought it best not bring that up.

'So, what's your point, Decurion? Are you concerned I'm nothing but some blood-crazed lunatic, desperate to step out of my father's shadow?'

He turned back to the decurion with a savage grin that split his lips, and his eyes were glazed like a frozen lake. 'Because if you are, you'd be right. We're here, let's go.'

Albinus led the charge up a steep and narrow path, forged of old tree roots and dry mud. The incline was short but steep and brought them out directly at the rear of the enemy. No one looked their way, at least initially. And why would they? They held the high ground and had the Fourteenth Legion pinned down on the grassy slope to their front. There was nothing behind them but rocks and air.

Cresting the cliff, Albinus saw the injured stretched out on a large flat plain. They were dressing each other's wounds, talking in low tones and drinking water, so much blessed water, they had barrels of it. One was open, not ten feet from Albinus, and the temptation to run through the Germani warriors and dunk his head straight in was almost too much to bear. He swallowed dust and hauled his sword free, raising it above his head.

'ROMA!' he bellowed, in the loudest voice his parched throat would allow.

The two hundred men of the Ala Noricorum followed suit, the last of them staggering and panting their way up the incline. Albinus charged, heedless of whether Bassus and his men were following.

They were.

The Roman sortie slammed into the backs of the massed Quadi warriors. Bassus had given quick orders to the rearmost twenty men to take care of the wounded, while the rest followed Albinus and hit the unprotected backs of the barbarians in a tidal wave of death and iron.

Albinus thrust his sword through the first man's back, his next blow hacked into an unprotected neck. Then he was in amongst them, swiping his sword from side to side as he drove a deeper hole. He could sense Bassus at his shoulder. The auxiliary fought with a long *spatha,* and he used the added reach and weight of the longer blade to devastating effect. A bearded warrior lunged for Albinus with a spear, but before he could even react, Bassus had turned the spear aside and slashed through the barbarian's throat. Albinus blocked a swipe from an axe with his shield before stabbing at a pale-skinned groin then letting his momentum carry him forward and lunging his blade into an open mouth.

The Germani ranks were thinning now, men spilling to the sides as they tried to avoid the crush. The Ala Noricorum had formed a wedge behind Albinus, and they had funnelled a path through to the Fourteenth Legion, who were attacking with vigour up the steep ridge.

Albinus saw Fullo in the front rank of his century, Bucco at his left shoulder. Albinus caught his *optio's* eye for a heartbeat, and they shared a manic grin. They were winning. Rejoining the men of his century, slotting in the line between Fullo and Bucco, Albinus ordered the horn-blower to sound the general charge, and with a manic roar, fuelled by bloodlust, the Fourteenth made one final effort to gain the ridge.

It was over in heartbeats.

The Quadi streamed to the west, where all they would find was more Roman iron ready to take their lives. Albinus hunched down on all fours. He was, as far as he could tell, unwounded, but his stomach cramped and his calves burned from the charge after the run through the clifftop path. He heaved in lungfuls of air before making his way unsteadily to the open barrel of water he had seen when he had first crested the ridge. He untied the straps of his helmet, let it fall to the floor before plunging his head into the barrel. He had known many pleasures in life: the touch of a woman, the unbridled joy of fatherhood. Each seemed both distant and unimportant at that sweet moment. The water massaged the sweat from his scalp, and he drank so much, he briefly worried it would go straight to his lungs. When he had drunk his fill, he stayed there a moment longer until the cold tingling around his neck grew too intense.

He rose and breathed deeply, feeling as if he could begin the day's fighting over again. Looking around, he saw other men from both the Ala Noricorum and the sixth century all doing the same. Water fights broke out, grown men giggled in glee as they playfully splashed each other. Each man seemed to forget a battle still raged just to their flank.

It took him a moment or two to notice that the light from the scorching sun had faded. He looked around, confused at first, for surely it could not be dusk already? Looking up, he saw thick, black clouds rolling in from the east. They tumbled and swirled before coming together in a crash of thunder. Lightning bolts scarred the great abyss of black, and then the rain fell and washed away the last remnants of his exhaustion.

# CHAPTER III

**January, 193 AD**
**Carnuntum, Pannonia**

It is the morning after their late-night feast on the street. Faustus walks the frozen cobbled streets of Carnuntum, his toes numb at the ends of his boots. He is wearing the military-issue ox-hide boots, even though he promised himself he would not. His other pair are thin and well worn; small holes have appeared on the soles. In this weather, they are the kind of boots that will see you come down with some sort of coughing illness, and that, he does not want.

He walks out of the eastern gate, the pale yellow sun shining almost white in a cloudless sky. A memory tugs at him: he is sitting in a hot bath in a villa just north of Rome. His father is there, looking resplendent in gleaming mail, polished *phalera* sitting proudly in their harness. His father had worn three of the coveted disks, all awarded to him by the Caesar Commodus for bravery in battle. Faustus rubs his chest, remembering the savage cough that had seen him bed-ridden for a whole month. A physician named Galen, who is known throughout the empire as a man of medicine, stands over him. He is a learned man who does not believe all ills are brought on by the gods or that they can be cured by prayer or sacrifice. He believes in medicine and what he can see and touch. As Faustus lies in the scalding bath, he sees the respect in his father's eyes, the deference he shows the physician, even in Faustus' presence. Usually, his father is so protective of his son, will not let anyone except Meredith

41

even speak to him. But Galen can speak, can listen to his breathing and touch his chest.

'Your son has phlegm on his lungs… It is the cold air,' he says. Faustus remembers he spoke Latin with a lisp, and sometimes he paused mid-sentence, trying to find the right words.

'What can we do?' his father says. As he speaks, he reaches down and takes hold of Faustus' hand. Faustus remembers the warmth of that touch, the calloused palms rough on his child-smooth skin.

'Keep him inside and keep him warm. Make him eat lots of fruit and fresh vegetables and limit his exercise. No running or… any other unnecessary exertions.' He waves his hand as he speaks the last words, unable to think of what else a boy at the tender age of four would be up to.

'Thank you, Doctor,' his father says. Faustus remembers payment is offered and declined; the emperor himself will be paying for the physician's time. Even now, all these years later, the thought of the emperor of Rome paying for his medical treatment makes him smile. *How far I have fallen,* he thinks, and the smile sags into a frown.

'Has someone taken a shit outside your front door again? You seem as miserable as sin.' Calvus appears at his shoulder. He walks with a heavy limp, his right hand – the good one – clutches a wooden staff that he leans on heavily. His back is stooped, the curve of his spine sticking out from the back of the blue cloak Faustus had given him the previous night. He wears an old off-white tunic unbelted so it falls to his bare ankles, which Faustus thinks look as fickle as kindling.

'No, Uncle,' Faustus says with a gentle smile, 'I was just reminded of a moment from my childhood, of my father…' he trails off, his mind wandering. Calvus is speaking, and with effort, Faustus shakes the haze from his mind and brushes the glaze from his glistening eyes. 'Sorry, what?'

'Ha! You are a daydreamer, lad. I was just saying that you should tell me of your time in Rome. I know so little of it.'

'Really? Did Meredith not speak of it?' He is surprised at this. He was there for a number of years, along with Meredith and Marcus. Marcus and he grew up in the eternal city's honeycomb streets. He can still smell the excrement now.

'No, not in any detail, anyhow. She was lonely, I think. A foreigner in a strange land. Much as she was here, I suppose.'

Calvus' daughter had been born in Britannia just south of Lundene. She had been forced into slavery and shipped out to Pannonia where, quite by chance, she had bumped into her father. Calvus had quickly seen her freed – with brute force rather than coin, if the stories were to be believed, and when stories were about Calvus and violence, they were most certainly true – and she had stayed with him till her death. Another stab of pain in his chest, another frown.

'But you saw my father once we had left Rome, out east?'

'I did, yes,' the old man nods. There is an anguish in his voice, a pain in his eyes that Faustus cannot read and isn't sure he wants to. 'But that, my lad, is not a story for today. Are you coming to the *ludus* with me? I want another look at my man before next week.'

There were to be games for two days the next week. They had originally been scheduled in honour of the Divine Emperor Commodus, but now that he was dead, it was not certain whether they would still be going ahead.

'Yes, Uncle, I'll come, although you know I detest such places.'

That was not quite true; gladiators had formed a big part of his childhood whilst he was living with the then Caesar Commodus and his retinue. As a child, he had sat in the wooden stalls that surrounded the small indoor arena the caesar would train in day after day. The finest gladiators from around the empire would be brought to Rome just to tutor Commodus for an hour.

Faustus remembers the divine emperor as he was. Young, fearless, determined. So different from the man he was said to have become. They walk through the doors of the *ludus* and the smell, once more, brings him back to his childhood. Sweat and oil, ox-hide and body odour. Muscled men walk the chambers in nothing but loincloths, their bodies shaped like an army officer's cuirass. The floor is sand, and through his boots, Faustus can feel it is damp. It is, he thinks, colder in here than it is outside, if that is even possible. His breath misting the air, he sees a small fire in a corner, its flames dancing from an oval iron bowl. He stands by the fire, blowing slowly onto his frozen hands. Calvus is well known here – and well liked.

It appears he is acquainted with every gladiator that calls this place their home. One slaps him on the back before grasping his arm. Faustus studies the man, evaluating him. He is of average height and not particularly well-built. Looking around at the other gladiators, Faustus wonders how this man has managed to stay alive, competing against men so much bigger and stronger than he.

'I did what you said, sir, and it worked! I let his momentum shift his weight forward then spun from my position and rammed my blade home in his side. He was dead in heartbeats!' the gladiator is shouting, pure joy in his dark eyes. He grabs Calvus by the shoulders and shakes him, and Faustus worries the old man will not be able to cope with such vigorous physical contact, but then he remembers who he is, what he has done.

'I told you it would work, Brennus! We are of a similar build, you and I. Fighting bigger men is what we do. The key to it is to make their greater weight and strength their weakness. Speed is our friend. Lure them in close, make them stumble, then stick 'em where it hurts!'

There is so much *life* in Calvus' eyes, they sparkle, a spark of colour against the dark, drab walls. Faustus smiles to see it, he has not seen him so happy, so animated and passionate about anything, in months.

Not since they died.

'Faustus, Faustus, always daydreaming, this kid. Come here, lad, come here and meet Brennus.'

Faustus reluctantly leaves the warmth of the fire and walks into the centre of the chamber. He holds out a hand which is firmly grasped – too firmly for his liking – by Brennus. 'Brennus is from Gaul,' Calvus says, a hand on each of their shoulders. 'Brennus, this is Faustus, he has some of Gaul in his blood himself, on his mother's side. I fought with both his grandfather's back in the day, and of course, his father is—'

'A legend! Every man in Carnuntum knows of Centurion Albinus Silus! A warrior to be feared if the tales are to be believed.'

'Oh, they are,' Calvus says. Faustus is saved more talk of his famous father by a bell tolling. 'Time to train, young Brennus. I shall leave you to your preparations. I have good coin placed on you for the upcoming games, so you make sure you practise hard, your mind as well as your body.'

Once the gladiator is gone, Calvus ushers them to the stalls. They take their seats on the top row where the air feels warmer and the smell of sweating men is fainter. There is another fire flickering in a brazier, and Faustus drags it across the floorboards so it is nearer Calvus.

'Oh, I almost forgot to ask. Was it true, what you told me last night? Was it really my father that turned the battle against the Quadi?'

Calvus nods, a mischievous glint in his eye. 'Aye, so they say. I was not present, of course, but that is the story I heard.'

'You told me it was "God" that won the day for the Fourteenth! You cheeky old bastard, I nearly believed you as well.'

Calvus cackles, and it brings on a small coughing bout. He reaches within his cloak and pulls out a small pendant hanging from a chain. The pendant is made of bronze, it is circular in shape, the thin oval band surrounding a crude portrait of a fish, the symbol of the Christians.

'Jupiter best and greatest! Do not show that in public! They'll be crucifying you at the damn games if you're not careful!' Faustus moves his hand and grasps the pendant, thrusting it back into the old man's cloak.

'*Jesu* will protect me. As he did your father that day.'

'I think it was his shield that protected him, Uncle. Anyway, you said God, or *Jesu* or whatever you call him, brought on the storm which saved the legion. Sounds very much like it was father that did the saving before the storm even hit!'

'Ahh, but who was it that revealed the path through the rocks around the bare cliff and onto the enemy's unsuspecting rear? God, that is who.'

Faustus snorts and shaking his head he says, 'Well, I guess it is another story about my immortal father I will be hearing about for the rest of my life.'

'You could always go and ask him yourself…?' Calvus says in a small voice.

Faustus does not reply but shakes his head.

'Okay, lad, no more talk of your father. Would you like to hear about what I was getting up to whilst your father was beating the shit out of the Quadi? Now that *is* a rare tale.'

Faustus smiles in delight. Calvus has rarely spoken of his life in the immediate years after he left the legions. 'Yes, Uncle, I would be delighted to listen. Unless, of course, it is a grand tale about another *miracle* your god conjured up.'

Calvus tries to look serious and fails, and they both laugh. 'Sit comfortably, lad, and let me tell you about my journey across the breadth of the empire.'

# CHAPTER IV

**Spring, 172 AD**
**Thessalonica, Macedonia**

It was around the Ides of March. Habitus and I entered the great city of Thessalonica. I had seen many cities before, of course, but nothing of that magnitude. I would, when I got to the east, but we shall get to that in due course.

We were tired and footsore, as even twenty-odd years ago, we were by no means young men. The journey from Pannonia had been hard. There were deserters from the army, hundreds of the buggers at that time, camped in the woods and hills on the roads that we travelled, and twice we had to fight them off. By the time we entered the great city, we had passed nearly six hundred mile markers – six hundred!

We had left Carnuntum in January. Your father, Albinus, had just formally taken command of his new century, and my old comrade, Bucco, had gone with him. Albinus had appointed his friend, Fullo – who, sadly, you may not remember – as his *optio*. Meredith had settled into the very apartment you still dwell in, and you and Marcus were both hale and strong. She was sad, Meredith, though she tried to put on a brave face. I could see the pain in her eyes, the fear in the twitch of her fingers. She was a single mother to two boys in a foreign city, a foreign country. Her Latin in those days was broken, and I knew she fretted over the simple things: shopping in the market, paying her rent to the landlord, making friends with fellow new mothers. I had asked my tribune, Pompeianus, to watch over her. He did that and far much more. You know he took her shopping twice a week for her first few weeks alone, explained carefully and gently our currency, taught her the art of haggling, showed her which vendors sold the best products and who could be trusted to not try and rip her off. He even came around to the apartment on the first day of the month with eight armed men and stood at Meredith's shoulder as she made her first rental payment. Ha! By God, I'd have loved to have seen the old landlord's face! He must have needed to change his loincloth when he got home.

But anyway, Habitus and I walked through the gates of Thessalonica and immediately found a tavern. After our second jug of wine, the first decent drink we'd had in nearly two months, Habitus said, 'So, when does the ship leave?'

I was caught off guard and momentarily blubbered like a fish out of water.

'Cut the crap, Calvus. You have our journey all planned out, I know it,' said Habitus. 'When we stopped at Arrabo, you waited half the night to take a piss. Don't talk, just listen. We sat in that tavern, and you watched the latrine door like a hawk. When you knew it was empty, you went in, and moments later, someone followed you.'

'That's ridiculous! It was probably just another customer going for a pi—'

'He wore military boots, had his tunic belted, and there was a short sword strapped to his back. I could see it under his cloak. Don't bullshit me, Calvus, he was either passing you orders or you were giving him instructions. Wait, I'm not done yet. In Mursa, someone passed you a scrap of parchment in the street which you read when you thought I had stopped to admire the goods of that trader who was selling jewellery. You read the note then threw it in the nearest brazier. That night, I saw you scribble a reply when you thought I was asleep. I also saw you tuck it into the hand of a passer-by on the road the next day.'

'That's farcical!'

'He pretended to bump into you, and the note passed from your right hand to his. Shall I go on?'

'Okay, okay, you wi—'

'In Narona, a fisherman, flogging his latest catch, put another scrap of parchment in the bundle of fish you bought. And I knew full well there was something going on there because you hate fish!'

'Something "fishy", you might say,' I said with a smirk. Habitus fought back the smile but couldn't contain it for long.

'There have been other little instances on the way. A carving in a tree and suddenly you want to change direction, your insistence we stay at certain taverns, even when there is clearly a better and cheaper option over the road. I've known you for twenty years, Calvus, we marched together, fought together. God's brother, we were in the same *contubernium.* I know you inside out. Now, tell me, what exactly have you got yourself involved in, and how deep in it are you?'

I've always been pretty bad at lying. I once tried to hide from my mother a loaf of bread I had stolen. She stormed into the small house I had grown up in and demanded to know why the local auxiliary centurion was looking for me. I shrugged, said I had no clue, but she saw straight through my quivering eyes, the stupid nervous smile that would always fix my face. I looked down to try and hide my eyes from her, and there were breadcrumbs all over my tunic! Ha! She beat me black and blue.

I knew I was wearing that same nervous smile as Habitus' eyes locked onto mine. It felt as though he was looking *into* me rather than at me, as if he could read the lies that were carved onto my soul. 'I cannot tell you everything,' I said, not wanting to tell him anything.

'You are *frumentarii,'* he said. It wasn't a question.

'Yes. Taurus put me up for the position when I had been discharged from the army. You remember how low I was, the drinking, the gambling…'

I really loved being a soldier. I know, young Faustus, that the mere thought of it gives you the shudders, but there really aren't many better ways for a man to make a living. See, the actual fighting is a tiny proportion of your career. Some men can go the full twenty-five years without drawing their sword in anger. All depends where you get posted, I suppose. Most days is nothing more than hanging out with your brothers, the odd march, bit of sentry duty, it really isn't a bad life.

'I was introduced to Tribune Pompeianus, and he set me up with a little mission, a test if you like. I was to help uncover the plot against the emperor, and as you may have noticed, in December, whilst you and the rest of the Fourteenth were on parade, I succeeded.'

'That was all you?' Habitus said through the rim of his wine cup. His grey-green eyes sparkled then, and it was good to see so much life in them.

Habitus had served nearly thirty years by the time he was eventually discharged. See, the army only pension off the greybeards every other year, for fear of thinning out their numbers of hardened fighters too frequently. The year Habitus was supposed to be discharged, it appears his papers were lost, and it took them a further four years to rectify it! *Jesu* knows he was angry, and the abuse we gave him… well, it's a wonder he didn't do for us all.

He had got no joy from his belated discharge though. In the last battle of the year before our journey east, Longus had been killed. He was young, not much older than you are now, Faustus. Italian by birth, he had been an animated young man who had fitted in well with the rest of us in the *contubernium*. Habitus and he had grown close, some of the lads even thought it was sexual, though I'm fairly sure Longus, at least, only had eyes for the ladies. Habitus would have probably taken anything he could get. Anyway, the lad's death hit Habitus hard. His once-golden skin had grown grey and haggard. His dark hair thinned and turned duller than iron, and he grew a long shaggy beard that didn't suit his small, round face.

He was not a big man, in fact, he was the shortest of us and was twig thin, though he had a wiry strength that was rarely bested in a shield wall. He always carried a bow; his father taught him how to shoot before he could walk, or so he said. He was deadly with it, would be firing arrows at an enemy from a hundred paces or more, long before the rest of us could hit them with our *pila*. He had not originally planned to go back to his homeland after retirement, I think he was only doing it for Longus.

Longus had always dreamed of retiring in Syria, opening a tavern beside the sea and having it filled with luscious serving girls and the finest wines. He would never realise that dream, so Habitus would do it for him.

'Yes, well, some of it was,' I answered Habitus. 'But I found out things, things I never wanted to know…'

'Licina?'

I nodded, unable to find the words. 'The tribune wants her found.'

'What will they do to her if you bring her back?'

I gulped. This will not be easy for you to hear, young Faustus, but in some people's minds, your mother was a traitor. Don't speak, Faustus, just listen. That day – when the Fourteenth had been on parade in Carnuntum, celebrating the victories over the tribes and the surrender of Balomar – I had seen your mother in a heated argument with a man I had been following. That man was named Cocconas, and he was in the service of Alexander of Abonoteichos, an apothecary who thought to make himself emperor. You recognise the name, yes? The maniac had even been so confident in his plans that in the centre of the forum, right here in Carnuntum, he had a statue erected in his image. The whole thing was covered in giant sheets of canvas so we were unable to see within, but once I had arrested Cocconas and Alexander's plans had been laid bare at the feet of the Divine Marcus Aurelius, the emperor ordered the canvas hauled down, and there he was.

Alexander was the founder of a religion based around the snake god, Glycon, who he claimed had hatched from an egg after he had dreamed it would. He was a fraud, of course, but had built quite the following. Ex-soldiers, gladiators and various criminals formed his entourage, and it was not until later we discovered the true extent of the power he held over certain senators. Marcus Aurelius, of course, ordered all his correspondence to be burnt as soon as it was found, for he had a particular hatred of persecuting members of the elite.

Once Alexander had been killed, Pompeianus ordered me to go after your mother, so I tagged along with Habitus. How did I know she had gone east? Well, I'm not certain I did, but I had a hunch. She had, of course, already travelled to the far north, and I knew she would have no wish to return there. So, I took a chance.

'You know what they do to traitors,' I said to Habitus.

'What will you do?'

A good question and one I had no ready answer for. 'I do not know, but I do know I must find her before someone else does.' I was not the only agent that had been sent to find her, of that I was certain. And there was another reason, too, but I could not share that with Habitus. 'We have a ship, it leaves Thessalonica at dawn, the day after tomorrow. We have passage booked, it will take us directly to Ephesus where I will receive further orders.'

The ship was named *Neptune's Wings*. The captain said she soared through the waves like an eagle through the sky. If only that had turned out to be true. She was a fat-bellied merchant ship, short and wide, and rode the waves of the Aegean like a constipated donkey.

We had arrived at the great docks of Thessalonica just before dawn. I was tired and irritable, for I had been up most of the night. Thessalonica is a special city for us in the Christian faith, for it was once visited by Paul the Apostle. Go there for yourself, walk the streets, look out for the fish signs painted on the sides of taverns and shops, follow the way they point.

The small house I had arrived at was old and half in ruin. Water leaked through a hole in the roof, even though there had been no rain. But there were candles aplenty, its inhabitants were peaceful, and I found it the perfect place to pray to our Lord, the first time I had managed to so since we had left Carnuntum. Habitus, of course, knew of my devotion to the one true god, but did not like to speak of such things.

The captain of *Neptune's Wings* was a snivelling little Greek called Rastus, who stank of fish and salt and had skin the colour of sand. I assumed his skin tone was because of his constant exposure to the sun, but another passenger on the voyage remarked to his companion that there must be something wrong with his liver. I wasn't really sure what a liver was!

We were all sent down to the hold, which was to be our quarters for the trip. The wooden ladder was old and bent as I placed my weight down. On closer inspection, mould patches could be seen on the thin strips of timber, and I worried it would not last the journey. The hold of the ship stank of neglect and decay, dead animals and human waste. At the rear was the cargo, stacked up in crates, and amphora that Rastus was hoping to sell when we reached Ephesus. To the front were small rectangular segments, partitioned off with rank old sheets, and these would serve as our rooms.

Habitus was moaning, as he always was, but I was not listening, my attention caught by voices behind the sheet to my right.

'Fuck this,' the first voice said. 'Cassius promised us a cushty journey east, and what do we get?' There was a pause and I imagine the speaker was gesturing around him. 'We get some shitty little merchant ship that stinks of dead animals and old farts, and to make it worse, we don't even get a fucking room! You sure we're doing the right thing, Cletus?'

I could not see the men, just the silhouette of their shadows through the white sheet, but even their shadows looked military.

'Peace, Timon. You know Cassius as well as I. He would not intentionally allow his men to travel in squalor. He has done right by us so far, let us see what he has to say when we reach Egypt.'

Egypt? Now that was interesting. It was common knowledge that there had been a rebellion in Egypt and that senator Avidius Cassius, governor of Asia, had been given the title of *Rector Orientis* and charged with clearing the vital province of the rebels before they could disrupt the grain supply to Rome.

'And how long is that gonna bloody take? First this stinking ship then a long wait in Ephesus followed by a longer voyage on another stinking ship! We better get paid and paid fucking well!'

'How many times, Timon! We will be paid once we arrive, paid again once the rebellion is put down and then receive the payday of our lives once we have accomplished our mission! We shall live like kings, brother. Just be patient.'

*We shall live like kings?* The words swirled around my mind. As I said, I had more than one reason for following Habitus to the east, finding Licina was just one of those. I had to get close to these men, earn their trust and loosen their tongues. The one named Timon seemed as dumb as an ox, a typical soldier, he would speak after a few cups of wine. The other, Cletus, sounded more refined, his Latin pure with little trace of an accent. He would not fall for any cheap trick I might try on him.

'Habitus,' I said in a voice too loud. 'Fancy a game of dice? We haven't played a round since we left the legion!'

That silenced them next door, as I knew it would. Habitus' face lit up, and he rummaged in his pack for his dice and cup, bringing them out and blowing the dust off with glee. He beamed at me. 'I know you got a load of coin hidden somewhere in that pack, brother, time for me to deepen the old retirement pot!'

There was a whispered conversation the other side of the sheet, Timon clearly eager to join in the game, Cletus reluctant. Their muted argument did not last long, and when the sheet was pulled aside moments later, I was able to put a face to both their voices. 'Ave, brothers. Care to allow a couple of fellow soldiers to join the party?' Timon said with a gap-toothed grin.

The day went by, not that we saw the sun rise and fall. We drank strong wine, supplied by our two guests, and ate our way through a couple of loaves of stale bread and a chunk of ham I had bought the day before. To start with, our conversation was polite but reserved, as each pair tried to get an understanding of the other. They were veterans, like us, but had signed back up for three years to serve under Cassius in his war against the rebels in Egypt.

'Why does Cassius need to be recruiting retired veterans to fight the bandits?' Habitus asked through a mouthful of bread.

Cletus had shrugged and said, 'His legions are the same as every other, I imagine. The plague has stripped them down to bare bones, men retire, fewer recruits sign up every year. I hear it is the same across the empire.'

I nodded in agreement, for the situation had been much the same on the northern frontier. The Fourteenth Legion alone had been under strength by a thousand men when we had left Carnuntum; black smoke rose from pyres all around the city as the ravaged victims of the plague were burned to prevent the putrid air from their rotting bodies from spreading the disease.

It is different now, I know, for men your age, Faustus; the plague is nothing more than a story. But ask anyone who lived through it, they will tell you of the years they spent checking their bodies for puss-filled lumps, the cold touch of death one felt when they were succumbed by a minor nosebleed. It was bad being in the army then. We lived at such close proximity to one another that when you saw a comrade fall ill, you thought it an impossibility that it would not infect you in turn.

'What legion did you serve with?' I asked, hoping to steer the conversation on from plague and death.

'The Second, mostly. Had a spell with the Thirteenth early in my career. Timon here served on the Rhine with the Twenty-Second before being promoted to centurion, where he was transferred to the Second. We commanded the second and third centuries in the first cohort throughout the eastern wars under Varus.'

I shared a look with Habitus before replying. The Second had been the legion that had attacked Seleucia after it had surrendered. Seleucia was where the plague had originated. 'So, what's enticed you from retirement? Need the coin or just got bored?'

'Bit of both for me,' Cletus said. 'I retired to a small village, about half a day from Thessalonica. It is okay, you know, though I thought I would have found myself a wife by now, but…'

'You're ugly as sin!' Timon put in.

'Yes, thanks for that, brother!' We all laughed, and then our mirth-tired Cletus said, 'Guess I just wasn't ready for it, you know? After twenty-five years, you'd have thought I would have had enough, suppose I'm not quite done yet.'

'I know how you feel,' I said, holding up the stump of my left hand. I, too, had been lost when the Fourteenth had been forced to discharge me. I felt as if I had no home, didn't belong. We spoke for a while about how I had lost the fingers, shared stories of battles we had fought in, overexaggerated our heroic valour, the usual. I had to excuse myself after a time and climbed the rickety ladder onto the deck and sucked in some fresh air.

Rastus was still pacing the small deck, sailing the ship with nothing more than the light of the moon to guide him. As much as he was a rat of a man, and I would never have trusted him as far as I could have thrown him, I did appreciate the fine skill of being able to navigate by nothing more than the sun and stars. Most ships, to my understanding, would hug the coast and never leave sight of land, therefore avoiding ever losing their way or being sunk by a sudden storm. Rastus, though, seemed to have no such qualms. There were five other ships, all in formation behind us. As I stood and leaned over the rail, enjoying the peaceful sound of water swashing off the hull, he took great pleasure in bragging to me that the captains of those ships were paying him a hefty fee for the privilege of being allowed to follow him. Apparently, they would arrive at Ephesus two days earlier than their rivals who hugged the coastline and would, therefore, be able to drive a higher price when they sold their wares.

I was just preparing myself to go back down into the hold when I heard a commotion from below. There were raised voices followed by the splintering of wood and a wet crunch, which sounded as though a dense object had connected with a skull, and then silence.

'What in Neptune's sea is going on down there?' Rastus said as he sped past me, throwing himself down the ladder. I followed the captain as quickly as I could, though I was not as trusting of the ladder as he. The light was dim in the hold; for obvious reasons, Rastus did not want too many candles lit on his wooden ship. As I reached the bottom, I saw a crowd had formed around our partition, and there was a man lying prone on the floor. There were maybe fifteen other passengers aboard: a couple of old men who seemed to be physicians of some description, a large family with eight children, one of which was screaming, another clinging to her mother's skirt. The last group were all male, all young. They appeared to be of military stock but showed no sign of being armed.

I pushed through the crowd, heart thudding, blood pumping, and came face to face with Habitus, holding what appeared to be one leg from a shattered wooden stool. 'Habitus,' I whispered, although in the deathly silence of the hold, there could be no privacy. 'What in God's name have you done?'

'He was using a loaded dice!' he said in a frantic voice. 'Look, I'll show you.'

Habitus bent down and retrieved two bone carved dice from the floor. 'Bet you an *aureus* these both land on six,' he said, before dropping both on the floor. Sure enough, both dice landed on six. I retrieved them myself before rolling, and once more, the dice landed on six. Closer examination showed the edges around the six to be curved where the others were angular and lateral. This meant that when the dice were thrown, they were far less likely to land with the six face down, as the momentum of the throw would help it roll past the curved edge.

'Well, they're not loaded, brother, but they have been tampered with.' I pointed out the difference in the edges around the six.

'Well, that is no reason for your friend to behave the way he has,' Cletus spat. He was on his knees, Timon's head resting on his lap. 'Timon is barely breathing, I think his skull may be cracked.'

I moved away from Habitus and knelt by Timon, pressing my ear to his mouth to check he was breathing.

When I raised my head, all was chaos.

Cletus had a knife in his hand and an evil glint in his eye. Without his eyes leaving mine, he lunged the knife forward, and only years of military training saved my life. I arched my back and lifted my head, and the knife whistled past my neck. Always move – a slow man is a dead man. I rolled and sprang to my feet, my right hand already on the hilt of my own knife. Before I had even pulled it free, Habitus had crashed into Cletus, and the two men rolled across the swaying floor. Cletus fell into the pack of children before their father could pull them free, and one of them was sent flying backwards, knocking over a single candle.

By some cruel twist of fate from the Lord, at the very same time, the ship lurched forward, and we were all sent sprawling to the bow. Rastus had the wares he was transporting packed in tight, and great lengths of rope secured them in place. But a single amphora rolled free and bounced across the floor before cracking open and spilling its contents right next to the dropped candle, which had landed on a cloak that was beginning to catch fire.

'Oil! It's fucking oil!' Rastus bellowed and ran for the ladder. The ship lurched again and sent him flying toward the rear of the hold, and then he was lost to my sight, for all I could see was the savagery of fire.

Black smoke engulfed us, the fire was a living organism, it pulsed through the hold of the ship and held us in its deathly embrace.

Coughing and spluttering, I kept my head low and crawled through the blackness, dimly aware of where Habitus had been when he fell. Reaching out, I grabbed hold of what I thought was an arm but turned out to be one of Habitus' skinny legs. 'Can you move?' I asked him with a wheeze. He nodded, not wanting to take his hand from over his mouth. Slowly we rose to our feet and began to move towards the ladder, or where the ladder had been. Looking up through the hole in the deck I could see anxious faces looking down at us, the ladder nothing but ashes.

'Help!' I screamed, but the faces just disappeared, and I imagined I could hear the soft splashes of the panicking crew as they abandoned ship. Habitus was gripping my shoulder hard, and I turned to him as he pointed frantically down to his legs. I looked down and saw a large piece of splintered wood protruding from his left leg, dark blood pouring from the wound, a puddle forming beneath his feet. 'We have to get out of here!' I said pointlessly, for that was obvious!

We moved away from the ladder, and with me leading, we staggered to the edge of the hold, our backs against the ship's side. The fire was growing, red and yellow flames burning through the deck above us. It would not be long before the ship collapsed, sealing our fate. I turned my head left then right, desperate to see *anything* that could help us: a length of rope to swing through the hatch to the deck, some sort of long wooden beam we could perhaps shimmy up – though the likelihood that we could do either with my hand and Habitus' injured leg was low.

Still, we stood there, me racked with indecision and him writhing in pain. A shadow stumbled from the smoke, and as I leant out to help the silhouette regain its footing, I saw it was Cletus, and he was dragging an unconscious Timon away from the flames. For the second time that night, our eyes locked, and we both went for our daggers and both found nothing but empty scabbards at our belts. He had been dragging Timon by the arms, but he let his friend go and delivered a right hook that sent me spinning. I landed on Habitus who spun me back around in time to catch another blow to the face. I fell to one knee and never managed to get back up.

There was a loud groan, like the ship was giving one last scream of defiance, before water erupted between the crumbling wooden beams. In moments, it filled the hold of the ship, dragging us down in a deathly embrace. I grabbed hold of Habitus and he grabbed me, and we fell into the dark abyss.

# CHAPTER V

**January, 193 AD**
**Carnuntum, Pannonia**

*Will this winter ever end?* Faustus thinks as he wanders the market in the forum. He has a little coin in his pouch, thanks to some work he has been doing for the tavern across the street. The Sword and Sheath has forever been a popular watering hole with the men from the Fourteenth Legion, and for that reason alone, Faustus has tended to avoid it.

But the owner is an old widower, and she struggles with some of the more laborious tasks involved in the day-to-day running of the place. Her staff is made up in its entirety of pretty serving girls, which leaves no muscle to heave in the heavy barrels of booze or dispose of the empties. There had been a Thracian slave whom she owned, but he had caught a fever in the autumn and never recovered. They had dug him a small grave on the outskirts of the city and even paid a mason to make him a small headstone. He had been a good man, honest and true, it was the least he had deserved.

Faustus had been desperate for coin and had agreed to do the heavy lifting. The day before, he had been in nothing but his loincloth come lunchtime, despite the cold. He had huffed and puffed as he rolled the wooden barrels off the back of a horse-drawn cart, the driver choosing to sit inside by the fire rather than help unload. When the girls had arrived for work around noon, he had felt their eyes burning into him, appraising the tight muscles that knotted his stomach and arms. If he hadn't been burning red already, he was by then.

He is still shy around women, unable to hold their gaze, and struggles to find the right words whenever he must converse with one. The serving girls, especially, are particularly attractive. The widower is called Attia and had once been a serving girl herself in the same tavern. She had married the son of the previous owner and, therefore, had spent most of her life behind that bar. Calvus says she was a rare beauty in her day, flowing red hair and pale eyes that could pierce your heart with a glance. There is an echo of those good looks when you see her now. Her hair has thinned and is as white as snow, age lines crease her face, and her spine has curved so she has a constant stoop. But her eyes still hold a glint of magic, the sparkle of youth and life. Faustus has seen her, too, looking at him appreciatively as he labours under her watchful eye.

He is thinking of her as he wanders between the stalls, oblivious to the hustle and bustle of the crowd around him. A vendor shoves a fresh fish in his face, it is so long, its tail droops over the man's shoulders. Faustus ignores the opening offer on the fish, thinking it was large enough to feed a small family for a week. He adjusts his body to squeeze past a semi-circle of punters all bidding on a poor boy who has been thrust onto an empty barrel and is being sold for a pittance. Faustus can see, just from a glance, that the boy is deathly pale and shivering in the freezing air, wearing nothing more than a rank old loincloth wrapped around his midriff. There is a stain running down his leg, and it is all Faustus can do not to stop and take the boy from the stall. He imagines he has been taken from his family, thrust into the back of a wagon and transported halfway across the empire just to be sold on a freezing January day to some poor farmer who needs another labourer come spring.

He pauses, his eyes fix on the boy's, and he is just about to shout his bid when he feels a slight touch on his left hip. When he looks down, he sees a small silver blade cut through the thong of his purse, and then both vanish into the crowd behind him.

'Hey!' he shouts. 'Hey, hey, you! Stop! Stop that man!'

The thief is short and slim, hooded against the cold. Likely it is a child just trying to steal some coin to take home to his starving mother, not that Faustus cares. He barges people from his path and stumbles clumsily after the thief. He bellows for the guards to help, but they just stand slouched, leaning on their spears. *Fucking soldiers,* he thinks as he charges into the back of an old man and stops to grab hold of his body to prevent him falling to the floor.

There is space ahead of him now. As he leaves the forum, he sees the thief, donned in a dark brown cloak, scurry down a honeycomb alley. Faustus darts after him, his hobnailed boots ringing off the flagstones. So intent is his gaze on the hooded thief, he does not see the patch of black ice on the cobbles, and as he adjusts his body to turn right, his legs go from beneath him. There is a flash of sunlight that offends his eyes before he hits the ground, head first, and sees nothing but white light.

Stunned, but blood still pumping furiously, he leaps back to his feet, ignoring the glaring pain behind his eyes, nausea rising within him, and staggers into the darkened alley.

'Took your time,' a voice rasps as Faustus grinds to a halt.

As his eyes adjust, he makes out the shadows of four men, two to his front and two circling behind. *Jupiter best and greatest. Jupiter best and greatest.* He prays in silence and tries to slow his breathing. His mind is filled with thoughts of Marcus and Meredith, standing in an alleyway not too different to this one. He remembers the screams, the blood…

'Thought you were gonna hurt my lad, did ya?' one of the men to his front says, stepping forward from the shadows. He is not tall, this man, a full head shorter than Faustus, but his shoulders are wide, his hands like hams, his face a crisscross of white scars. 'Well? Did ya?'

*Fuck you!* He wants to scream it but doesn't find the courage. He has been here before, knows what will happen. He doesn't think he will survive it a second time.

'He stole my purse,' he says in a mumble and immediately regrets it.

'*Oh, he stole my purse,*' the scarred man says in mock, strutting along the alley. '*I was overpowered by a child, someone help me!*' he whines in the highest pitch his voice can reach.

Tears prick Faustus' eyes, he swallows and to his horror, tastes the bile that rises from the pit of his stomach until… he vomits over the cobbles. His face burns with the shame.

There is a cacophony of laughter, in which even the child thief partakes. Faustus slumps to his knees as his legs go to jelly, his breathing is shallow, his heart pounds in his chest. He is pressing his weight on his hands, but there is no strength in his arms, and they begin to quiver.

'You're not some sort of pervert, are you?' a quiet voice says at his back. Faustus feels hot breath on the back of his neck, a looming presence over his left shoulder. 'We don't like boy fuckers round here,' the voice says in a gruff whisper.

A fire is lit deep inside Faustus. A raw and visceral energy pulsates through him, and before he can stop himself, he is surging to his feet, screaming incoherently. His sudden shift in weight takes the man behind him off guard and Faustus elbows him on the jaw. There is a loud snap followed by a groan and the would-be attacker flops to the cobbles.

*Always move, be the predator, not the prey.* Once more, he thinks of his childhood, of Commodus and the great gladiators of Rome as they sparred in the confines of the small amphitheatre just north of the eternal city.

There is a rush of wind past his right ear, and Faustus turns in time to block a thrown fist with his forearm. Pain shoots to his shoulder, but he grits his teeth and pushes himself forward, hitting his assailant with a punch of his own. The man staggers back, and Faustus glimpses a shaggy beard, the colour of rust, framing a toothless mouth. His right hand is aflame from the punch, so he kicks the man on the knee, forcing him from his feet. He is about to land the finishing blow to the temple when arms grapple him from behind, and he is off his feet, flying, before crashing into a red brick wall.

Stars circle overhead, a blinding pain cripples him, but he is conscious enough to feel shame as his leg warms to the touch of his own piss. Something hard hits him on the cheek, a fist or a rock, he knows not. He hears voices, but they are faint, distant, muffled: 'Go on son, you 'ave a go. That's it, yeah, let 'im 'ave it.'

He recoils as something smaller hits him repeatedly, he is not being hit especially hard but consistently in the same place. *Beaten by a child,* he thinks as he slumps to the shit-stained cobbles, willing the darkness to take him.

On the precipice of consciousness, he hears running footsteps, a blade being drawn, the screams of dying men. A man stands over him, old and wrinkled, dark-eyed, his face set in a frown. 'Can't leave you anywhere, can I, lad?' a gruff old voice rasps in broken Latin.

'Uncle,' Faustus whispers, before succumbing to the dark.

The sun is strong in the pale blue sky when he wakes. A chill breeze rushes in from an open window. He opens his eyes a fraction, but the pain is intense. The sun is flat and low in the sky, its white light blinding as it shines directly on his face.

'He's awake. Close that shutter, quickly now.'

Faustus groans, bile rises in his throat, but he has nothing left in him to vomit. He moves his hands to his head, trying to smother the pain, but all he can feel is the rough fabric of tightly wound bandages.

'Gently, lad, gently,' the voice says, and he feels hands pressed lightly on his arms.

'Where am I?' Faustus says, it hurts to speak.

'You are in the fortress, at the hospital. I didn't know where else to bring you.'

Faustus groans again. He would rather be back in the alley than in the fortress. He would rather be at the bottom of the Danube than in this cursed place. 'How long?' he says.

'Two days. You are quite lucky to be alive, according to the surgeon, anyway.'

'How did you find me?'

'The good Lord guided me,' Calvus says, gripping Faustus' sweaty palm with his own dry, calloused one.

'Then Fortuna is with me,' Faustus says, managing a smirk even through the pain.

'Your father's favourite, Fortuna, do not take her name in vain.'

'She was. I remember.' He tries to sit, but Calvus pushes him down.

'Don't be stupid, lad, you are in no condition to move. Just lie down, try to stay still.'

Faustus relents and lies back on the cot, keeping his eyes squinted shut. 'Did you kill them?' he asks.

There is a pause, the silence stretches. 'God help me, but yes, I did.

The child is here, working in the kitchens. It seems his father and his gang of thieves were his only family.'

'Poor child,' Faustus says with a cough that hurts so much a tear escapes and streaks his cheek. Despite what he has been through, he feels a deep pang of sympathy for the boy and the bleakness of his future.

'I know. He will be looked after. I still have friends here, they will see he comes to no harm.'

'Anyway, speaking of Fortuna, how in the name of all the gods did you survive that burning ship?'

Calvus chuckles, it drives him to a small coughing fit, as laughing always seems to do. 'God certainly had a hand in that, I can tell you. Truth is, I don't really know how we made it to the surface. One moment we were lost in the deep dark of the Aegean – the silence was surreal, as was the cold. The shock of going from the intense heat of the flames to that icy embrace was nearly the end of both Habitus and me – and then we were at the surface, a rope was thrown from one of the ships that had been following Rastus, and we were hauled to safety. You know, I've never had much time for sailing since.'

'I wonder why,' Faustus says with a wry grin. 'So, what did you do when you made land?'

'Oh, that is a long story, lad. I am not sure I am ready to speak about that just yet. What about your father? You want to hear more of him? You know it was not long after the battle against the Quadi that he first met Commodus.'

'I do not appear to be going anywhere, Uncle! Yes, please, I would love to hear more of him.'

'Well then, settle down young Faustus, get comfortable and listen.'

# CHAPTER VI

**October, 172 AD**
**Carnuntum, Pannonia**

It was the Ides of Hercules, the fifteenth day of the month of October. Autumn had cast its first blow against the summer, and wilted leaves turned a golden yellow and ripe orange, making for a beautiful sight across the windswept plain.

Centurion Albinus Silus stood to rigid attention at the front of his century as the Fourteenth Legion stood on the parade ground, awaiting the emperor. His chest filled with pride as he glanced at the silent ranks of men to his back, each turned out in immaculate kit, their mail glimmering in the light of the pale sun.

They were, of course, the most junior century in the legion and, therefore, stood at the rear of the parade ground on the eastern side, nearest the river Danube. Already, there was a distinct chill in the air, and Albinus had heard the veterans talk of the coming winter and how it was sure to be harsh. On the coldest of winters, the river Danube had been known to freeze over, and one could simply walk from one bank to the other, though Albinus had never known it to be so in his lifetime. But he was feeling the cold and wished he'd had the foresight to put one of his spare tunics under the one he was wearing, just for the extra warmth.

A gust of wind shot through him, and Albinus heard his teeth chattering, felt the scar on his left cheek burn as it always did in the cold. A surgeon had told him it was because of the distress to the joint and that the sensation would never fully go away. Bucco had said it was at least better than being dead, which he supposed was true.

'How long is he going to keep us waiting?' a voice said at his back.

'Not long now, brother,' Albinus said with a reassuring smile. 'With Fortuna's blessing, we shall be back in the *castrum* tucking into the noon meal before too long.' Albinus looked affectionately at his *optio*, Fullo. He had been Albinus' closest friend since they were young boys, and the two had formed a bond as tight as that of their fathers. Silus had rarely been seen in his army days without the ever-loyal Vitulus at his side, and they had grown even closer in retirement. Albinus hoped he and his friend would live as long to tread the same path.

'What you smiling at?' Fullo said with a scowl. He was still the same youth he had been before the two of them had signed up to fight under the Fourteenth's eagle, six years before. His blonde locks were an unruly mop atop his head, and the same thin, white scars ran across his forehead. He was proud of those scars, Albinus knew, for they were the lasting impression the dreaded plague had left on him. He had more, all over his torso, where the puss-filled lumps had formed and then been drained. Albinus could remember the fear he had felt for his friend, so soon after the despair of losing his mother to the same cursed illness.

Sometimes the gods were cruel.

'I was thinking of our fathers,' Albinus said. 'Of what they would make of us if they could see us now.' It was a confusing feeling, Albinus mused. Even now, years after his father's death, he still wondered if he had done enough to make the grizzled old veteran proud. And still he felt a burning shame that he longed for that reassurance.

'They can see us, brother,' Fullo said, putting his hand on Albinus' shoulder, 'and they are proud.'

A horn sounded, then another, and all around the parade ground, the quiet muttering ebbed and men stood straighter, eyes dead ahead. Albinus could hear the studded hobnails of soldiers' boots on gravel, and then a half-century of Praetorians marched past him, looking resplendent in their white tunics and black cloaks. They wore no mail, which Albinus thought strange, and already he was imagining what Fullo would have to say about that when this was over.

There was a gap behind the column of Praetorians, and then the emperor himself walked through the centre of the legion. He did not rush, nor did he dither. He merely strode at a steady pace, his eyes focused on the raised dais ahead, his back straight. His left arm was across his chest, holding the folds of his purple striped toga, his right arm hung at his side. It was the first time Albinus had seen the emperor since the parade inside the walls of Carnuntum the previous winter – he thought he looked older.

He was trailed by a youth Albinus had not seen before. His boyish features showed him to be no more than ten or eleven, but his physique was incredible for one so young. He stood as tall as his father, stiff-backed with rigid movements. He wore a thin golden crown around long, dark hair. He had tired eyes, set slightly too far apart. His nose was long and curved like a bird's beak. A golden cuirass gleamed beneath a white cloak. There was no mistaking his identity, he was Commodus, heir to the empire.

The emperor, followed by his son, climbed the steps to the raised wooden dais, passing the stone statues that showed the likeness of them both. Albinus had to squint against the sun's light as they were greeted by three priests from the temple of Jupiter and Legate Maximianus. The auguries were swiftly taken, and it was Commodus who severed the neck of the bull that had been waiting impatiently to be slaughtered.

The entrails were checked, the priests conferred. Even from a distance, Albinus could read the signs of impatience on Aurelius' stoic features. Eventually, it was agreed they were favourable, and Maximianus strode forward, one hand on the hilt of his sword.

He addressed the legion, his words swift and punctual. They had been parading that day to award the Divine Marcus Aurelius Antoninus Augustus the title of Germanicus, thanks to the recent victories won against the northern tribes. The Fourteenth Legion proclaimed him Germanicus without the slightest hesitation, just as the Tenth at Vindobona had the week before and the First Adiutrix would at Aquincum when the emperor arrived there the following week. From there, he would continue his tour back west to Noricum, where the First and Second Italica Legions, still under the command of Publius Helvius Pertinax, would be expected to do the same.

When the ceremony was over and Albinus could feel the impatience of the men around him, desperate to be away from the growing cold, something unexpected happened. Marcus Aurelius himself stepped forward on the raised dais, his face expressionless.

'Men of the Fourteenth Gemina legion,' he said in a clear, unbreaking voice. 'I wish to commend you on your fine work this summer and thank you for the victories you have won in our name. Details of your valour were read aloud from the floor in the senate house and were greeted with cheers both from the benches and from the people outside in the streets. You are heroes, one and all.'

There was a murmur of excitement. Albinus could hear his men whispering about rewards as their hopes began to shine the colour of silver.

The emperor continued. 'I wish to publicly express my thanks to a certain centurion amongst your ranks. This man, this brave warrior, was responsible for turning the tide against the Quadi, breaking their left wing and forging the path to victory. Step forward, Centurion Albinus Silus.'

To a man, the men of the sixth century, tenth cohort, erupted into raucous cheers. Fists were thrown towards the sky, and one man even threw his helmet.

Albinus didn't move. He was stunned, his jaw slack, tongue resting on his bottom lip. *Did he just say my name?*

Hands on his back pushed him forward, Bucco and Fullo whispering urgently in either ear, though he didn't register what either man said. He walked down the centre aisle between the waiting ranks of legionaries in a daze. Staring wide-eyed at a smiling Maximianus, he was treated to a bear hug from Taurus, who stood at the bottom of the steps leading up to the platform. 'Enjoy it, lad,' he whispered in his ear as Albinus trudged past.

Up the steps and he met the salute of his legate with one of his own before falling to his knees at the feet of Marcus Aurelius.

'Rise,' the emperor said. Albinus obeyed.

'For your bravery in the face of the enemy, for your cunning in outmanoeuvring them, for your part in the victory which has left the Quadi almost entirely beaten, I award you this.' Aurelius stretched out his arm and took hold of the medal harness that Albinus wore over the top of his mail. There was only one medal on it, which had been given to him, along with the harness, on his promotion to centurion. Now, Aurelius placed in one of the empty pockets a golden disc, the face of which portrayed a snarling lion.

'You are proving yourself to be quite the soldier, young man. Stay alive, you will achieve great things, I feel it in my bones.'

Albinus was speechless. He tried to form words of thanks but just blubbered like a fish. He knelt once more, head bowed, covering the tears of pride that stung his eyes. A Praetorian stepped forward and ushered him down the steps, and greeted by the cheers from the entire legion, he marched proudly back to the head of his century.

General Claudius Pompeianus stepped forward then, resting his hands on the wooden railing of the raised platform. 'Soldiers of Rome.' He spoke in a deep voice that reverberated around the parade ground, silencing the elated soldiers. 'You have done honour to your emperor, awarded him the most deserving of titles. Now, it is the imperial majesty's wish that you extend that honour to his son and heir.'

The proclamation was greeted with silence. Only once in the history of the Principate had a son succeeded his father as emperor. Life for a boy in the imperial family was fraught with danger. The same way the Divine Augustus himself had killed the republic and carved himself a throne, men had always sought the ultimate power of the purple. Emperors had been murdered, their families quietly killed off, new men had ascended to the highest position on earth. There had even been four emperors in a single year once. But it seemed Marcus Aurelius sought to make those turbulent days a thing of the distant past. This was much more than a statement; Aurelius was thinking beyond the boundaries of his own mortality. His reign would be the first in a dynasty, which would rule Rome and her empire for generations to come.

Through the silence stepped forward Maximianus . Albinus could make out the sparkle in his grey-green eyes, sensed the pride the man was feeling as he knelt before the boy in the golden cuirass and in a loud, clear voice, named him caesar, second in line to the throne.

The sun had set when Albinus finally made it to the door of the centurion's mess. He still felt uncomfortable upon entering, a sense of unbelonging lurked at the back of his mind. He was amongst the newest batch of recruits to the centurionate and by far the youngest. Twelve others had been promoted on the same day as he, and each had been a grizzled veteran that had served as an *optio* for several years. Albinus had only been an *optio* for a few months before being awarded his promotion, a feat that had caused some unrest with certain veterans, both common soldiers and officers alike.

He knew that without the support of Taurus, the first spear centurion in the legion, he would have faced much stauncher opposition than he had. He was grateful to his friend and mentor, who had served under Silus, Albinus' father, before getting his promotion. But he could never shake the feeling that he had only risen to where he was because he was his father's son and not because of what he had achieved. He insisted on his friends calling him Albinus rather than Silus, just to help distance him from that famous name.

The mess was crowded and smelt of sweat and dried leather. He eased his way through the throng, leaning on the bar and raising his hand to the bartender who acknowledged his presence. As he stood there, waiting to be served, he felt a burning sensation between his shoulders, and the hairs on the back of his neck prickled.

'There he is, fucking golden boy,' a voice muttered.

'Just another provincial, ain't he? Not got any proper blood. And we're meant to laud him as some sort of hero? Do me a favour.'

Albinus resisted the urge to turn. His fingers itched for the comfort of his sword hilt, though it was back in his room at the *castrum*. He had been ridiculed, when he had first entered the mess, for still being armed and armoured, men joking that he was fearful of an attack in the centre of their own fortress.

'Ain't like he's done something the rest of us couldn't have done. Must have been a fucking field day, attacking the backs of those barbarians. Even ten of the greenest recruits could have turned that battle.'

'Aye. And you know full well if that had been me or you that led the attack, then no more would have come of it. But old golden cock there gets a fucking medal from the emperor, no less!'

'I'm surprised he ain't wearing it now, and his mail!'

Albinus didn't need to turn around to discover who the two voices belonged to, he recognised them well enough. The first belonged to Marius Pullo, the senior centurion of the second cohort. Of pure Italian stock, he wore a chip on his shoulder when it came to officers from the provinces. He had never seen eye to eye with Taurus, and he often positioned his cohort in direct confrontation with the first when it came to training exercises, hoping to get one up on his *primus pilus*. He rarely did.

'People like him everywhere now, though, ain't there? You know, I had a letter from my brother, who's still in Rome. He says that one of the consuls for this year is from Africa. Africa! What the fuck is an African doing as the head of the senate! Ain't right, I tell you,' Pullo said.

'I hear you,' said the second voice. He was Titus Verrens, another Italian. He had served nearly twenty years under the eagle and had most likely spent at least three of those carrying out some form of punishment. He was known throughout the fortress to be the man to go to if you wanted to place an illegal bet on the next gladiatorial games and had twice been caught smuggling contraband into the fortress. Despite all this, he had been promoted to centurion in the fourth cohort at the same time Albinus had been given his own century. 'Problem is, there's just too many of the fuckers now. We're outnumbered, brother. Just look at this one legion, down to about three and a half thousand fighting fit, two thousand of them must be from the provinces, and the rest are made up of freed slaves and ex-gladiators. The gods are deserting us, slowly but surely.'

Albinus went to move away from the disgruntled pair, eager to be parted from their discriminatory views and desolate outlook on the empire.

'Oh, I think we offended her,' Pullo said with a snigger.

Albinus stopped in his tracks, lowered his wine cup gently onto the bar. The barman had overheard snippets of the conversation, and his eyes shuffled nervously from Albinus to the two centurions. Albinus met his eye and shook his head slightly, indicating there was no need to worry.

'Salve, brothers,' he said as he turned. 'I trust you are having a good evening? If you get too warm in here, I might suggest you take a turn outside, get some good Pannonian air into your lungs. You can't beat the open air out in the provinces, wouldn't you agree?'

'Who the fuck you calling brothers?' Pullo said, rising to his feet. He had a typical soldier's build, short and squat, shoulders like barrels and a deep chest atop a wide waist. His hair was mud brown, flecked with grey, his nose wide and flat like a pig's snout, his big mouth framed with thick lips. 'When you address a senior officer, you call him "sir". Or do you think you're so fucking special these days you don't need to follow protocol?'

Albinus smiled, a full and genuine beam that only angered Pullo more. 'I apologise, sir,' he said, rasping a salute, much to the delight of the crowd that had gathered around the growing confrontation. 'I could not help but overhear your disgruntlement at "provincials", as you called them, being promoted to positions of authority. And clearly, you have taken some small offence to the award I was presented with today by the emperor himself.'

The crowd around them growled, anger directed at Pullo. Albinus sensed the room gathering behind him and smiled again. Most of the centurions were from Pannonia or Noricum or another of the northern provinces. It would be the same for the other legions dotted along the river Danube. The legions had been in their provinces so long, they had become part of the local community. The soldiers that fought in them did not fight for faraway Rome, they fought for their families that lived on that very frontier, they fought for the people of the provinces. In their mind, Pannonia was as much Rome as Rome was itself. Pullo and Verrens should have been more careful about where they let fly their prejudiced remarks, a lesson they were about to learn the hard way.

'What in Mithras' name is going on here?' boomed first spear Centurion Taurus as he barrelled his way through the throng. He stood between Albinus and Pullo, eyes darting from one man to the next. His *vitis,* the badge of office carried by all centurions, was in his right hand. Albinus knew all too well he would not hesitate to use it.

'Nothing to worry about, sir,' Albinus said in a calm voice. 'Pullo here was just explaining to his friend how he thinks it's a disgrace that men from the provinces are allowed to be officers and how he resents serving under someone who has no "real blood".' Albinus, of course, knew full well he had mixed the truth with his own fiction, but he didn't care. Once more, he beamed at Pullo, whose shocked expression quickly turned to anger.

'That's bollo—'

'You do not believe men from the provinces should be allowed to serve as officers, hey?' Taurus arched an eyebrow. Albinus could see the glint in the first spear's eye. This was going to end very badly for Pullo. 'By a show of hands, who here is from the northern provinces? Or from anywhere outside Italy for that matter?'

Every man in the room raised their hand.

'That's what… fifty hands? Would you say so, Albinus?'

He nodded but had the sense to wipe the smile from his face.

'So, out of the fifty-odd centurions in the room, you two arse-wipes are the only two actually from Italy. How do you think you would fare commanding the entire legion by yourselves?'

Neither Pullo nor Verrens spoke. Verrens had, it seemed, found something very interesting about the laces of his boots.

'Think, before you speak, you half-baked fool. Men hadn't been levied from Italy for I don't know how many years until the First and Second Italia were formed. Without men from the provinces, there would be no legions or auxiliaries. Who then, would stop the barbarians from crossing the Danube, the Rhine? Who would crush the Britons when they revolt every other year? Who would hold back the Parthians? I wouldn't be so precious about your Italian blood if I were you, Pullo, your "provincial" commander may need you to spill it soon, all in the name of Rome, of course.'

Albinus could barely hide his delight as Taurus turned from Pullo to him. 'Wipe that smirk off your face, lad. The legate wants to see you, now.'

'You've made an enemy there, Albinus. Watch your step. A loud-mouthed fool he might be, but Pullo's dangerous, you hear me?'

'I know. It was stupid. He just wound me up, I should not have let him get to me. What does Maximianus want with me, anyway?'

'Ahh, speaking of dangerous,' Taurus said with a tight smile. They were walking down the *via principalis* that ran from east to west through the heart of the fortress. The smell of woodsmoke and baking bread wafted through Albinus' nostrils, reminding him he had not eaten since the midday meal. There was a southerly breeze that whipped off the Danube, and Albinus drew his cloak about him tighter. He felt the cold more than the average legionary. He was taller than most and a darn sight thinner too. It did not seem to matter how much he ate or how far he marched or how hard he trained with sword and shield, his twig-thin frame seemed destined to stay with him for the rest of his life.

'What?' Albinus said, nerves shooting up his spine. They were walking past the *quaestorium,* where the legion's *quaestor,* or quartermaster, kept the spare weapons and armour under lock and key.

'You'll find out soon enough. How's young Faustus getting along? You had a chance to pop down and see him?'

Albinus brightened at the mention of his young son, who was being well looked after by Calvus' daughter, Meredith, in Carnuntum. 'Yes, I spent the morning there yesterday. He's getting so big, can even stand on his own two feet now! He looks so much like my father.'

'Ha! He looks like you, you mean. Come on, we're here.' They passed into the *praetorium,* under a wooden colonnade with a tribune's house to either side, and through a small passageway that opened into a courtyard with legionaries standing on guard at every corner. Outside the door to the legate's office were two Praetorians standing rigidly to attention. They saluted and moved aside as the two officers approached.

Albinus did not have time to question why there were Praetorians in the fortress as he was thrust swiftly down to his knees by Taurus the moment he had ducked through the door. Taurus knelt beside him, muttering the words, 'Imperial Majesty.'

His eyes fixed on the floorboards, Albinus sensed the people in the room rather than saw them. Legate Maximianus stood to his right, Felix, the camp prefect beside him. To his front was a man seated on a wooden stool, the purple folds of his toga covering his feet. He risked a glance up, and the eyes of the most powerful man in the world met his.

'Please, rise,' said Marcus Aurelius.

Albinus and Taurus both stood rigidly to attention. Taurus moved off to Albinus' right, standing next to his two senior officers, leaving Albinus alone.

'I hear, young Silus, that you are quite a remarkable young man,' Aurelius said, a small smile playing on his lips.

'Th-thank you, Divine Augustus,' Albinus said.

'Please, young man, be at ease, there is no need for formalities here. I am not the tyrant some of my predecessors were. I do not believe myself to be a god, and I do not take offence to people conversing with me as one man to another.' He gave a dry chuckle, which was quickly followed by the other men in the room.

Following a noise to his left, Albinus looked to see Claudius Pompeianus, general of the northern armies and Aurelius' closest advisor, standing with his hands on Commodus' shoulders. Commodus himself seemed nervous, unsure. His eyes darted around the room before settling on Albinus. He nodded to Albinus who returned the gesture.

'You must be wondering why you are here?' Aurelius said.

Albinus' throat felt drier than burning sand. He tried to swallow but couldn't. He nodded to save himself the embarrassment of trying to speak.

'I have a favour to ask of you, young Silus. This is no mere passing request from your emperor but is a task of monumental importance to me. One that will change the course of your life forever and may well put it in some considerable danger.'

*Merciful gods.* 'Anything for you, Emperor,' Albinus managed to croak out.

'My son,' Aurelius said, motioning for the caesar to step forward, 'is still a boy, but a boy who will one day hold the ultimate power and will command armies in the field, as I have.'

Albinus nodded again. It was true that Aurelius had been present on more than one battlefield since the beginning of the war against the tribes. His white horse and billowing red cloak had bolstered the Romans' morale on several occasions, spearheading them to victory when defeat had seemed imminent.

'It is important to me that he is exposed to the life of a common soldier so he comes to develop a better understanding of the people he will once hold the power of life and death over. You, Silus, shall be the man to give him such exposure.'

*Merciful gods. Me?*

'Your legate,' he gestured to Maximianus, 'speaks very highly of you, as does your *primus pilus,* Taurus. Maximianus is a man with proven experience and sound judgement, he assures me you are more than up to the task.'

Silence. *Am I supposed to speak?*

'You could, perhaps, look a tad happier, Centurion. Your emperor is showing you great favour, after all,' Aurelius said with a wide smile.

'I – I… I am honoured, Imperial Majesty, truly. I just do not understand why I have been selected when there are many more experienced officers than me in this legion, let alone the whole army.'

Again, Aurelius laughed. 'There are many factors, young Silus, political mostly, that I shall not bore you with now. But to put it bluntly, I feel my son would be much safer with the men of the Fourteenth Legion, under the command of the *loyal* Maximianus.'

The added emphasis to the word 'loyal' was not lost on Albinus, who looked to his legate for guidance. Maximianus merely nodded to him, a tight smile betraying his nerves.

'Then it shall be my honour, Imperial Majesty. From one father to another, I swear before Jupiter, best and greatest, that I shall protect your son as I would my own.' Albinus prostrated himself on the floorboards, his heart thudding wildly.

'That, my dear boy, is all a father can ask for.'

# CHAPTER VII

**January, 193 AD**
**Carnuntum, Pannonia**

Memories haunt his dreams. His father hoists him onto his shoulders and marches through the fortress at Carnuntum. Together, they inspect the men of his century, who stand at stoic attention as their centurion gives their kit and weapons a once-over. They relax when he passes, slapping Faustus' palm and pulling funny faces, making the boy laugh. Albinus pretends to be angry, shouting at the men in mock anger, threatening to redden their hides with his rod of office.

Faustus is happy when he is with his father. The days seem brighter, the air tastes sweeter. He feels invincible, high up on those shoulders. Every man in the legion, it seems, knows his name. Every man says he is the son of a hero, says his father is brave and fearless, a warrior of rare skill.

He dreams his father is leading his men into battle. They form a square around him, red shields glinting in a strong and relentless sun. They hold the high ground, atop a large knoll in the land. All around them barbarians circle; big, bearded men on large horses. Some have swords, others carry lances, around and around the Roman square they ride, taking pot-shots at the tiring legionaries whenever their shields droop.

Albinus stands in their centre. Faustus can see through the haze that he is wounded; his left shoulder hangs impotent, his hand lifeless. He screams at his men, bellows at them to raise their shields. There is a man beside Albinus, a single red crest atop his helmet. Faustus can see the edges of cropped blonde hair, jagged scars like lightning bolts across his forehead. He carries a large wooden pole, and Faustus knows him to be Fullo, though his memory of the man is vague. A barbarian lunges at Albinus on his unprotected left side, and Fullo leaps past his friend and knocks the lance away with his pole. But he is tired, his reactions slow, and he can do nothing to block a sword cut that takes him high in the shoulder, shattering his mail and leaving behind a torrent of blood.

He drops from view without a sound.

One by one the other men drop, their cries of agony lost in the mist. Eventually, it is just his father left standing alone on the hilltop, beset by enemies. He does not try to defend himself, he merely stands, head raised to the heavens, and in that moment, Faustus and he lock eyes. Faustus screams, writhes, desperate to reach his father, his rock. But every step he takes closer, it seems Albinus moves another two back. He watches in despair as Albinus raises a hand in salute, his eyes moistened by glistening tears.

And then he is gone, lost to the charge of the savage horsemen, and Faustus is all alone…

'Faustus, Faustus, can you hear me, lad? It's okay, okay now, I've got you. Old Calvus has you.'

It is the third time he has had this dream since the fever that grips him took its hold the week before. Waking, Faustus recoils from the light, though the room is lit by nothing more than a single, flickering candle. 'Uncle,' he murmurs, his sweaty palm reaching out. It comforts him when Calvus grips it.

'You've got to fight this, lad. Don't let it take a hold of you. The doctor says that it's partly in the mind, this sickness. You've got to *want* to get better, you hear me?'

'What have I got to fight for, Uncle?' Faustus says in a whisper. 'I should have fought that day in the alleyway, when those… bastards killed them. But I didn't because I am a coward. What is there left for me now?'

'Me! You still have me, Faustus, and I still have you. If anything were to happen to you, how could I ever face your father, look him in the eye?'

'I fear I will be meeting him be—'

'In this life or at heaven's gates themselves, I swear to our Lord I will not allow myself to face your father knowing his son had died on my watch. I promised him, Faustus, *swore* to him I would protect you with my life. I cannot live knowing you are no more. You hear me? If for nothing else, fight this sickness for me.'

Time passes. Weeks, days, hours, he knows not. The sun is out when Faustus wakes, but the chill that sweeps in through the open window tells him winter still grips the land. He blinks rapidly, eyes adjusting to the light, to the sights he feels he hasn't seen for an age, as if he has spent half a life covered by a blindfold.

He tries to sit but has no strength in his arms, so he just lies, looks, listens. The familiar sounds of the legionary camp fill his ears: centurions shout at hapless recruits, studded boots rattle off gravel paths, a hammer strikes an anvil. It is the sound of his childhood, and tears stain his cheeks before he can control them. He thinks once more of his father, relives the dreams that haunted his fever-induced coma. He has spent years trying to distance himself from all things military, treating the soldiers in the red cloaks as if they were the flame and he the moth. In sudden realisation, he knows why he will not let them draw him in, why he must be forever in the shadows.

His father. It is obvious, now he is prepared to admit it. He has never made peace with his father, never forgiven him for leaving when he needed him most. With a heavy sigh and a few more tears, he faces up to the facts. He must make peace with his father, with the demons of his past, if only so he can move forward.

There is noise beyond the chamber door, the awkward shuffle of an old man. Calvus appears in the door frame, and his face lights up to see Faustus awake.

'Can I get you anything? Do you need another pillow? Are you hungry? Wine! You need wine, lad, that'll get you back on your feet.'

'Uncle, Uncle, peace, please!' Faustus says with a smile. The old man settles on a stool by the bed, his eyes never leaving Faustus.

'It is good to see you awake, lad. You had me worried for a while there.'

'How long was I asleep?'

'Two weeks, on and off. You awoke occasionally, but never for very long, and you were delirious when you did.'

Faustus nods, dismayed to have wasted so much time passed out in a bedchamber. 'How are you?' he asks the old Briton.

'Me? Don't worry about me, dear boy! It is you that has fought your way back from Hades' gates.'

'Hades' gates? Surely, such a place does not really exist?' Faustus says in mock.

'I see your usual ill humour has returned. I will fetch food and drink, you must be ravenous.'

A short time later, the old man returns with a tray of vegetable broth and water. 'Eat slowly, and no wine I'm afraid, just water for now, doctor's orders.'

They sit in silence whilst Faustus eats, slowly at first, but soon his appetite gets the better of him, and before he can stop himself, he is licking the bowl dry.

'I still feel so weak,' he says as he struggles to a sitting position.

'You will for a while yet, lad, I'd wager. But no matter, we can sit and talk as you recover. They cancelled the games, by the way, due to the emperor's untimely demise. There is a new man on the throne now, Pertinax, if you can believe it. Pertinax indeed, what a time to be alive.'

'I've heard of him, he fought in the northern wars, did he not?'

'Aye, and in the Parthian wars before them. He is a good man, a good leader, but he will not last long on the throne, mark my words.'

'I shall ask no more. Why don't you tell me what in Neptune's name you got up to in the east, after you rejected his kind offer of a watery grave?'

Calvus cackled. 'Ha! Reject it I did! Now then, let me think, we eventually made land at the port of Ephesus. By God, young Faustus, I could talk about that city all day...'

# CHAPTER VIII

**Spring, 172 AD**
**Ephesus, Asia**

It must have been around the Ides of April when we staggered ungainly down the gangway and finally onto dry land. As I said to you before, young Faustus, how in the name of our Lord we managed to escape from the blazing inferno that had been *Neptune's Wings*, I'll never know, but escape we did.

Habitus' leg wound had been bad, but thankfully he had managed to avoid infection. He had been reliant on a crutch for the remainder of the journey, but that bright afternoon, he walked unaided onto the quay, not helped by the mass of locals there to greet us.

They shouted and they screamed, they thrust their wares into our faces, you know, one man even held a live chicken right under my nose and would not take the wretched thing away until I poked him in his side with my knife.

After some time, we finally broke clear of the masses and followed the harbour round to the north. Warehouses dotted the skyline ahead of us. To this day, I find it hard to credit they were just warehouses, for up here, in the north, they would have been considered palaces. Their walls were a terracotta clay, their roofs red-tiled. I do not think I exaggerate when I say those walls rose higher than the ones that surround the fortress we sit in.

Our rescuer from the icy hell of the Aegean was a young captain, another Greek by the name of Loukios. He had paid a fortune to Rastus to guide him across the Aegean Sea and had also agreed to share a healthy portion of his profits with his fellow merchant. You would have thought him to have been sombre, dejected, distraught at the death of a comrade.

I swear, in all my years, I have never seen a man so happy.

'So, he was actually on fire when the ship sunk?' he said through a smile full of gleaming white teeth.

'For the hundredth time, Loukios, I do not wish to speak of it. We are very grateful for you and your men pulling us out of the water. But listen up, and listen well, I never wish to speak of that night's events again.' My conscience was preying on me. It is not the loss of that opportunist Rastus that bothers me, and certainly not the timely demise of Cletus and Timon. But there were many innocent people aboard that ship. To this day, I can see the face of the girl as she clung to her mother's skirts, the flames flaring up between us, condemning them to a most horrific death.

There was no way anyone else had escaped that cursed ship, of that, I was certain. All night, the crews of the other ships in our small fleet had stood on the rails, their ships at anchor, desperately seeking out signs of life. None had been found. Nothing but the odd scrap of timber had surfaced after Habitus and me. By God, we were lucky.

'Gods, I wish I could have seen that bastard die! You know what he demanded of me when I asked if we might follow him across the Aegean? Forty per cent of my profits! Forty per cent! That, on top of the fee I had to pay him upfront. The man is a pirate, I tell you.' He stopped then, turned to me and flashed another dazzling smile. '*Was* a pirate, I should say,' before laughing gayly and carrying on towards the warehouses.

I thought of killing him then, that measly merchant who thought so little of death and suffering. If I had learnt one thing from the events of the days previous, it was never to trust a Greek. Shame I didn't heed my own advice.

'You know somewhere we can stay?' Habitus asked Loukios as he hobbled along.

The heat was unlike anything I had experienced before. Sure, the summers here get a bit hot under the collar, and even back in Britannia, I remember one or two that were almost unbearable. But you have not felt heat until you have set foot in the east. The humidity was incredible, breathing was a labour, let alone walking and talking. And it was only April! Habitus, of course, barely felt it, him being from Syria. In fact, when I remarked that I thought I might be melting, he just laughed and said he had known warmer temperatures at Saturnalia. Saturnalia in the simmering sun, can you imagine?

'My crew all stay in the warehouse I rent here on the quay, I'm sure we will have a couple of spare cots for you.'

'No, we couldn't possibly impose. You have done more than enough for us, Loukios,' I said, and to be fair, I meant it. But we had no coin. I had travelled with a purse full of silver, given to me by Commander Pompeianus. But that, of course, had sunk to the bottom of the sea along with everything else we had stored in our packs.

Habitus nudged me discreetly, gently slowing the pace so a gap opened up between the two of us and Loukios. 'This guy's a wrong'un, ain't no two ways about it. But us being lacking in money and all that, might be worth seeing how far we can milk him.'

I made to protest, for the more time I spent with Loukios, the more he gave me a bad feeling. Habitus, though, cut me off. 'What else we gonna do, Calvus? Sleep on the street? Steal food from the markets? We'll take a cot and some provisions from the pirate, and in return we'll do him a favour, bit of labour, carry some goods from his ship or something. Gives us a roof over our heads until you can get hold of your contacts, don't it?'

God forgive me for ignoring the feeling in my gut and for the terrible events that were to occur on the basis of my decision, but I agreed.

For four days, we toiled under the merciless sun. Loukios may have only commanded a small vessel and a handful of crew, but by God, he turned a good profit from that old bucket. I hauled countless amphorae, filled with the finest Italian vintages, from the ship and onto the wharf. That was followed by more amphora, fish sauce, olive oil, dried figs… I could go on. There were crates full of cheaply made terracotta oil lamps which, to my horror, I realised were very similar to the one that had been knocked over and caused the fire on the *Neptune's Wings*. There were tapestries wrapped in cloth to protect them, one said to be worth more than an entire year's salary for a soldier.

And that was just the goods we *unloaded* from the ship. Going from the warehouse to the ship were perfumes, silks, ivory, even large slabs of coloured marble. Truly, in all my years as a soldier, never before had I appreciated the vastness of the commerce of the empire, the money to be made in having the right product at the right time. I asked Loukios how he was planning to sell the warehouse full of goods once it had all been safely stacked away. He just laughed and took me over to the nearest amphora and showed me the inscription, written in ink, along the top. It had a name on it, I can't remember whose now, all these years later, but the point is, he had *already* sold all these wares on his last trip to Ephesus the previous summer.

'My customers tell me what they want – I simply go and get it and bring it back for them. You will see, my friend, once word spreads around the city that I have returned, they will flock to this warehouse like crows to a battlefield, hungry for their feed.'

The man was making a fortune just on these deals alone. Then there were the cheaper goods he had brought along – wine from northern Gaul, more olive oil from southern Spain – that he sold at the markets, all for a huge profit. It was a dangerous profession, as our episode at sea had proven, but if you got it right and avoided sinking your ship, you could set yourself up for life in just one season.

So, as I was saying, for four days, we hauled goods wherever we were told, and on the fifth, Loukios said we were free to explore the city. And let me tell you, young Faustus, Ephesus is one hell of a city.

We left the warehouse just after daybreak, still wearing the same stained and ragged clothes that we had escaped from the Aegean in, and to be honest, we didn't cut a particularly impressive sight. We walked along the harbour, our pace slow as Habitus was suffering badly with his wounded leg. The manual labour of the previous days had put him under some strain, and on the second day the wound had reopened, and he had spent the remainder of the day confined to his cot in the warehouse.

The main road from the harbour into the city proper was known as the street of Arcadius, and that is the route we took. It was a bustling, busy street, even at that early hour, and we had to fight our way through the throng as we headed deeper into the city.

Market stalls lined the pavements to each side of the road, and the sights and smells were incredible. One vendor was selling nothing but silks, God only knows what the total value of his wares were, but suffice to say, he had around him four heavily armed bodyguards who looked as though they were well versed at using the long spears they carried. Another stall sold spices, and I swear I could have stood there all day just sniffing the produce, for the aromas were so rich and wonderful, let alone enjoying the sight of the patchwork colours.

All the while, we could see the imposing sight of the theatre in the distance. The great semi-circle of stone-built seats rose almost as high as the mountainous terrain that backed it. The plaza, with the stage and small changing rooms for the actors, was in front of it, and that, too, looked grander than anything I had seen before.

It was to be just the start of the wondrous sights that this city had in store for us.

All the while we were enjoying the fabulous delights of the east, we were on the lookout for a tavern that I had been ordered to present myself at when I arrived at Ephesus. It was called The Ox Hide, presumably because it had, at one time or another, been home to a tanner, and after a short walk, we found the place on the left-hand side of the street, a small sign above the door depicting an ox, predictably.

We entered cautiously, unsure of what to expect. I was still finding my feet in the *frumentarii,* not quite sure how I was supposed to behave. My contact was a man named Crassus, not to be confused with the famous old millionaire who had marched his legion to their deaths somewhere not too far from where we were.

'I'm here to see Crassus,' I said as I propped an elbow on the bar. The place was dimly lit and smelt like old leather, confirming that it had, indeed, once been used to transform rawhide of ox into usable leather.

'And who might you be?' the bartender replied in good Latin. Everything about him screamed ex-military. He had marched from the other end of the bar to greet us, his hobnailed sandals ringing off the timber floorboards. He was average height, solidly built and had a perfectly round head as bald as an egg. His nose was squat and broken, and he spoke with a slight lisp, a whistle if you like, thanks to his two top teeth being missing.

'My name is Calvus. I'm a friend from the north,' I said.

I felt Habitus shift uncomfortably next to me, could sense him gripping the hilt of his sword which he wore under a heavy cloak, despite the heat. I was unarmed, unable to bring myself to wear more layers. The old brown tunic I had on was causing me to sweat profusely.

'The candelabrum burn brightest on the darkest of nights,' the bartender said.

'All the better to spot the thief,' I replied.

I know what you're are thinking, what a poor excuse for a passcode. But I had insisted there be something more substantial than the usual watchwords used by the legions. Tribune Pompeianus had laughed at me and told me to come up with something on the spot – that was the best I had managed.

After a tense pause in which the bartender looked Habitus and I up and down, probably wondering why a *frumentarii* agent would arrive for a meeting in such a sorry state, he finally laid down the small towel he had been holding. There was a heavy clunk on the bar as the knife the towel had been concealing was laid to rest.

'I'm Crassus, come with me.'


'You don't look like much,' Crassus said, lounging on a small chair behind a dusty old desk in a tiny office behind the bar.

'We haven't had the easiest of journeys,' I replied, settling myself down on a round stool. Habitus had stayed at the bar, not willing to be involved in imperial business, and to be fair, I didn't blame him.

'If I didn't know better, I'd say the two of you swam half the way here. Most of the dye has run from your clothes,' he said with a crooked grin. I wondered for a moment if he knew of our plight at sea, it must have been common knowledge around the city by now that *The Neptune's Wings* had not made it across the Aegean, but how could this man have known we were on it?

'Well, you wouldn't be completely wrong, to be honest.'

I proceeded to tell him of the catastrophic events aboard the *Neptune's Wings* and of our current moneyless state and our reliance on Loukios.

'The two soldiers on the ship,' he said to me when I had finished, 'they were on their way to serve Cassius in Egypt?'

'Yes,' I said. 'Why?'

Crassus leaned forward before he spoke, his eyes scanning the open doorway behind me, making sure we were not being overheard. 'I've heard whispers coming out of Egypt. Cassius seeks to make himself emperor. We're unclear at this moment as to when exactly he will strike, but seems like it could be soon.'

I swallowed nervously. I had – in case I haven't made this clear to you as of yet, Faustus – not wanted a career in the *frumentarii.* I had no business discussing the affairs of senators or members of the imperial court. They were patricians, 'cream' as the soldiers called them, referring, of course, to them being the cream of society.

'I was told of this rumour before I departed the north,' I confirmed, deciding I had no choice but to trust this Crassus.

It is difficult, when acting the role of a spy, to know who around you can be trusted and who can't. Especially when you have been sent to an entirely new continent with no trusted allies to call upon. I had Habitus, of course, but he was just one retired soldier. I had no idea what sort of storm I was blindly lumbering into.

'Well, this *rumour* is growing in substance by the day. Cassius has all the high rankers in the east on his side, all apart from the ever-loyal governor Publius Martius Verus, who so far, has remained aloof. One of our agents managed to intercept correspondence from Verus to Cassius, politely refusing to acknowledge his bid for the purple, and says he is giving Cassius time to renounce this nonsense, as he calls it, before he tells Aurelius himself.'

'What about the rest of the east?' I asked, fiddling with the hem of my tunic. Being caught up in a civil war was not high on my agenda, to say the least.

'Well, Syria, of course, backs him. Cassius is himself native of the province, being born in Antioch. So, from both Syria and Syria Palaestina he will get five legions.'

'Five legions!'

'From Mesopotamia, he will get another, plus a shitload of auxiliaries.'

'Well, surely they won't all rally to his banner—'

'From Asia, he will get another two legions.'

'That's eight legions!'

'Quick maths, my friend,' Crassus said through that crooked grin of his. 'And throw into the mix Armenia, the Paphlagonions on the coast of the Black Sea, Assyria has thrown its lot in, from what I hear—'

'How many men, Crassus?' I spat. Sweat poured down my forehead, for this dire news, coupled with the heat, had given me a fright.

'Forty-five thousand men, including auxiliaries.'

'God above,' I muttered. I had, unconsciously, withdrawn my small fish amulet from beneath my tunic and was fiddling with it.

'You might want to keep that hidden, friend. Christians aren't treated too kindly around here,' Crassus said.

In a state of panic, I grabbed a stylus that lay on the desk between us and leapt to my feet, ready to use it as a dagger.

'Hey, easy there, brother, you'll get no judgement from me,' Crassus said as he held his hands high above his head.

My stool had fallen to the wooden floor with a crash, and no sooner had I relaxed my posture and framed my mouth to offer an apology, Habitus sprang through the open door, sword naked in his palm.

'Get the fuck away from him, you bastard! If you wanna take him, you'll have to go through me first!'

After a moment's pause, Crassus and I burst into laughter, much to the annoyance of Habitus who looked as though he might do for us both with his trusted old *gladius*.

'Peace, Habitus,' I said, laying a calming arm on his shoulder. 'Crassus here saw my amulet, and for a moment I panicked he might try and have me arrested. But he won't. Please, put the sword down.'

Habitus did as I asked, still scowling at Crassus.

'He's on our side, Habitus. And by the sounds of it, we are going to need all the friends we can get.'

Habitus sheathed the blade and turned to me. 'What's going on then? You two have been in here whispering like lovers for an age.'

His breath stank of wine, and I wondered how long we had indeed been cooped up in that little office. Habitus, it seemed, had wasted no time in reacquainting himself with the local vintages of the eastern provinces.

'I have work to do, it seems.'

'I haven't told you all of it, yet,' Crassus said, him too rising to his feet. 'Come on, now your friend has joined us, we might as well go through to the bar and get ourselves a drink.'

We followed Crassus through and settled down at a small table in the corner. There were only three other customers in the tavern, for the hour was still early, and there was little danger of us being overheard.

'So, now you know how many legions Aurelius is likely to be facing in the field. But what you don't know is that Cassius has also been recruiting some of his veteran officers, some of whom are currently in Ephesus. I've had a message from your tribune, Pompeianus, is it? Well, he wants you to try and get close to one of them, see if you can get him to talk.'

Habitus and I shared a look.

'As it happens, we have already met a couple. Timon and Cletus were their names. Both Greek. They were on their way to Egypt to sign back up and serve,' Habitus said.

'I know, Calvus has already told me. Do you think they survived the sinking ship?' Crassus asked.

'Not likely. Habitus had knocked one of them out cold, and I'd had a scuffle with the other. When the hull collapsed on us, the one named Cletus was dragging an unconscious Timon across the floor. I think it's safe to say they are both food for the fish,' I said. Habitus nodded his agreement.

'Good,' Crassus said. 'That's two fewer we have to worry about then. I'll give you some coin, as much as you need. Get yourselves some new clothes and start doing the rounds of the local taverns, see what you can come up with. Me and my lads are too well known in these parts, someone will expose us in a heartbeat if we try and do it ourselves. You two are our best hope.'

'Okay,' I said. 'We'll do it.'

'What?' Habitus exclaimed. 'I'm not here as some sort of spy! I'm a retired soldier, on my way to Syria to open a bar! You want me to risk my neck, going on some wild goose chase for fellow soldiers who may or may not be traitors? Leave me out!'

He turned for the door and had almost made it when Crassus said, 'You bring me information, and I'll tell you the whereabouts of a certain red-haired girl from Gaul who passed through here not too long ago.'

Habitus stopped, turned back slowly. Our eyes met.

'What makes you think I am here looking for a red-haired girl from Gaul?' I asked.

'I know a lot more than you think, mate.'


We took the offered pouch of silver from Crassus. Leaving the tavern at around midday, we spent the afternoon refilling our bags with supplies. Of course, we even had to buy new bags.

After a couple of hours, we had bought enough dried meat and bread to last us a few days, a few jugs of fine wine, new clothes and sandals, and were making our way back to the warehouse where we planned to politely thank Loukios for giving us a bed for a few nights before heading back to the city to book into the finest-looking tavern we could find.

'Where do you think we should stay?' Habitus asked me as we were walking through one of the gates that led into the harbour. There was a soldier on guard, whistling a tuneless melody as he rocked back and forth on his feet. He smiled and nodded my way, and I returned the gesture.

'I've no idea,' I said. 'Got no way of knowing where any of Cassius' supporters will be staying. Guess we just find a tavern, book in for one night and try a different one every night.'

I patted the money pouch on my newly acquired belt, just to reassure myself the coin was still in place. There must have been three years' pay for a legionary jingling inside the leather, I was anxious to get it inside a locked room.

The Aegean glistened in the orange glow of the setting sun, the air warm and salty on my face, blown in by a gentle breeze. I felt happy, peaceful, in fact, the happiest I had been since we had departed Pannonia. There was money once more in my purse, a faint hope of finding Licina and the prospect of playing a small role in putting down a revolt against the emperor, which did fill me with some kind of nervous excitement.

So content was I, as we made our way up the gentle incline to the warehouse, that I paid no heed to how quiet the harbour was. At all hours, day and night since our arrival, there had been people bustling about the quay: merchants haggling their crew as they observed their cargo being unloaded from their ships; prostitutes flaunting themselves to the sailors, looking to earn themselves some easy coin; off-duty soldiers playing dice; opportunists looking to sell their stolen goods from leather satchels, I could go on.

That evening, there was nothing. Neither Habitus nor I had noticed the silence outside Loukios' warehouse. It was only when I put my hand to the door and it came away bloody that I felt the first tingling sensation of fear gripping me in an icy embrace.

I pulled my hand away, staring at it in wonder. I looked from it to the door, which was coated in a thin film of claret. It swung open slowly, and I stepped inside in a stupor.

Loukios lay dead on the floor, his head nearly separated from his body. Around him were his crew. The torrent of blood was so thick, it almost came up to the top of my toes. The smell was horrific. I swatted a fly from my face, scrunching my nose against the stink. I was about to turn back to Habitus, but a voice stopped me in my tracks.

'Ahh, well, if it isn't our old friends, Calvus and Habitus. We've been waiting for you to come home, haven't we, boys?'

I looked up, grimacing, for at once, I had recognised the voice of the speaker. Cletus was grinning like a wolf, Timon standing at his shoulder, his eyes sending flying daggers at Habitus. And all around us, armed men crept out of the shadows, their blades naked in their palms.

# CHAPTER IX

**February, 193 AD**
**Carnuntum, Pannonia**

It has been a week since Faustus first woke from his fever-induced dreams. He feels stronger now, is able to rise from his bed and venture outside, though the cold bites at his bones when he does.

He is sitting in the portico of the hospital, taking in the sights of the day-to-day life of the army. A small column of miserable-looking recruits is force-marched past, a surly old centurion encouraging them on with a whip of his vine stick. Faustus winces as one youth, who is struggling to keep up the pace, is lashed across the back of his knee. There is a loud snap as the wooden rod strikes skin, and with a howl of pain, the youth drops to the ground like a sack of grain.

In moments, the centurion has him back on his feet, forcing him on, always forwards. 'If you stop, you die,' the centurion barks in the youth's ear, and Faustus hears an echo of his father in those harsh words. Life in the army is hard, nothing but the monotonous routine of barracks life in peacetime and the constant danger of battle during war. The youth will have to learn quickly if he is to survive.

Not for the first time, Faustus contemplates his decision to shy away from the army. His grandfather had been the *primus pilus*, or first spear centurion, of the Fourteenth Legion, his father also serving with distinction as a centurion in the same legion. Why is it he feels no longing to follow the same path?

He thinks back to the fight in the alley, to the rush of pure anger he had felt as he cracked his elbow into the first attacker's jaw, the savage joy of seeing the body flop to the cobbles. That is what it is to be a soldier, that is how it feels to kill. But then he remembers the beating, lying helpless on the cold ground, fists plunging into him, striking bone, breaking skin. He remembers the fear, the loneliness, and despite the chill breeze, he begins to sweat. That is what it is to die on the battlefield or in the arena. It does not matter if you are surrounded by your comrades, your brothers, in the end, each man meets his maker alone.

Faustus snaps his eyes open and realises he has been dozing. His face still hurts, though he is told the bruising has faded. Miraculously, he has no broken bones. With a wry smile, Faustus remembers the father encouraging his son to punch him. He thinks that was the only thing that saved him further punishment.

There is a presence to his right, a shadow lurking around the corner. Faustus sits back in his chair and tries to study the shadow without turning his head. It is a boy, no more than ten years old, judging by his height. He sees the hint of a pale face as the child edges around the corner of the hospital before darting back into the shadows.

'Hello?' Faustus says, his head fully turned now. There is no reply, but he senses the boy is still there. He thinks he knows who it is – Calvus said the boy from the alley was working in the fortress, and he doesn't know of anyone else that would seek him out.

With a wince, Faustus rises from the chair. Shedding the blanket, he walks to the edge of the portico and looks around the corner, but there is no one there.

One week later and Faustus is strong enough to take a lap of the fortress in the morning, although it leaves him feeling weak. He has not seen or heard from Calvus in that time and is starting to worry about the old man. An orderly has been keeping him well fed, though he does not attempt to make much conversation and can answer none of the questions Faustus fires his way.

After another two days, Faustus feels well enough to bathe. He walks down the gravel path from the hospital to the bathhouse. Part of him wishes he could have gone into the city to bathe, as he knows he would feel more comfortable around fellow civilians rather than soldiers, but he knows he does not have the energy for the walk. He enters the small bathhouse and undresses in a dark corner of the changing room, trying not to meet anyone's eye.

He walks into the main room, relishing its warm embrace. The steam seems to soak into his bones as he moves sheepishly through the throng of off-duty soldiers. It seems to him that each man there is twice his weight, and their loud comradery makes him uncomfortable. He slips from the towel that has been concealing his manhood and plunges into the pool. The water is hot, soothing, protective, like armour shielding him from a blade. He allows himself to be drawn in by its calling and slips deeper underwater until he hears nothing but its swirling, sees nothing but a murky blue.

After a time, he rises and sucks in a lungful of clammy air, immediately feeling more alive. He feels an aching in his cheeks and with a bark of laughter, realises it has been caused by a broad smile that has deserted his face for too long.

He scrubs himself, gently at first but more firmly as he sees the white skin come to the fore as weeks of dirt and grime are washed away. Eventually, he rises from the pool and walks hurriedly to the next room where he sucks in a deep breath before diving into the cold bath He doesn't stay here long, just long enough for the sweat to stop and the icy grip of the water to work its way into the pores of his skin.

Once more, he feels the odd sensation that he is being watched. There is a boy leaning against a pillar in the corner of the room. He is wearing a dark-coloured tunic and appears to be chewing his fingernails as he observes. Faustus feels his neck burn and the hairs on his arms stand on end, though it has nothing to do with the temperature.

Quickly, he rises from the water and wraps himself in a towel before moving to the last room in the bathhouse. Here, a slave leads him to a wooden table and instructs him to lie on his front. The towel is removed from his waist and warm oil is sprinkled on his back and legs. All the time Faustus feels the presence of the boy, senses the wide eyes that never leave him.

Massaged and scrubbed clean of oil, Faustus leaves the baths a new man. He is more energised, still smiling and ravenous with hunger. As he walks back to the hospital, he even finds it within himself to nod to a couple of passing soldiers. One asks him how he is, says he was there when he was first brought in. They talk for a small time, Faustus thanks him for his concern and assures him he is much recovered.

'By the gods, you look like your father,' the soldier says as the two men part. 'It is a wonder some of the boys don't stop and salute you as you walk past.'

Faustus smiles at the comment, but inside, he winces. *As long as I am here, I will never escape him.*

To his relief, Calvus is in his room when he returns, sitting by the window, drinking a cup of wine. They embrace, and Calvus talks of how well he is looking. Is he hungry? Will he take wine? Is he warm enough? Faustus shrugs off the questions and eases the old man back into his seat.

'Where have you been?' Faustus asks. 'I was starting to worry. I kept asking the orderly if he had seen you, but it seemed as though you had disappeared.'

'I know, lad, I know, I'm sorry. Bit of business came up, that's all. I knew you would be well cared for here, though.' He shifts on his chair as he speaks, clearly uncomfortable with the question.

'What sort of business?' Faustus presses. He knows, of course, full well what line of work Calvus was in once he had been discharged from the legions. He does not know, however, how involved the old man still is with the *frumentarii* and their work.

Calvus hesitates before he speaks. 'Imperial business. I can't say much more than that right now, I'm afraid.'

'Are you in danger? Is there to be a war?' Faustus blurts before he can control himself.

'Danger?' Calvus says through a laugh. 'What danger could an old man like me get into? No, lad, it is not me that could be in trouble, but the empire itself. You remember I told you Pertinax had taken the throne for himself?' Faustus nods. 'Well, it seems as though he may not be there for long. Across the empire, men are springing up, staking their claim for the purple. There will be a civil war, lad, mark my words. Maybe as bad as after Nero took his own life.'

Faustus sits in silence as he contemplates the news. Wars need armies, and armies need men. There had been no conscription to the army since he had been a baby and Marcus Aurelius had ordered the northern legions to get themselves up to full strength, no matter what, after the long war and plague had combined to ravage them of fighting men. But now, Faustus was imagining rogue generals riding at the head of large columns of men, scouring every town and village for boys of fighting age and donning them in mail. He does not want to fight, doesn't have the mentality to cope with that life, that much he knows.

'They won't make you fight, Faustus,' Calvus says, as if he can see into Faustus' soul.

'They might,' Faustus says, bile rising in his throat as he speaks. Once more, he is back in that alley, standing immobile as the woman that raised him and his best friend are murdered. 'I will not survive if they do,' he says.

'Enough of this!' Calvus says, slapping his thigh. 'Let us talk of other things. The sun is shining, you are hale and your strength is growing, and soon, an orderly will be round with more wine and food to fill our bellies. Now then, shall I tell you what happened to Habitus and me after we had been taken by those two Greek curs, Cletus and Timon?'

'Gods, yes!' Faustus says, and the smile returns to his face. 'I still do not believe they were alive.'

'Neither did I, lad,' Calvus says with a dry chuckle, 'but alive they were, and not in the best of moods with us!'

# CHAPTER X

**Spring, 172 AD**
**Ephesus, Asia**

We were bound and gagged and led from that blood-soaked warehouse a matter of moments after we had entered.

Cletus and Timon did not speak to us nor approach us, just ordered their henchmen to bind us and led our column out into that glorious evening. We were marched back down the quay. The harbour appeared as deserted as it had been just moments before when we had arrived. I quickly found out why. At the main gate into the city, Cletus slipped a small money purse to the soldier who was on guard duty, who took his payment with glee. He had nodded amiably to me, that guard, as Habitus and I had walked past him from the city to the harbour. Clearly, he had been ordered to keep everyone out, except us.

The sun was setting now, behind us to the west. I looked back as we were forced through the gate and saw its dying red light as it dipped beneath the ocean, and wondered if I saw my own life thread ending with that light.

Struggling against our bonds, we walked down the Street of Arcadius with the towering structure of the theatre plaza to our front, the bare rock of the mountains looming in the shadows behind it. 'Where are you taking us?' I asked Cletus, hoping my voice did not betray my fear.

'You will see soon enough, traitor,' Cletus replied.

'It is you that is the traitor, you maggot!' I spat. 'You who would turn your back on your true emperor, your country.'

'My *country?*' he said, almost vomiting over the second word. 'Rome is not my country, Greece is. We were kings of the world once, pioneers that civilised half the barbarians you now deem to be *Roman.* Do not insult me, barbarian, we Greeks shall one day rise again.'

I made to retort, but Habitus threw his weight into my side. 'Save your strength, brother,' he whispered. 'I do not plan to die a coward's death at these bastards' hands, you hear me?'

I nodded, I too had a reason to live, a person to find. You know now who I speak of, Faustus, I'm sure. We reached the end of the Street of Arcadius, the night now fully dark. Torches lined the buildings to every side, the great plaza of the theatre had one hung outside almost every window, illuminating it in a brilliant orange glow. We paused there, at the crossroads in front of the theatre, Cletus and Timon to our front, seemingly having a hushed disagreement about where they should take us. Timon was pointing left, to the north where the road led past the gymnasium, and eventually, to the giant stadium and stables that housed the chariot racing. The Greens were big in Ephesus at the time, their driver being a local. Almost every bar and store had green awnings draped over the doors, and some homes were even painted green to show their support for their hero. Cletus, however, insisted we go right, deeper into the city.

Cletus won the muted row, and right we went, south, deeper into the sprawling city. We passed the Agora on our right, the home of the local city government. Even then, at that late hour, men in togas stood deep in discussion on the stone steps. Litters waited with sweating slaves who wished their masters would stop dawdling so they could whisk them home and be discharged of their duties for the day.

One such man nodded to Cletus as we walked down the street, his eyebrows knitted together in question when he saw Habitus and I being dragged by a throng of armed men. He made a beeline for Cletus, but, 'Not now, friend, later. I will call on you and explain if it pleases you,' was the only answer he got to his unspoken question. I wondered at the power Cletus had then, if he was able to dismiss a city official so easily. Did Cassius have every city in the east this deep in his pocket? If he did, then the emperor, and maybe the empire, were done for.

At the next junction, our captors led us left past the Gate of Mithridates, another cursed easterner who had sought dominance over Rome. It had taken three of the republic's greatest generals: Sulla, Lucullus and, finally, Pompey the Great to bring him to his knees. We carried on in the darkness, the air growing colder with every step until I could see my breath in the torchlight.

On we walked, in total silence now. Eventually, the torches lighting our path stopped with the last of the houses, and we were nothing but shadows, silent and cold. After a time, we stopped at the walls of a limestone building, a small wooden door the only feature. Cletus knocked three times then paused for five heartbeats and knocked three times again.

The door was opened by someone I could not see, and we were ushered into a cramped room that stank of rotten timber and damp. There was a sound like grating iron, like an old lock being opened for the first time in a generation, and Habitus and I were thrust into a cage, the rusty door locked behind us.

No one spoke to us, no one offered food or water. We just sat on the damp floor, shivering in the dark. Eventually, we both gave in to sleep.

Dawn must have broken over the eastern horizon, though no light filtered into our damp cage. I woke slowly, groggily, as if I had drunk my body weight in wine the night before. My back and neck were in tatters, my arms numb. I tried to move onto my knees, raise myself to a standing position, but my legs could not support my weight.

'Habitus?' I croaked through a dry throat. 'Habitus?' I said again, this time coughing violently.

'I'm here, brother,' came a wheezy reply.

'Are you okay?' I asked.

'As well as I can be. I can't turn my neck; my spine is burning, and my fingers are numb. You?'

I laughed, despite the peril we were clearly in. 'About the same, brother. No fun getting old, is it?'

These days, you know, I smile to think that back then, twenty years ago,

I thought myself as old. Though, if you'd have met me back then, Faustus, you would have thought it so.

'Well, it seems Fortuna has had her fill of us, brother, and she will not let us get any older.'

'I am sorry, old friend,' I said. For the first time since we had been captured, it was not fear I felt then, but sadness. I had promised Habitus I would accompany him to the east, stay with him as he set himself up in Syria and built the foundations for his new life. He had been delighted for the company, even though he knew too well that my motives were not as clear as they appeared. Now, it seemed, he would not get to see the sun rise on his homeland, smell the salt of the sea on the shores that he had been away from for so many years.

'I'm a soldier, Calvus,' he said. 'I've spent my whole life fighting, seeing my friends cut down and wondering why they were taken and I was left here, on this earth. Do not be sorry for me, brother, I shall be glad to see my old comrades once more and gladder still that you will cross the river with me.'

There was a noise then, a bolt being slid back from an unseen door, and a burst of light blinded us.

I turned my head, squinting my eyes shut as the light sent a shockwave of pain through my skull. Footsteps, the grate of hobnails on wet stone, hushed voices. 'I shall see you on the ferry, brother,' I said to Habitus as I opened my eyes.

The chamber was lit now, bathed in the golden light of the sun. We appeared to be in some sort of disused warehouse, locked in a small iron-barred cage in the corner. The walls were red brick and the ceiling bare plaster, the floor a zigzag of old, broken cobbles. There was a leak in the roof on the other side of the room, the cause of the wet floor. The ground was not completely flat, and our cage was situated on the lower ground, small puddles forming atop the cracked flagstones around us.

I looked then at the men who had come to take us to our execution, for surely the only thing left for us now was to hope for a good end, a soldier's death. Four men, all draped in brown cloaks, hoods up to conceal their faces, stood facing us on the other side of the iron bars. That they were military was in no doubt; they wore no armour, but their off-white tunics were belted at the waist, the unmistakable bulge of swords at their sides, the pommel protruding from their cloaks.

Once more I tried to stand, but still my legs were like wet sand under the weight of a rock. 'Who are you?' I said instead. Cletus and Timon were not among the four men. I guessed they did not feel the need to come and end us themselves. We were nothing but a minor inconvenience to them, a mosquito to be swatted aside.

'I knew you two would give me grief the moment I laid eyes on you,' a voice said. He stood slightly closer to us than the other three men, and I saw the shadow of a smile dance across his crooked lips.

'Crassus?' I said, confused, not wanting to believe he had betrayed us.

'Salve, brothers,' he said. 'I must apologise to you both. It would appear we were overheard in my tavern when you came to visit. One of my men, he was not who he seemed.' He lowered his hood then, fully revealing his crooked mouth and the deep tan of his skin. 'I tortured the man in question, turns out he has been on Cassius' payroll for some time. I had no idea, please believe me.'

'I believe you, friend,' I said, for in reality, I had little choice. 'Can you get us out of here?'

'Yes, I believe so, anyway. You are in a disused gymnasium, in the southeast corner of the city. It seems Cletus has been using this as a base of operations. There are ten men here, including your two *friends* Cletus and Timon. Cletus, it appears, has been negotiating with the local government for a peaceful transition into Cassius' rule once he has declared for the purple. Most of the officials are in his pay now, we have to move fast.'

'What do we do?' Habitus spoke. He rose slowly to his feet, swaying as if he was on the deck of a rolling ship.

'Behind this building is a gate that leads east out of Ephesus and into Asia. We shall have to travel by road, the journey will be long and hard. Are you both up to it?'

I looked at Habitus and he at me. He surprised me then, this reluctant old soldier that wanted nothing more than to go home. 'Let's do it, brother.' I returned his nod before speaking.

'And the girl? You said before you would help us find her? You will keep your promise?'

'I will,' Crassus said. 'You have my word.'

'Then for Christ's sake, get us out of here.'

Crassus smashed the lock of the cage with the pommel of his sword. There was a loud bang and a clatter as it fell to the cobbles, splitting into three pieces. I thanked God then that the owner of the gymnasium had allowed the iron to turn to rust, for had been maintained, we may never have broken out of there without the key.

One of Crassus' men moved forward and with a flick of his knife, freed us from our bonds. I knew pain then, intense and hot as if my hands had been thrust into the heart of a roaring hearth. Blood pumped beneath skin that had swollen and coloured a purple shade of blue. I gasped, biting my tongue till I tasted blood in my efforts to not shout out with pain. Through watery eyes, I could see Habitus enduring the same struggles, though he seemed to recover faster than I and was already experimenting with the dexterity of his fingers.

'Can you hold a sword?' Crassus asked. He made no effort to introduce us to his men, and to be fair, in the line of work we were all embroiled, that was no bad thing. You cannot give a man up under torture if you do not know his name.

'Do you have an axe?' I asked. I have always preferred a short-handled axe to the gladius that I had been trained to use for twenty-odd years. I had taken to carrying one with me always when in the legions, after my fifth year when I had served as an engineer. It is a much more effective weapon in the shield wall, the press of battle, I find. Standing shoulder to shoulder with my brothers, I would hook my axe over the rim of my opponent's shield and pull it forward, exposing his neck and torso. One of my shield brothers would then skewer the man with the point of his sword, and we would step over the corpse and repeat the exercise with our next victim.

'Here,' one of Crassus' men said, unhooking a single-headed, wedge-shaped axe from his belt. 'It's not the sharpest, but it will do the job just fine,' he said.

I thanked the man and gave him a quick once-over. He was tall and broad with a great shaggy mane of dark red hair. His eyes were light brown, his skin pale, reddened by the heat of the sun. I thought he could well be from Britannia, like me, though there appeared to be no trace of an accent in his Latin.

'You have a plan?' I asked Crassus.

He sucked his teeth before replying. 'To be honest, I'm rather making this all up as we go along. It has only been a few hours since I learned of your capture, the spy that had followed you back to the warehouse had to fight his way back to me. We managed to sneak in here unobserved, but we are on the western side of the complex. We need to cross the small courtyard and enter the building on the eastern side, which is where our *friends* are currently situated. I'm afraid the only thing for it is to fight our way through to the gate.'

'You were spying on us?' I said.

'Of course,' Crassus said, as if I had just asked him if he took wine with his dinner.

'So, I am sent east to spy. When I arrive, I meet the only ally I have in the entire region, and he, in turn, decides to spy on me. But when the spy sent to spy on me is doing his spying, he is, in turn, being spied upon by our mutual enemy. Have I got that right?'

'Not to forget that the spy who was spying on my spy was actually a double agent, taking his pay from both me and our enemy.' He smiled then, looking at my dumb-stricken face. 'I get the feeling you are still new to all this.'

'I wish I were back in the army,' I said with a sigh. 'Life was so much simpler. An enemy to your front, a sword in your hand and your comrades to either side. Good times.'

'I hear you, brother,' Habitus said, testing the weight on a gladius he had just been passed. 'Let's get this over with, shall we?'

We edged out of the door from the chamber into a small, square courtyard. It was an old training square where, at one point, men would have met to wrestle and run, throw javelins and box. The floor was sand, my feet still unsteady, and I wobbled as I walked. The silence was absolute. I wondered how far we had walked down that dark road the previous night, after passing the Gate of Mithridates. The streets had been teeming with people then, surely they would be now, but I could hear no sign, just the gentle rustle of the breeze as it swept inland from the sea.

Crassus ordered us into a skirmish line, and we stepped as quietly as we could across the sand, our eyes fixed on a wooden door in the southeastern corner. It was not closed; I could see a sliver of light that crept in through the small gap between the door's edge and the frame. Before long, we were alongside the door, our backs against the wall. Crassus sent forth one man, a small man with a bald head, skin darker than Habitus' which marked him out as a native of these lands. He crept to the threshold and got down on his belly before peering into the small crack. I wondered, for a moment, why he had lain down and then saw the brilliance in it. If he had remained standing, his body would have blocked out the light which could have alerted the men inside. On his belly, it was just his head that would cause a shadow on the cobbles, and it would not protrude far into the chamber.

'All clear,' he mouthed at Crassus as he shuffled back behind the door and rose to his feet.

'What could you see?' Crassus asked.

'Nothing,' the man whispered. 'Just an empty room. There is light coming from the other side, a doorway in the far right corner, must be the way to the gate.'

Crassus nodded, he stepped away from the wall and looked up at the sun, judging its position and the direction we needed to travel. 'Right then, I'll lead, single file behind me. Stay silent.'

Crassus edged the door back and we padded in after him, myself and Habitus at the end of the line, for we were the weaker of our party and likely to be a liability in a fight after our ordeal the night before.

The chamber was well lit and better maintained than the one Cletus had used to store us in. The flagstones under my feet were level, and there was a smell of cement and plaster, as if the building had just been refurbished. The walls were full of faded paintings of men stripped to the waist, muscled torsos exaggerated as they threw javelins and wrestled on sand. One even had a man riding a lion, wearing nothing but a loincloth.

At an order from Crassus, we moved over to the right-side wall and pressed our backs to it, waiting, breathing. There came the faint sounds of men from around the corner, the indistinguishable murmur of deep voices, the rich aroma of a cooking pot. My heart was thudding as Crassus stuck his head around the corner. My palms were slick with sweat, and I had a sudden and desperate urge to defecate.

And then we were moving, at a jog now, our hobnailed sandals clattering on the flagstones. Through a short and narrow corridor and into a large, open chamber that had a portico on the eastern wall, allowing in the heat from the rising sun.

We saw them then, ten men, lounging on straw cots, the cooking pot steaming in the centre of the room above a small fire. Most wore just their loincloths, one was completely naked and was drying himself with a towel, clearly having just bathed. Two were playing dice in the corner, and it was one of those men who raised the alarm as he saw us.

'Get them!' Crassus shouted, not wanting to let the moment of surprise go to waste.

Crassus and his four men lurched forward, weapons bared. I hung back, aware that my muscles were still not fully functioning. I saw Timon engage with the man who had given me the axe. The big Briton forced him back a pace with a savage overarm swing which Timon only just managed to block with his own blade, still in its sheath. Timon kicked the Briton in the groin, and only then did he have time to draw his sword. He swiped at the Briton from right to left, and without thinking, I leapt forward and stopped the blow with the shaft of my axe.

'You're a dead man,' Timon snarled at me. He had taken a step back, and the two of us circled slowly, each looking for a weakness in the other. I was too weary to speak, just the simple act of blocking his strike had taken the wind from me.

Behind Timon, the giant redhead was, once more, fighting for his life, fending off two attackers who leapt for him, armed with nothing but their eating knives. I had no idea how the battle was faring elsewhere, I could not take my eyes from Timon.

'I'm going to be a rich man once Cassius is on the throne,' Timon said, a mirthless grin fixed on his lips. 'You should have stayed at the bottom of the ocean, you maggot. At least your end would have been painless.' With that, he stepped forward, and his sword darted out faster than a viper's tongue, and only my reactions saved me. He had lunged high, aiming for the meat in my right shoulder. I ducked and swivelled on my feet, rolling to my left, and the blow struck nothing but air. Even as I moved, I changed the grip on my axe so the blade was cutting the air as I swivelled, and as I turned full circle, I kept swinging, and the axe dug into Timon's hip with a wet slap.

Dark blood erupted from the wound. I felt the bone of his hip break under the weight of the axe. He screamed – a high-pitched yelp that was at odds with his usual gruff voice – and lost his grip on his sword as he crumpled to a heap. *Never hesitate*, that's what they tell you in the army when you're soaked in sweat, swiping a wooden practice sword at a straw target.

That training never leaves you.

Once more, I adjusted the grip on my axe, and hefting it high above my head, I sent it crashing into Timon's neck. He was dead before I wrenched it clear.

I was panting then, sweat streamed down me, my hands shook. I took in the rest of the fight and saw that just two of our opponents remained. Cletus was one, fighting hand to hand with Crassus. They appeared to be equal rivals, matching each other stroke for stroke. Habitus was fighting the other man, and even as I watched, he dummied a thrust to his opponent's groin before reversing it and driving his blade through the helpless man's heart.

To my dismay, when I took in the rest of that blood-drenched chamber, I saw that there were just the four of us left standing. The red-haired giant lay in a pool of claret, a knife sticking out of his groin. The two men he had been fighting were both down; one still had a sword in his chest. The small easterner, who had cunningly peered in through the crack of the door just a short time before, was gazing up at the ceiling, lifeless eyes glazed over. Crassus' two other men were slumped together in a corner, four dead bodies littered the ground around them. So much blood, so much death, just to save Habitus and me.

'It's over, Cletus,' Crassus said as he stepped away from the Greek centurion, breathing hard.

'Over?' Cletus spat. 'You think that your victory here is going to stop the storm that is coming? Nothing will stop Cassius getting what he wants, *nothing*. Aurelius is as good as dead, he just doesn't know it yet.'

'We will stop Cassius,' I said, limping forward. I had taken a wound to my left leg in the disastrous battle the Fourteenth had fought against Balomar in Pannonia five years before. The wound was, of course, fully healed by then, but by God, it throbbed as much as it had when I had first taken it – I had to stop and check it hadn't reopened.

'Ha! You three? Against the might of his armies? When he marches, he will have fifty thousand fresh men at his back. What will your master have? Four tired legions he will be able to spare from the northern front? There can only be one outcome.'

'I will kill him before it comes to that. I will sacrifice my life if necessary, to ensure peace remains throughout our lands.' I was quite taken aback by how *true* those words were, even as I spoke them. Me, a retired old legionary from Britannia, an unwilling *frumentarii* agent, I really would have risked it all to stop Cassius and his devious plans. If only because I knew Cletus and his cronies would be turning in their graves as I did.

'Good luck with that,' Cletus said. He raised his sword one last time, and I saw a flicker of fear in his dark eyes. He was going to meet his gods, was realising his own mortality. Even though I did not like him, I respected his resolve to die well.

He lunged forward with the blade. It was a slow and tired lunge, and I deflected it wide with my axe with ease. Before I could even bring the axe back to my body to make the killing blow, Habitus stepped between us and stabbed Cletus in the heart. He thrust so hard, the blade went right through Cletus' chest and erupted in a spray of blood from his back. And so was the end of Cletus, a good soldier, I'm sure, who died for a master who had probably forgotten he was alive in the first place.

# CHAPTER XI

**April, 193 AD**
**Carnuntum, Pannonia**

Faustus' heart pounds as he runs. On and on he goes, past the limit of his exhaustion, beyond the boundaries of his fragile stamina.

He does not know why he subjects himself to this punishment day after day, but his constant tiredness leaves his brain no power to torment him with thoughts of his father, of Marcus and Meredith.

When he runs he is free, as free as the wind that blows off the river and cools his skin. Too long has he been a victim, too long has he lain on his cot, dark thoughts filling his mind. Today, he has pushed himself further than ever. As he stops at the southern gate to the fortress of Carnuntum, it completes his tenth lap of the fortress. He stands there, panting, hands on his knees, wondering how many miles ten laps would be.

'You're looking stronger,' a voice says at his back. He turns and sees the first spear centurion of the legion, Terentius Varo, leaning up against the parapet, wearing just a belted tunic.

'Thank you,' Faustus says, 'I feel it.'

'Walk with me,' Varo says, gesturing into the fortress, 'I'd like to speak with you.'

Faustus pauses, eyeing the centurion with suspicion. 'Has Calvus put you up to this?' he asks.

Varo laughs. 'Nothing gets past you, hey? Yes, he did. But that's not the only reason I'm doing it. Come, I promise not to bite.'

They walk under the arch of the gate and into the fortress itself. Faustus watches Varo from the corner of his eye, already steeling himself for the inevitable army propaganda that Varo is about to shower him with. Things have taken a turn for the worse in Rome, and fear and disorder is rife throughout the empire.

Publius Helvius Pertinax Augustus has lasted just three months on the throne. As Calvus had predicted, he did not adapt well to being the most important man in the world and has been murdered by his own Praetorian Guard after they rejected his motion to reform their pay and implement harsher disciplinary procedures to the misbehaving men in their ranks.

As if that is not shocking enough, Rome then watched on as two men held a bidding war for the purple. Senator Didius Julianus rushed to the barracks of the Praetorian Guard once he heard of Pertinax's demise and found himself to not be the only man to have the same chain of thought. Pertinax's father-in-law, Sulpicianus, was also there, negotiating the bribe he would pay the Praetorian tribunes to make him emperor. A bidding war ensued, and the Praetorians duly sold the empire to Julianus, who, it seemed, had deeper pockets than his rival.

So, that is the state of play within Rome itself. But across the Roman world, other men are emerging from the shadows, their lustful eyes set on the throne. In the east, Pescennius Niger, governor of Syria, is said to be raising an army, paid for from his own vast funds. He has made no official declaration yet, but it is clear to those in the know – Calvus at least – that he will make his move when he is ready.

But what disturbs Faustus most of all is that Septimius Severus, governor of Pannonia and commander of the Fourteenth Legion, has also declared himself emperor, without the permission of the senate, and is hell-bent on starting a civil war. Calvus has also spoken of a senator named Clodius Albinus, who was originally offered the throne after Commodus' assassination, as being yet another potential rival, though Faustus has now shut his ears to what his old guardian has to say on the state of political affairs, he finds it all too overwhelming.

This is doubtless what Varo wishes to speak to him of, to lay the groundwork for Faustus to enrol in the Fourteenth Legion, to fight in the coming war.

'You seem lost in your own mind, young Faustus,' Varo says. His tone is cheerful enough, and he smiles as he speaks, but Faustus sees the edge in his eyes, the uncertainty in his gaze.

'I was just thinking about all that is going on in the world. My own problems seem insignificant by comparison.'

'We are all insignificant when compared to the fate of the empire,' he says.

Faustus studies him once more, trying to decide whether he is a man to be trusted. He is shorter than Faustus, but then most men are. Squat built, stocky legs and scarred fists the size of hams. His hair is black, shot with grey, and he has a livid white scar running across the bridge of his nose, over his left eye and onto his cheek. On closer inspection, you can see the left eye is glazed, milkier than the right. It is said throughout the fortress that he lost sight in the eye completely when he took the wound, but nothing is ever uttered to his face.

'Do you support Severus' claim to the purple?' Faustus asks.

'Of course. He is the best man to take the empire forward, to bring us back from the years of neglect and corruption suffered under Commodus. He will restore the empire to its glory years, make us strong again.'

'But he intends to do that by making us weaker, surely? He is starting a war, do not object Varo, you know what I say to be true.'

Varo gives Faustus a thin-lipped smile before slowly nodding. 'Yes, it is true, there will be a war. Whether it be Niger in the east or Julianus and the senate themselves, conflict is inevitable now. Severus has gone too far to withdraw, he must see this through to the end.'

'And that end will either be him on the throne or every man in this fortress dead, the legion disgraced and its eagle melted down and turned into coin with another man's head portrayed on the front.'

Varo barks a short laugh. 'That is true, but what care is it of yours if the Fourteenth is retired in disgrace? From what Calvus tells me, you are no lover of the army, this legion in particular.'

'True enough. But, as you well know, my family has a lot of history inside these walls. I would not like to see their memory tarnished for another's benefit.'

'It is of that history that I wish to speak to you. Come, we are here.'

They turn off the road, and for the first time, Faustus notices where they are. Varo pushes open the door to the centurion's mess and ushers Faustus inside.

'Am I even allowed in here?' Faustus asks.

'No, but I'm sure my fellow officers can turn a blind eye to your presence, just this once.'

They enter the small timber building, the ceiling low over Faustus' head. He is aware that a hush has fallen over the room, the cacophony of many conversations evaporating into a stifling silence.

'Brothers, for those of you that have not met him before, this is Faustus, son of Centurion Albinus Silus, grandson of the revered first spear Centurion Silus, a man whose memory will live forever in this legion.' There is a murmur of approval in the room, men nod to Faustus, two men step forward and grip his arm in the warrior's embrace. 'Come, Faustus, let us get a cup of wine and talk.'

Time passes, Faustus does not know how much. When he had first entered the mess, he had been conscious he wore nothing but a sweat-stained tunic, he was even bereft of shoes or sandals, preferring to run in bare feet. But the wine has numbed the embarrassment, the conversation and comradery of the centurions cheering his mood.

They are on their third jug now, Faustus and Varo, and for what feels like hours, they have spoken of much, little of consequence. For the first time in his life, Faustus finds himself enjoying the company of soldiers. One man tells him stories of his grandfather, of the time he single-handedly held back a barbarian horde, whilst his *optio* rallied the rest of his cohort, another of how he marched alone into Germania and challenged a chieftain to single combat in front of his tribe and duly defeated him. Faustus laughs at such stories, which are clearly the works of someone's imaginations or have been exaggerated over time as tales of fallen heroes often are.

Then one man speaks of his grandfather's death, of how he and one hundred retired soldiers had fought a war band of five thousand Germanic warriors and laid down their lives so their families could escape. 'They charged them, or so the story goes. One hundred greybeards against five thousand of the nastiest bastards from across the river. Silus ordered them into a wedge, and they tore through their ranks, killing five or six men each before they began to fall. Silus was the last man standing, or so they say. When they found his body the next day, there were heaps of dead Germani warriors around him, three deep in some places. A greater warrior this legion has never seen.'

Faustus feels tears begin to well in his eyes. Looking around, he sees some men are already weeping unashamedly. Varo himself has to wipe his eyes. He wonders if it is strange for a chamber full of men to be weeping so openly for a man that lived and died before their time. He decides there is not and that there is something quite beautiful in it.

'Thank you,' Faustus says, 'all of you. I have been finding life quite hard in recent months, even more so since the attack. You have cheered my spirits. I owe you all a debt of gratitude.'

'You owe them nothing,' a voice says from behind him. Turning, Faustus sees the door to the mess is open. Sunlight streams through, conquering the shadows of the windowless room. A light breeze caresses his face, the air suddenly feels lighter, easier to breathe. 'Your family have given so much to this legion, to the army as a whole, it is us that should be thanking you.'

The speaker is a dark silhouette against the backdrop of devasting light. He wears nothing but a plain white tunic, belted at the waist, with a dusty old cloak thrown back over his shoulders. There is no gold at his neck or wrists, no rings aligning his slim, long fingers. His hair is not powdered or greased but dishevelled and unkempt. He wears a cropped black beard, flecked with grey that, coupled with the lines that run like crevices in the land through his face, place his age somewhere between forty-five and fifty. He is of average height and build, but as he moves forward out of the light, there is an authority in his step, a distinct resonance in every footfall.

His profile is clearer now, and even if Faustus has doubts as to his identity, the thirty centurions that leap to their feet and offer a salute should be proof enough of who he is. Septimius Severus, governor of Pannonia, commander of the northern legions and would-be emperor of Rome, smiles down at Faustus who still sits, dumbstruck, in his seat.

Slowly, Faustus stands. He is unsure as to what he should do. He is not a soldier, therefore, has no need to salute. But this is a man who seeks to make himself emperor of Rome, should he offer some sort of bow?

In the end, Severus makes the decision for him. 'Faustus Silus, if I am not mistaken. It is an absolute pleasure to meet you, young man.' He leans in and offers his hand, which Faustus takes limply in his own.

Faustus tries to speak, but it feels as though his tongue is stuck to the roof of his mouth. He stammers something unintelligible, feels his cheeks reddening as his gaze meets with Severus, and he sees the amused glint in the other man's eyes.

'Tell me, young Faustus, what do you think of my attempt to rise to the purple? Would you consider me to be worthy of the title "Emperor"?'

Again, Faustus stammers. He knows little enough of the political situation in Rome or across the empire. What business is it of his who sits on a golden throne and rules over the senate in faraway Rome? For the little people, like him, life goes on regardless.

'And more importantly, of course, would your father have fought for me?'

'My father?' Faustus asks, dumbfounded.

'Yes. I hear lots of stories about him from the legate and the first spear here,' he pauses, motioning to Varus, 'and, of course, our mutual friend, Calvus, never ceases in his stories of days gone by. His ones about Albinus have always been my favourite.' Severus' brown eyes seem to sparkle as he speaks. As his dark skin creases into smile lines, Faustus glimpses a full mouth of perfectly white teeth.

'Calvus? *You,* know Calvus?'

Severus booms out a laugh so loud and deep, Faustus is sure he can feel the timber beams of the mess reverberate above him. 'My dear boy, there is not a man or woman in Pannonia, prostitute or senator who is not familiar with old Calvus. Why, he must be the one man in this province who is more famous than me! And people say the *frumentarii* work in the shadows.' Once more he erupts into laughter. This time, Faustus can see specks of dust falling from the beams above him. It seems this man needs nothing more than his voice to shake the world around him.

'His best story, of course, is the one about the battle on the ice against the Iazyges. Now, *that* sounds like a battle I would like to have fought in.'

'I have never heard it,' Faustus mutters.

'You mean to say Calvus has never told you of the battle on the ice? Gods above, sit down, young man, in fact, sit down, all of you,' he roars to the chamber of centurions, all still standing to attention. 'And Varo, get us some wine. This is a story none of you shall want to miss.'

# CHAPTER XII

**January, 173 AD**
**Pannonia**

The snow bit deep at Albinus' bones, the old scar on his jaw burned, his chattering teeth caused the joints in his face to ache so fiercely, he could concentrate on nothing else.

He eyed the auxiliary cavalrymen that trotted alongside the convoy with envy. They wore thick woollen trousers beneath their mail, warm-looking gloves covered their hands, and instead of iron helmets, they wore fur caps. As their decurion passed him down the line, Albinus saw beads of sweat on the man's forehead. He scowled, praying to Vulcan to share with him some of that heat.

Gazing up toward the sky, Albinus saw nothing but low-lying cloud rolling ever south. They were dark and vicious, and every few heartbeats, they were illuminated by a flash of lightning.

They had been out on patrol for five days now, going east along the frozen Danube. It seemed the storm was following them, chiding them for their folly, for surely, no tribesmen would be daring enough to raid in this weather?

The convoy consisted of five hundred infantry and one hundred and twenty cavalry, commanded by a tribune, a youth of no more than eighteen, named Corvinus Falco, who had impressed Legate Maximianus sufficiently to be given an independent command.

The infantry consisted of the tenth cohort of the Fourteenth Legion, commanded by their senior centurion, a sturdy old warhorse by the name of Valerius Sura, a Thracian who had served for over twenty years. Albinus liked him; Sura was honest and upfront, quick to praise and always made time to educate Albinus when there was a task he had forgotten or his men were stepping out of line.

He was still growing accustomed to being a centurion, even though he had held the post for nearly a year. The instant fear he could bring out in a legionary still shocked him. A few months prior, he had caught his century's resident clown, Pavo, prancing around the small fire outside his tent, doing an impression of Albinus and Fullo to his tent mates. Albinus had been horrified and more than a little intimidated. He had caught Pavo right in the act as he walked between the tent lines. If he could have turned around and run in the other direction without having to confront the soldier, he would have, but Pavo and his seven spectators had all clearly seen him. To walk away would have damaged his reputation beyond recovery.

Albinus had steeled his nerves and approached the small group, telling them all in a quiet but authoritative tone that they would be on latrines for the rest of the month. No one had complained, in fact, Albinus later heard, through Fullo, that they had respected him for the way he had handled the situation. There were many centurions who would have had their vine sticks in their hands before they uttered a word, and the legion's hospital would suddenly receive several new patients. Albinus knew his father would have chided him, called him a coward for not beating the men. But Albinus prided himself in not being the man his father was and had always tried to distance himself from that name and the inevitable comparison. Although, in this legion, it was unavoidable.

That incident, coupled with his handling of the century in battle throughout the summer campaigns, meant he had a fairly relaxed relationship with his men. But his command, of course, did not stop at them.

'Gods, it's cold,' Commodus said through chattering teeth. He had a great skin of bear fur wrapped around his shoulders. The bear's head was over his, and the fur ran down his body and legs, dragging in the snow behind him. Beneath, he wore the same as the legionaries that marched around him: a short-sleeved tunic, chain mail and leather boots.

'That it is, Caesar. We will be home soon enough though, another six days or so.'

'Six days? What are we going to achieve in six days? We're marching to nowhere, for no reason. There's no one out here, just snow, ice and misery.'

There was a low rumble of 'aye's from the legionaries in earshot, each as disgruntled as the young prince about being kept from their winter fires. Albinus was as reluctant as them all to be out in this storm. His feet were frozen, and when the feeling came back, the soles of his feet ached and cramped whilst he slept. The base of his back was a ball of fire, his shoulders were sore, his neck too, such was the heavy toll life on the march took on a soldier. But he was an officer, supposedly above such trivial things as aching limbs, and he could not let his discomfort show to his men.

Albinus silently cursed the boy. He had behaved himself well enough in the short time he had been in his charge. He was quiet, thoughtful and clearly extremely intelligent. But it appeared this winter patrol was bringing out the worst in him, and Albinus knew full well he could not allow his bitter comments to lower his men's morale.

'Do you know how this war began?' Albinus said.

Commodus shrugged. 'When Balomar sent a mob of blood-crazed barbarians into Italy?' The comment caused muffled laughter from the men. Albinus bit back his irritation when he saw the caesar's smug smile.

'It began by the Germani raiding Pannonia on a day very much like this one. They slaughtered a whole village of people, my father among them.'

The smile vanished from Commodus' face. Despite the cold, his cheeks burned red.

'Aye, mine too,' Fullo chipped in. He was huddled in his cloak, his wild, curly hair draped across his face, weighed down by snow and rain.

'The Germani don't wait for spring to start raiding. They're hungry, restless, eager for silver and cattle, and they strike when they think there isn't a Roman force close enough to confront them. That is why we are here. Even if we meet no raiders, word will spread over the river that we are patrolling, that we are alert. When the tribes hear, that may just be enough to keep them in their huts, huddled around their fires. Just by us being here, in this cursed storm, we are saving lives.'

Silence greeted his words, just the howling of the wind and another burst of lightning. Albinus moved ahead of his century, tears pricking the corners of his eyes. It was true, what he had said. If the legions had been doing patrols such as this throughout the winter seven years before, then his father may still have been alive. But Rome had been at peace with the tribes then, and there had been no need for the army to break from their winter camps and brave the harsh conditions. Or so they had thought.

'I'm sorry,' said a small voice, uttered so quietly it could have been nothing more than a whisper on the breeze.

Albinus turned to find a shamefaced Commodus as his shoulder. He seemed to have shrunk further into the bear fur. 'You have nothing to apologise for, Caesar. You didn't know.'

'But all the same, I am sorry. It must have been hard for you when he died.'

Albinus stopped and steered Commodus out of the line of marching men. 'Yes, it was. You know, I never wanted to be a soldier, never dreamed I'd end up a centurion in the army, let alone the protector of the heir to the throne! But… sometimes you have to just roll with the punches the gods throw at you. Anyway, I'm happy enough.'

Commodus shifted from foot to foot in the snow. Albinus could see him working his toes under his leather boots, trying to keep them from going numb. 'My father will die soon, at least that is what they say in Rome.'

'The emperor? Don't think that, Caesar, he's not an old man yet.'

'No, but he is sickly. His body is weak, even if his mind remains strong. One day soon, he will rise to the heavens, and I will be left for the vultures.'

'You will be emperor, supreme commander of all the legions Rome can put in the field. I don't think you have to worry about the vultures,' Albinus said, putting a reassuring hand on the boy's shoulder.

'You really think I will be allowed to take the purple? You believe the senate will support my claim? Then you are naïve, Centurion. They will put their own man on the throne, an experienced governor or a successful general, from one of the oldest families in Rome. I will be exiled if I am lucky, murdered more likely, along with what is left of my family.'

*Gods, when I was twelve, all I had to worry about was being up in time to help feed the animals! No wonder the boy is so serious.* 'What about your father's *amici*? His friends? They will have all sworn an oath to ensure you succeed him, they will not go back on that lightly.' He wanted to console the boy, to raise his spirits, but it was hard to find the right words in the midst of a storm as ravenous as that one.

'True. But they are my *father's* friends, not mine. If I am to survive, I need to build my own *amici*, my own circle of friends and advisors. I need more men like you, Centurion Albinus.' Commodus reached out and touched Albinus' arm as he spoke, it was the first sign of affection Albinus had seen him show for anyone.

'Me? I am nothing, nobody. I am the lowest-ranking centurion in the Fourteenth Legion. There must be a thousand more just like me across the army. Why on earth would you want me in your inner circle?'

Commodus smiled. Albinus was a little taken aback by the genuine warmth he saw in his dark eyes. 'You are much more than that, Centurion. You are respected by your seniors, admired by your men and, from the stories I have heard, ferocious in battle. You are destined for big things, I think.'

Albinus watched as the young Caesar walked off and rejoined the marching column. He didn't know whether he admired the boy or was afraid of him. Either way, he felt his determination to keep him safe and fulfil the duty placed on him by the emperor grow stronger than ever.

The sky was a wall of grey the next day when Albinus stepped from his frozen tent, stretching his back and shaking some feeling into his legs. He had slept in nothing but his cloak, his small fold-up cot stuck with half of the column's baggage train a full five miles behind their camp. Only the tents and the packhorses carrying provisions had made it through, which meant they had been unable to construct any sort of marching camp.

Just as the last of the light was fading, tribune Falco had ordered the men to build a windbreak to the north, along the bank of the frozen river, where a biting gale was barrelling into the rain-sodden men. So, in the absence of equipment, the five hundred men of the tenth cohort had set to work with nothing but their bare hands. They had erected a wall of snow and ice nearly eight feet tall. Albinus had stood and watched his century work and had been shocked to see Commodus there, shovelling snow with the rest.

It seemed it was not just the generals and senators he sought to win favour with. Albinus thought it would do the boy no harm to win the support of the rank and file. One day, after all, he would need them to fight for him.

As he walked from his tent, past the huddles of soldiers, all trying and failing to get a cooking fire going, his thoughts turned to his own son. He had not spent enough time with Faustus, who had recently passed his first birthday. Meredith was doing a fine job of raising him, alongside her own son, Marcus, but Albinus could not help feeling his life would be far richer if he were with his mother.

*Licina.*

Day after day, hour after hour, he did his best to keep that name from his lips, her image from his mind. But he had found it harder in the last few days, out here in the wilderness, with nothing but the endless snow and countless milestones to focus him. His men needed little from him, and what instructions were needed, Fullo took care of. He had nothing to occupy his mind, no administrative duties to fulfil, no drills to run, no inspections to do. The days seemed to pass so quickly when in Carnuntum as he rushed from one meeting to another. Out here, he was alone with his thoughts.

He could picture her form so clearly: the fiery red that was her hair, flowing in locks down her back. Green eyes that sparkled in the moonlight, her full lips, long legs…

'Morning, sir,' a voice said, waking him from his daze.

'Fullo, morning, brother. Sleep well?'

'What do you think?' Fullo replied with a sarcastic grin. 'I think I managed to drift off somewhere between the third and fourth hour, I was up again by the fifth.'

'Aye, wasn't the most comfortable I've been, either. Still, we'll have worse at some point, I'm sure,' Albinus said with a wink. 'See to the men. Get them fed and ready to move. I'm just off to the morning briefing.'

Fullo gave a small salute and was about to move off when he turned back and said, 'Oh, will you be bringing the caesar with you?'

Albinus paused. Taking Commodus along hadn't even crossed his mind. 'Yes, I think I probably should. Where is he?'

By way of reply, Fullo pointed to the nearest cooking fire, where Commodus was handing out bowls of warm broth to an orderly queue of freezing soldiers.

Albinus smiled. 'Leave him be, *optio*, he's making friends.'

It seemed to grow darker as Albinus moved through the marching camp – if it could even be called that. Snow drifted lazily from the low-hanging cloud, letting the bitter wind determine its destination. Hauling in his cloak to try and maintain what little warmth he could, Albinus almost ran to the command tent, ignoring the salutes and greetings of the men from the other centuries. He was tired, footsore, half-frozen and miserable and wanted nothing more than to huddle next to a roaring fire with a heated cup of wine in his palm. Instead, he knew he would face another day of braving the elements.

He was, it appeared, the last to arrive as he threw back the canvas flap to the giant leather tent that had been Tribune Corvus' home for the night. In usual circumstances, this one tent alone would have been bigger than all the tents from the tenth cohort put together, with a separate entrance hall, a sleeping chamber and a greeting room. Given the conditions the detachment had been combatting, just the greeting chamber had been erected the previous evening, and Albinus thought it was somehow colder in there than it was outside.

The tribune was standing slightly apart from the other officers, observing them as they huddled around a single brazier, each fighting to be closest to the flickering flames. Albinus, in turn, watched him. He was short and slight with soft, pale skin that had a purple glow in the winter air. His eyes were large and round, his hair grown long in the latest fashion, and when in barracks, it would be perfectly curled, but out here, with no barber to maintain it and a helmet being thrust upon it daily, it was wild and dishevelled.

Corvus nodded to Albinus when he saw the centurion studying him and moved to greet him. Albinus cursed himself softly for his own inquisitive nature, he was in no mood for making small talk with his commanding officer.

'Salve, Centurion,' Corvus said as he approached, in a high pitched, soft voice. 'How is our caesar this morning?'

'Morning, sir. He is well. I left him breaking his fast with the men.' Albinus thought it best not to mention that the heir to the empire was actually *serving* breakfast to the common soldiery.

'Good. Is he coping well with the march? It's not been easy for any of us.'

'Well enough, sir. A few grumbles, but nothing you wouldn't expect from one so young.'

Albinus was still standing to attention, his thumbs hooked in his belt, eyes fixed at a point above Corvus' head. He could see the tribune studying him once more, could make out the amber flecks in his brown eyes.

'Why is it, do you think, that the caesar has been passed into your care?'

So that was it, Albinus thought. Corvus, he knew, came from an ancient and noble line; his ancestry could be traced back to the republic and had been prominent members of the senate for generations. Corvus was jealous, jealous that someone so insignificant had been handed the care of the emperor's son, rather than a young man of standing such as him.

Albinus was, however, spared from answering the intrusive question by the arrival of Decurion Flavius Bassus of the Ala Noricorum, the cavalry detachment for the convoy. His were the cavalry unit that had ambushed the Quadi with Albinus the year before, and Bassus nodded respectfully to Albinus before presenting himself to the tribune.

'Sir, one of my scouts has spotted a column of tribesmen heading north and east, roughly five hundred warriors strong, about two hours from our position. The scout said they were all mounted and appeared to be laden with captives and loot. If we leave now, we can be on them by midday.'

Bassus spoke with a stoic calmness as if he were remarking on nothing more than the weather. Albinus, however, felt his heartbeat quicken, his mouth ran dry, and his palms dampened with sweat. It did not matter what rank you held or how long you had fought under the eagle, every man felt the same rush of fear at the prospect of facing the enemy in battle.

'They are all mounted? How will we catch them when most of our force is on foot?' Corvus asked. Albinus thought he seemed to have shrunk at the news, his high voice cracking in terror.

'They will be moving slowly, sir. If they have captives, plunder and cattle, then they won't be able to move at a pace faster than a slow walk. Our lads will be able to close the distance without too much trouble.'

Every man in the room was listening intently to the decurion. There was a low rumble of murmured talk as the centurions whispered guesses as to what the tribune would do.

Centurion Sura moved towards Corvus, saluting respectfully and saying in a quiet voice, 'Sir, we must attack, sir. The whole reason we are out here is to try and protect the people that live on the northern frontier. From what the decurion has said, it sounds as though they have already attacked our people. We must get them before they cross the river.'

Sura looked to Bassus and Albinus, widening his eyes and making a small gesture with his hand – a silent plea for help.

'Sir, if I make speak,' Albinus said. 'Centurion Sura is right, sir. The main task of these patrols is to be a deterrent. If we do not attack an enemy column when we know its position, then it will only encourage the barbarians to raid south of the river. We must attack.' Despite his fear at having to fight, especially in the current conditions, Albinus knew it was the only course of action.

'Right then,' Corvus said, visibly steeling himself. 'Make ready to march, at once.'


They set off within the hour marching at double pace, the slow dog-footed jog a legionary could maintain all day and cover up to thirty miles from sunrise to sunset.

Commodus jogged beside Albinus whilst Albinus, in turn, fretted as to what to do with the boy when they closed with the enemy. 'You go straight to the rear, understand? I don't want to see you anywhere near the front.'

'Yes, you have said a thousand tim—'

'Actually, stay in the centre, the men in the middle ranks will see you're safe, that way, you won't get hit by a stray arrow or javelin.'

'You're sure you want me in the centre? Would I not be safer with you? It is *you* who have been charged with my protection, after all.'

'Absolutely not. I am a centurion, and I lead from the front. Having said that, I don't want you to leave my sight as I don't trust you not to get into trouble, so stay right behind me at all times.'

'But you just sa—'

'Yes, I knew very well what I just said! Jupiter's shining cock, I didn't actually think I would have to fight a battle with you at my side when I agreed to protect you!'

'So, where do you want me to go?'

'Oh, I don't kno—'

'Enemy to the front, battle formation, NOW!' Centurion Sura's voice pierced through the ranks of running soldiers like a well-thrown spear.

Albinus and his century were at the back of the column, due to them being the lowest-ranking century in the cohort. Albinus craned his neck to try and see over the top of the marching column but could see nothing save the cohorts' standards and the crests on the helmets of his fellow centurions.

The column widened and split as he watched, with the first three centuries forming the front line, the last three forming up behind them. Albinus and his men found themselves behind the second century, who had taken the right flank, with the first in the centre and the third on the left. The fourth was next to him and the fifth on the left behind the third.

Looking left, Albinus could make out Quirinus Marinus, the centurion of the fourth century. Marinus had been promoted the year before Albinus and had served for just two years longer. Native to Hispania, with dark hair and olive skin, he had become a friend to Albinus since his promotion. Marinus gave Albinus a nod which he returned, taking comfort from the fact he was around friends.

'Tie your helmets, check your armour and your laces. Don't want any of you falling over,' Albinus called over his shoulder. He breathed deep, held it, trying to slow the blood that rushed to his ears. The air smelt of impending action, a pungent scent of leather mixed with rotting bowels that even the howling wind could not dislodge. As always, he fought the growing urge to piss his breeches, his guts growled at him, and he wanted to vomit.

Shouts to his front forced the needs of his body to the back of his mind. The cavalry was charging, their target still hidden to him. Without an order, the tenth cohort picked up the pace, men running with their shields in their left hands and javelins in their right. It was no easy thing to do, and after just ten steps, Albinus felt his wrists burn and his shoulders sag as if he carried the hopes of his whole command on his back. In a way he did.

Sura barked an order, far to Albinus' front, but it was lost on the wind. Soon after, a horn-blower sounded the order to loose javelins, and the sky darkened as the lead-weighted *pila* ripped through the air.

Albinus still could not see the enemy, but alarm bells were beginning to ring in his ears as he realised that the thick snow they had been trudging through was thinning, and now he was standing on bare ice. He snapped a look left and right, dread welling inside him as he saw he and his men were running straight *onto* the river Danube.

The ice creaked and groaned, seemingly unhappy to burden the extra weight of five hundred men in armour.

'Albinus, right, look right!' Fullo cried from the rear, and Albinus followed the instruction, fear rocking him as he saw a column of mounted tribesmen riding straight for his men.

'Form up to the right, at the double!' he screamed in a voice cracking with terror. His men wheeled without conscious thought, years of training and iron discipline taking over when fear or indecision could lead a man to hesitate.

Albinus thrust his way through the ranks until he stood in the reformed front line, heartbeats before the cavalry charged past, a whisker away from the Roman shields.

'They won't charge right at you, the horses will be reluctant,' Commodus said, peering through a gap in the shields.

'Get back, Caesar, for the love of the gods!'

'I'm just saying, they won't charge. They'll keep circling you, picking you off with their spears.' Commodus spoke in such a calm and detached voice, Albinus thought he could have been remarking on the flight of a bird or the new roof on a temple. He was, however, quite right in his observation.

Once more, the barbarian cavalry swept past, warriors hanging low in their saddles, spear tips lashing out like snakes' tongues as they galloped by. The ice groaned once more, the lonely cry of a husband watching on as his wife burns on her funeral pyre. Snow began to fall again, softly at first, before tumbling in a torrent.

'Form square. Don't throw your javelins, use them as spears. Keep your shields up, and don't give them anything to aim at. Fullo, Fullo! You command the rear of the square, keep the men in line.'

Fullo replied, but Albinus had already turned his attention back to his front. He was isolated from the second century to his left, who seemed to be in a shoving match with another horde of barbarians. He could not see the fourth century to his back and had no idea where the Roman cavalry was. His only option, as far as he could make out, was to keep moving north, their left, and join up with the second.

'On my order, we move left, but keep facing this way. Ready? Step!'

And so it began. There was no great distance to cover, thirty paces at most, but the ice was treacherous, and even the legionaries' hobnailed boots could gather no grip on the pristine white ground. The Germani wheeled back around, and as the ice shuddered under their charge, the man to Albinus' right slipped and fell, exposing himself to the barbarian spears. Albinus reached down to haul the man to his feet, but as his arm clasped onto his comrade, a spear exploded through his chest, covering Albinus in his lifeblood. He dropped the soldier's arm and carried on moving.

Ten paces further and two more men were down, speared by the rampaging Germani warriors. 'Halt!' Albinus called. 'This is hopeless. We hold our ground, keep the formation tight.'

The square quickly became a circle, as more and more horsemen surrounded them, jabbing with their long spears. The Romans replied with their shorter javelins, and every now and then, caught a complacent barbarian in the leg or arm, but the Romans were falling in droves.

Bucco was at Albinus' left shoulder now and plastered in Germani blood. With a roar, he stepped outside the circle of shields and launched his javelin at a group of mounted barbarians, hitting one square in the chest. He slipped and struggled to regain his footing as he rejoined the isolated Roman formation.

'What do we do?' he said to Albinus through heaving breaths.

Albinus turned full circle, reaching up on his toes as he tried to make sense of the battle.

'I've no idea what's going on. We can't move as we have no grip, and this ice feels as though it could break at any moment.' As if on cue, the ice shuddered and moaned aloud once more. Albinus knew that if it broke, it would be the death of him and his men. The water would be freezing, and even the strongest swimmers among them would be sucked to the depths in heartbeats by the weight of their armour.

'So, what do we do?'

'Stand on your shields, the wood should give you more grip.'

Commodus was, once more, at Albinus' back, the centurion shocked to realise he had forgotten about him completely.

'Stand on our shields?'

'If you stand on your shields, you will have more grip,' he repeated. 'As you just said, you cannot move anywhere, so you may as well stand and try to fight. All you're doing currently is dying. Start fighting back!'

The outmost rank of the circle stood on their shields, while the men on the inside held theirs aloft above their comrades' heads, giving them at least some protection. For the first time, Albinus was glad of the snow and wind, for, without it, the enemy would surely have picked them off with arrows. As it was, arrows were useless.

The snow had turned to sleet, driving straight down at them, seemingly impervious to the wind. Albinus felt the added weight of water on his helmet, his lining cap soaked beneath, and every time he moved his head, it was a strain on his neck. His calves burned as he kept his legs braced, unwilling to relax as he stood on the curved edges of his shield. He had a javelin in his left hand, its leaf-shaped point blunted by constant use, his yet unbloodied sword in his right.

The barbarians had not attacked for a while, and Albinus was starting to feel the cold. His first wave of adrenalin had worn off, and the old wound on his left cheek was a pulsing ball of agony. They still had made no contact with their comrades, and visibility was bad due to the sleet and wind. Fullo had reported thirty men from the sixth were dead already, and a further ten wouldn't last the day.

Albinus felt despondent, waves of guilt weighing him down, surely dragging him toward a watery grave. His men were dying in front of his eyes, picked off one by one by the enemy cavalry. His century was isolated, separated from the rest of the Roman formation. It would not be long before the rest of his men were bleeding out on the ice, too.

Squinting through the sleet, Albinus saw, once more, the barbarian cavalry readying to charge. For a moment, the wind dropped, and through the sleet, he could see huddled shapes sitting on the frozen river, cattle being driven off toward the northern bank. For the first time, he understood the enemy were not able to throw their whole force into the battle, as some men were needed to guard the spoils from their raids.

'I need a volunteer,' Albinus said, coming to a quick decision. 'Quickly now, don't make me pick someone.'

Legionary Pavo shuffled through the ranks, saluting in front of Albinus when he presented himself. 'I'll do it, sir,' he said.

'You don't know what *it* is yet, soldier,' Albinus said through a half-smile.

'All the same, sir, I'll do it.' He nodded to his centurion. Even Albinus could see the respect the man held for him in his eyes.

'Very well, thank you, Pavo. I need you to find the tribune as fast as you can. Tell him that the enemy has the hostages and cattle to my century's front, I *think* east of our position, though this weather is making it almost impossible to tell.' Once more, Albinus squinted through the sleet, but all that was to be seen now was shadows and ice. 'Tell him they are unable to commit their whole force to battle and that if we form a line across the river and try and advance on them, our cavalry could outflank them and attack their rear. Understand?'

'Yes, sir. We will do what is ordered and at every command will be ready.' With that, he was gone.

'They're coming back,' Bucco said, as Albinus watched Pavo disappear into the storm.

Albinus turned and watched as the Germani mounted their horses and prepared for another charge. The overburdened ice gave another groan, and panic welled in Albinus' belly.

And then, seemingly from nowhere, his mind forced upon him a memory of Licina. They were sitting by this very river, it was summer, their feet swishing in the green-tinted water. Licina was speaking of her father, who had been long dead even then. She said she could remember him fishing on the river in winter, using his sword to carve out a circular hole in the ice. He remembered laughing when she had said she'd asked her father if all the fish would be frozen, trapped underneath the ice.

An idea sprouted, budding and beautiful, like the first blossom of spring.

'Axes! Does anyone have an axe?' he asked frantically. Two men raised their hands, then passed them through the ranks. Once Albinus had them, he handed one to Bucco. 'You know how you promised my father you would always protect me?'

'Sometimes you're too much like your old man for your own good,' he said, taking the axe, grasping at the straws of his centurion's plan. 'Come on then, *sir*, let's go get ourselves killed, shall we?'

Forward they ran, into the storm. The cold bit at Albinus' frozen fingers, just keeping a hold on the axe was a challenge. His boots scratched and slid on the ice, and looking down, he felt a pang of terror, glimpsing the dark water below. It seemed to look back up at him, its black eyes smiling, eager to draw him down.

They had gone thirty paces when Albinus called for Bucco to halt, and they readied their axes. 'Are you sure about this, lad?' Bucco called through the raging storm.

'We've got to get them off their horses, can you think of a better way to do that?'

'If this gets us killed, I'm going to be really pissed off with you,' Bucco replied, a savage grin fixed on his face.

Albinus grinned back and looked up at the enemy, who were just beginning their advance. 'Let's do it!'

Bucco swung first, the axe glinting in the dull light as he held it above his head before it crashed down into the ice, making no sound other than a dull chink. Albinus swung after. He was startled by how thick the ice felt and how little impression the axe blade had made on the surface.

Swing after swing, they took turns at hacking the ice to shreds, Albinus acutely aware that the barbarians would be getting closer with every beat of his heart and that there would be nowhere to run if the ice did not break.

But it *was* breaking. Albinus raised his axe once more as Bucco thumped his down, and there was a low rumble, followed by a shudder. Albinus felt sick, his arms were numb, and he was beginning to feel dizzy. He was freezing but sweating from his exertions. As he willed his tiring muscles to swing the axe once more, he nearly lost his footing, and there was no power at all in his blow. The axe, however, went straight through the ice, forming a small, rectangular hole.

'Yes! Come on, Bucco, keep going, we're nearly there!'

'Aye, and so are they,' Bucco said, pointing to the enemy who were no more than fifty paces off.

Frantically now, they swung with no cohesion at all, and strike by strike, the hole got longer, wider, and a crack began to form on the surface across the breadth of the river.

'One more each, then we run like we're late for the races,' he bellowed, hefting the axe, willing his body to give him the energy for one last blow.

Two blades struck the ice, then two sets of legs pumped into action, as Bucco and Albinus ran like villains from the gallows.

Thirty paces felt like thirty miles as Albinus skidded along the ice, Fullo urging him on, his men forming up to face another charge behind him.

The ice rumbled once more, the shaking causing Albinus to lose his footing again. He hit the frozen surface hard, shards of pain tearing through his right shoulder, the dislocation taken in first battle coming back to haunt him once more.

Slowly, he got to his feet, Bucco beside him, hauling him up. The ice was vibrating, cracking, groaning, distressed at the burden of the rampaging horses charging toward the Roman line.

And suddenly, with an almighty crack that almost seemed to shake the earth, it broke.

The noise was horrific, an ear-splitting crack so powerful, even the howling storm seemed to recede in its wake. The ground shook, as if Albinus were standing on a volcano preparing to erupt and shatter the earth around it.

Albinus was on his back once more, the constant shuddering vibration making it impossible for him to rise. He turned back, seeing nothing but shadows through the driving sleet, hearing nothing but the screams of the dying on the wind which seemed to carry the perishing men's fear with it.

'We need to move, Albinus,' Bucco called. He had risen unsteadily to his feet and was slowly inching towards his centurion. 'The ice is cracking under us.'

Albinus reached out with a palm, his bare skin almost numb as he caressed the glistening surface. But Bucco was right, he could feel the small cracks sprouting underneath him, sense the weakness in the ice.

*Get up.* A voice screamed at him in his head. *Get up, boy!* His father's voice. Transported back to the training square, wooden sword in hand, lying in the dust after Fullo had put him down.

He was on his feet in heartbeats, the old anger and hatred he had felt towards his father driving him on. He made the ice Silus. He would not let the old bastard beat him this time. Twenty painful paces later, he fell into the arms of Fullo who ushered him through the ranks. 'Better get ready to fight, sir,' Fullo said, 'the bastards are still coming.'

Through the sleet and the wind, the odd flash of lightning illuminated the barbarians. They advanced on foot now, their horsemen all condemned to a cold and watery end. Over the shards of ice they advanced, impervious to their comrades who floated, lifeless, in the river. The ice had not broken fully, as Albinus had hoped it would, but a large hole had formed in the centre of the river, leaving plenty of room for the footmen to circle around the edges.

'Is Pavo back?' Albinus asked, hoping in vain that the remnants of his century would receive backup.

'I am, sir. The tribune is dead. Centurion Sura has command of the rest of the cohort, and they are engaged a few hundred paces to our west. He said he would send reinforcements as soon as he could.'

'And our cavalry?'

'He has no idea where they are, said he hasn't seen them since the fighting began.'

Albinus swore and forced himself to stand taller, concealing from his men the fear he felt. 'Right, we hold here. The ice still feels solid, and stand on your shields again, it will give us an advantage. Everyone still got their javelins?'

There were nods and shouts. Albinus nodded, silently praying to every deity he could recall. 'We have to hold them here, lads. If they get through us, then they will be onto the rest of the cohort, and it sounds as though they are facing the other way.'

He looked behind his century, in the direction Pavo had said their comrades were. He could see nothing through the haze, hear no signs of combat, as the wind was coming from the east, vanquishing all in its path.

Albinus pushed through his men until he was standing in the front line. He was exhausted, freezing, but he forced himself to focus on the task in hand.

The barbarians were twenty paces off when he could first get a good look at them. Covered in furs, armed with longswords and axes, they slipped and skidded as they charged, any order long since lost. Most did not have shields, perhaps fearing the extra weight on the unstable surface, but it appeared as though they would not miss them. There were hundreds of them.

More and more men streamed from the cover of the storm, each screaming a war cry. Albinus gripped the hilt of his sword a little tighter, his javelin long gone now. Bucco was at his left shoulder, Pavo his right. He could hear Fullo issuing orders behind him, the Roman line curving until it became a circle once more. Albinus thought it a sensible decision and cursed himself for not making it himself, as there was no way they could avoid being outflanked. And then there was no time left to think, just to fight.

The first man to come at him lunged with a sword for his groin. Albinus swayed on the curved edge of his shield and the sword tip kissed his hip as it passed him. Armed with just his short sword, Albinus leant forward and grabbed hold of the barbarian's outstretched arm and heaved him in. The German could get no purchase on the ice and fell into Albinus' arms, helpless as he took a blade through the heart.

Albinus threw the body to the ground and just had time to bring his sword up to block a chop from an axe. Its bearer was a huge man, naked from the waist up. His tattooed body was thick with muscle, and flecks of grey speckled his red hair. This was a warrior of experience, a survivor. The axe chopped down again, and once more, Albinus brought his sword up to meet it, this time, instead of just blocking the cut, he returned one of his own. The axeman tried to use his own weapon to block the blow, but the sword missed the axe blade and cut through the shaft instead, sending it toppling to the frozen ground.

Not wasting any time, Albinus leant forward as much as he dared and cut the German across his face. Blood spurted from the open wound, thick and dark, and it poured down the warrior's face as he fell out of sight, screaming.

Pressure on his back, Albinus tried to turn and see what was happening behind him, but as he craned his neck he was pushed again, and he toppled from his shield, hitting the ice with a thump.

His training kicked in, and he rolled onto his back, sword held up in front of his face. A shadow appeared over him, a wicked smile revealing stumped, yellow teeth. A blade flashed down, and Albinus couldn't bring his own to block in time. He screamed, a thousand memories whirling through his mind, his son's face painting itself on his eyelids. But the death blow never came. When he opened his eyes once more, there was another body standing over him, his attacker falling lifeless to the floor.

Commodus knelt down and put a hand on Albinus' shoulder, his other holding a bloody sword. 'Are you okay, my friend?' he asked, his voice still as calm as a summer sea.

Albinus nodded and rose gingerly. Looking around, he saw his men had advanced over his stricken form and were wrestling the barbarians on the ice. The battle had drifted away, it was now being fought by pairs.

Bucco was grappling with a man in a great coat of fur. They rolled on the ice, Bucco coming out on top. He grabbed his opponent by the neck and rammed his head repeatedly on the ice until it broke.

Fullo was ten paces from him. Sword gone, dagger in hand, he slashed at a face then rammed the short blade into another's ribs.

Albinus just stood, breathing hard, nausea winning its battle over him, holding him in a trance. He vomited a foul-smelling liquid onto his feet, swaying, vision going blurry. He slumped down to his knees, head spinning.

'We need you to get up, Centurion,' Commodus said. He knelt down beside Albinus, his dark eyes boring into him, imploring. 'Your men need you. Get up, your caesar commands it.'

More barbarians were streaming in from the east, out of the shadows. This time though, they were not howling a war cry, most did not even have weapons. They were looking behind them. Albinus saw most were bloodied; one man even had a spear protruding from his left shoulder.

The ground rumbled, the ice shuddered under heavy impact. It groaned once more, like a wild beast, rearing its head for one final charge, and out of the mist came the Roman cavalry, swinging their long swords, Bassus at their head.

'We've done it,' Albinus whispered. 'Thank Mars and all his legions, we held them.'

# PART II

# THE ETERNAL CITY

# CHAPTER XIII

**July, 193 AD**
**Rome**

Faustus breathes deep, steeling his nerves as he slows his mount to a walk. Ahead of him lies the Milvian Bridge and past it, to the south, Rome.

He is still not entirely sure why he agreed to accompany Rome's new emperor, Septimius Severus, on his march from the northern frontier to the eternal city, but he has. Memories from his childhood creep up on him, unbidden, as he gazes at the sprawling city that opens up before him. It has been eighteen years since he was last here. He thinks of the twists and turns the thread of his life has taken in that time. His father's face is fixed in his mind, and he struggles to hold back tears. He has never allowed himself time to grieve, to move on, the ghosts of his past still dog his every step.

The previous night, Severus and his entourage had stayed at the villa just off the Via Clodia, once occupied by Commodus and his retinue. It is the villa Faustus still thinks of as his childhood home. He can still recall the stink of sweat from the gladiators, the sweet scent of wafting perfume Commodus used to insist was spread across the villa. He had been unable to enter the villa itself, the wave of intense emotion crushing him even as he entered the grounds. He had spent the night in the stables with the half century of men from the Fourteenth Legion that had acted as the emperor's guard.

He can see him now, Severus, sitting easily astride his horse, a broad grin stretched across his sun-darkened skin. Every step of the journey south has been hampered by crowds of cheering citizens, all desperate to catch a glimpse of their new emperor. Faustus had not known there were so many people in all of the empire, let alone Italy. It seemed that at every milestone on the Via Flaminia, another crowd had gathered, led by the local magistrates.

'So, that is Rome, then,' Calvus says, steering his horse alongside Faustus.

'Aye, I had forgotten you have never been here.'

'Been a lot of places, me, but never Rome. First time I've been in Italy at all.'

'Strange, is it not? All you have done for Rome in your life, in the army and then the *frumentarii*. And yet, you have never seen the city you seek to protect.'

Calvus smiles, rubbing his mount's neck as the beast shifts and whinnies, impatient to be on its way. 'Rome ain't just a city, lad. It's a belief, a way of life. To be Roman is to be civilised, to be better than the barbarians that live in the wilderness, outside the frontier.'

'Do you know, Uncle, not once have I ever heard you called *civilised* by anyone,' Faustus says through a grin. 'And the only culture I have ever seen you take joy in is the weekly bloodbaths they offer up in the arena.'

Faustus laughs as Calvus offers an expression of mock offence. 'They've got a big arena here, haven't they? The biggest in the empire, or so I hear.'

'Yes, Uncle,' Faustus says, still chuckling. 'The Flavian amphitheatre is quite something. You can see it, just past the Palatine Hill,' he says, pointing to the south. 'The Circus Maximus is well worth a visit, too. I can picture you on the stalls, throwing a punch at someone who is cheering for a different chariot faction.'

Up ahead, on the south side of the bridge, the masses that have travelled north out of the city are being ushered out of the road by the cudgels of the Praetorian Guard, and a body of men are moving in a slow procession, each with their heads down, hiding their sombre expressions.

'Which team did Commodus follow?'

'Green. It is quite common for emperors to favour the Greens, from what I remember anyway. What's going on here then?' Faustus nods towards the procession of plainly dressed men.

'They are the senate, here to greet Severus,' Calvus says with a smirk. 'Severus, as you have probably heard, has taken to calling himself *divi commodi frater,* the brother of the Divine Commodus. Those old farts are unhappy enough about Severus assuming the throne, they've got no idea of the shit storm he is going to rain on them.'

'They have supported his claim though, have they not? I mean, Severus has come to Rome on their invitation.'

'Ha!' Calvus barks a laugh. 'How naïve you are, my young friend. When we left Pannonia, Severus was just another usurper, ridiculed by the senate. But the further we marched, more legions threw their lot in with Severus, they had no choice but to abandon Didius Julianus and side with him. They will pander to him now, escort him through the city to the palace, but tonight, when they leave for their homes, they will already begin conspiring behind his back.'

'Makes you wonder why anyone would want to be emperor at all,' Faustus says, thinking it hasn't even been six months since Commodus himself was murdered, and Severus will be the third man to have set himself up in his palace and put on the purple-striped toga. Pertinax murdered in the palace, and the same fate had befallen Julianus, just the previous month. Both the senate and the Praetorian Guard had abandoned the man who had won the empire at auction upon hearing of the size of the army Severus was bringing to Italian soil. Faustus had also heard the men of the Fourteenth speaking of Pescennius Niger, who had been declared emperor by his troops in the east. A confrontation between the two was said to be inevitable.

'Severus is going to make Clodius Albinus his caesar, or so I hear,' Calvus says. He's biting on an apple, chewing loudly. Faustus realises his own hunger and is about to ask the old man where he got the apple from when Calvus throws one over to him. 'I'm told you haven't been eating,' he says with a pointed look.

'The governor of Britannia? He thinks himself an emperor as well, does he? And no, I haven't really. Since getting the hit round the head, I haven't had much of an appetite. I'm okay though, no need to worry, Uncle.'

'Well, you make sure you eat, lad, I have a feeling you're going to need your wits about you in the coming months. And yes, Albinus is the governor of Britannia. By all accounts, he was a big supporter of Julianus. Seems Severus is just trying to secure his rear when he marches east to face Niger.'

Faustus is only half listening, he's watching the senators, who are lowering themselves to their knees, one by one, as Severus dismounts and walks among them, raising the men he knows and shaking their hands warmly. That wide grin still fixes his face, but even from this distance, Faustus can detect the iron glint in his eye.

'Will you go east?' he asks Calvus.

'Aye, if I'm asked. It will be good to revisit some of the places I saw when I was there with Habitus, even better to not have to spend my time looking over my shoulder and sleeping with one eye open.'

Faustus smiles, giving his old guardian a shrewd look, 'You really must tell me the end of your story, Uncle. I feel it is a tale with many threads still left to untangle.'

Calvus shifts uncomfortably in his saddle, and Faustus sees a small quiver in his lips. 'It's not a tale with a happy ending, lad, but yes, I will tell you the rest of it soon. But since we're going to be stuck here for the best part of the afternoon, sweating like pigs in this blasted heat, why not tell me a story of your childhood? Tell me more about this sprawling cesspit that people say is the centre of the civilised world.'

# CHAPTER XIV

**JANUARY, 175 AD**
**ROME**

Albinus sat under a shaded portico in a small courtyard just outside the palace on the Palatine Hill, letting the biting winter wind cool his skin. It was just before midday, and he and his men had been hard at work all morning, marching and weapons training. As always, Albinus had not just stood and watched as his men sweated in the January sun, but joined in, led by example.

His shoulder ached, as it always seemed to every time he practised with sword or spear, the old wound seemingly growing worse. It had been a few years now since the joint had first dislocated, but it seemed as though the injury would stay with him forever. He sighed, rotating his right arm slowly, wincing as the pain rose and fell like the tide. Commodus had arranged for the emperor's own physician, Galen, to take a look at the arm, and the old Greek had taken less than an hour to confirm there was no cure, although he did recommend Albinus leave the army at once and find a less physically taxing profession.

Albinus smiled at the thought, wondering what Commodus would have said if he had brought a petition to the caesar. In short, he was fairly sure the answer would have been a resounding 'no', followed by a few expletives and a rant about how he needed his best men around him. Albinus had still not grown accustomed to the lofty heights he had risen to and remained uncomfortable with the power he was able to wield and always hesitated to use it.

After the near disaster of the battle on the ice against the Iazyges, Marcus Aurelius had made the decision to send his son back south to Rome. Commodus had requested Albinus, along with his century, be allowed to go with him and act as his bodyguard. It seemed the caesar was not to be denied in this, pleading with the emperor to allow his 'closest friend and advisor' to stay on as his protector. And so, Albinus and his century found themselves on prolonged detached duty from the Fourteenth Legion, and Albinus the only man in Rome in a position to grant an audience with the caesar – even the Praetorian prefect had to seek his permission to be admitted into royal presence.

It was not that life was bad in Rome. Apart from the constant stink the populaces conjured up, the city was vibrant and full of wonders. Albinus had been unable to put his feelings into words when he first stepped out onto the balcony of the royal box at the Flavian Amphitheatre. Thousands upon thousands of people were crammed in, the top benches so high, Albinus couldn't make out the individual people sitting there, just a blur of colour. The Circus Maximus too was an awe-inspiring sight, and for the first time, Albinus had developed a love of chariot racing and had grown very passionate about his favourite team, the Blues.

That was before he took in a play at Pompey's theatre – which was still a structural marvel, despite its age – the sights and smells at Trajan's forum on market day and the sheer feeling of invincibility he had felt walking up the steps to the temple of Jupiter on the Capitoline Hill.

A child's scream behind him roused him from his musings as little Faustus and Marcus came tearing through the courtyard, wooden swords in hand. Meredith came out behind them, hissing for the boys to be quiet. Albinus smiled as Faustus ran up to his father, almost striking him a glancing blow with the sword as he ran into Albinus' outstretched arms.

'I'm so sorry, sir,' Meredith said. Her face was flushed, and her red hair had a golden glow in the sunlight. 'I've tried to calm them down, but they are full of it today. Jupiter knows what was in their porridge this morning!'

'It's okay, Meredith,' Albinus said through a broad grin. 'They're children, they should be allowed to play as much as they want.' He picked Faustus up and raised the boy above his head, whirling him around in circles.

'Me next!' Marcus called, hugging Albinus' leg, nearly causing him to lose balance. Albinus obliged and squatted down once he had finished, drawing both boys into him. 'Are you two causing mischief again?'

'Yep,' Faustus said with a satisfied grin. 'We playing swords, I'm better than Marcus though, I am.'

'No, he's not! He beat me once, but I beat him twice,' Marcus said with a scowl.

Albinus dragged the warring pair apart before it could come to blows, still laughing as he did. 'Easy there, little soldiers. Now, stand to attention.' The two boys stood erect, their feet apart, arms rigid by their side, just as he had taught them. 'I have a special mission for the two of you, one that you must succeed in at all costs.'

'What's *succeed* mean, sir?' Marcus asked, his tongue fumbling over the new word.

'It means you must not fail, understand? Good. Now, your mission is to obey Meredith at all times and to do everything she says. Do you both understand?' Both boys nodded. 'Excellent, now off you go, and remember, obey every word.'

The boys ran off, back into the palace via the door they had erupted from, Meredith watching them disappear.

'Are you okay?' Albinus asked her. He felt slightly awkward alone in her presence and made sure it didn't happen often. It wasn't that he disliked her, for she was very agreeable and the perfect mother figure to bring up his son. It was that, no matter how hard he tried to force the thought from his mind, she reminded him of Licina.

Both women had flowing hair a golden red, both were slim built and long-legged, though Meredith was a full head taller than Licina. She had hazel eyes, whereas Licina's were emerald green, her nose was flat and wide, like her father's, and thick lips surrounded a mouth of white teeth.

'Yes, I'm fine, thank you, sir,' she said, giving a little curtsy as she spoke.

'I've told you before, Meredith, you can dispatch with the formalities when it's just us. You are a slave no more.'

'Yes, sorry, sir, I keep forgetting.'

A pause of silence. Somewhere in the distance, a loud crack split the air, immediately followed by a cacophony of raised voices.

'Another cart broken, it would seem,' Albinus said with a shy smile. He took a step towards her, reached out an arm and touched her shoulder. 'Are you sure you're all right? Have you heard anything from your father?'

'No, why, have you?'

Albinus shook his head. It had been three years since he had said his goodbyes to Calvus and Habitus as they headed off for the distant east. Not a day went by without him sending a swift prayer to the heavens for their safety. 'Is that what worries you?' he asked.

'No, it's not that, my father is more than capable of looking after himself. It's just…' she trailed off as two legionaries marched through the courtyard, both saluting Albinus and nodding politely to Meredith.

'Is it the men? Albinus asked, noticing the wary look she had given the passing soldiers. 'Is someone bothering you, because I'll crucify any bastard that thinks he can touch you—'

'No! No, sir, it's not your soldiers…' she said, raising her eyes to meet his.

They stared at each other for a moment, a flicker of knowledge passing from her to him. 'Oh gods,' Albinus said, his face colouring with rage, 'not Commodus?'

'Yes, sir.' Tears welled in her eyes as she spoke, her body shuddered, and Albinus moved to wrap her in his arms. 'He has *invited* me into his private chambers for a drink with him and his whores twice now. I have managed to avoid it by saying that I have to look after the children, but I can *feel* him looking at me sometimes as if he is undressing me with his eyes.'

'And he wonders why people hate him,' Albinus muttered, still holding Meredith tight. 'I will speak to him today. This will stop, I promise.'

'Thank you. Please don't get into any trouble over me. I had better go, Juno knows what those boys are getting up to unattended.' She moved away, her hand lingering on Albinus' arm as they parted. Albinus stood in the courtyard after she had gone, her scent still lingering in his nostrils.

It was under a copper sky that Albinus accompanied Commodus to the baths of Nero later that day. It was not a long journey from the Palatine

Hill to the Campus Martius in the west of the city, which had once been nothing but a sweeping valley, used to house the pens for the senatorial elections. In the years since Augustus had seized power and the republic transformed into an empire, more and more buildings had risen to join Pompey's magnificent theatre, so now there was barely any of the green grass among the foundations of the towering buildings.

Commodus, of course, rode in a litter, with Albinus and twenty men on foot around him, all wrapped in their winter cloaks. Through a sprawling mass of side streets and alleys, they went by the fastest route, a soldier from the Praetorian Guard leading the way. Albinus thought he would never get to grips with the sheer geography of the never-ending city. As they entered the Campus Martius from the east, he could see the circular building of the Mausoleum of Augustus in the distance, remarkable due to its grass-green roof. Lined with trees, it stood out amongst a skyline of red brick and stone. Across the river was another circular structure, even more magnificent: the Mausoleum of Hadrian, built over fifty years before. The Emperor Hadrian had clearly decided that Augustus' Mausoleum had reached its capacity and commissioned an even grander building to be constructed, one fitting to house his remains.

It struck Albinus that since the days of the republic, the aristocracy of Rome had been intent on outdoing each other, with powerful men all eager to have their names linked to a monument that would last a thousand years or more. The bathhouses themselves were a fine example of this. As they marched past the baths of Agrippa, surrounded by scaffolding with builders and stonemasons scrambling up and down flimsy-looking wooden ladders, Albinus could not help but think there had probably been nothing wrong with the existing baths when Nero had commissioned his own . But he wanted to build something grander, something he would be remembered for. And what he had built was truly a marvel.

Commodus stepped from his litter onto the back of a squatting slave, surveying his surroundings in the twilight. This would usually be the time of day where men were expelled from the bathhouse – or *thermae,* as it was known – and women would be allowed time to bathe in private as the sun bled out and the first hour of the night approached.

He nodded to Albinus, who returned the gesture but kept himself rigidly erect, his thumbs tucked into his belt. Privately, he hoped he would not be asked to join Commodus in the baths and, therefore, avoid an hour of uncomfortable conversation. He had been thinking all afternoon how he could broach the subject of Meredith, whose temper was growing more and more erratic. It was not something he looked forward to.

'Bucco, you and Servius guard the doors,' Albinus said, nodding to his old friend. He was doing Bucco a favour, and both men knew it, for standing in the heat of the baths in armour was extremely uncomfortable, and even remaining outdoors and being exposed to the worst the winter could throw at you was preferable.

'You will join me, Centurion?' Commodus asked, his dark eyes slits, giving him a menacing look.

'Certainly, Caesar,' Albinus said, silently cursing. 'We had a hard morning's training, it would be good to give my shoulder a soak.'

They walked through the main doors into a vestibule that would not have been out of place on the Palatine itself. All was red granite and white marble. In the centre of the vestibule stood a giant fountain in the shape of a bowl, carved entirely from granite. The walls were covered in erotic frescos, some so crude it made Albinus blush to look upon them. Commodus, however, revelled in the bare flesh that had been so elegantly brought to life. He studied them as they walked through into the main complex, pointing out his favourite drawings.

They made their way through to one of the dressing rooms, just off the side of the main bath, and Albinus felt uncomfortable as he shed his clothes in the presence of his caesar and four of his men, who stood guard at the door. Commodus, though, appeared to show no shame, letting his tunic fall to the floor before removing his loincloth and scratching his groin.

This summer would see Commodus turn fourteen years of age, and not for the first time, Albinus had cause to wonder what sort of man would emerge – and what sort of emperor. Albinus had worked tirelessly in the years since his appointment as the caesar's chief protector to mould him into a leader, a man his soldiers would follow. He had no real idea if that is what he was meant to be doing with the boy, but it was the only thing he thought he could do. He reasoned that if his men grew to love him, if they would give their lives to save his, then surely Commodus would have grown into a man worth dying for. And if you were not prepared to die for your emperor, then the wrong man was wearing the purple.

Commodus, however, had changed rapidly from the quiet and curious child who had been thrust into the heart of the legions three years before. Since returning to Rome, he seemed to have grown in confidence, being back on home soil making him more comfortable to express himself and force his will on others. In fact, the only reason they had come to the baths of Nero was because Commodus had become frustrated with the temperature of his own bath in the palace and had dismissed four of the slaves from his service, forcing them out on the street. He had been going to execute them until Albinus had jumped in at the last moment and begged him to reconsider. And to make matters worse, he treated the noblemen of the senate no better.

'You seem lost in thought, brother,' Commodus said, his dark eyes fixed on Albinus.

'Sorry, Caesar,' Albinus said, recovering quickly, 'just got a bit on my mind, is all.'

'Oh? Well, do tell. Is it to do with that soldier of yours? Pavo, I believe his name is.'

'Pavo?' Albinus stopped short. 'Why would Pavo be bothering my mind?'

They walked from the dressing room and into the *caldarium,* the main bath, where the water was kept fiercely warm. Commodus dived straight in, emerging from the steaming waters with his dark curly hair plastered down his face. Albinus eased himself in, part relishing and part dreading the extreme temperature of the water. He was sweating before his thighs were fully submerged, and he looked back at the four men of his century who had followed the two of them into the chamber, giving them a sympathetic smile. *At least I don't have to stand there and sweat in all that armour.*

'Yes, Pavo,' Commodus said, pushing the hair off his face. 'He was on guard in the palace this morning with two black eyes and what appeared to be a raging hangover – the smell nearly put me off my breakfast.'

'He was on guard half cut?' Albinus boomed, his voice reverberating around the chamber. It was a grievous crime to be drunk on duty, whether the soldier was guarding a prisoner destined for the execution block or Caesar himself.

'Yes, I was just walking into the triclinium and overheard your *optio* giving him a bit of a tongue lashing, something about being out gambling down the Aventine again. Oh, I haven't even told you the best bit, he had no helmet, sword or shoes!'

'*What!*' Albinus spluttered, sweat pouring down him now as he raged.

'I believe that was why he was *excused* from the drill this morning? It would appear you need to have a quiet word with your *optio*, Centurion,' Commodus said with a smirk. It was Albinus' one consolation that he knew Commodus would have found the whole thing to be amusing; another man could have had Pavo executed on the spot.

'I will, Caesar,' Albinus said, wondering why Fullo would keep something like that from him. Pavo had always been the joker of the century, the one most likely to cause Albinus grief, but never had he turned up for duty drunk or missing half his kit.

'So, if it isn't Pavo bothering you, then what is?'

Albinus steeled himself, forcing his erstwhile legionary from his mind. He knew he had to say something, but it didn't make the task any easier. 'It's about Meredith.'

'Your childminder?'

'Yes, Caesar. She has said to me that you have made certain... advances towards her.'

'So what if I have?' Commodus said. He was lying on his back, floating in the water, his arms rotating in circles above his head.

'She is important to me to me, Caesar, to little Faustus, too. She is the only mother he has ever known. I would not be able to fulfil my duties without her,' Albinus said, hoping that if he focused on that, Commodus would listen, as he knew he would not be sympathetic towards his son.

'How is your son?'

'Faustus? He thrives, thanks to Jupiter.'

'I am glad to hear it. I often see him and Meredith's child at play, it makes me sad in a way, that I never got to have that kind of childhood.' Commodus drifted off, his eyes glazing over. Albinus felt a pang of sympathy for him. Despite the extreme wealth and privilege Commodus had been raised to take for granted, he had never been given the opportunity to experience the simple pleasures of being a child.

'Life was hard for me growing up, especially after my brother died.'

Albinus lowered his head, gazing at his feet through the water, embarrassed to hear the caesar speak of such things in his presence. Commodus had, Albinus knew, been born a twin. Titus Aurelius Fulvus Antoninus had been the elder of the two and had passed from this world some ten years previous.

'Do you have any siblings?' Commodus asked.

'No, Caesar,' Albinus said, wishing the conversation would move on but having no idea how to initiate it.

'Why ever not? I cannot imagine your mother and father set out to have just the one.'

Life was different in the provinces than it was in Rome. Albinus could see that, coming from Pannonia and into the eternal city, where unwanted children were just left on street corners in the dead of night, either for the wild dogs to ravage or a barren wife to pick up and raise as her own. The city was overpopulated, property was at a premium and all most families could afford was a two-room apartment seven or eight floors high in a hastily erected tower block. No one wanted more than one or two children, for rent was usually paid not for the space you lived in but for how many people lived within it, no matter how cramped.

In the country, it was different. Even a small farmhouse could winter four or five children. With luck, the produce from the land would see enough coin trickle in to get the family through to spring, if the gods were kind.

'I'm not sure, Caesar.' Albinus shifted in the water, uncomfortable with the question, as he was with any question relating to his parents. 'My father was in the army. He didn't spend much time with my mother and me until he retired. My mother died shortly after that, plague…'

Albinus did not think of his mother much. Thinking of her now made him realise how much he had ceased to remember her, the musical pitch of her voice, the way her smile lit up a room. Since the murder of his father and his hasty enrolment into the legions eight years before, his only thoughts of family had been of his father, Silus, though he comforted himself that it was mainly down to his comrades' obsession with the man and not being able to go a day without Bucco regaling him with a tale of his youth, usually with his father ending the story a hero.

'Cursed plague,' Commodus spat. 'Did you hear there has been another outburst in the east? They say the flames of the pyres in Syria can be seen from the Acropolis in Athens.'

'I had,' said Albinus with a worried frown, his thoughts drifting to Calvus and Habitus, whom he had still received no word of. 'So, about Meredith, Caesar,' Albinus said, hoping to steer the conversation back to its original direction.

'Message received, Centurion, loud and clear. Meredith is off the table, forbidden fruit, a poisoned chalice. If I pursue her, then I risk losing you, which is something I am not prepared to do. I need my friends, Albinus, now more than ever. The wolves are circling. Each week, it seems, another report from the senate is read out in the forum, each clearly stating my father's waning health. I need you here, brother, at my side.'

'I'm sure your father is fine, Caesar. There have been rumours regarding his health for years now, since the war first began. And on the day he passes from this world, you shall ascend to your rightful place, ruler of the empire, you'll see.'

'Not if the senate get their way.'

Albinus opened his mouth to reply but then quickly closed it. He had an opinion on this, but he had to word it carefully. 'The senators are proud, fickle old men. Since the Divine Augustus seized power, they have seen their influence ebb. Your father understands this and does well to treat them as equals, to show them the right respect. It is, I think, something you have to learn.'

'You seek to lecture me, soldier?' Commodus spat, his dark eyes fixing Albinus with a challenge.

'No, Caesar—'

'Is it you who is heir to the world? Or me?'

'You, of course, Caesar—'

'And is it you that has received the finest education money can buy? You who has been schooled about imperial politics since he was old enough to speak, you who has had to listen to endless lectures from an *all so wise* father?'

Albinus said nothing.

'It is not! And yet you seek to lecture me? To *educate* me? I am the rising sun, I am the one who will take Rome into the greatest age of wealth and glory she has ever known! And the people will love me for it. The senate? They shall unite behind me or fall on their own, the choice is theirs. Leave me, Centurion, I feel the need to be alone.'

Albinus rose from the bath, offering a small bow before turning and making for the dressing room. Inside, he dressed quickly, declining the offer from the waiting slave to have his body oiled and massaged. He stormed from the bathhouse, not even stopping at the door to speak to Bucco. He made for the Palatine, remembering with a grimace that he had a certain drunken soldier to deal with.

# CHAPTER XV

**July, 193 AD**
**Rome**

*Don't dawdle, but don't hurry. Never look back, and if the worst happens, never hesitate.*

The words ring through Faustus' mind as he treads steadily through a winding alley, deep in the Subura, Rome's poorest district. He has been in the city for two weeks, the first week passing in monotonous boredom as he paced between the four walls in the small room he had been allotted at the palace. Severus had been stamping his authority on the city and the senate, still preaching to anyone that would listen he was a brother of the revered Commodus, and he would do what it took to rehabilitate his memory and have him deified by the senate. Upon his assassination, the senate had ruled that the reign of Commodus should be wiped from history, all images of him were to be destroyed, all buildings or monuments commissioned in his name were to be either torn down or his name erased from them. It was the rule of that wise council that a hundred years from now, no man alive would remember the name of the cruel and vindictive man that had caused the death of so many innocents. They had ridiculed him for claiming to be a god, though, in truth, he had done nothing that emperors before him had not been doing for a generation and more. *A de facto damnatio memoriae,* they called it, condemnation of memory, a punishment Faustus knew Commodus would have considered worse than his assassination itself.

He could remember the man who clearly thought himself a god. Though, in truth, when Faustus had known him, he still wore the tunic of a child. It was only after the rebellion of Avidius Cassius in the east that the revered Marcus Aurelius had officially made his son a man, another clear indication that it was his intention for his son to inherit the purple once he had departed this world.

Faustus could indeed remember Commodus drunkenly accusing Albinus of 'betraying a god' when he was deep in his cups one evening, though he could not remember what his father had done to anger the young caesar so.

It is with a start that Faustus realises his wandering mind has carried his feet to his destination. He breathes deep, despite the overpowering stench of piss and shit on the street. Overhead, a shuttered window opens, and a woman leans out, emptying her overflowing chamber pot onto the street. She barks an apology when she notices Faustus, who feels warm urine splash up his shins.

It is around midday, but the sun's light does not reach this part of the city, where shadows rule and even the Praetorian Guard stay well clear unless they are specifically ordered. The Subura is run by gangs, owned by gangs, it is, in effect, its own mini-city, mini-empire, with rival leaders all vying for power over the desperately poor and overcrowded population.

There are no villas with magnificent views over the city and its seven hills, there are just tower blocks, built of timber and finished in concrete. When Faustus looks up to the window that the woman with the chamber pot has retreated back into, he sees the space between that and the window of the opposite apartment on the other side of the street is no more than six feet. No wonder there are so many people on the street, he thinks, where else do they have to go?

Reaching the end of the alley, he turns right, out onto a wider, paved street. To his right is a tanner; large ox hides block the cobbles on the road, rolled into cylinders and tied off with string. Two boys emerge from the door and, between them, heft one off the floor, one spluttering obscenities as they struggle with it through the threshold.

Faustus sees this from the corner of his eye but refrains from turning to look. *Don't look like a tourist, act as if you belong. You are just a man treading the same well-worn path you follow every day. Do not stand and gawp at the locals – that will give them cause to pay more attention to you. Remember, you are a ghost, no one must be able to recognise you in a crowd.*

It all sounded so easy when Calvus had begun to drill him on the ways of spying. He had only agreed to accompany his old friend to the Camp of Strangers, the home of the feared *frumentarii,* in the south of the city at the start of their second week in Rome, out of boredom. He had not thought he would leave that dark and secretive place as a trainee agent. But he had not planned on coming south with Severus at all. It seemed there was something deep inside him that was spurring him on as if his life were being guided by a higher power. He thinks again of his father, of how he would have coped with this sort of mission. *I am not my father.*

The sharp smell of vinegar invades his nostrils as he passes a tavern which seems to have no name, just a faded canopy over the door and a dozen empty amphora stacked up against the wall. Faustus sees a red stain on the bare concrete next to the door. He does not stop to see if it is wine or blood, he just assumes the latter.

Two steps past the tavern and he sees his mark walking towards him. He knows it to be her as she is wearing a strip of yellow cloth tied around her neck – the agreed signal that the exchange is to take place.

*Now for the hard bit. You need to walk towards your mark but not directly. When you come together, it needs to appear to anyone watching that it is an accident, nothing more. Contact between the two of you should last for no more than a couple of heartbeats, then carry on just as you were.*

Faustus keeps his eyes dead ahead, his expression neutral, but inside his heart is thrumming, and already, his palms are drenched in sweat. He carries on along the flagstones at the same steady pace, weaving slightly to the right in the hope the girl will notice him. He tries to study her face from the corner of his eye, get some sort of signal from her that she has noticed him. He too is wearing a colour, a patch of blue, sticking out from his belt on his right hip. Has she noticed? He doesn't know. Panicking now, Faustus quickens his pace, fighting the urge to wipe the sweat that pours down his face. The girl has stopped and is examining a vase on display outside a small pottery shop. He sees his chance.

He slows as he approaches the shop, his eyes fixed on the merchandise. He picks up a small urn and turns it in his hand, feigning to admire the craftsmanship, which he can tell just from touch is poor; the clay is rough and has an unfinished feel. He edges closer to the girl, who stands a few paces to his left. Their heads never turn, eyes never meet, but each shuffle of the feet closes the distance.

*This is too slow.* Faustus can feel the rhythm of his heart in his ears, his tunic has stuck to his back, and he's too scared to put the urn down as his hands are shaking so violently. The girl takes another step, her foot now just inches from his, and then she takes another, and before Faustus knows what has happened their arms are entwined, and she is stumbling into him, and it is all he can do to prevent her from falling over.

'I'm so sorry,' he says as he feels her hand slip beneath his belt, leaving something behind as she withdraws it.

'My fault entirely, now, if you'll excuse me,' and she is gone, away down the road without a backward glance.

'I told you all would be well. By Jesu, lad, stop shaking will you, you're creating a draught!'

'How do we know I wasn't seen?'

'Seen?'

'What if they were watching? Do you think anyone would have noticed?'

'And who are *they* exactly?'

'Well, you know, our enemies.'

'Enemies?'

'Gods, Calvus, I don't know! You said there would be someone watching, that I would have to make it look innocent as if we had bumped into each other by accident. You said it was imperative no one saw her slip me the piece of parchment. What's on it anyway?'

'On what?'

'The parchment! What is it?'

'What do you think it is?'

Faustus pauses, his mind racing at the possibilities. 'A list of senators conspiring against Severus?'

Calvus barks a laugh, 'The parchment would be longer than me if it were!'

'A list of the legions that have gone over to Niger in the east? A rough estimation of his army?'

'Now why would a list of Niger's armies be in the Subura of all places? Do you not think that list would come from somewhere out of Asia? Some serving girl in Rome is hardly going to have come across that, is she?'

'How do you know she is a serving girl?'

'Really? That's the first question that springs to your mind?'

Faustus throws his arms up in frustration and leans back on the parapet. They stand on the roof of the main building of the Camp of Strangers. Inside there is no light, no one is permitted to speak above a murmur, and no one speaks at all until commanded by a superior officer. Every man Faustus has seen appears to be identical, bald and short, well-built and scarred. He thinks he would most likely pass them all on the street without a second glance, it is only in the dark confines of this hellish place they look so foreboding. But of course, if that were not so, then they would not be as good at their jobs.

Calvus seems to have eased into the life of an agent in Rome. Despite having never visited the city before, he had been greeted as an old friend at the gates to the Camp of Strangers. In fact, he had increased the pace up the Caelian hill as it had come into view. Once inside, he had made it his business to learn the names of every man he came across and even managed to bump into two clerks he had been having correspondence with for nearly twenty years but had never met in person. Faustus has been wondering if the old man ever intends to leave or whether he has come to Rome to die.

Faustus breathes in deeply, trying to put an end to his growing frustration, he knows it will get him nowhere, especially with Calvus. From the rooftop balcony, he can see the Flavian amphitheatre to the north, the Circus Maximus to the west and the Palace just behind it. The air seems to be clearer up here, the stench of the streets seemingly unable to rise from the cobbles as if some force holds it down there. 'So, what do we do now?'

'Dinner.'

'Dinner? No, I mean, what do we do with the information on the parchment? Do we take it to the emperor?'

'Nope. We take it to dinner.'

Calvus is laughing, Faustus can see his stomach convulsing from the corner of his eye. Eventually, Calvus can hold it in no more, and he howls in his mirth, tears stream down his creased face.

'Fuck you, Calvus.'

'I'm so sorry,' Calvus manages to breathe in a hoarse whisper. The parchment appears in his hand – in his rage, Faustus has not seen where from, and he snatches it from his friend. It is a menu for a tavern a few doors down from where they are standing.

'It was all a game, wasn't it?'

'No, not a game, a test. And you passed, my young friend.'

'Who was the girl? And how do you know I passed anyway, there was no one there watching me, I'd have seen.'

'The girl is one of us, she works solely in Rome, I'm told. And you *were* watched, me and four of the lads were on your tail the whole way. You did well, Faustus. If I hadn't known what I was watching, I would have thought it completely innocent. Come on, smile! You're one of us now, a *frumentarius*.'

'You'll pay for this, you sly old bastard,' Faustus says with venom, but already, there is a smile creeping on his face.

'I shall start by paying for dinner.'

'And a story, you still need to finish your tale. I would like to hear more of Habitus and your younger self.'

Calvus nods, the smile fading from his face. 'Okay, lad, I owe you that, I suppose. But it is a long road, the one that brought me here, full of treacherous passes and shrouded in shadow. I do not think now is the right time to retrace those steps, but soon I shall, lad, I promise. Tell me more of this city, of your childhood, and I shall tell you more of the mission our new emperor has recently entrusted me with. I am hoping you can be of some assistance.'

Faustus raises an eyebrow in question, not for the first time wondering

159

exactly who this old man who has been such a big part of his life really is, and what he has done with his long years to earn the trust of an emperor. 'Very well, but I will hear the end of your story, old man, even if I have to fight Hercules himself for the privilege.'

# CHAPTER XVI

**January, 175 AD**
**Rome**

'Start again from the beginning, and this time, don't leave anything out.'

Albinus sat on the edge of the cot, Pavo lay under a blanket, his face ashen and pale, his red eyes sunken. 'I told you everything, sir.'

'No, you did not! Don't fucking lie to me, Pavo, you've caused me enough grief already. Now tell me the whole story, right from the beginning.'

It was just after dawn, the day after Albinus had displeased Commodus in the bathhouse. Albinus had returned to the palace in a rage but had found Fullo to have gone out with a couple of the men, that night being his night off, and Pavo in a deep sleep in the small room he shared with the other seven men of his *contubernium.*

As angry as he was, the centurion had still been unable to force himself into the small sleeping chamber, rouse the men and turf out the seven innocents. Pavo had looked awful, slumped as he was in his cot, breathing unsteadily. Albinus had reasoned with himself that he was being sensible, letting the man get some rest before putting him under questioning, for surely, in the morning he would be in a better condition to talk? Deep down, he knew it to be just a cheap excuse to hide his cowardice. His father would have been in there in a heartbeat, vine stick drawn, whipping any man that did not get out of arm's reach quick enough. Taurus too, though Albinus knew himself to be a very different sort of man to both his father and his protégé.

A man. It still seemed strange to think of himself as a full-grown man, though he had the stubble and the scars to prove it. This year would be his eighth under the eagle and his twenty-third in this world. Most boys that signed up at the age Albinus and Fullo had didn't survive to see their mid-twenties. Very few lived to be granted their *honesta missio* and the retirement bonus that came with it. Even in times of peace, disease was a constant companion to an army camp, especially on the frontiers that lacked sufficient drainage for human waste and bathhouses. When the imperial physician Galen had been attending to his shoulder, he had said that one in three babies born in Rome doesn't live to see their fifth birthday. Albinus had raced to Faustus and hugged him tightly on hearing that, always fearful his beloved son would wake one day with a cough that wouldn't shift or a fever that would never break.

'Come on, Pavo,' Albinus rasped in the deepest voice he could put on. 'I've always known you to be a bit stupid, but I've never thought you a complete idiot. Tell me what is going on. Let me help you.'

'*Optio* Fullo knows, sir. Ain't you spoken to him?'

'No, I want to hear it from you,' Albinus spat, anger rising in him at the reminder of yet another of his weak moments. A stronger officer would have awoken his delicate *optio* in the last hour before dawn and demanded to know what on earth he was playing at, protecting one of the men from punishment. But, true to form, Albinus had marched right past his room on his way to see Pavo that morning. Angry as he was, he still hadn't the heart to rouse his old friend from his slumber. *Soldiers respect discipline, a unit without discipline is nothing and that starts with its leader.* A memory from his childhood, his father lecturing some poor man on the state of his men's kit, though Albinus could not remember who it was or what had been wrong.

'It all started a few weeks ago, sir,' Pavo said with a weary sigh, sitting himself up with a wince. 'Me and a few of the lads had taken to going down the Aventine when off duty – the wine is cheap, the whores decent. In one of the taverns there, we were approached by a man, said he was in with the Greens and that they ran a dice circuit in the basement, asked if we would like to come down for a few rounds and a couple of jugs of good wine.'

'Gambling is, of course, illegal within the city walls, as I am sure you are aware.'

Pavo laughed – it turned into a cough, and blood seeped from a cut inside his mouth. 'You been to the races yet? Or the arena when the gladiators are on? Everyone does it, even the cream.'

Albinus had indeed seen the 'cream', the senators and other elites of the city, gambling on the outcome of the gladiatorial matches. 'Point taken, carry on.'

'So, there we are, in this sweaty basement, the people seem friendly enough, there's even a few veterans amongst the crowd, we talk, we drink, we fuck, all is well.'

'These men from the Greens, they would be the same gang that cause trouble throughout the city? Starting fires, fights and gods knows what else?' It was well known that the racing factions had long morphed into full-blown gangs, whose tribal wars across the city had caused huge amounts of damage on multiple occasions.

'Well, yeah,' Pavo said, looking sheepish. 'But we haven't been involved in any of that, sir, promise! We went the one night, then the following week, went back. The same man met us in the bar upstairs and invited us down again. Except, this time, there was somewhat of a different crowd there.'

'Different?' Albinus was already beginning to feel exasperated. He was tired, frustrated with both Pavo and himself. He just wanted to get this resolved so he could concentrate on Commodus and not have to worry about his men getting themselves killed on the street.

'There were senators there, sir. Men who went only by nicknames and kept their hoods up. No one actually *said* they were senators, but I knew they were, I recognised them.'

'Who?'

'Gaius Vettius Sabinianus. I was on guard duty at the palace when he returned to Rome a short while ago. He'd come from the northern frontier, though I don't remember hearing the name when we were there. They called him The Owl.'

Albinus paused, letting the information sink in. He had met Vettius once himself, two weeks previous when he had been invited to dine with

Commodus. The caesar had introduced Sabinianus as a dear friend of his father's and a man that could be trusted. It had seemed he had been sent back to Rome for a particular reason, though Albinus never did find out what that was.

'And the others?'

'One was Claudius Dryantius, they called him The Mouse. The other was Avidius Maecianus, son of Avidius Cassius, governor of Syria. They called him The Fox.'

'Dryantius is married to Cassius' daughter, is he not?' Albinus asked, his face creased in a frown.

'How in Jupiter's name would I know?'

'I wonder if it's all linked,' Albinus trailed off. 'Sorry, Pavo, carry on.'

'So, there we are, four of us from the Fourteenth, a gang of rogues, and The Owl, The Mouse and The Fox. The dice start rolling, and to begin with, I'm doing well. A few coins on six, couple on four, but then I start to see a pattern. All even numbers coming up – not once did anyone roll a one, three or five. Now, I've been under the eagle for nearly twenty years, and once you go an hour or two with the same numbers coming up trumps, I know too well—'

'The dice were loaded,' Albinus finished for him.

'Exactly. So, I start to bet big on six, knowing full well if it don't come up the first time, it will the second or third, and guess what? I start winning, big time. So, the more I win, the more I bet; the more I bet, the more I drink, and before I know it, I'm blind drunk, grinning like an idiot, hoarding a pile of silver.' Pavo stopped, wincing in pain as he sipped water from a wooden jug.

'They swapped the dice, didn't they?'

'You bet your fucking arse they did. Lucius will tell you. Ask him, he saw them do it, just as I did,' Pavo said, pointing to the empty bunk that belonged to Legionary Lucius. 'So, I call them out on it, fucked if they're cream or not, I'm not having that! But they deny all knowledge, say I'm talking bollocks and tell me to roll again. So, I rolled.'

'How much did you put on the roll?'

'All of it.'

'*All of it?*'

'Yep.'

'Pavo, I'm no expert on the arts of gambling, but surely it's bad form to put everything you have on one throw of the dice?'

'Yeah, but I was blind drunk, weren't I? And fucking angry to boot, I wanted those fuckers to pay for trying to stitch me up.'

'So, you lost all your money?'

'Yes.'

'And your kit? Your sword, shoes? And those shiny black eyes, how did they happen?'

'They said I could roll again to win the money back. I bet on three, thinking it would be another odd number, but it came up six. They must have changed them back again, but I didn't see it.'

'So, they took your weapon, your shoes and beat the shit out of you?'

'That's pretty much it, yes. I'm so sorry, sir, I can't believe I've been so stupid.'

'What about Lucius and the others? No one else seems to have been fighting?'

'They were dragged upstairs and chucked onto the street. Only took a few heartbeats to deal with me, then I was out there with them.'

'Bastards.' Albinus thought desperately of a way to get even with the men that had done this, but he didn't think Commodus would offer him any protection if he was caught waging a war against one of the racing factions, let alone men of the senate.

'These three men, The Owl, The Mouse and The Fox, what connection do they have to the Greens?'

'I'm not sure exactly, but they were being treated like kings. My guess would be they help fund them, or get them an audience with other powerful men, men who would not usually accept a visitor from off the street.'

'The Owl is wise, The Mouse quiet, The Fox is cunning...' Albinus trailed off, deep in thought.

'Sir?'

'Sorry, Pavo, just thinking. Do me a favour, and don't breathe a word of this to anyone, understand? Get yourself down the armoury as soon as you're able and replace your lost kit, and for the love of the gods, stay out of the Aventine. In fact, stay on the Palatine until I tell you otherwise.'

'Yes, sir, as you command. But, sir, am I not in trouble, sir?' the soldier asked anxiously.

Albinus smiled, putting a hand on Pavo's shoulder. His father would have had the legionary fined and whipped, Taurus would have knocked out half his teeth, but Albinus was his own man, and his men were his family. 'No, Pavo, you're not in trouble, although for the record, you are a halfwit. Give me a few days, let me come up with a plan, then I'll come back to you.'

'A plan for what?'

'Why, revenge, of course! No one messes with the Fourteenth, Pavo. No one.'

It was under a sky of low rolling cloud that Albinus trailed The Owl through Rome that same afternoon. The wind howled and carried with it the smell of street food and river water. He could taste the impending rain on the air.

He had shed his military cloak and tunic, and only his standard-issue sandals remained that could give him away as a soldier. After speaking with Pavo that morning, he had retreated to his rooms, broken his fast with Faustus, Marcus and Meredith and pondered his next course of action. Commodus, he knew, would still be sleeping off the hangover he had inevitably earned himself the night before. Bucco had informed him the caesar had drunk himself into a stupor after their confrontation at Nero's bathhouse.

Commodus would need to be avoided at all costs for the next couple of days, until the boy needed Albinus for something and he would be summoned to his imperial presence and treated as though nothing had happened. Until then, he was on his own.

Two things troubled the centurion's mind: firstly, the man he was trailing, The Owl, as he had been nicknamed, was none other than Gaius Vettius Sabinianus, a known *amicus* of Marcus Aurelius. Could it really be possible that one of the emperor's inner circle was entangled in a plot to bring down the emperor and put their own man on the throne? Pavo may not have heard of Sabinianus when they were in the north, but Albinus certainly had. He was known as a 'fixer', a man who could solve any problem. He had been given command of troubled units early in the war, men whose metal had been tested and found to be brittle with rust. He had succeeded where others had failed, his star shining brighter by the month.

The second thought that troubled him was the presence of the other two men. Both Claudius Dryantius and Avidius Maecianus were tied by blood to Avidius Cassius, governor of Syria. There had long been whispers that the governor sought to seat himself on the throne. There was even a rumour that the traitor Alexander of Abonoteichos had named him when he was captured and tortured in Pannonia, though nothing was ever confirmed, and if Cassius had been found to have been guilty of any crime, then Aurelius must have dealt with him lightly indeed. But Albinus had a feeling in his gut, a nagging doubt that something about this wasn't right. Why would the man that had proved himself time and again to his emperor return to Rome just to get involved with a racing faction? Money was the obvious answer, but maybe there was more to it.

Sabinianus walked slowly up the Esquiline, surrounded by retainers and a few armed guards. He stopped to speak to certain merchants on his journey, and Albinus watched with interest as coins changed hands after whispered conversations. He assumed these were the senator's clients, men who were loyal to Sabinianus and would gladly give him information in exchange for his support in the day-to-day running of their business. Relationships like that made perfect sense for both parties, as the merchants would be privy to vital political information through street gossip that the senator might not otherwise hear until he reached the steps of the senate house the next day.

Scandal was always rife in Rome, and it paid dividends to know which senators had money troubles, whose wife was being unfaithful or whose son was serving in which legion and under whom. In the world that Sabinianus lived, it all came down to leverage and influence. If you had leverage over someone you could influence them, and if you could influence enough of your fellow senators, you could influence the outcome of bills of law, what was debated in the senate house that day, who would be allotted which province when the time came. It was a world Albinus knew very little about and had no real interest in learning more of. He was a soldier, a simple man who liked his enemies to his front and his friends in a shield wall at his side. Life was simpler on a battlefield and often less bloody.

He carried on shadowing the column of men, who seemed to stand as if in military rank behind Sabinianus, with his closest advisors or those in favour huddled around him, those less important bringing up the rear. It was as the first soft splashes of cold rain hit his face that Albinus began to realise he, too, was being followed. The irony that the hunter had unwittingly become the prey was not lost on him, and his attention turned from the senator to his front to the hooded figure at his back.

Albinus stopped at the same market stall Sabinianus had and pretended to examine the cheap wares on offer. There were bracelets and necklaces, poorly made rings and a single brooch. He picked up the brooch, turning it over in his hands, eyes scanning the street behind him.

'That would make a lovely gift for your wife, if you don't mind me saying,' the merchant said, scurrying over to Albinus like a rat. He was short and overweight, his back hunched, hands clasped together in front of his chest. Looking into his face, Albinus saw a dishevelled character under unwashed skin, slippery eyes and a tongue that sporadically darted out from thin lips.

'I'm not married,' Albinus said, returning the brooch. He moved a little further up the street, his pace slow, willing himself not to look back to let his hunter know he had been spotted. Up ahead on the right, he saw an arched entrance to a public garden. Increasing his pace, he darted through the stone archway, pressing his body into the shadows, waiting for his tail to catch up.

Albinus breathed deeply and counted the beats of his heart. He cursed himself for not bringing his sword, but his palm brushed the hilt of his military dagger reassuringly – he was not completely defenceless. If there was to be violence, it would have to be swift and silent, for bloodshed in daylight on the streets of Rome would attract the Praetorian Guard like honey to a bee, and Albinus had no intention of spending the night in a prison cell.

He had reached a count of fifty when a hooded figure peered cautiously around the arch, the man's face masked in shadow. The rain fell from the heavens with purpose now, the drops making a racket as they bounced off the cobbles. Albinus stayed rooted to the spot, unconsciously holding his breath, as if his stalker might hear it over the driving rain.

The man took two more steps under the archway, his hands hidden inside his cloak, and Albinus wondered if he was armed. One more step and the man was level with Albinus but still peering into the gardens. Seizing his chance, Albinus leapt from the shadows and grabbed the man by the neck, pulling him back into the darkness and throwing him bodily against the wall. In an instant, Albinus had his knife in hand, pressed up against the man's throat.

'Who are you? Why are you following me?' He spat the words into the man's face.

'Juno's… tits… Albinus… it's… me,' the man wheezed, almost breathless with the shock and pain.

Albinus stepped back, unnerved that the man knew his name. Slowly, he reached forward and threw back the hood of his would-be assailant. 'Fullo?'

'Salve, brother,' Fullo said, bending forward to help catch his wind. He brought a hand up to his throat and winced as his fingers ran over the small cut Albinus had made with his knife. 'It's good to see you, too!'

'What in Jupiter's name were you doing following me like that? I thought there was someone trying to kill me!' Albinus had broken into a sweat, his cheeks puffed red, the relief pouring out of him.

'I spoke to Pavo this morning. He told me you'd already been to see him. Then Bucco told me of the argument you'd had with the caesar last night, and when I couldn't find you at the palace, I figured you'd gone off to do something stupid, so I found you and followed you.'

'And you didn't think to approach me? To let me know you were there?'

'I was going to, but then you marched off, and I lost you. What were you doing anyway? Following senator Sabinianus?'

'Yes. You know, of course, that he was one of the men behind Pavo losing all his money and kit?'

'To be fair, I think most of the blame is on Pavo himself, but yes, I did.'

'You knew about it, and you didn't tell me. Why?'

Fullo sighed, still clutching his throat, 'I thought I could handle it myself, thought there was some way I could get it back for him without bothering you.'

'I'm your centurion, Fullo. If one of my men has been stupid enough to gamble away all their coin, that's their problem, but if they have lost their kit, then I very much need to know about it. Commodus saw you both yesterday, and *I* had to find out from *him* that one of my men was drunk on duty, missing his sword and sandals!'

'I'm sorry, sir,' Fullo said, hanging his head in shame. 'I just wanted to try and do something myself, rather than referring to you all the time.'

Albinus paused, thoughtful. He and Fullo had been close since they were small boys, since they were the same age as Faustus and Marcus. In fact, Fullo had always been the soldier born, better with the sword, built like a warrior. It was he that was meant to grow up and have a glittering career in the legions. Albinus had been too tall and lightweight, more interested in growing crops and caring for livestock. Albinus wondered if his friend felt somewhat overshadowed by his rise in the ranks and whether he felt Albinus had pitied him by making him his *optio* when he was given his first command.

'You want more responsibility?' Albinus asked.

Fullo shifted, clearly uncomfortable with the question. 'Just always thought that it was me that would be the soldier, never really thought you were in it for the long haul when you signed up. To be honest, I kind of thought it would be me looking after you throughout our service, but yet, you've taken to the role of centurion like you were born to do it. I swear, some days, Albinus, you're so much like your fa—'

'Don't finish that sentence, please.'

'I know you don't like people mentioning him. I'm just saying I feel a bit inadequate, and I'm getting restless here in Rome.'

Albinus nodded, he could understand that. He wouldn't be surprised if more of his men felt the same way. Legionaries were not meant to be cooped up in cities; they were built for the march, the open air. 'You know, if you want to go back to the legion, I can always get you a transfer. Taurus would be delighted to have you back, I'm sure.'

'No! No, I won't leave you here with *him* on your own. We're brothers, you and I, and family stick together.'

Albinus held out his hand, and the two men locked wrists. 'Glad to hear it, old friend. Now then, how are we going to get Pavo his coin and kit back?'

# CHAPTER XVII

**February, 175 AD**
**Rome**

Rome was silent in the dead of night. Albinus heard nothing but the distant wail of a baby as he crept up the Esquiline hill, Fullo, Bucco and Pavo in tow.

It was the fifth hour of the night, and they did not have long before the sun began its gradual ascent and another grey dawn broke over the sprawling city skyline. It had snowed the day before, and thick and fluffy powder covered the cobbles, making their ascent up the slope perilous.

'At least we aren't tramping over this stuff with a thousand barbarians trying to spear us in the back,' Bucco said, his face flushed with the cold.

'Aye, what a bloody day that was,' Fullo replied, his voice muffled by the scarf he wore wrapped around his face.

Albinus grunted in reply, not willing to speak due to the burning pain in his cheek; the old wound was always worse in the winter, and that night was truly freezing.

For two weeks, Albinus and Fullo had worked on a plan to sneak into the home of senator Sabinianus and try to recoup Pavo's lost money and kit. Pavo was convinced it was the senator himself who had taken possession of his belongings, claiming Sabinianus had been the ringleader of the men of the Greens and the one most keen to see Pavo stripped of all he had in the world. Albinus had cursed his drunken soldier and made sure he had been on hand to help the palace slaves with the worst of the tasks they had to perform on a daily basis, ever since he had been able to rise from his cot. He was still angry with Pavo now, angry about what he was about to do, but he could not see any alternative.

Commodus had ignored the centurion ever since their argument in the bathhouse, which suited Albinus just fine. He felt happier, lighter, when he did not have to spend time around the boy who would one day have the power of life and death over him. He found keeping up with his mood swings exhausting. He was worried for the safety of Faustus, Meredith and Marcus and wondered if the time had come to ask to be allowed a transfer back to the Fourteenth Legion and get back to some honest soldiering.

But first, he had a score to settle.

Their plan was a simple one. Fullo had bribed a slave in Sabinianus' household to open the door for them in the dead of night. The soldiers would then sneak into the house, take back Pavo's possessions and steal whatever coin they could get their hands on. It wasn't perfect, Albinus knew, but it was the best he could come up with. He knew there would be consequences and that in the morning, Sabinianus would march directly to the palace and preach to Commodus that a man from his honour guard had broken into his house and taken his coin. But there, in part, lay the beauty. If Sabinianus were to do that, then he would be showing his hand, admitting he was in league with the Greens, admitting he had gambled and drunk with the lowest class of citizen Rome could offer and taken a legionary's weapon – a legionary who was sworn to protect the sacred body of caesar.

Albinus knew it could get uncomfortable for him, but he was determined he would make any accusation Sabinianus could throw at him just as painful for his accuser.

'Not having any second thoughts are you, little brother?' Bucco asked as he increased his pace to walk beside Albinus.

'No, just enjoying the thought of this bastard turning up at the palace tomorrow, accusing us of robbing him.'

'What if he does?' Pavo asked, a tremor in his voice that sounded to Albinus more like nerves than the cold.

'You let me worry about that, Pavo. How are you feeling?'

'Better, thank you, sir. A bit of bruising still, but I'll be all right.'

'Glad to hear it. I'm thinking we should get ourselves back up north soon, do some proper soldiering, what do you think?'

'Fuck, yes. I've had enough of this stinking city, would be good to get back home, at least the air is clean there.'

'Couldn't agree more, Legionary Pavo. Now then, let's get this over with, shall we?'

They stood at the gate to the senator's home, and a short walk later, they were at the threshold. Fullo knocked on the door, a distinctive pattern that was the signal for the slave to open up. Albinus counted the beats of his heart as they waited and tried to control his breathing.

'What do we do if this whoreson doesn't answer?' asked Bucco. Albinus was still counting his heartbeats, thinking the same thing as the beat struck fifty.

Fullo knocked again and this time, was rewarded instantly with the muffled sound of the locking bar lifting. The door opened silently, a sparsely lit vestibule slowly coming into view. A small man poked his head around the door, his face masked in shadow against the backdrop of the lantern he held. 'The Fourteenth,' he whispered.

'Marshal and victorious,' Fullo replied.

'At least he'll never know it was us,' Bucco breathed, trying to stifle a laugh.

Fullo turned and scowled at his old friend, but Albinus put a hand on his shoulder before he could retort. 'Don't listen to him, brother, we needed a password, and Sabinianus will know who did this anyway.'

'I won't tell, if that's what worries you,' the slave said in a murmur.

'And why should we trust you?' Pavo challenged in a hissed whisper.

'I was not born a slave, soldier. My father was a free man, a stonemason and a damn fine one. He and my mother made a good home for me, raised me well, saw I received an education. Life was good until Sabinianus came along, coaxing my father to invest his money into some crazy venture, a new temple to be built on the Campus Martius. My father was all for it, saying it would be the grandest building in all of Rome. It was only after he had paid up that Sabinianus pulled the plug, voting against the build in the senate. My father lost everything, ended up a slave. Want to guess who bought him?'

'Ouch,' was all Bucco could say.

'My father died a slave, working stone for that bastard who sleeps upstairs. My mother did not cope well and took her own life shortly after being sold, or so I am told, anyway. She was sold to a different house, a farm north of Rome. Not a day goes by that I don't miss her. You do not have to worry about my loose tongue, soldiers. I may be the one man in Rome that wants the senator dead more than you do.'

Albinus felt a pang of sympathy for the man but hardened his heart. He had, after all, his own tragic past. 'If you sell us out, I will kill you, understand?'

'I do,' the slave said and stepped aside to let the four men in.

Albinus stepped through the threshold first, relishing the warmth that greeted him.

The slave closed the door and in a hushed voice, gave them directions. 'There is a strongbox in the main reception room, though it will be locked, and the master sleeps with the key under his pillow. Anything else of value will be in the study. If you follow me, I can lead you straight there.'

'I'll go to the study, you three see what else you can find. And for Jupiter's sake, be quiet.'

Albinus followed the slave through the vestibule and into the atrium. The large reception room was lavish, with sculptures of marble and stone lining the walls which were painted in vibrant colours.

'My father made these,' the slave murmured, pausing by one and rubbing his hand over a sculptured torso. Albinus studied the sculpture, seeing what he thought was the face of a young Lucius Verus on a body that Hercules himself would have been proud of.

'I don't know your name,' Albinus said as if it was suddenly important.

'Aegeus is my slave name, Marcus was my birth name, Marcus Ambrosius. I was born just after Marcus Aurelius was named heir to the empire.' It was not unusual for the populace of Rome to name their children after either the ruling monarch or a member of his family.

'Why do people always give slaves Greek names?' Albinus said. He realised he was only speaking to hide his growing nerves, and that he really should be keeping his mouth shut. If he and his men were caught here, they would be executed, even if Commodus did have a mind to save him.

'To make us sound more intelligent? I do not know, Centurion. Here we are, the master's study.' Aegeus stopped and opened a heavy wooden door that squealed as it opened, and Albinus flinched.

'I shall await you in the vestibule, but be quick. The master has a couple of gladiators that guard him throughout the day, and they will arrive just before dawn.'

Albinus padded softly into a small, warm room. The walls were lined with bookcases, a candelabra in the corner the only light. Unconsciously, Albinus felt his eyes drift to a desk set against the far wall, under the double shutter of a window. Walking over, he saw the desk covered in a disorganised pile of wax tablets and papyrus. Picking up the one on top, he walked over to the candelabra to take advantage of the flickering light. It was a letter from none other than Avidius Cassius to Sabinianus. Albinus gasped in shock as he read:

*To senator Gaius Vettius Sabinianus, from Governor Avidius Cassius, greetings.*

*I hope this letter finds you in good health and that your journey from the north to Rome was both smooth and pleasant.*

*I was thrilled to receive your letter and delighted your efforts in the northern cause have not gone unnoticed by our usually ungrateful monarch.*

*In answer to your question, I have so far fulfilled everything that I promised to you and our allies some months ago. Egypt is fully pacified, the rebels dead to the last man. The legions of the east stand ready to acclaim me emperor and fight their way west to see me safe to Rome.*

*As well as cementing support from the most influential men in Syria, I am confident I have won over the prominent citizens of Asia and Bithynia as well as prefect Gaius Calvisius Statianus in Egypt, who is, of course, most grateful for the military support I have given him in the last two years. Cappadocia remains an obstacle but one I shall soon overcome. Governor Publius Martius Verus thinks me a fool, though soon we shall teach him such a lesson!*

*I have now returned to Antioch as I plan my next steps, but I* can confirm I plan to use Egypt as my rallying point when I have been proclaimed emperor, with Antioch and Cyrrhus also holding particular importance.

It really is a stroke of good fortune that Aurelius has sent you south. I am certain that when he hears of my rebellion, he will order you to take command of all available military resources and hold the city – which I hope, of course, you do until I arrive.

To be sure, you will hear from me soon with further instructions once I have moved our plans forward. Oh, the future, my dear Vettius, does look golden indeed. Together, we shall bring Rome back to the glory days.

To end on a rather humorous note, I wrote a short while ago to Herodes Atticus, a distinguished senator, as I am sure you are aware, who has now retired to Athens. I asked him what the feeling was in Greece and if he would be willing to offer me some support, rally my banner, as it were. His reply to me was both short and clear: 'You are mad,' was all he said. Mad! If nothing else, it did make me chuckle.

For now, I must go, but please know that I shall be forever grateful for your efforts and am very much looking forward to seeing you well rewarded when I am in my rightful place.

Avidius Cassius, governor of Syria, future ruler of the world.

Albinus reread the letter, put it down then picked it back up and read it again. Could this really be true? His hands shook, his tongue lolled, the hairs on the back of his neck stood on end. Avidius Cassius really was planning to usurp the throne, and Sabinianus, a trusted friend of the rightful emperor Marcus Aurelius, was in on the plot.

Torn with indecision, Albinus stood rooted to the spot. Should he take the letter to Commodus? To do so would be to reveal the foolish thing he had done, but if he said he'd done it on the pretence that he expected the senator of being a traitor, would that get him off the hook? Albinus doubted it. The Praetorian prefect would want to know why he hadn't been involved, as would the *frumentarii* in the Camp of Strangers. *Too many lies.*

If nothing else, Albinus had always been honest, it was the way he had been raised, the only way he knew how to be. He put the letter down and turned to leave but stopped. This was not some trifling issue; details about a senator's affair or poor credit. This was the possible usurpation of the throne, the murder of a monarch that Albinus both liked and respected. He thought then of Maximianus, his legate. What would he think if he knew Albinus had uncovered a plot against the emperor and done nothing to stop it? What would his father have thought? No, there was no question of leaving the letter here. Whatever the cost to himself, Commodus had to see it.

He scooped up the parchment, rolled it tight and tucked it into the back of his belt. He was just leaving the study when Fullo poked his head around the door, startling his already frayed wits.

'You'll never guess what we found?' Fullo said with a mischievous grin.

'Tell me later, we need to get out of here, now. Where are the others?'

'They are in the vestibule. Albinus? What's happened?'

'I'll tell you back at the camp. Right now, we need to get out of here before—'

Albinus never finished his sentence. There was a loud thud from the direction of the vestibule, followed by a scream and the distinctive sound of a blade being drawn from its sheath.

Not allowing himself to hesitate, Albinus set off at once, drawing his own sword from under his cloak as he did. In the vestibule, he was greeted to the sight of Bucco and Pavo clashing blades with what appeared to be two gladiators.

The one battling Bucco was short and broad. His hair was cut short, and in the dim light, Albinus could see it was streaked with grey. The gladiator snarled and leapt at Bucco, jabbing his sword at the soldier's chest. Bucco brought his own blade up and swept the weapon aside. Turning defence to attack, he charged the gladiator, shoving him from his feet. Raising his blade to deliver the killing blow, Bucco bellowed a war cry and then chopped the sword down.

But gladiators do not grow old enough to turn grey without knowing every trick in the book. He kicked out with his leg, a crunching blow with his left boot into Bucco's groin, who groaned as his sword clattered to the tiled floor. He fell down shortly after it.

Albinus raced into the fray, launching himself at the gladiator before the man could get to his feet. He swiped his sword at outstretched feet, catching flesh and bone. Now, it was the gladiator that groaned, but as Albinus leant in to strike the killing blow, his face hit a thrown fist, and he, too, was catapulted to the flagstones.

Dizzy, disorientated and quashing the sudden urge to vomit, Albinus rose unsteadily, bleeding heavily from a broken nose. He tried to breathe but couldn't, opened his mouth and was engulfed by a stream of his own blood. He staggered, frantically trying to regain his focus. He was dimly aware that Bucco, too, was back upright and once more blade to blade with the first gladiator. Albinus staggered right, away from the warring pair, and crashed into the back of an unseen body.

Back down he went, collapsing on top of a man his own height and build. Their eyes locked, each man as shocked as the other. The gladiator reacted first. He had a knife in his left hand, his sword arm trapped beneath Albinus' weight. He raised the knife and slashed at Albinus, carving a deep gash in the centurion's left side.

Crying out with pain, Albinus rolled away just in time to dodge a heavy cut from the gladiator's sword. Albinus lay back on the tiles, rocked by the open wound in his side. He put a hand to the cut, and it came away dark with blood.

The gladiator was on his feet, looming over Albinus, sword already falling towards Albinus' stricken form. Shutting his eyes, he just had a moment to picture, one last time, the face of his beloved, the long red hair, the dazzling green eyes…

With his eyes scrunched tight, Albinus waited in agonised anticipation, but nothing happened. When he opened his eyes once more, Fullo was standing over him, his sword drenched in blood. Pavo was on his knees beside him, a wicked gash on his cheek. Bucco stumbled over, murmuring incoherently. Frantic hands patted Albinus, putting pressure on his wound.

'Did we win?' he muttered, faintly aware he was losing consciousness.

'We won, lad, we won. Now, let's get the fuck out of here, shall we?'

Bucco lifted Albinus to his feet. Fullo stepped in to support his wounded side.

'I'm sorry, brothers,' Albinus wheezed, every word an effort. 'I don't think I'm going to make—'

And then he fell into darkness.

'I'm sorry Caesar, I just don't think he is quite ready for visitors yet,' a voice said, muffled as if it travelled through water.

'Not ready for visitors? I saw his son come out of there this morning, so do not tell me he is not ready when I am not even the first visitor he has had today!'

'Caesar, he has not even woken up yet. His son merely went in to watch him. Caesar, I implore you—'

A door crashed open, bringing with it a flood of light that stung Albinus' eyes. He blinked rapidly, immediately aware of an acute burning sensation down the left side of his body. 'The light,' he managed to croak out, covering his eyes with his hands.

'Shutter the windows, quickly now!' a voice said. 'What in Jupiter's name have you gotten yourself into?'

'Huh?'

'Don't play dumb with me, Centurion. Five days you have been locked away in here now, and I can't get a single word out of your men. What were you doing in the house of Senator Sabinianus? Tell me this instant!'

Albinus blinked again, moaning as the fog that clouded his mind was replaced by a thumping pain. Slowly, the memories came back to him, the house of Sabinianus, the slave, the study. The letter.

'I... I...' he tried to speak but his tongue would not follow his brain's commands.

'I am waiting, Centurion,' Commodus said, standing over the bed.

'Caesar, please, the patient is still weak. Perhaps tomorrow—'

'Galen, you are a fine man and a good friend to my father.'

'Thank you, Caesar.'

'But I swear to the gods, if you do not leave me with this man, I will have you locked in the dungeon and the key thrown to the depths of the Tiber!'

'Yes, Caesar.'

'Albinus, concentrate this instant, and tell me what is going on.'

Albinus lolled, fixing Commodus with a confounded stare. 'Caesar?'

'The one and only.'

'Plot… kill your father… Sabinianus… the letter.'

'Yes! The letter! Centurion, where is the letter? Centurion? Can you hear me?'

But Albinus could not hear him. He laid his head back on the pillow and passed once more into obscurity.

It was another two days before Albinus woke again. A soft orange light crept through the shuttered windows, and as Albinus came back into consciousness, his first thought was that the day was either beginning or drawing to a golden close. The pain in his head had subsided, his tongue was swollen and felt like a ball of leather in his parched mouth. 'Water,' he muttered, straining to move himself to a sitting position. There was a jug on a bedside table, a small wooden cup placed next to it.

With shaking hands Albinus poured himself a cup of water, spilling plenty in the process. He drank greedily, immediately refilling the cup and emptying it once more. With his thirst quenched, he looked around the room, pleased to find he was in his own sleeping quarters. He had a vague memory of being awoken by Commodus but decided that must have just been a bad dream.

There was a chamber pot in the corner of the room. Tenderly, Albinus rose from the bed, an intense, burning pain emanating from the left side of his torso that reverberated through his whole body. Step by painful step, Albinus made it to the corner of the room and sighed with pleasure as he relieved himself.

He was just climbing back onto the bed when the door to his room was thrust open, and a small child poked his head through the threshold. 'Daddy?' a voice called.

'Faustus, come here, my boy, it's ok.'

The boy scurried in, leaving the door open in his wake. He clambered onto the bed and leapt upon his father, burying his head in Albinus' chest. 'Are you okay, Daddy?'

'I'm fine, son, I'm fine. How are you? Have you been worried about me?'

The boy nodded, tears pricking the corners of his eyes. 'Meredith told me not to come in here, but I wanted to see you.'

'I'm very glad that you did,' Albinus said, cupping the boy's face in his hands. 'Are Meredith and Marcus okay?'

Faustus nodded. 'Still sleeping. Marcus sleeps too much,' he said with a scowl.

Albinus laughed. 'And you don't sleep enough! What hour is it?'

'I don't know, but it's morning. Can I have breakfast?'

'I'm sure we can arrange that for you,' Albinus said, laughing again. 'Come on then, let's find some breakfast.'

They were sitting on a balcony, bellies full and Faustus showing Albinus how good he had become with his little wooden sword when the physician Galen found them. 'Centurion, should you be out of bed?'

'Galen, good to see you. I am feeling much better, thank you, and I assume I have you to thank for that.'

'I did nothing apart from stitch you back together. The wound in your side was long but shallow, and your nose reset well enough. You must rest well for the next few weeks, no more… exertions.'

Albinus put an experimental hand to his nose, wincing at the pain of his own touch. The wound in his side hurt so much, he had not even realised his nose was broken. 'I shall do my best. I assume Caesar is still asking to see me?' The longer Albinus had been awake, the stronger his mind had become. He could well remember the desperate fight with the gladiators in the vestibule at the house of Sabinianus as well as the letter and what it contained.

'Caesar has been most insistent that you call on him the moment you are able. I do not know what you have done, Centurion, but he is most unhappy with you. I would advise you get yourself out of Rome as soon as you can, get back to your legion.'

'Do you often advise soldiers to get back to the front line of war as soon as they can?'

'I think this is a first,' Galen said with a laugh. Albinus liked the old physician, he was slight of build and short of stature, a balding head with the odd wisp of iron-grey hair, olive-coloured skin covering an honest face. He had treated Faustus a few months before when the boy had come down with a persistent cough and a fever, and Albinus had been worried he was losing him.

'It may be that I take your advice. I thank you again. I am, once more, in your debt.' Albinus rose and offered a small bow before grasping Galen's outstretched hand. 'Did I, by chance, have a letter on me when I was brought back here? Parchment, tucked into my belt?'

'There is nothing to thank me for, my friend. But you would do well to heed my words. As for the letter, I believe your *optio* will be able to assist you with that.' With that, the physician left.

Albinus left his son with Meredith and went in search of Commodus, finding him in his office, a room he barely frequented. He was seated on a couch. Opposite him was none other than Gaius Vettius Sabinianus.

'Ahh, Centurion,' Commodus said, rising from his couch and putting an arm on Albinus' shoulder. 'How are you?'

Albinus hesitated. His eyes fixed on those of Sabinianus, and the two men held a moment of silent communication over Commodus' shoulder. 'I am much recovered, Caesar, thank you.' Albinus saluted and stood to attention, waiting to be asked to either sit or leave.

'Sit down, Centurion, have some wine. We three have much to discuss.'

Albinus sat on a couch opposite Sabinianus. Commodus stayed standing, pouring wine into three cups before handing two to his guests. 'Now, who would like to go first?'

'This man broke into my house and stole from me! He also killed two highly trained gladiators – ones recommended to me by your good self, Caesar, I hasten to add – before escaping. I demand there be a trial, I wish to see this villain hung by the neck! I shall prosecute him myself if needs be!' Sabinianus had risen to his feet, and his chubby face had grown flushed with the exertion of his accusation.

'This man,' Albinus said before Commodus could respond, 'This man lured three of my soldiers into an illegal gambling den on the Aventine hill, a tavern that is used as the base for the members of the Greens. This man proceeded to get my men blind drunk and then robbed one of all his money. Once the money had run dry, he then confiscated his sword and sandals, leaving him with no weapon the following morning when he was charged with protecting the sacred body of Caesar!' Albinus too had risen to his feet, the wound in his side aching, and he worried he had ripped the stitches rising from the couch, but the furies had gripped him, and he did not care.

'This man is involved in a plot to kill the emperor and overthrow him with a man of his own. That man is Avidius Cassius. I found the letter, you bastard.'

Albinus took a step towards the senator, who shrank away and covered his face with his hands. Commodus called for guards, and to Albinus' surprise, Fullo, Bucco and Pavo raced into the study from a side door and restrained Albinus before he could reach the senator.

'Ahh, good, now the whole gang is here. At ease, gentlemen,' Commodus said, a wicked grin fixing his face. 'In fact, be seated, all of you, I shall pour more wine.'

The tension in the room was palpable, the silence oppressive, nothing but the sound of heavy breathing. Albinus studied Sabinianus as they sat, taking in his overweight frame, his flushed face, a swollen nose, more purple than red, indicating his love of a fine vintage and his tendency to overindulge.

Fullo, Bucco and Pavo clattered in their armour as they lowered themselves onto the couch. Albinus stifled a smile at the uncertain look on Bucco's usually bold features, he did not think he had ever seen his father's old friend look so afraid.

'Now then,' Commodus said, handing the stunned soldiers each a cup of wine, '*Optio* Fullo, I am told by the imperial physician, Galen, that you have a certain letter, a letter you took from Albinus for safekeeping after the centurion was carried back to the palace. I am also told that this letter contains details of an uprising against my father by the governor of Syria, Avidius Cassius. Does that sound about right?'

Fullo flushed and looked at his feet. Albinus wondered if he had actually had a conversation with Commodus since they had returned to Rome two years before; he doubted it. 'I have, Caesar, yes.'

'Could I have it? If you give it to me now, maybe we can gloss over the fact that you have been withholding information critical to the safety of his imperial majesty. What do you say about that?' From within his robe, Commodus had produced an ornate dagger, the hilt, solid gold, embedded with jewels. It was not a killing weapon, not a soldier's weapon, but from where Albinus was sitting, the blade seemed to be of iron, and sharp.

Fullo risked a glance at Albinus, his desperation written all over his sweating face. Albinus nodded to his old friend, wishing there was more he could do to comfort him. 'It's in my quarters, Caesar,' Fullo said in a voice that shook like a leaf on the wind.

'Go and get it.' Commodus did not look up from the knife as he spoke, just twirled the blade in his hands. 'Maybe you two should go with him and leave the centurion and the senator to explain the rest to me.'

The three soldiers shot up from the couch, slamming their untouched wine cups onto a table and leaving the room with a snappy salute.

As the door slammed behind them, Commodus turned to Albinus and Sabinianus, Albinus saw the malevolent look in the caesar's eyes and wondered if he would use the dagger after all.

'So, who wants to start?'

Sabinianus went to speak, but Albinus cut him off before he could spill any lies. 'The senator is embroiled in a plot to kill your father and place Avidius Cassius on the throne. In his study, I found a letter from Cassius himself, outlining his progress and what supporters he has already won over in the east. Cassius believes that when word reaches the emperor, Sabinianus will be tasked with seizing control of all armed forces in Italy and holding Rome, which he will do, for Cassius.' Albinus spluttered out the facts as he knew them, leaving out the minor details, such as he and three armed soldiers breaking into the senator's house in the dead of night.

Albinus stared intently at Sabinianus as he spoke, each word another dagger he metaphorically plunged into his heart. He tried to judge the senator's reaction, was he afraid? If he was, he was hiding it well.

'Caesar, may I speak?' Sabinianus said, sitting upright on the couch, chin held high. Swooshing the cloth of his toga around his shoulder, he looked every inch the patrician.

'I think you'd better, Senator.' Commodus had sat down behind an ornate oak desk, both grand in design and stature. It had been polished to perfection, the dark wood gleaming in the sunlight that flooded through an open window behind Commodus.

'It is true, what the centurion says.' Sabinianus waved a dismissive hand at Albinus, looking down on him from above his bulbous, purple nose. 'But everything I have done has been on the order of your father and with the guidance of the *frumentarii* themselves.'

'Lies,' Albinus spat before he could control himself. Once more, his side pulsed with blinding pain. Putting a hand there, he could feel the damp patch spreading beneath his tunic. He cursed under his breath, not wanting to let his discomfort show in front of the traitorous senator.

Commodus rose from his seat and walked around his grand desk, sitting on its edge and leaning forward so his face was a hand's breadth from Sabinianus. He still twirled the dagger in his right hand. 'You are telling me that my father is aware of the threat from the east and has not bothered to inform his son?'

'Precisely,' Sabinianus said, giving Commodus a distasteful look. 'Says a lot about what he thinks of your potential, does it not?'

Albinus saw the anger flicker through the young Caesar, the devil within fighting to be unleashed. 'Prove it,' Commodus said.

'I have no need of proving myself to a mere boy. If you want proof, go up to the Camp of Strangers yourself, speak to Verenus, he'll confirm everything I have said.'

'Does Perennis know of this?' Albinus asked. Sextus Tigidius Perennis was the prefect of the Praetorian Guard and the man who should have sole responsibility for safeguarding Caesar whilst he was in Rome. He had reacted bitterly when Commodus had whisked into the eternal city from the north accompanied by Albinus and a century from the Fourteenth Legion. He saw it not only as a slight on his men but on him as well. Albinus had never had a good relationship with the man.

'Only his imperial majesty's most *trusted* advisors are in the know, so I wouldn't imagine so, no,' Sabinianus sniffed, lifting his head high and looking down his purple nose once more at Albinus, who wanted nothing more than to batter it flat.

'Vettius, I think you had better leave us,' Commodus said in a low voice, his tone menacing. 'On your way out, please find Saoterus and Cleander and ask them to attend me.'

The senator rose from the couch, offering Commodus a bow that was nothing if not mocking, and swept from the room, leaving the door open behind him.

'Caesar,' Albinus said, clearing his dry throat, 'I really must apologise—'

'Apologise? Whatever for, dear man? You have uncovered a plot on my father, I am in your debt.' Commodus leant forward and placed his hands on Albinus'. 'Although, one day, my friend, you will tell me *exactly* what you were doing in Vettius' house in the middle of the night when you stumbled across that letter.'

Albinus returned the smile that was offered and rose to his feet gingerly, left hand clamped to his flank. 'Think I left my bed too early,' he said in response to Commodus' concerned look. 'I had better go and find Galen, see if he can stitch me back up. He won't be happy, told me to take it easy.'

'Rest, Centurion, I feel I will have need of you in the days and months to come.'

# CHAPTER XVIII

**April, 175 AD**
**Rome**

'Watch your left,' came a scream from behind him, and Albinus immediately brought his sword across his body, blocking a savage thrust from his opponent. The blow was powerful but clumsy, and Albinus used his strength to knock it aside, and his momentum carried him forward onto the unguarded flank of his opponent. He shouldered into his adversary, using his advantage in height and weight to knock the man from his feet, nearly falling to the floor after him.

'Got you,' Albinus panted, holding the edge of his sword to his opponent's neck.

'Fortuna's tits!' Commodus spat dust and blood onto the sand, 'I almost had you then!'

'Almost, Caesar, you're getting stronger.' Albinus held out a hand, hauling Commodus to his feet.

'Yes, quick too, my lord,' Cleander said, applauding from the wooden rails that circled the makeshift training field. He clapped enthusiastically, drowning out his compatriot Saoterus, who was trying to speak.

'You really think so?' Commodus asked, taking a water skin from Saoterus and drinking greedily.

'Certainly, my lord. I think with another few months' training you shall be a match for any warrior in the empire.'

Albinus turned his back to hide his sneer and walked over to Fullo and Bucco who stood watching, leaning against the opposite rail.

Cleander was the same age as Commodus, a slave bought by the imperial household some time ago, from Phrygia, east of the Aegean. It was not known how the provincial came to be a slave, and Cleander had never expressed a desire to share his past. He had dark skin, raven hair and shifty eyes that reminded Albinus of a slithering snake. He was cunning and cruel and had wormed his way into the centre of Commodus' inner circle in a matter of weeks.

Saoterus, on the other hand, was different. Born a slave, he had served the imperial household his entire life. His parents were from Bithynia, but unlike Cleander, his complexion was pale and his hair a light brown. He had a delicate appearance, light and frail, a thin face with large, honest eyes. It was clear to whoever saw the two together that Saoterus worshipped Commodus, and there were even rumours that the young caesar had taken him to his bed.

'That man gives me the creeps,' Bucco said, passing Albinus a water skin.

Albinus drank deeply before tipping the remaining water over his head. It was warm for the time of year, spring already giving way to a summer that promised nothing but torture for the confined citizens of Rome. They were at Commodus' villa, north of Rome on the Via Clodia, where, at least, the air was cleaner.

'I know, and Caesar's behaviour has become more erratic ever since he started spending time with him,' Albinus said, looking cautiously at Cleander, who was stroking Commodus' arm whilst whispering in his ear. 'I fear for what will become of Commodus when his father is gone.'

'Why?' asked Fullo.

'Because what he says is right. Once Aurelius dies, the vultures will circle. There are more men than Cassius in the senate who fancy themselves in purple, you can mark my words.'

'You heard any more about Cassius?' Bucco asked.

It had been two months since Albinus, Fullo, Bucco and Pavo had sneaked into senator Sabinianus' house and Albinus had discovered the letter on his desk. Albinus was still not sure whether he believed the senator's story, but Commodus most certainly did and was still outraged that he had not been informed of the plot against his father. Despite strong counsel from Albinus, Commodus had written to his father, venting all his fury that Aurelius could treat him like such a child when the lives of all their family were at stake.

'No, nothing. Commodus hasn't had a reply from his father, and Sabinianus has made no effort to share any more information with us. I don't like it, this not knowing. I have tried to persuade Commodus to quit Rome and go back north, but he will hear nothing of it.'

'What good would that do?' said Fullo.

'It would get us out of the cesspit that is Rome for a start,' Albinus said, 'and hopefully get Commodus away from his hangers-on. He motioned once more to Cleander, who was still locked in conversation with Commodus.

'Daddy, Daddy, you won!' came a shout from his right. Turning, Albinus smiled as Faustus came running from the stalls, slipping under the wooden fence that surrounded the training circle, and hugged his father's leg.

'Daddy always wins,' Albinus whispered into his son's ear as he bent down to hug him, breathing in the boy's scent deeply.

'Will you teach me to fight like that?'

Albinus laughed, 'One day, lad, yes. But you need to grow big and strong first!'

'Like you did?'

'I think I'm still waiting to grow strong myself! Your grandfather, my father, was the strongest man I ever met.'

'Strongest man most men ever met!' Bucco chipped in.

'You don't have a daddy,' Faustus said with a frown. 'Just like I don't have a mummy.'

Albinus recoiled as if he had been hit by an arrow, his heart missed a beat, and he found it hard to catch his breath. Never before had Faustus asked about his mother, and even now, over two years since she had fled, Albinus still longed for her.

'You do have a mummy,' he said eventually, 'and she loves you very much.'

'Where is she then?' Faustus asked, his small face scrunched up, ready to burst into tears.

'Wherever she is, lad, I know she's thinking about you,' Bucco said, reaching down and scooping Faustus up. 'Come on, let's get you back to Aunt Meredith, shall we?'

Albinus stood slowly, hands shaking, knees weak. He would have cried were it not for the fact the caesar was just paces behind him, or closer, in fact.

'Are you okay, Centurion?' Commodus asked, putting a hand on Albinus' shoulder. 'I heard what the boy said. You're going to have to talk to him.'

'I'm fine, thank you, Caesar. We should be washed and ready to go, we have a meeting at the Camp of Strangers this afternoon.'

'I know my own diary well enough, thank you. You don't have to come with me if you do not wish to. Spend the day with your son if you'd like?'

Albinus smiled a sad smile that did not quite reach his eyes. Moments of genuine warmth between him and Commodus had become very rare. They had grown apart in the years since they had travelled south to Rome. Albinus thought it a good thing, at least, that Commodus was still capable of showing affection. 'Really, I'm fine, Caesar. Faustus has every right to ask about his mother, just as I have every right to be upset about it. Meredith is a fine woman and has done a superb job of helping me raise him, but—'

'She is not the boy's mother,' Commodus finished, his arm still resting on Albinus' shoulder.

'No, it is not the same.'

'And she has her eye on you. I see things, you know, I am not the complete fool some people take me for.'

'As I said, she is a fine woman.'

'But she is not your wife,' Commodus said, moving away from Albinus. 'Get yourself ready, Centurion, this afternoon, we find out just how far this plot against my father has stretched.'


The chamber was windowless, airless, and stank of damp and decay. Albinus sat on a small wooden stool, huddled next to the single brazier that was the only source of light. Three men sat around a small, round table. Commodus, heir to the greatest empire in the world; Sextus Tigidius Perennis, prefect of the Praetorian Guard; and Verenus, who had no other names that Albinus knew of, the head of the *frumentarii*.

Albinus had not known what to expect as they had approached the gates of the Camp of Strangers, the headquarters for Rome's secret service, but he was not sure he had expected what he found. The building was large enough to be a palace but was, in essence, one giant torture cell. All the windows were barred, and there were few enough of them. Men in plain tunics seemed to guard every corridor, all armed with a sword. None had even so much as nodded when Commodus had walked past, which Albinus considered a grievous insult to the man who could order them dead if he wished. Commodus, though, seemed not to notice, such was his focus on the task in hand.

'So, what can you tell us?' Commodus said, opening the floor for Verenus to speak.

'Little enough, I'm afraid, Caesar. The letter your man over there *acquired* from Senator Sabinianus Vettius is the most solid piece of intel we have on Cassius and his intentions. We have nothing concrete on any of Cassius' known friends and family. If I were, however, able to ask his son some questions—'

'There is no way I am allowing you to torture the son of a senator. My father would never condone it, even if the evidence against Cassius was unsurmountable.'

'I understand,' Verenus said with a reluctant nod, as if he had expected nothing else.

'So, what do we do?' Perennis asked, leaning back on his chair and sighing. Perennis was a bull of a man, and Albinus suspected he had risen to his lofty position from his use of brawn rather than his brain.

'That, my dear prefect, is what we are here to decide.'

'We have made some progress in the east, though. I have men over there keeping as close an eye as they can on Cassius.'

'Who?' Commodus said, leaning across the table, visibly desperate for some good news.

'My man in the east is an old soldier named Crassus. Nearly three years ago now, he helped spring two veterans who had gone east from Pannonia from the clutches of two of Cassius' men. My man Crassus claims these two men had discovered Cassius was recruiting veteran soldiers, first to help put down the rebellion in Egypt and then to fight their way west and put Cassius on the throne.'

Albinus sprang to his feet and his stool clattered to the flagstones. 'The two veterans from Pannonia, what are their names?'

'Centurion? What is the meaning of this?' Commodus said, rising to his feet himself.

'Their names, Verenus, what are their names?'

There was a pause as Verenus looked to Commodus for permission. Albinus stood on shaking legs, his heart pounding, unable to catch his breath. Commodus nodded and Verenus pulled a roll of parchment from his belt. 'Calvus and Habitus. The one named Calvus has been *frumentarii* for a while, been working for Tribune Pompeianus in the northern provinces.'

'Calvus, Habitus,' Albinus whispered as he slumped to the floor, barely noticing the cold embrace of the flagstones. 'They're alive.'

'Should they not be?' Verenus asked.

'I believe the men in question are old friends of the centurion here. They served together in the Fourteenth Legion,' Commodus added, walking over to Albinus and putting a hand on his shoulder. 'Are you quite okay, my friend?'

'I'm fine,' Albinus said, a smile spreading across his face. 'That's the best news I've heard in years. Verenus, tell me everything you know, what have they been getting up to?'

Verenus spoke. He told them of a sunken ship and a desperate escape from Ephesus, he spoke of two years of travelling the eastern provinces on horseback, stumbling from one lead to the next, one eye always over their shoulders, waiting to be discovered. 'Was a time when Crassus practically owned the east, could walk into any governor's home and be treated with honour, such was the reputation of the *frumentarii*. Now...' Verenus trailed off, throwing a hand into the air in exasperation. 'Now, my men get nowhere. Every route of enquiry seems to be blocked, every lead they chase ends with a corpse. Crassus was all for giving up, even wrote as much in one of his reports. But around a year ago, they made a breakthrough.'

Silence in the airless chamber as Verenus cleared his throat.

'Well?' Albinus said, unable to contain himself.

'There is a woman, a woman who has embedded herself in Cassius' household. Your friend Calvus seems to know her, Crassus even says he is fond of the girl. I don't know her motivation or what it is she desires, but she seems to have sold herself into slavery in order to get close to Cassius.'

*Thud. Thud. Thud.* Albinus felt his heart the way an anvil felt a hammer. *Thud. Thud. Thud. A woman? Could it be?* 'The woman, what is her name?' he asked in a ghostly whisper.

'I don't know,' Verenus said, frowning down at the parchment still clutched in his hand, 'Crassus just calls her "Red".'

*Red.* More words were spoken in that chamber, plans were formed and then discarded, Commodus schemed and Verenus presented counter-arguments, though once they had staggered back into the blinding daylight, Albinus could not remember what they were. His mind was full of the image of a woman with blazing red hair and emerald-green eyes.


Trajan's basilica teemed with people. It was two days since they had visited the Camp of Strangers, two days since Albinus had discovered Licina was still alive.

He had been lost in a fog of thought and regret, unable to eat or sleep. It had been so long since he had last seen his wife that it was an effort to picture her face and hold it in his mind. She would come to him in his dreams, or flashes when he least expected it when awake, but when he tried ot focus on her face, his memory failed him.

He sat on the step under the portico, gazing listlessly at the throng of people that waited impatiently for their entitlement of free grain. Commodus had insisted on coming here and handing it out to as many people as he could personally, as rumours continued to spread like wildfire across the city.

> 'Cassius has seized Egypt and is holding back the grain ships!'
> 'Aurelius is dead! Cassius marches west to seize the throne by force!'
> 'War is coming! Rome is unprotected! Aurelius must come back south!'

Albinus listened to them all without hearing; he was numb. Commodus stood to his right, dressed, as always in public, in the tunic of a boy, as his father had still not named him a man, a fact that was a constant irritation to the young caesar. 'Most lads my age are married, some even have children of their own! How long am I to be treated as a child?' he was saying even now, though Albinus did not hear.

'She is alive,' Albinus whispered. He toyed with a small gold ring, the one she had placed on his finger on their wedding day. It was not the ring of a rich man, just a simple, thin gold band, all that they had been able to afford. He had given her one almost identical to his.

'For the love of Apollo, Centurion, wake up!' Commodus snapped, handing out yet more bowls of grain to the teeming masses. 'The future of the world is at stake here. I know you have your own problems, but for Jupiter's sake, man, the next few weeks could well determine the fate of us all!'

A line of Praetorians stood between Commodus and the populace, who heaved against the soldiers' shields with their arms outstretched, screaming for the caesar to acknowledge them, to give them their precious grain next. There was a commotion in the middle of the crowd as two hooded men robbed a woman of her grain dole. She fell to the floor screaming in fear and rage as they took the grain at knifepoint and ran off, instantly losing themselves in the endless sea of people.

'Centurion? Are you even listening to me?' Commodus called, having to raise his voice over the tumult.

Albinus gazed up, trying to escape from the torture cell that was his mind. *She is alive. All this time she has been out there, and what have I done to find her?*

Commodus motioned to a Praetorian, ordering him to keep giving out the grain. He sat down next to Albinus, running his eyes over the crowd. 'It would be a simpler life, would it not, to be among them,' he said, gesturing with a hand, 'worrying about nothing other than getting their grain, keeping their small homes clean, scratching out enough of a living to ensure their children get some form of education. See, hard work, Centurion, hard work and oppression leaves the mind too exhausted to worry about anything other than the simpler things. Bread, work, rent, survival. That is the limit of their ambition.'

'Is there a point to this lecture, enthralling as it is?' Albinus asked, his voice dripping with sarcasm.

'My point, dear friend, is that all the time you are sitting here, wallowing over the past, you are unable to see into the future. You have your whole life ahead of you, Albinus, a life that will contain more freedom and choices than, say, mine ever will.'

'Freedom? Well, for starters, I've got another twenty years' service in the army to survive, not much freedom there, Caesar.'

Commodus chuckled. He rested a hand on Albinus' shoulder. 'True enough, I suppose. But you will survive it, I think, live to retire on your father's farm, perhaps?'

'I'll never go back there. I cannot. Too many demons rest in that cursed valley.'

'Then where will you go? Tell me, Centurion, where will you retire to?'

Albinus thought for a moment, closing his eyes and breathing deep, thinking of nothing but his breath, in and out, in and out. 'I will live by the sea, somewhere warm. I will wake each morning to the sun kissing my face, I will swim before I break my fast, then once more before the sun slips beyond the horizon. I will be at peace.'

'A beautiful vision. Maybe I will live long enough to join you. I can picture us as old men, sitting under a portico, eating dried figs and drinking a fine vintage, complaining of the heat and how the cursed summers seem to get hotter every year.' He broke off, and both men smiled.

'I will die in battle, of that I'm certain,' Albinus said after a while, a sudden conviction in his voice. 'Just like my father and his father before him. Us that bear the name Silus do not tend to enjoy the tranquillity of retirement.'

'Your father did, for a time.'

Albinus shook his head. 'My father's whole life was a battle. In the short time he had after his service, he lost his wife and fought plague and growing fears of starvation.' Albinus shook his head, a wry smile brushing across his lips. 'The only time that man was ever at peace was when he had a good sword in his hand and an enemy to bring down. Truly, he was a formidable warrior.'

'So I have heard. But did that make him a good man?'

'No. He was never a thinker, never one to dwell on past mistakes or think on how his actions or words could make other people feel. Being a leader of men was who he was, but men only followed him due to his reputation, not necessarily his deeds.'

'But follow him they did. Indeed, some men loved him so much, they journeyed with him over the river Styx. Sure, they fought for their families, but I'd wager there was a large part of every man that stood in that final shield wall with your father with no other emotion than pride. Pride to be fighting to the last with their centurion, their commander. Why? I hear the question on the tip of your tongue. Love, Albinus, nothing simpler, nothing purer. Love.'

Suddenly, Albinus was transported back in time. He was sitting by the fire in the great hall at the farm. Drunken men swayed on benches, there was laughter, boasting, comradeship at its basest form. Silus was the beating heart of the night, moving from table to table, slapping backs and chinking cups with every man. Eyes followed the centurion wherever he went, old soldiers desperate to get a moment alone with the man they had marched with for so many years. Love. Was it really love? Or just a desire to be closest to the man on the top rung of the ladder, a desperate need to be recognised, acknowledged in front of your peers as a friend of the famous warrior.

'You may be right,' Albinus said.

'I am. And the way those men thought of your father, your men think of you.'

Albinus laughed, 'Hardly. I'm no hero.'

'But you are! It amuses me that you are so blind to the effect you have on those around you.'

'And what effect do I have on you, Caesar?' Albinus asked, not entirely sure he wanted to hear the answer.

'You have made me a better person, that much I know. The time I spent in the north with you and your men, it showed me the worth of true friendship, brotherhood, if you like. That is why I have distanced myself from the senate, surrounded myself with men I can trust, not snakes like Sabinianus.'

'You think you can trust Cleander? That man is a vulture.' Albinus winced after he spoke, hoping he hadn't gone too far.

Commodus sighed. 'You may be right there, Centurion. Cleander has ambition, a burning desire for power.'

'What will you do?'

'Give it to him, of course. I have no doubt that one day, he will try to betray me, but right now, I need him.'

Albinus paused, trying to get his head around the statement. 'Why would you place your trust in someone you know full well will one day betray you? Do you think that of me?'

'No, brother. Never in my darkest dreams could I picture you going back on the oath you made to my father. I hope, one day, when he is gone, you will make another oath, to me directly.'

'Another oath?' Albinus asked. He was desperate to return to the north, to the honest and stable life of a frontier legionary, even at a time of war. Rome was a vipers' nest with enemies lurking at every corner. He yearned for the open plains and the clean air of the north.

'Would you stay with me if I asked it?' The hope in Commodus' eyes was almost too much for Albinus to bear. He could lie, of course, say he would be honoured to and spend the rest of his days a glorified bodyguard to the emperor. Surely, that would come with some perks? But in the end, he had to be true and follow his heart.

'I belong in the army,' he said gently. 'I'm a soldier, built for life on the frontier. Rome is… has been… difficult for me, my men too.'

'They want to go home?' Commodus asked.

'Yes. Yes, they wish to return to the legion, as do I. But I will not leave you unprotected. You must find men in the city that you trust, men who will watch your back, watch the people closest to you.'

'Like Cleander?' Commodus said with a wry smile.

'Yes. Him especially.'

'I will think on what you have said, Centurion. Luckily, it would appear I am going to have nothing to do but think in the coming weeks.'

Albinus let the silence stretch on. The grain was all given out now, the crowd ebbing away. He thought it funny how no one was seemingly interested anymore in the boy who sat on the basilica step, the boy who would one day rule over them all. 'Go on then,' Albinus said eventually. 'I'll bite. Why will you have nothing to do but think?'

Commodus didn't reply, he just reached into a pouch at his belt, pulled out a scroll and handed it to Albinus.

Albinus took the parchment, the wax seal already broken. He opened it up and read, a slow smile spreading across his face as he did. 'I'm going home?' he said.

'It would appear so, my friend,' Commodus said.

The letter was from Marcus Aurelius, addressed to his son. In it, he ordered Commodus to travel north with due haste. Aurelius was worried for his son's safety, concerned Cassius may target him whilst he is alone and vulnerable in Rome.

'When do we leave?' Albinus asked.

'Tomorrow. Dawn.'

Albinus moved his horse just off the road and watched as his men filed past, smiling as he overheard their high-spirited jokes, saw the look of pure joy on their faces. Three years they had been in Rome, three years was more than enough for all of them.

He reflected that when a man signed up to serve under the eagle they changed. It did not matter their background, their upbringing or child-hood dreams. From day one, the drill masters of the legions took the raw flesh and bone of young volunteers and moulded them into the best men they could possibly be. Strong, tough, fit. But it was not just the body that was changed during the forced winter marches, the endless drills with the heavy wooden practice sword and wicker shield. The mind changed too.

Within a year, each man that had joined was changed forever, and each year thereafter, they changed a little more until they were programmed how to think, how to behave. Battle pushed them further from the boys they used to be and towards the men they would become. Killing changed men, it was irreversible.

Would his father have been a better man if he had not fought up and down the empire for twenty-five years? Would he have been a better father?

A carriage rolled by, and Albinus smiled and waved at Faustus and Marcus who hung outside the window. Meredith was visible behind them, trying, without much success, to pull the boys back inside. Albinus looked at Faustus and felt nothing but burning love, a love so intense, tears welled behind his eyes. Did his father ever feel the same when he had looked at him? Albinus didn't think so. Silus had served too long by the time Albinus had been born, seen too much death.

A horse pulled up beside him. Commodus, draped in a purple-edged cloak, spoke into the dawn, 'You are finally going home, Centurion.'

'And you are once more leaving yours. Are you okay?'

'I'm fine. It will be good to be among family once more.' Another carriage passed them on the road, Cleander and Saoterus inside. Cleander bowed his head reverently as they sped past, though Albinus thought he could see a wicked glint in his eye.

'I mean what I said about that man,' Albinus said.

'And so did I, Centurion. He will betray me when he feels the time is right. It would seem I must betray him first if I am to survive. My father told me once that I would never have any friends, not real ones, anyway. Men will flock to me, shower me with praise and promise me the world. Though, when all is said and done, they will do it only for their own personal gain. It is the destiny of all rulers to be alone, no matter who they are surrounded by.'

'I am your friend.'

Commodus smiled. A single tear ran down his cheek. 'That you are, Albinus Silus, that you are. You have been honest and true, shown me what it is to be a leader of men. I will forever be grateful to you. I look forward to visiting your villa one day, many years from now. To sit in the shade of the portico and watch the ships sail by on the horizon, the breeze cool on our faces. It is a dream I will keep close to me, no matter how slowly the years go by, no matter the distance between us.'

Albinus bowed his head, a deep feeling of shame washing over him. How could he leave this young man to his fate, exposed to the predators of Rome? Who will watch his back, give him honest feedback and keep him on the right path? He feared for the young Caesar, of what would happen when his father eventually journeyed to the realm of the gods. Commodus would have to mature quickly if he were to survive, let alone succeed.

So lost was he in his thoughts, he didn't notice Commodus rejoin the road and canter off. Neither did he notice that the road was now empty, their small convoy all disappearing into the north. Shaking his ruminations from his mind, he looked back south one last time at the sprawling city that was Rome. He could make out the Flavian Amphitheatre, the magnificence of the imperial palace. To the west, he could see the top of Hadrian's Mausoleum, and once more, his thoughts returned to blood and death.

All men die, that was one of life's few assurances. It was how you chose to live that mattered. He turned his horse and looked north. Somewhere, there in the distance, were the open plains of home. He smiled and gave the beast a nudge in the flanks.

Three years in Rome was enough for any man. He was going home, back to Pannonia, to the Fourteenth. He would never see Rome again, of that he was certain. Of that he was glad. He did not look back.

# PART III

# FIRE IN THE EAST

# CHAPTER XIX

**January, 197 AD**
**Gaul**

A lot has happened to Faustus in the last four years. He has immersed himself into the life of a *frumentarii* agent, made the shadows his ally, cloaked himself in anonymity.

Yet more has happened to Rome.

In the four years since Faustus had been introduced to Septimius Severus, the would-be emperor of Rome, he has watched from the shadows as Severus has taken the Roman world and shaken it to its core.

Pescennius Niger, the former governor of Syria, had been officially proclaimed emperor by the eastern legions just weeks after Severus' initial arrival in Rome. War between the two rivals had been as inevitable as winter, though a more brutal winter had never been seen.

Severus, in an effort to protect his rear, had named the governor of Britannia, and another rival to the throne, Clodius Albinus, as caesar, giving him all the honours but none of the power of the prodigious title. Word was that Clodius had been happy to take the title, but all had known his satisfaction would not last forever.

So, Faustus had been sent north whilst Severus and his army, joined by a vast network of spies – including Calvus – had boarded ships and aimed their prows to the east. Battles had been fought, though Faustus had heard little enough of the detail. But in the end, after near on two years on campaign, Severus had finally been victorious. Niger and his followers were dead, his legions broken up, sent home in dwindling numbers in disgrace. Some had even been made an example of, their standards burnt, never to grace a battlefield again, their eagles melted down and redistributed as coin marked with Severus' head.

Faustus had missed all the action; of that, at least, he was grateful. But for him, the tumultuous years of civil war across the empire had passed largely in isolation and boredom. He had received no personal mail, not conversed with another human for anything other than business.

He had been part of a four-man team sent by Severus to Britannia, their purpose there to keep tabs on Clodius and his movements. Being the newest member of the *frumentarii* on the four-man team, Faustus had been given the unenviable task of journeying north as far as north goes, all the way to the Antonine Wall. And there he had stayed, relaying troop movements back down the country in coded messages, keeping track of who commanded which unit, who was broke and who could be bribed when the time came.

He had found the work interesting at first and had even enjoyed the isolation to an extent. His cover story had been that he was a wool merchant from Pannonia and sure enough, three times a week, he had appeared at one of the many markets along the great turf-built wall and bought and sold all the wool he could get his hands on.

Four years later, he still knew nothing about wool.

However, he had found the tribesmen of the far reaches of Britannia *did* know a lot about wool and were always keen to sell their wares. Faustus had found it surprising at first, arriving as he had, midway through a blistering hot summer. By December, he had a much better understanding as to why they found it so precious. Winters in the far north of the world are brutal.

Finally, just as he was beginning to think he could handle the isolation no more, a message had reached him, urging him to travel south with all haste. He had not hesitated.

Reunited with his three brother agents, they had journeyed back across the narrow sea just weeks in front of Clodius and his armies. Clodius, of course, had heard of Severus' victory in the east and judged the time right to launch his own bid for the purple. Faustus thought it a shrewd move.

Severus' army, though still high on victory, was said to be heavily depleted from constant battle. Clodius had used the time wisely, steadily building up allies in the west. He could call on no fewer than seventy-five thousand men now, all fresh troops, all ready for war.

So it is that Faustus sits in a crowded tavern on a chilly January night in southern Gaul. The coastal city of Massilia teems with merchants and travellers alike, all desperate to get out of Gaul as quickly as they can. Clodius landed his ships on the northern shores just before the Ides of December and quickly went about securing his position. The legions of Gaul marched straight to him and offered their allegiance, Faustus assumes, with the promise of a large amount of coin. The Rhine legions, though, have thrown their lot in with Severus.

Severus made his name as a general on the northern frontier, battling the Germanic tribes as they continued their quest of gaining a foothold south of the Danube. Commodus had treated with them upon the death of his father, wishing to bring the drawn-out hostilities to a close. The treaty had not lasted long.

The legions on the Rhine were all too aware of Severus and his reputation, many legionaries had even served under him before. They had required no coin to go over to his service. They are led now by Legate Virius Lupus, who has long been a supporter of Severus and has been sent ahead to Gaul to take command of the German legions and do what he can to disrupt Clodius and his preparations for war.

Faustus has met with Lupus and told him of what he knows. He has told him the weakest links in Clodius' chain of command, which legions are understrength, which men have done nothing but garrison duty for the last ten years. These are the legions that will be targeted on the field of battle, these are the men who will die first.

His duty discharged, Faustus had been at a loss as to what to do next, having received no further orders from the Camp of Strangers in Rome. But then a letter had reached him, asking him to travel to Massilia. It had been signed by 'Uncle'. He had left at once.

So now, he sits in the tavern and shivers, the single fire in the stone-and-thatch-built building being on the other side of the room. He has a cup of warmed wine, though it does nothing to take the chill from his bones. His cloak is drenched from the torrential rain outside, but still, he is reluctant to shed it. He has grown a shaggy beard in his time in the north, it itches him constantly, and he fears the lice have come back to torment him. Scratching at it absently, he fails to notice the tavern door swing open and the old hunch-backed man stagger in out of the rain, a wooden staff supporting him, grasped tightly in a frozen hand.

'Sweet Jesus, lad, I thought I'd had a hard time of it. You look as though you've been living in the forest for the last four years,' a gruff old voice says, the tone edged with humour.

Faustus stumbles to his feet, his lice-ridden beard and numb bones forgotten. 'Uncle!' he says, taking two giant strides towards the newcomer and engulfing him in a bear hug. 'By Jupiter, it's so good to see you.' Before he can control it, tears are streaming down his face, his throat is choked with raw emotion, and it's all he can do to stay on his feet.

'I've missed you too, son, God knows I have,' Calvus says, kissing Faustus on the head and looking him up and down. 'You've grown, I can feel the muscle under that cloak. What have they had you doing up in the far reaches of the world?'

Faustus laughs, 'Lugging wool around mostly. Oh, Uncle, I've been so lonely, starved of news and company. Sit, have some wine, try and warm yourself best you can.' They return to the table Faustus has been frequenting, and the young man rushes to the bar for a jug of warm wine, returning with a fresh cup for Calvus. 'Tell me everything. I have heard almost nothing of what has happened. Where have you been? Did you see battle? How did Niger die? How are Severus' men? Are they strong enough to win another war?'

'Easy, lad,' Calvus says with a cackle, pouring himself some wine and savouring the warmth of his first sip. 'Truth be told, I didn't get to see much action myself. Severus had me mainly in the cities, trying to raise support amongst the rich and powerful. Not that he needed their help in the end, of course.' He drains his cup and refills it; Faustus can see his lips are blue, his eyes red-rimmed with exhaustion.

'How long have you been travelling?' he asks.

'Three months, more or less. We left Ephesus just as the weather was turning. Glad we did, too, the crossing was choppy enough as it was. What about you, lad, how did you find the country of my birth?'

'Blistering summers, freezing winters, rain in-between. Pretty much as you always described it,' Faustus says with a grin.

'Aye, glad to hear nothing has changed. Where were you posted?'

'The Wall of Antonine. Four years I was stuck up there, trudging from east to west, pretending to know a thing or two about wool! It was okay, though the gods know I was bored.'

Calvus nods, a slow grin spreading across his face. 'I thought you always said that the quiet life was for you. No interest in being a soldier, in spreading your wings and diving out into the wide world. Look at you now, you've travelled across half the known world, lived in Rome, learnt the way of a *frumentarii*, and you're complaining you're bored!'

Faustus joins in the laughter, appreciating the irony. 'You are quite right! I just feel as though so much has happened in these last years, and I have missed it all.'

'Things happen across the Roman world every day, have been for hundreds of years. Why do they interest you now?'

Faustus pauses, considering the question. He finds himself at a loss, unable to give a coherent answer.

'I can tell you why, lad,' Calvus says, leaning across the table. 'You have *knowledge* now, and knowledge is power. Before you met Severus, before you were wounded and I took you to the fortress at Carnuntum to be healed, you had no notion of what went on in the world. War in the east? What do you care? Rebellion in Britannia? What's it to you? But now, you know Severus, now, you know the men who fight for him and the men who will fight for Clodius Albinus against him. Now, you're invested in this war, and the course of your life could well change depending on who is victorious.'

'And who will win, Uncle?'

'Severus, of course. He has developed a knack for winning. Good habit to have, if you ask me.'

'Why? Why will he win? You have no notion of this Clodius, his forces, how capable they are. His army has declared him emperor in the field, he has thousands of soldiers at his back who are willing to risk their lives to see him draped in purple. Why can he not win?'

Calvus considers the question as he refills his wine cup, taking a generous swig. Eventually, he replies. 'I did not say Clodius *can't* win, I just said he won't. I'm not sure I know how to fully explain myself, but I shall try. Severus has marched all over the empire, beating Niger in battle after battle until he eventually surrounded the pretender in some shithole town – I forget its name – and bombarded its walls until Niger had no choice but to fall on his sword, and what remained of his army surrendered. Clodius has not yet had to strike a blow. Right now, he is living with his head in the clouds. His army has marched south and crossed the narrow sea, and the men of Gaul have gone over to him without so much as a skirmish. So far, he has not struggled, so far, he has not had to fight. Soon, he will fight, he will force a battle with Virius Lupus, and he will win—'

'You just said he will lose!'

'I said he will lose the war, but the first engagement, he shall win.' Calvus speaks with a mischievous glint in his eye, an amused half-smile on his old, weathered face. He speaks as a man who knows things Faustus does not, things a man can only learn from a lifetime spent in the arena of war.

'In the first battle, he will fight an army that is outnumbered, an army that does not have its figurehead there to lead it. As experienced as the Rhine legions are, and as competent as I'm sure Lupus is, Clodius will win, no question.'

'But then Severus will land his men in Gaul…'

'But then Severus will arrive,' Calvus agrees with a nod of his head, 'and the tide will turn in his favour. Their armies will be evenly matched in numbers, but Severus will have battle-hardened troops, men who have bled across the empire for him. They won in the north, they won in the east, I promise you, dear boy, they shall not lose in the west.'

'I am to be with Lupus when he meets Clodius in the field,' Faustus says, a nervous edge in his voice.

'Why?' Calvus asks. 'Surely, he does not expect you to fight?'

'No, he wants me on his staff. I have been given a week's leave, then I am to present myself to him, me and the other three men who have been in Britannia.'

'He wants you there for your knowledge, a shrewd move.'

'Not very shrewd on my part, if I am on the losing side!'

'You will not be harmed, lad. The soldiers will do the dying, you may just have to do some running away at the end! Better to run and live, lad.'

'I did that once before,' Faustus says, remembering the shadows of the alley, the glint of knives, the screams of Meredith and Marcus. *I ran away then; I ran away as they died.*

'I have never blamed you for the deaths of my daughter and grandson, and I never will. You were a child still, Faustus, attacked by some thugs in the dead of night. It was not your fault.'

'Your sympathy just makes it worse,' Faustus says.

'You must stop looking back, Faustus, that is not the way you are going.'

'I do not have much to look back on, Uncle, I know so little of where I have come from, of who I am.'

Calvus pauses to pour more wine and swirls it around in his cup before raising the stump of his fingerless left hand and stroking the scarred knuckles. 'You want to hear of your mother?' he says.

'Yes,' Faustus replies in a hoarse whisper. 'My father never spoke of her, not once. I know her name, I know she was beautiful and had red hair that shone like the sun. Aside from that, I know nothing.'

'And will it make you feel better, to know what I know?'

'Why don't you tell me, old man? Then I can decide for myself.'

Calvus continues to stare into his wine cup. Eventually, he speaks. 'Okay, lad, okay. I shall tell you everything that happened. When was it we last spoke? Where had I got to in my story?'

'You had been rescued from captivity by Crassus and his *frumentarii*, and you killed Cletus and Timon in the fight.'

'Ahh, yes. Well, you might be forgiven for thinking that after Habitus and I had survived a shipwreck, fought our way free of Cassius' agents and ridden off into the desert, we were quite entitled to head off into the sunset and find that tavern Habitus had been dreaming about buying. Unfortunately, it didn't quite work out that way for us…'

209

# CHAPTER XX

For three years, we stalked Cassius. Three years of chasing rumours and ghosts. First, we heard he was moving gold from Egypt up to Mesopotamia by land, then it was to Cyzicus by sea. Three years, and we had no concrete evidence to show for our efforts.

We lived on horseback, a new experience for both myself and Habitus and one that was, on the whole, unenjoyable. Crassus seemed like a man born in the saddle, though he always denied he had spent any time with the cavalry during his army days, saying he would have rather served in the marines than with those 'tunic lifters' as he called them.

But after three years of constant riding and sleeping under the stars, my thighs had toughened and scarred, my groin was swollen to twice its original size, and despite this, I think I may have been the fittest I had ever been.

Habitus, though, was showing his age. His hair was thinner and the colour of dull iron. He had never been a big man, but now, his back had stooped, and the wiry muscles in his arms had withered. His skin was sagging and seemed to glow a strange mix of grey and green in the sunlight. He needed water constantly and had to relieve himself almost as often. Food had become hard for him to digest, and he complained of stomach cramps daily and found it hard to pass a stool. I was concerned for his health, guilty that the lifestyle I had forced upon him had caused this deterioration of his physical form. His mind, however, remained as sharp as his sword.

'Fuck me, I'd do anything for a skin of wine right about now,' he said as we sat in the shade of a stone portico, just outside the palace in Alexandria.

'You'd neck the lot in less time than it takes you to piss it out, then you would moan of stomach cramps for an hour before heading off behind the nearest bush and groaning for another hour as you tried to have a shit,' I said, my eyes never leaving the palace gates.

'Yeah, but still, at least I'd be a bit pissed as I was trying to squeeze one out,' he said with a shrug. 'How long we going to stay here for? I'm roasting.'

'We have already told you, my impatient friend. We will stay for as long it takes,' Crassus said, his bald head buried in a straw hat.

'Yeah, but for as long as *what* takes? Gods, it's hot.'

'For as long as it takes us to find a way into that palace and put a sword through the heart of the man that is about to cause a civil war the size of the one that saw three emperors dead inside a year,' I said in exasperation. 'You were there when we were forming this plan, right?'

'Actually, he wasn't,' Crassus said with a smirk. 'He was in the latrine, trying to have a shit.' Crassus and I both stifled a laugh as Habitus coloured, anger clear on his face.

'In all seriousness, how are we going to get in there?' Crassus said, motioning towards the gates with his head. 'The place is a fortress.'

And in truth, he wasn't wrong. From our vantage point, we could see a whole century of auxiliaries on guard at the gates, legionaries patrolling inside and more armed men on the roof. It was the same around the entire perimeter. Cassius had his home locked down, no one was getting in or out without him knowing about it.

I, though, had another plan, one I thought was secret, one I did not truly want to act on.

'We use the girl, obvious, ain't it?' Habitus said.

Silence. I looked down at my feet and counted to ten, hoping they both weren't going to be looking at me when I rose my head. They were. 'We can't use her,' I said.

'We're going to have to do something, brother. No way the three of us can sneak into there unnoticed, let alone back out once the deed is done.' Crassus did, at least, have the dignity to look troubled as he spoke.

The girl, of course, was your mother, Faustus. Licina.

I had first seen her the month before when we had arrived at Alexandria. She had been following Cassius as he inspected his troops on the parade ground just to the south of the city. Cassius had been atop a fine white stallion, cloaked in purple and wrapped in shining armour. It had been the first time I had seen him for myself, and even from a distance, I could see why it was that men would follow him to war. He was overweight and had less hair than me, if you can believe that. But he had something about him, an easy charm, an aura, you could say. He rode up and down in front of the ranks of men, giving a speech I could not hear, though I could hear the men's laughter and cheers. She walked behind him, a towel in one hand, a flask of water in the other, ready and waiting for his call.

For the last month, I had caught glimpses of her through the gates at the palace and out and about in the streets of Alexandria, but she was always well guarded. I wondered how it was she had come to be here, how she could have possibly survived her journey east alone. But one day, two weeks previous, it had all suddenly clicked.

I realised that every time she left the palace to go into the town, she was accompanied by the same troop of soldiers: a centurion and eight men. I had not paid the slightest bit of attention to the centurion the first time I saw him, just another face under a helmet. But the second time, I thought I recognised him but struggled to place where from. The third time, however, I knew for certain.

'We'll never be able to get to her, she's never alone. *He,* on the other hand, we should be able to reach,' Habitus said, his eyes fixed on mine.

'The centurion?' Crassus asked. He didn't know who it was we spoke about, and before then, I hadn't realised Habitus had noticed him too, though like I said, his body might have been failing, but his mind was as strong as ever.

'Julius Decanus,' Habitus said. 'He is Licina's lover, or was, anyway. Not much of a stretch to imagine he is again, considering he just *happens* to have earned himself a transfer to one of Cassius' legions at the same time she disappeared off the face of the earth and ran east.'

Another pause. Once more, I looked down at my feet in despair. How could I ever look Albinus in the eye again, knowing what I knew? I hadn't written to your father once since Habitus and I left for the east. As we walked away from Pannonia and the Fourteenth, I had promised myself I wouldn't write unless I had news. Well, now I had news, but not news I could share. I knew it would break Albinus' heart.

'Licina is the girl that is married to your friend though?' Crassus asked, frown lines creasing his face.

'Aye,' I said.

'And you both knew she had a lover before you left Pannonia for the east, where she ran from, and your friend still lives? So, I'm assuming your friend also knows about—'

'Just leave it, Crassus, it's a long fucking story, all right?'

'It involves an unsanctioned winter march through Germania, a few fights with a load of barbarians, a one-to-one fight to the death with the man who murdered our friends' father and a desperate rescue to bring back a lost lover from across the northern sea. Have I left anything out, Calvus?' Habitus asked with a smirk.

'I wouldn't know, brother,' I said, raising the stump of my left hand, 'I cut my own fingers off to escape a mountain pass in a storm and spent the rest of the winter in a fever-induced coma.'

'Okay,' Crassus said. 'Three years and I haven't heard this story. I feel as though I'm missing out.'

'Later there'll be time for stories,' I said. 'First, we follow Decanus, understand his routine. Then we get him alone.'


Four days was all it took to get our opportunity. Decanus, it seemed, was a man of routine, and that routine involved a run through the streets of Alexandria at dawn. We awoke in the small one-room apartment we had been renting as the sand clocks turned for the last hour of the night. Easing our way onto the streets of the Jewish quarter of the city, we picked up our prey as he ran south, away from the palace.

As he came to a junction at the end of the main street, Crassus pounced, leaping from the shadows and bringing him to the floor in one fluid motion. Habitus moved quickly to wrap a sack around his head, and between the three of us, we lifted his squirming body and carried him down the nearest alley.

The sun was lighting the rooftops as we set him free from the sack, and he lay on the floor blinking rapidly as his eyes adjusted to the growing light. 'Who the fuck are you?' he spat, rising unsteadily to his knees.

'You know who I am, boy,' I said, squatting down so our eyes were level. I saw the moment his pupils widened as he recognised me.

'Calvus, from the Fourteenth Legion. What, in the name of the gods, are you doing in Alexandria?'

'I am retired from the legions, mainly due to the fact that I lost four fingers scampering through Germania on my way north to bring Licina back to Pannonia after you had taken her over the northern sea and away from her husband, my friend, Albinus.' I spoke with all the gravel I could muster, a pent-up rage I didn't know I had been withholding poured free. I felt lighter as if a weight had been lifted.

'On retirement, I took employment with the *frumentarii*, and now, I am part of a large team working tirelessly to bring down Avidius Cassius before he starts a civil war with his audacious attempt to take the purple.'

I was panting, sweating in the early morning heat. The word 'tirelessly' caught in my throat, and I think, for the first time, I acknowledged just how tired I was. Tired of spending my days on horseback, tired of sleeping under the stars. I was old – gods, young Faustus, even then, twenty years ago, I was an old man! I wanted nothing more than for it to be over, to take Habitus and find his tavern, to end my days sipping iced wine in the sunshine.

'Gods, brother,' Habitus said as he came up behind me, 'I'm no spy, but telling the man we've just kidnapped who you are and what you're planning don't seem like the best way to go about it!'

'Aye,' I said, wiping sweat – or was it tears – from my eyes. 'But in this instance, I think it's the best way to proceed. See, Decanus here, he wants the same thing as us, don't you, mate?'

'Yes,' Decanus said after an awkward pause.

'And why would he want that?' said Crassus as he loomed over Decanus, knife in hand.

'Tell them,' I said.

Decanus nodded, shifted slightly and raised himself, no longer the cowering dog. 'I came here to kill Avidius Cassius. I came here to avenge the horrific crimes he has already committed against our emperor and his people.'

'Already committed?' Habitus spat, the anger of a man not in the know.

'We have been victims to those crimes, brother,' I said, my eyes still locked on our captive.

'Is anyone going to explain exactly what is going on here?' Crassus said, in a tone full of exasperation.

See, young Faustus, I had already begun to piece together the puzzle. Unfortunately for my two comrades, I had been selfish and hidden from them some of the pieces, so they were a few steps behind me.

Habitus and I had spent our lives in the Fourteenth Legion, trudging up and down the Danube and putting down rebellion after rebellion. Tribes turned their backs on their treaties with Rome every year, but never in our lifetime had the tribes united under one banner and made a real push south over the river.

That happened, as I'm sure you know, on the fateful day your grandfather was killed. There were six thousand or so of the bastards on that winter raid, and over the following years, the army was hard-pressed to keep them back. Your father fought them right up until the day he was ordered to accompany Commodus back to Rome, and his comrades fought on in his absence.

Now, the story these days is that the king of the Marcomanni, Balomar, was the co-ordinator of the tribes. They say he banded them together, oaths were made, sealed in blood and gold, and as one people, they marched south and attacked. Now, this is true, in part. Balomar was the king that united the others under his banner, but it was Roman gold that paid for his allies.

Alexander of Abonoteichos, a man I'm sure you have heard of, was arrested and executed for treason. But he had many allies in his quest to leap from soothsayer to emperor, and his biggest was Avidius Cassius.

Maybe as far back as when he fought under Lucius Verus in the eastern wars, maybe even as he ordered the sacking of Seleucia, Cassius had been planning this. Step by step, year by year, he gathered allies, bribed senators, won over legions. Alexander, I know, thought he was playing Cassius, thought he had the man eating out of the palm of his hands. How do I know this, you ask? I know, Faustus, because I was there, in Carnuntum of all places, when they tortured him.

It was him and his followers that caused your mother to flee east. She had been caught up in their conspiracy, forced to pass on information she gained by dishonest deeds she was forced to do. All of this she was ultimately doing for Avidius Cassius, but at the time, she just didn't know.

Alexander was always going to fall; Cassius was counting on it. All he had to do was lie low, let the fallout from his capture die down and wait whilst the rumours of Marcus Aurelius' ailing health grew by the day – although I'm convinced at least half of those rumours were spread by his agents.

And when the time was finally right? When vendors on every street corner across the empire were shouting that the emperor was dying or dead? He struck.

'I am here because I believe Cassius has been funding the wars in the north, that he has been putting gold into the Germans' pockets, encouraging them to continue their struggle against Rome. I am here because if he is not stopped, thousands will die, all for one man's greed,' I said.

I turned to Crassus, ignoring Habitus' dumbstruck face – for all his qualities, he really was no spy – and concentrated on Crassus. 'For years, we thought Cassius was serving Alexander of Abonoteichos, what if all the time it was the other way around?'

Crassus was silent for a while, his face a crease beneath his habitual straw hat. Finally, he nodded. 'It fits,' he said. 'I've had news from Rome recently, from the Camp of Strangers. It would seem Commodus has been there, discussing conspiracy theories with my superiors. Your friend was there too – Albinus Silus,' he said as an afterthought.

'Albinus, in Rome?'

'We shall talk later, or you can speak to him yourself when he escorts Commodus east.' Habitus and I shared a look. Clearly, it was my turn to be the one not in the know. 'But right now, we need to come up with a plan to rid us of Cassius. Decanus, do you have anything? You must have been here a while.'

And so, it began.

# CHAPTER XXI

**July, 175 AD**
**Alexandria, Egypt**

I met with your mother twice before we put our master plan into action. The first was in a wine bar overlooking the sea. I sat in the shade, awaiting her, nervously rubbing the stump of my left hand. By then, it had been three years or more since I had last seen her on a cold and blustery December day as the Fourteenth Legion had paraded through Carnuntum, victorious in their battles against the Marcomanni and their king, Balomar.

When she arrived, it was without fuss or fanfare. She was accompanied by Centurion Decanus, and not once did his hand leave the pommel of his sword as he directed her through the crowds on the street. She saw me and walked over, her head bowed, demeanour weak, guilty.

I stood, held out my arms ready for her embrace, but she merely took the seat opposite me and sat, her eyes still downcast.

'How are you?' I said into the silence. I got no reply.

Your mother, Faustus, had always been so full of life, her emerald-green eyes sparkled in the sun, her pale skin shone in winter. When I saw her then, it hurt me to see how far she had fallen. This woman, this magnificent woman, had not only survived capture and slavery after the winter raid which had started the northern wars, but had seemingly revelled in it. She had escaped her captors, run north, across the entire length of Germania and then done what few Romans had ever done before: sailed across the northern sea and made a life for herself in a country ruled by ice and snow.

And now, here she was, a slave once more in the blistering heat of the east. With the Lord as my witness, young Faustus, truly, no woman has ever lived a life quite like your mother. But it seemed all that living had finally taken its toll.

'Licina?' I said, my right arm stretching across the table, 'are you okay?'

When she eventually looked up, I did not recognise the face I saw. Her hair was no longer the golden red of autumn, but dark and drab like a January morning. Eyes that had once sparkled were dull and void of life. She appeared to carry the fears of emperors in the dark bags underneath.

'Faustus?' she whispered, in a meek, croaking voice.

'Is alive and well,' I said. I felt a spark of anger then, I have to admit. Anger that this woman would have the audacity to ask after a child she had abandoned with no hesitation, abandoned to lead a quest for no other purpose but revenge. But I quashed it down, buried it deep, for truly, I could not blame her for what she had done. I felt my own guilt for her departure, I still do to this day. Surely, there must have been more I could have done? Once the parade was over and Alexander of Abonoteichos was in custody, I could have gone to her, rather than follow my superiors to see him tortured. But I didn't, I was not smart enough to see the damage that had been done. I thought only of myself, of reward and advancement. Truly, men are selfish creatures, brittle to our core.

She wept, your mother, she wept for so long, it seemed her tears would join with the sea and together they would drown us all. Three years she had been gone, three years, starved of news from home with the ghost of her absent son tormenting her every step.

'And Albinus?' she said.

'Still alive, last I heard,' I said with a small smile, hoping to spark some of the old life into her.

'In Rome?' Decanus asked. He stood over Licina, one hand clamped firmly on her shoulder. He was her rock, I saw, her guardian and also her captive. He wore a deep frown on his face, clearly irked by her asking after Albinus. Despite myself, I felt some small sympathy for him, for I too have loved a woman and known the bitter taste it leaves when she does not love you back.

219

'Yes, he has been in Rome, with Faustus, Meredith and her child, Marcus.'

'Meredith,' Licina said in a whisper. 'She is his lover now?'

'Licina, I think we must focus on the task at hand—'

I silenced Decanus with a glare, matching his anger with my own. His knuckles whitened on the pommel of his sword, his left hand clamping Licina like a vice. If he'd have bared that blade, he would have killed me in a fair fight; he was in his prime, I was not. But with God as my witness, I'd have fought him all the same. 'Licina has every right to ask after her *family*,' I said, putting all the emphasis I could on the last word.

'Why are they in Rome?' she asked. She spoke to me but looked at Decanus, her eyes betraying for a moment her mistrust of him. It told me all I needed to know of their relationship, that Decanus knew of Albinus' movements, and she did not.

'Albinus was given the unimaginable honour of being a guardian to the caesar, Commodus. Albinus and his century looked after him whilst he was in the north with his father, and when he was sent back south, caesar himself asked for Albinus to accompany him. From what I hear, he thrives and is a celebrity in his own right.' Okay, so he wasn't a celebrity, but I couldn't pass up the opportunity to have a little dig at Decanus, could I?

'Gods, I miss them,' Licina said, once more breaking down into tears. 'I thought I did the right thing in leaving, truly I did. But now, now, all I want is to go home, to hold my son, to kiss my husband.'

Decanus moved away at the word 'husband', and once again, I had the strange sensation in my gut, feeling sympathy for him but not wanting to.

'Why did you come here?' I said, eager to talk to her whilst Decanus was out of earshot. 'You didn't need to leave, you had done nothing wrong.'

'Yes, I had. I gave them information for months. Cocconas stalked me, making me pass on troop movements and supply routes. I had access to it all at the Basilica, I didn't know what else to do. I was all alone,' she said, her shoulders slumped.

'No, you weren't. I was there. I could have helped you. Why did you never tell me what was happening?'

'I don't know,' she said, her voice a quiver on the sea breeze. 'You were going through a tough time yourself, discharged from the army, getting used to living without the use of your hand. And anyway, you never told me you had been recruited into the *frumentarii*, if I'd have known that, I would have reached out to you!'

Harsh, but fair. I had, in fact, been stalking Cocconas even as he harassed Licina, though I hadn't realised it was her he was trying to see. Once more, I wish I had been better. 'So, we both made mistakes,' I said. 'But now, we have a chance to put them right. Tell me how you came to be here, a slave to Cassius.'

She spoke. She told me of her journey south and then east, of how Decanus had caught her on the road just two days after she had departed Carnuntum. They had fled north together, the two of them, and he had been her companion when she had learnt the ways of spear and shield in the frozen lands of the distant north. He had fallen in love with her then, she, in turn, had been fond of him, though, in truth, I think she just needed a friend.

Decanus had accompanied her on the rest of her journey, turning his back on his comrades in the Fourteenth Legion. He had no loyalty, not like your father or his grandfather before him. Decanus had only joined the Fourteenth to stay near to Licina, even as she was reunited with your father. When they had eventually arrived in Egypt, he had presented himself at the nearest legion fortress as an *optio* being transferred from the Fourteenth. Every legion was the same back then, numbers depleted from the plague. I doubt many questions were asked – every legion was just desperate for more manpower, especially officers with experience. It seemed it did not take him long to reach the rank of centurion.

It had been Licina's idea to be sold as a slave into Cassius' household. Much like Crassus, Habitus and I had done for days after arriving at Alexandria, she had watched the palace gates and wondered how on earth she would ever get in to get to her man.

'I knew he was behind it all,' she said with venom. 'Cocconas spoke of him often, always said that he had been Alexander's closest ally in the senate. Who else would be able to keep the fight going after Alexander's capture and death? The more I thought about it, the more I realised it must all have been part of Cassius' plan. Let someone else do the dirty work, expose themselves and get caught, and then just as the dust settles and everyone thinks it's safe for the emperor once more, strike.'

'As he did.'

Licina nodded. I poured her a small cup of wine, and she drank greedily. I poured her another. 'It was his agents that spread the rumours of Aurelius' death,' she said.

'We suspected that much.'

'Did you also *suspect* that Cassius and Faustina are lovers?'

I sat, dumbstruck, gaping like a fish. 'Surely you don't mean…'

'Faustina, the empress.'

'No!'

'Yes. And I can prove it.'

'How?'

'He corresponds with her; the letters are all in his office.'

'Sweet Jesu,' I whistled, the ramifications whirling like a storm through my mind. If the empress really was the lover of Cassius, then the roots of his rebellion dug deeper than any of us could have imagined.

'He has to die. Soon. We can't let him leave Alexandria.'

I nodded, my mind still reeling from what she had said. 'What is your position in his household?'

Licina blushed, once more, her eyes seeking out her feet.

'I understand,' I said, not wanting to embarrass her further. 'But that means you are alone with him?' She nodded. 'So, if we could get you some form of poison? Nightshade maybe?'

'Already tried it,' she said. 'Decanus got us some, I spiked his wine, but all it seemed to do was loosen his bowels.'

'Loosened his bowels? Nightshade?'

'He must have built up some sort of immunity to a variety of poisons, it's not unknown, and remember, he was a friend of Alexander the apothecary.'

I nodded, beads of sweat racing down my face. I knew what she was going to say.

'It has to be a blade.'

'But it doesn't have to be you,' I said, my eyes locked with hers.

'He has taken everything from me. You do not understand, Calvus, I have no reason to live. Not without my son. Not without Albinus.'

Once more, Decanus flinched behind her, his pain visible, face set in a grimace as if he had just taken a wound in battle.

'Okay,' I said after a time, keeping my eyes downcast now, thinking how I could possibly explain to Albinus that I had finally found his wife, only to lose her once more. 'So, when and where?'

We met once more after that, a short and bitter reunion in a darkened alley. We finalised our plans and said our goodbyes. I will not reveal the details of that meeting now, not to you, young Faustus. I will only tell you this: as she hugged me tight, bidding me a final farewell, her only words were for you. 'Tell him I love him, tell him he is my whole world and that everything I do is for him.'

# CHAPTER XXII

**January, 197 AD**
**Gaul**

The wind is sharp, it assaults his body, cutting deeper than a blade. Atop his horse, Faustus shivers under his cloak. He is uncomfortable in the armour he has been forced to wear, he clanks and chinks with every movement, buckles and straps dig into his skin. Already, he can feel they have rubbed through in places, and he is bleeding onto his tunic. The day has only just begun.

Around him, the army of Legate Virius Lupus forms for battle, facing north, lining the top of a valley from east to west. Here is where they will make their stand, here is where they will hold Clodius Albinus and his vast armies, here is where Faustus believes he will likely die.

He shudders as another gust of wind rips through him. The gelding beneath him snorts and rolls its head, sensing its rider's discomfort. It is a small horse, the gelding, unnamed, as far as Faustus knows, but he is told it will ride like the wind. He hopes it will not be as savage.

He is not a skilled rider, had not sat atop a horse until he left Rome and began his journey to Britannia. As a child, they had frightened him, as an adult, the fear has receded but only a little.

He is just to the right of the command tent, close enough to be near the legate when he is called, far enough away to be out of earshot of the officers as they huddle around a brazier, plotting their moves for the day.

He has never seen an army on the cusp of battle before. Marching columns he has seen many times in Pannonia and Britannia, an endless line of trudging men, packs yoked over their shoulders, helmets swinging from their belts, swords resting in scabbards. Now, he sees the same men, but they are so very different.

No one has their pack with them, they have been left back in camp. Helmets are fastened to heads with leather straps, shields are out of their leather protectors, newly painted, glistening in the weak winter sun. Swords are freed from scabbards, men swinging them in the air, checking their edge, whetstones passed from one man to another. There is no artillery, something Faustus is aware the legate is deeply unhappy about. They were carted up and put on the road back on the Rhine frontier, but in the far corners of the empire, the roads are not as they are in Italy, and they have not survived the journey.

He finds the colours of the different legions interesting and studies them, taking his mind off the cold and the horrors the day promises to bring. On the left flank is the Twenty-Second Primigenia, resplendent in white tunics and matching shields. To their left is the Thirtieth Ulpia Victrix, in the centre are the Thirteenth and Seventh Gemina legions, on the right, the Third Italica. There are many cohorts of auxiliary mixed in with the legions, but Faustus has no notion as to their names nor their key strengths.

The army has no cavalry to call upon, apart from a small unit of around one hundred men and a handful of messengers to deliver orders throughout the battle. This is where Faustus fits in. He has told the legate all he knows of the enemy, of their strengths and weaknesses. Now, he must do his part in the battle, his stomach rolls with fear, he feels a very sudden and desperate need to shit. By the stink rolling off the field, it would appear he is not the only one.

So, five legions will face the army of Clodius Albinus, some twenty-five thousand men all told. They will not be enough. Faustus knows this, and the gods know he is no military man. But Virius Lupus has been charged with holding Clodius back, keeping him at bay until Severus can bring his field army to Gaul. No one will say he has failed in his duty.

The army of Severus will fight on the defensive, hold the high ground on the pass through which Clodius must march his army. They are in the north-west of Gaul, somewhere to the south of Rotomagus, Faustus is not entirely sure where. He knows only that it took him over a week to ride

225

from Massilia, and that it will be another week at least before the saddle-sore starts to calm down and the constant itching fades.

The pale winter sun has risen almost to its highest arc when the enemy comes into view. Faustus thinks it strange to consider another Roman army as the enemy, then thinks that in recent years, Rome has fought more with itself than against anyone outside the empire, so maybe this is the norm now.

They draw closer, screened by mounted scouts who will be checking the standards that wave proudly in the sunlight, relaying to their commanders who holds which part of the field. Faustus is doing the same. He can make out the Thirtieth Ulpia Victrix and, once more, feels a profound sense of unease. These are men that he has traded with, drunk with during his time in Britannia. Now, he must watch them die.

He sees also the Thirteenth Gemina on the enemy left, a unit that once fought with his father. The Second Gemina, the Third Italica... their marching column seems to stretch on and on, almost back to the coast.

Orders are given, and men move. The air smells of piss and leather, horse shit and sweat.

'Faustus, stay close to me!' says a voice to his left. Faustus turns his head slowly, feeling strangely detached from the events around him. Lupus is there, mounting a huge black horse, waving Faustus over.

'I want you to stay close and point out anything I may have missed in terms of their approach. The Thirteenth Gemina on their left, they're mostly made up of recruits, right?' Faustus nods, again with a sense of detachment. He feels as though he is watching this at the theatre, that it isn't *really* happening to him. But it is.

'And the Third Italica? Their commander is new, right? Some senator's son?'

Faustus nods. 'His father is Julius Solon, or was, I should say.' Already, forty senators have been executed on the order of Severus, there will be many more when this is done. If he wins. *He will win, of that, I can assure you.* Calvus' words ring in his mind; how could the man be so sure?

Lupus seems content to let the silence between them grow as they watch the opposing army advance on their position. Faustus feels his stomach tense and tries to control his breathing. His hands shake violently on the reins of his horse, he tells himself it is just the cold.

He looks out at the mass of men who stand as still as marble, awaiting an onslaught they cannot avoid. He imagines his father amongst those ranks, as he had been on more occasions than Faustus would ever know. He could picture him, prowling through his century, checking armour and helmets, offering words of encouragement. He knows it is a role he can never fulfil. What courage he must have had, he thinks, to stand in the arena of death and have the words to rouse men to slaughter. Faustus thinks he couldn't be more different to his father if he tried. His thoughts drift once more to that alley, to the knives, to the screams of Marcus and Meredith. *I left them to their deaths.*

Trumpets blare across the field, and Faustus realises his concentration has drifted. He chides himself, he who can let his mind wander just as men are about to die to protect him. The two armies are separated by no more than fifty paces, and he can make out men readying to throw their javelins. Once more, the trumpets sound, followed quickly by the high-pitched keen of the centurion's whistles, and then it is as if the sun has set as the sky darkens with iron-tipped javelins.

Men from both sides hurl their missiles, and for a moment, there is nothing but peace, silence. Faustus watches them fly, his breath held tight. It is like a dance as they arc up in the air before death rains on the men of both sides. The javelins strike home with a thump that even Faustus can hear from where he sits, and then the screaming starts.

Men fall dead to the floor, only to be stepped over by their comrades in the ranks behind as the armies draw swords and move forward to fight. It is a strange sort of engagement, with both sides evenly matched with long swords and rectangular shields, and Faustus shudders at the crunch of impact as the two battle lines meet and the melee begins.

A pushing match ensues, dust clouds rise and swirl from the press, Faustus squints as he tries to make sense of what he is seeing, but it is hopeless. Next to him, Lupus is already issuing orders, and riders scurry off to allotted parts of the field, delivering them with utmost haste. Faustus just sits, oblivious to the shouts of the legate, and watches, stunned as the wounded start to file back from the front. Virius has set a small hospital beyond the rise of the valley he has chosen to defend, though even Faustus knows it is nothing more than a token effort. If his army does not hold the hill, Lupus will order his men to retreat, and the wounded in the hospital will be left to the mercy of the enemy. Some would say it was better to suffer a clean death in battle than to be captured. They may be right.

'Faustus, get over to our right flank,' Lupus shouts in his ear, his voice a booming presence amidst the cacophony of battle. 'Their cavalry is moving. There – can you see them?' he says, pointing beyond the dust cloud to the enemy's rear. 'I think they will try to force our flank, tell Aemilianus he must not let this happen. Go!'

Faustus goes.

He kicks his mount in the flanks, and at once, they are flying down the valley, Faustus heedless to the dangers of a galloping horse on a steep decline. He does not allow himself to think, to commit the orders to memory, he does not even know who Aemilianus is, he just rides.

He approaches the rear of the right flank and is greeted by gore-covered men, some weeping, others silent as they trudge up the hill, away to the sanctuary of the hospital. 'Aemilianus, where is he? I need Aemilianus, have you seen him?'

'Aye, lad, that'll be me. What orders?'

Faustus swivels his horse until he finds the man he has been seeking. An ageing centurion looks up at him, a long, thin cut running down his cheek from eye to lip. As Faustus dismounts, the centurion tips a flask of water onto his face and hisses at the pain. 'I said what orders, boy? I haven't got all day.'

'Legate Virius says to expect a cavalry attack on your flank. He says you must not let them past.'

'No shit,' Aemilianus replies with a wry grin, and the soldiers in earshot laugh. 'How many?'

'How many what?'

'Cavalry, lad, how big is the damn cavalry?'

'I… I don't know,' Faustus says in a small voice. 'It was hard to see through the dust.'

'Nice one,' Aemilianus says. 'Some fucking help you are. Right, lads, prepare to repel cavalry!'

But even as he speaks, the charge comes out of the dust. The cavalry comes in from the far right, the enemy left, and burst through the dumb-struck infantry who fall like barley under the sickle. The crunch of breaking bone is horrific, and Faustus staggers back, reaching out for the reins of his mount, but the beast panics and runs before he can reach it.

In full fright now, he runs, legs pumping as he surges up the valley, the rumble of hooves on the grass and the savage sounds of battle hot in his ears. He dares not look back, does not possess the courage to look death in the eye. He has lived a coward's life; he will die one.

He trips on something sharp and spirals to the floor, coming down hard on his left shoulder. His mail, its weight still alien to him, rebounds from the hard ground and digs into his skin. He lies there stunned, wind gone, struggling to breathe.

Eventually, he rises, and his blurred vision begins to clear. He has tripped on an abandoned sword. He picks it up unsteadily, gripping the hilt as if his life depends on it.

And it might. The cavalry has broken through the flank, he has not got his message to Aemilianus in time. The battle is lost, Lupus' army is broken up, each unit now fighting alone. Faustus rises to his feet and grits his teeth, raising the sword. He has lived a coward's life, a life devoid of responsibility and honour. Years he has spent distancing himself from his father's name, just as his father had done before him. And yet, both his father and grandfather achieved fame and glory in their own right on the battlefield; Faustus can, at least, honour them by dying on one.

A cavalryman spots him standing alone with his sword held high and alters his grip on his sword and charges. Faustus screams, searching deep within himself, trying to find his courage. He thinks of Calvus, regrets never telling the old man how much he cares for him, how he has been the greatest role model any man could ever wish for. He thinks of Meredith and Marcus, dying in that alley whilst Faustus did nothing but and run away. He will not run today.

Lastly, he thinks of his father and wonders if he is proud of him. *Is this what it was like for you at the end?* And he thinks of his mother, a woman

229

he has never known. He knows now how she died. Calvus wept as he told the tale. She died for *something* though. For vengeance and revenge. Most of all, she died for love.

The cavalryman closes and swings his sword back, ready to strike the killing blow. Faustus raises his own in what he thinks is a guard that will block the falling blade. But he is no soldier. The cavalryman adjusts his grip mid-swing and his sword sings over Faustus before he brings it back around and delivers a savage back cut to the top of Faustus' head, who falls silently to the hard ground.

# CHAPTER XXIII

**July, 175 AD**
**Alexandria, Egypt**

Licina awoke to the sounds of trumpets announcing, in all their glory, the rising of the sun. She rose from her cot quickly, rushing over to the basin in the corner of the room and splashing her face with cool water. The nights in Egypt at this time of year were so hot they were almost unbearable. Even in the slave quarters of the palace which were so deep underground, the sun's light never pierced the eternal gloom.

She dressed in a pale tunic and tied her hair in a loose knot behind her head, feeling loose threads pull away with her fingers as she did. She wasn't exactly sure when she had begun to lose hair, but if she ran her fingers across the top of her head, she could feel the bald spot growing at the top of her crown.

Stress and grief had aged her more than years ever could. She was in her mid-twenties and should be in the prime of health. Instead, she was ailing; in many ways, her journey across the river Styx had already begun. By sundown today, it would be complete.

It had been months since she had managed to summon the courage to look into one of the many mirrors that adorned the palace walls. The face she saw in the polished sheets of brass, glass and gold did not represent her, at least not the version of her she knew.

Age lines creased her once smooth skin, crows' feet circled eyes that had long since lost their sparkle. Albinus used to love those eyes. Her thoughts drifted, as they always did, to her estranged husband and their young son. Did Albinus speak to their son of her? Did Faustus even know who his mother was?

She felt a strong pang of jealousy as she remembered Calvus saying Albinus had gone to Rome and that Meredith had accompanied him. She tried to quash it down but failed. Were they lovers now? Had she taken Licina's place as Faustus' mother? Her jealousy soon turned to anger as she thought of Decanus. How long had he known? Why had he not told her? She wasn't surprised that he had been keeping tabs on Albinus, she was sure he would have arranged for information to be filtered through to him even before he had left Pannonia.

She knew Decanus loved her, but they both knew she did not love him. She thought she might have done once, in a time that seemed an age ago, as they had journeyed together across the northern sea to lands where Rome was just a name, a far-off people who had no effect on the day-to-day lives of the locals.

Licina had grown in the north. Hardened. She had spent her time there immersing herself in the ways of a Shield Maiden, learning to fight with sword and spear and even fighting with the ladies of the Heruli in a desperate battle for survival against a neighbouring tribe. She had been happy, in her own way, out in the far reaches of the world. She thought often of her friend Heide, the woman who had befriended her and taught her the ways of war, and wondered what she was doing now, whether she had married or had children of her own. She hoped she had.

She left the small room that had been her home since she had arrived in Alexandria and been sold as a slave to Cassius. She passed the threshold but closed the door without a backward glance. There was nothing of value in the room, just a small straw pallet and a basin of water. She would not be returning.

She moved through the darkened corridors of the lower reaches of the palace and climbed the stairs as if in a trance. Soldiers stood on guard at every corner, they knew her by sight now, and she them. Neither paid the other any heed. Reaching the top level of the palace, she knocked once on a golden door and stood back, awaiting a response. A red-cloaked centurion opened the door after a moment's pause, and she entered into a room of luxury.

The floor was marble, the walls decorated with lavish tapestries. The air was rich with the aroma of fresh flowers and incense. Avidius Cassius stood on a raised circular dais in the centre of the chamber, three slaves fussing around him, adjusting the purple striped toga that seemed like skin around his rotund body. His bald head gleamed with sweat; a small boy stood behind the would-be emperor, wafting a huge canvas fan, though all it achieved was to circulate warm air around the room.

'Augustus,' Licina murmured, prostrating herself on the gleaming floor.

'Ahh, Licina,' Cassius said, lowering himself from the dais with the help of a slave and walking slowly over to her. 'Today will be a momentous day, girl. You shall accompany me to the drill field, hear the speech I have prepared for the men. Tomorrow, we march to war.'

Licina nodded, mute. It was now common knowledge throughout the city that the true emperor, Marcus Aurelius, was not, in fact, dead and was gathering an army in the north, ready to strike east.

She did not know if this was all part of Cassius' plan, or whether the senator thought spreading rumours of the emperor's death would be enough to clear a path to the throne for him. She thought there had to be more, an assassin perhaps, sent north in secret to plunge a knife into Aurelius' heart or poison his wine. If there was, she had not heard of it.

Cassius, though, seemed not to care about the prospect of imminent war. He had amassed a huge force from the eastern legions who had almost all gone over to him without so much as a drop of blood spilt. He was confident and brash, ready for anything the world could throw at him. *But is he ready for today?* she thought with a secret smile.

They exited the palace through the main doors and into the intense heat of the courtyard. Licina's tunic clung to her, and she could feel the hungry looks of the soldiers as they drank in the sight of her slim figure. She paid them no heed. There was a time when she would have prickled in anger and embarrassment and would have taken comfort from Albinus at her arm, warding off any potential suitors with a flare of his bright blue eyes.

Now she didn't care what they looked at, the body hidden beneath the tunic was ragged and worn, lined and haggard. They could look all they wanted.

Cassius mounted in the courtyard, and Licina was handed a jug of water by a soldier. The soldier was Decanus, she knew without diverting her gaze from the floor though neither of them spoke. As she took the jug, she felt a small, thin object wrapped in cloth press into her palm, the edge of the blade rough through the fabric.

She held it tight, clasped to her breast, the water jug concealing it from prying eyes. Cassius steered his mount from the courtyard, and Licina followed with a small body of soldiers, Decanus leading them.

They made their way through crowded streets. Market was underway to one side of the main thoroughfare, and Licina could hear the people haggling and jostling as they competed with one other to get their hands on the local wares.

She kept her eyes on the back of Decanus, watching the horsehair crest on his helmet sway in the slight breeze, though the gentle wind did nothing to relieve from the scorching heat of the day. Not for the first time, she wondered how the soldiers coped in all that armour. Surely, it was torture just to stand guard in the shade of the palace, let alone parade in the full sun? And to have to fight in it? Unthinkable.

She thought of Albinus, of how he would shrug off his mail coat and wince, arching his back and rubbing a spot at the base of his spine. It was a soldier's ache, or so he had said. Every soldier succumbed to it at some point in their career, his time had just come early.

Looking up at the scorching sun, she closed her eyes for a moment and focused on his image. He had been her first love, her only love. She had wanted to give Calvus a message to pass on to Albinus, but when she had set quill to parchment, she had drawn a blank. How could mere words sum up what she felt for him, for their son? 'Tell them I will love them, always,' she had simply said to Calvus. It would have to be enough.

They entered the parade ground to the sound of trumpets and swords beating on shields. There must have been over twenty thousand men there to meet Cassius, their emperor. Each man in that dust-covered field had committed the highest of treasons by turning their backs on Marcus Aurelius and supporting Cassius in his bid for the purple. She wondered, for a moment, if they even knew the true emperor still lived or whether Cassius and his agents still held them brainwashed. Though surely, that was a task too great even for Cassius.

She thought it more likely the weight of the bribes in gold they had been paid was enough to keep them loyal. Decanus, for one, had been very vocal in his support for the usurper once his purse had been filled with coin – in public, anyway.

She studied the centurion in front of her more closely as they walked past the ranks of cheering soldiers. He had been in love with her for many years now, knowing deep down that she did not return his feelings. Could he be trusted? Would he betray her at the last?

She was about to find out.

Cassius stopped his horse in front of the massed troops and basked in their acclaim. The horse did not seem as appreciative as him, being stuck under all that weight. To say he was rotund would have been to give him a compliment. Licina, unfortunately, had first-hand experience of being trapped under that giant belly. It was not pleasant, to say the least.

But Licina had survived a lot throughout her life. She had even been sexually abused by another woman once, long ago, in the legion fortress of Carnuntum, when she had been a slave to the Marcomannic king, Balomar. With a start, she realised she had not thought of Aelinia in an age, and neither had Decanus mentioned his sister in her presence. Aelinia was Decanus' sister, and they had been captured together and sold to Balomar at around the same time Licina herself was delivered to his gates. Aelinia had swiftly worked her way into the king's bedchamber, turning her back on Rome and setting her sights on becoming a barbarian queen. It had not worked out for her.

Licina felt a burning desire to shout to Decanus, to ask after his sister. She longed to know if the woman still lived. She longed for a lot of things; she would not get them. Not now.

Cassius was giving a speech. She listened without hearing. Blood thumped in her ears now, and she savoured every frantic beat, knowing they would be among the last. She scanned the crowd, praying to every god she held dear she would not see Calvus or Habitus in there. They had promised they would be close, would get her out if they could. She had told them not to bother, life held no meaning for her now. She just had one task left to accomplish before she could complete her journey.

Cassius turned to her and signalled for water. She looked up at his sweating face, plum red and pulsing from the heat. She moved forward, the last steps she would ever take. As she approached, Cassius motioned to another slave who moved forward duly and knelt. If Licina had thought Cassius was ungraceful mounting a horse, then seeing him dismount was something like a comedy act in the theatre.

He huffed and groaned as he strained to lift one leg over the beast, before more falling than stepping from its back. The slave on his knees winced but, to his credit, did not cry out. Licina thought that act in itself a mark of the man's courage.

Cassius turned to her and held out a hand, his red face a river of sweat. Licina stepped in close, her hands shaking, mind a whirlwind. *This is it. My opportunity. Courage.* She had heard Albinus speak of courage a lot over the years. He used to think himself a coward, though all around him could see he was anything but. Yet, he had put himself down, tortured himself for not fighting off thousands of barbarians alone when their home had been raided and Licina taken. His whole adult life, he had felt the need to endanger himself, to somehow prove he was worthy of being his father's son.

Truth was, Licina had never known a stronger man than her husband. Sure, his father had been ferocious on the battlefield, but he had failed as a father because of it. Albinus had embraced every aspect of his life, thrown himself at every challenge put in front of him, and she knew she would be hard-pressed to find a man who spoke badly of him, even Decanus had a begrudging respect for him. *For you, my love, and for Faustus.*

She breathed in deep and imagined she drew her strength from Albinus. In her left hand was the water jug, the knife tucked in her palm behind it. In her right was the cup. In one motion she stepped forward, into Cassius' shadow. She dropped the cup, sending it clattering to the dust. Reaching behind the jug, she hauled free the blade from beneath the cloth and bared the knife. She had wanted to speak some words, to shout and scream and denounce Cassius for everything he had done to her and her family. None came to mind.

Cassius froze in shock, eyes wide and locked on the blade. *Never hesitate.* Heide had told her that on a long-ago day atop a frozen lake in what felt like another world. The advice still stood. She cast aside the water jug and drew back her right arm, her body remembering the nerve-tingling terror of impending violence. She thrust forward, screaming incoherently as she did.

The blade never struck home.

Just as she was about to pierce his belly she was thrown to the ground, spitting dust in a rage. She rolled and clambered up to her knees, men with swords surrounding her. Decanus stood next to Cassius, one arm around him.

'No!' she screamed, rage and despair tearing her apart.

'It has to be this way,' Decanus said through the ring of blades. 'Let her go, boys.'

The soldiers moved back, and Licina stood slowly, understanding creeping up on her. 'You cannot do this,' she said quietly, almost a whisper.

'It is how it has to be,' he said and turned to Cassius.

'Centurion, I cannot thank you enou—'

Avidius Cassius never finished his sentence, never spoke again. Decanus drew his sword, stepped back and slashed with all his might. The head of Avidius Cassius fell slowly to the dust, his eyes wide, mouth still moving.

Licina sank to her knees and looked up into the cloudless sky. She did not see Decanus die, though he made no sound, so it must have been quick. Men moved all around her, some shouting in anger, some despair. She stayed perfectly still. In her mind, she held a picture of Albinus holding their son. He lofted the baby high above his head and circled round and round. Faustus giggled in delight, his little arms held out in a welcoming embrace as Albinus pulled him back close. She smiled, a single tear rolling down her cheek. *I will be with you, always.* She did not cry out as the blade penetrated her skin.

In truth, she barely felt it.

# CHAPTER XXIV

**July, 175 AD**
**Alexandria, Egypt**

I tried to get to your mother, Faustus, God knows I tried.

We had secreted ourselves in the corner of the parade field. Habitus had disguised himself as an eastern merchant and wore long flowing robes which were perfect for concealing his small bow and a short sword. I was his slave, wearing nothing but a dirty old tunic, my pale skin burning in the heat of the sun.

Crassus was set apart from us, wearing full military regalia, stolen from the unconscious body of a centurion who just happened to be in the wrong place at the wrong time. Crassus had more front than a legion set in battle formation, or so Habitus used to say, and he stood in front of a small column of men, even had the nerve to put two of them on latrines for the state of their kit.

Habitus and I watched with baited breath as Licina approached Cassius. She looked so small and frail as she took what would be her final steps, her red hair shining in the sun.

Decanus was already moving towards her, and as she thrust the blade forward, he caught it, pushing her back in one motion. His eyes locked on mine then, he knew where to find me, it had all been pre-arranged. I was up in a flash, moving at a fast walk towards her. She was maybe a hundred paces from me, all I had to do was get there before the killing began.

But we did not make it. Decanus and your mother shared some final words before Decanus hauled free his sword and cut off Cassius' head with a beautiful swing. For all his faults, and as much as I did not like the man, his love for Licina was both pure and true. He knew she did not return his feelings; she was dependent on him, reliant on his love and loyalty. She had been playing on it for years, both knew it, neither would acknowledge it.

Cassius' head fell to the floor, and then all hell broke loose. Decanus was dead moments later, swords penetrating his armour front and back, and he sank to the ground like a stone in the sea.

Licina was on her knees, head raised to the golden sun. She was twenty paces away and I called her name, though my voice was hoarse, my throat as dry as the dust-covered plain. I shouted again, tugging free the small axe I had stuffed down the back of my tunic.

Ten paces away, the first blade struck home, hitting her high in the chest. I cried out in anguish. There was a twang next to me as Habitus let loose his first arrow. He only had five with him, I knew. The soldier that had struck her fell, letting loose a howling cry. More men turned to us, all of them snarling in fury.

Just as I reached Licina, one soldier came for me with shield and spear. I dodged the spear thrust, hooked my axe over the rim of his shield and pulled hard. He fell forward, stumbling into me, and I slammed the axe into his back, screaming a war cry as I wrenched it free and sought my next foe.

Habitus had spent his arrows now, five men lying dead on the ground. He had freed his sword and was dancing around two men with shields. Unarmoured like me, he used his speed and lightness to wriggle between them and killed them both with quick slashes to the throat and groin respectively. He always was a natural killer.

I moved so I stood over Licina, hacking and slashing at anyone that came within reach of my axe. I felt myself tiring alarmingly quickly, age and the intense heat wearing me down. Just as I was about to be surrounded, I heard a trumpet to my rear, and a heartbeat later, Crassus was at my side, ordering the men he had taken command of to form a shield wall and keep their swords sheathed.

'No more blood, brothers!' he bellowed. 'Peace now, peace! There has been enough death today.'

Slowly, the battle madness left us all, each man stood and sweated, panting. It was all I could do to stay on my feet, such was the overwhelming exhaustion that washed over me.

'Take the girl and go,' Crassus said quietly to me. 'There's nothing else to be done here.'

'What about you?'

'Don't worry about me. Take the girl, see to her remains. And once that's done, you go to the emperor and report everything that has happened here. This is not what we wanted, Calvus, she should not have died.'

I reached out and gripped his arm. He was staying and that was a death sentence, we both knew it. 'Gratitude, brother. Everything happens for a reason, and I reckon this is how she wanted it, anyway,' I said before turning to Licina and picking her up as gently as I could. I had no need to stop and check if she was breathing, or her pulse still beat out a rhythm. The wound to her chest was grievous, and blood poured from the gaping hole – there was no chance she could have survived. I choked back hot tears and began walking, my stride unsteady under her weight.

'We can't just leave him,' Habitus said, taking hold of Licina's legs as we stumbled off from the parade ground. 'They'll kill him!'

'I know, and we need to be as far away from here as we can when they do.'

We kept walking, not turning back as voices were raised behind us. I heard Crassus order his men to draw swords, and just after, there was the distinctive sound of iron on iron. The officers there would be coming back to their senses, the shock of what had happened wearing off. They would want to know who Crassus was and why he was letting two men go free who had just made slaughter on their soldiers. Once again, there was the clash of swords, once again, we did not stop.

We left the parade ground and made for the horses we had left tied under a tree, each with a heavy pack strapped to its back, full of provisions for our journey. Gently, we eased Licina's body onto the back of Crassus' horse, and for the first time, I had a chance to study her. Her eyes were open slightly, and I closed them for the final time. She looked peaceful, at rest, which offered me some small comfort. Her hair was thin, and I was shocked to see the pale skin of her scalp through the loose tangle of hair. I marvelled at her strength, her dignity, even in the face of death.

Truly, young Faustus, never have I met another woman or man quite like your mother. She was so strong and brave. She threw herself into every aspect of life, whether it was giving birth to you or embracing the life of a slave in Germania. Each challenge she saw as an opportunity to be grasped. She was truly remarkable.

We rode from Alexandria, heading east. That night, we bought wood from a lone farmstead and set your mother's body on a great pyre. I stayed up all night, just watching the flames dance under the stars. I prayed, but it was not to God that I sent my words. I spoke to your mother, I told her that she was loved, that Albinus would hear of her sacrifice, and he would be proud. I did not know if it was true. I did not know if he even still cared for her – three years is a long time, much could have changed. My final words to her were a promise. I promised I would find you, young Faustus, and that I would stand over you, watch you grow from boy to man, see that you were safe. It is a promise I have kept and have taken great joy in keeping. You are a fine man, Faustus, your mother watches over you, and she is proud.

The next day we set off with no real idea as to where we were going. We assumed Aurelius would be assembling an army and coming east, and for a while, I pondered whether he would march them from the Danube or sail across the Mediterranean. It was not until weeks later, in the coastal city of Antioch in Syria, that we got our answer and unexpectedly ran into an old friend.

# CHAPTER XXV

Albinus entered the city of Tarsus through the Gate of Cleopatra on the city's western side. He was saddle-sore and tired, irritable and generally in a bad mood.

He turned to Fullo who rode behind him and gestured angrily. 'Find accommodation for the men, and see to the horses. I'm going to get a drink.'

He dismounted and made his way to the first tavern he could find. Ordering a jug of cooled wine, he sat on a stool and winced at the pain in his thighs. He seemed to have spent the majority of the last six months on horseback, riding first home to Pannonia from Rome before being sent almost immediately out east.

The gods, it seemed, were in no rush to give him any rest. He sighed in pleasure as he swallowed the first gulp of wine, savouring the taste and the coolness of the liquid on his dust-dry tongue.

'Fullo said I would find you in here,' a voice said, and Albinus immediately leapt to his feet.

'Sir!' he said, snapping a smart salute and standing to attention. 'I was not expecting to see you so soon, sir.'

'Aye, it appears you were not,' Legate Marcus Valerius Maximianus said through a wolf-like grin. Shrugging off his riding cloak, he took a seat, gesturing for Albinus to do the same. 'I was told you were in a mood; thought I'd come and check you hadn't taken your anger out on the locals.'

'I'm not in a mood,' Albinus said, though his tone told a different story.

'Of course you're not. You seem in the highest of spirits.'

'I'm just a bit frustrated,' Albinus said after a pause. 'All I wanted was to go back to Pannonia and reacquaint myself with the legion and get some normality back to my life. Instead, as soon as we arrived, I was told to get back on my horse and come east with you. And then there's the fact that I'm forced away from Faustus. The gods only know when I will get to see him again.'

Albinus tailed off, burying his head in a wine cup. It was true that he seemed destined to spend life on the road. On returning to Pannonia, he had discovered the emperor to be preparing for war with Cassius in the east. The northern legions were in a poor state of morale, with the men not keen on fighting against their fellow Romans, especially as the war against the Germanic tribes was far from over.

Just two months ago, the Fourteenth Legion had been part of a famous victory over a Sarmatian tribe from the eastern steppe, who had fancied their chances of gaining a foothold south of the Danube. Rome had won the battle and taken thousands of Sarmatian warriors as captives, enlisting them into the military as auxiliaries and spreading them across the empire. Some had been sent west to Britannia and Gaul, the rest rode with the advanced force that moved east, commanded by Legate Maximianus.

Albinus had missed the decisive battle against the tribes as he and his century had remained in Carnuntum with Commodus, carrying on in their duty as his protectors. Albinus was envious of his colleagues when they returned victorious from the battlefield. It was a strange feeling to be jealous of men who had just done battle, risked their lives and slain men. He thought it a mark of how much he had changed from the cowardly boy who had run from battle when his home was raided nine years before, the boy who left his father to die for him.

'So, that is what frustrates you?' Maximianus said, 'being away from your son?'

'In part,' Albinus said, his face colouring. It was unlike him to sit in a tavern and drink wine with the commander of his legion, even more unlike him to unload his emotional baggage onto a man who had the lives of five thousand men on his conscience every day. Albinus took a moment to study his commanding officer. Maximianus had always been grey in colour, his eyes were cold and seemed to glow a soft silver. His hair and beard were iron coloured, they had both been black when Albinus had first met him, when he was a tribune serving with the Fourteenth.

War had been kind to Maximianus. He had seen his stock rise under the stewardship of Marcus Aurelius, and Albinus knew he was now one of the emperor's foremost counsellors in the war against the northern tribes. He also knew Maximianus thought very highly of him and this pleased Albinus. The legate had never served with Albinus' father, and Albinus always valued praise more from men who judged him for the man he was and not the legend that had been his father.

'And the rest?' Maximianus asked.

Albinus waved a frustrated hand in the air, unable to put his feelings into words.

'How goes it with Commodus?'

'He is a fourteen-year-old boy with almost unlimited power and more gold than any man could spend in a hundred lifetimes. How do you think it is going?'

Maximianus laughed into his cup. 'Not well then? I have heard mixed things from Rome.'

'What have you heard?'

'That the boy is petulant, prone to fits of anger and jealousy. He spends his time with freedmen, slaves and gladiators when he should be immersing himself in the politics of the empire.'

'True.'

'I have also heard that he can be kind and considerate, that when he is in the right mood, he can take counsel from those close to him.'

'He is close to no one, except maybe Cleander.'

'I hear differently. I hear he has a man at his side who no one dares cross, a man even the great men of Rome are wary of. A man who broke into a senator's home and uncovered information that proved a certain Avidius Cassius was making a move for the throne.'

Albinus was silent, but a small smile played on his lips. 'I hardly think the *great men of Rome* are wary of me,' he said.

'Oh, I believe they are. And rightly so, too. You are a formidable man, Albinus, it does you credit that you cannot see it.'

'I'm nothing more than a farm boy from Pannonia. The day after I retire, I will be forgotten, replaced by another faceless man in a helmet.'

'Oh, no, my friend, in that you are wrong, trust me.'

The two men sat in silence, each savouring the taste of the wine in the heat of the day. Albinus had never experienced anything like it. He thought the summers in Rome had been unbearable, but it seemed each step he took east made the airless furnace of the eternal city seem as cool as a spring morning on the Danube.

'Why are you here?' Albinus asked suddenly. 'Aren't you meant to be in Syria by now?'

'I was. I left a week ago, have been riding hard back west. I had no intention of stopping here, it was pure coincidence I bumped into your *optio* in the street.'

'Where are you going?' Albinus asked, his interest piqued.

Maximianus was leading a combined force of Roman and German auxiliary cavalry in a lightning strike east. His orders were to take the east, province by province, and judge whether the leaders were still loyal to the true emperor or had gone over to the usurper Cassius. So far, they had encountered no real resistance. Any governor or prominent citizen that had pledged their allegiance to Cassius soon changed their minds when Maximianus produced a scroll from beneath his cuirass, complete with the seal of the emperor. The scroll, of course, offered clemency to those whose loyalty had shifted, as was Aurelius' way. Albinus thought it admirable if a little naïve.

It shocked Albinus that so many well-educated men could actually believe Marcus Aurelius to be dead, but such had been the ferocity of Cassius' slander campaign that it seemed half the east had been fooled. Maximianus was to correct them in their ways or replace them with loyal men.

'I am going to find the emperor. I have news from Cappadocia – the governor there has remained loyal throughout the rebellion.'

'Couldn't you send a messenger?'

'No. Not with this.'

Maximianus turned and scanned the dark interior of the tavern. They sat in the far corner of the tavern, which was empty with the exception of the barman and a lone drinker who leant against the bar, clearly already deep within his cups, despite the early hour of the morning.

'Cassius is dead,' Maximianus said in a whisper.

'Jupiter's cock!' Albinus exclaimed, knocking over his cup as his hand rushed to his mouth.

'Way to play it cool, brother,' Maximianus said with a chuckle.

'When? How?'

'Some point in July, killed by one of his own centurions in Alexandria.'

'An assassin?'

Maximianus nodded. 'Of sorts. I cannot be the one to tell you more.'

'What do you mean?'

The legate shuffled uncomfortably on his stool, and Albinus saw his skin redden as he coughed quietly, clearing his throat. 'I was in Antioch when I met two men, riding hard themselves from Alexandria. They told me the news. They are… old friends of yours.'

The blood drained from Albinus' face, his heart beat so hard it hurt his chest. 'Calvus? Habitus?' he muttered in shock.

'Yes,' Maximianus said, nodding slowly. Albinus noticed his superior's face looked pained. 'I have asked them to wait in Antioch until I contact them. You should get there as quickly as you can. There are things you need to know, things only they can tell you.'

Albinus was on the road that same day, saddle-sores all but forgotten, his mind a torrent of dark thoughts. He left Tarsus at the gallop, heading east, a long line of soldiers riding in his wake.

His role in the strike east had originally been to report back to Commodus anything of significance he discovered as they travelled. Commodus was secretly already preparing for life without his father and had been keen to learn as much as he could about the eastern provinces and the men that ruled them, men who could, one day soon, serve him.

Though Maximianus had been supportive of the task he had been given, the strain of commanding such a mixed group had quickly taken its toll, and upon crossing into Asia, he had been forced to give Albinus an independent command.

Albinus had relished the task at first. He was to take his men south as Maximianus continued east, checking in on the coastal cities of Asia and Cilicia, ensuring the local politicians and soldiers alike remained loyal.

He had come across no real resistance, apart from a small band of soldiers in Attaleia who had refused to renounce their oaths to Cassius. Albinus had been forced to discipline the unit of auxiliaries, even going as far as to execute a centurion. It had upset him, but he had hardened his heart and seen the thing through to the bitter end.

Maximianus had been very clear on what action to take if he were to come across any resistance, especially as the convoy was largely made up of Germanic warriors, forced into serving Rome after being defeated in battle. They were to be shown exactly what would happen if they dared cross Rome again. Albinus had thought the sight of their brothers and fathers being killed in battle might have already done the trick, but he knew better than to go against a direct order from his legate, and it turned out that Maximianus was right to be cautious.

Besides, Albinus, had felt the need to show his new-found allies the true meaning of discipline, as the barbarian auxiliaries that accompanied him were, in fact, five hundred cavalry from the Marcomanni, their king, Balomar, among them.

'My king requests we stop a while,' a voice said behind him. It was around midday, the day after they had set off in a hurry from Tarsus. They were on a dust-covered road, dry, yellow grass slipping away to their left, the Mediterranean just visible on the horizon to their right.

Albinus rode at the head of the column, Fullo to one side, Bucco the other. 'We stop when I say,' he said without turning around.

'Maybe you did not hear me, Roman. I said my *king* requests we stop for a break,' the man said, venom oozing through his broken Latin.

'Your *king* holds no power here. *I* am in command, and I say when and where we shall rest. The day is still young, we have much ground to cover.

We shall take a break in due course.' Albinus hated the snooty tone in his voice, and he could feel Fullo at his side, itching to give him some stick the moment the German was out of earshot.

'You Roman dogs have no respect,' the man said, spitting on the ground and turning away.

'Not gonna let him get away with that, are you?' Bucco said, eyebrow raised.

Albinus inhaled slowly, held the breath before releasing. He repeated the act three times. 'There are eighty Roman soldiers in this convoy and five hundred Marcomanni warriors. I need to tread carefully.'

'We can take 'em,' Bucco said with a wink.

'They may be our *allies* for now but that does not mean I trust them as far as I can throw them. Don't forget, it was Balomar that named himself High King of the Germans and started this war in the first place.'

'With the help of Roman gold, obviously,' Fullo added with a sardonic laugh.

'With the help of *Cassius'* gold, not Rome's. But yes, he has been a victim in all this as much as us, I suppose. I wonder if that's why he elected to come south and serve with his men?'

'He didn't have to?' Fullo asked.

'Apparently not. He was instructed to provide five thousand warriors to serve our army. When he arrived at Carnuntum, he offered his own sword to Rome, not sure he ever said why.'

'Well, I for one ain't surprised,' Bucco said. 'You seen their women? Big, hairy creatures. He probably just wanted to get away from his wife!'

The three men broke into laughter, Albinus wiped a tear from his eye. He turned at the sound of hoofbeats, surprised to see the Marcomannic king himself approaching. So far, on the long journey east, Balomar had kept himself to himself, staying with his most trusted men at the rear of the column. He and Albinus hadn't shared so much as a word, which suited Albinus just fine. It appeared, though, that was about to change.

'Centurion,' he called, as his horse drew near. 'May I trouble you for a moment of your time?'

Albinus moved his horse to the side of the road, gesturing for Fullo and Bucco to continue. 'Of course, Lord King. How may I be of service?'

'My man, Adalwin, says you are a pig, your manners more suited to a brothel than the command of an army.'

Albinus smiled. 'He thinks that highly of me? Maybe I should invite him out for dinner?'

Balomar laughed, and Albinus took the opportunity to study him. He had seen the king before, once, whilst on guard duty at Carnuntum as Balomar had entered the legion's fortress for peace talks with the governor of Pannonia. That had been some eight years previous. Time, it seemed, had not been kind to the German.

Albinus always remembered him as being big, but what was once bunched muscle had now clearly run to fat. His hair was iron-grey, streaked with the red that had once shone bright. His beard was thin and patchy, his eyes red-rimmed from lack of sleep and too much wine, and his chin sagged, wobbling as he moved his head. He no longer wore armour; Albinus suspected he could not fit into it anymore, and once more wondered why the king had travelled south with his men. He was staring at a savage-looking scar on the king's right bicep when Balomar caught him looking.

'One of your lot did that,' he said.

'When?' Albinus asked.

'It was the strangest thing. I was wintering in Carrodunum, a small village in Germania. I had met a few of the local chiefs there and was hoping to cement their support for the following year's campaign. The evening went well, the chiefs pledged their men, and I went to sleep drunk and happy. We were awoken in the night by a small band of intruders, Roman intruders. They burst in, killed a few of our men, took the chief of Carrodunum's daughter and ran off into the night. Do you know, after everything that has happened since, I'm not sure I ever really found out why...'

Albinus felt his blood freeze. For a moment, he allowed his memories to control him. He thought back to his journey through Germania, seven years before. He and his seven tent mates had fought their way through the winter, desperate to reach the northern shores of the barbarian land.

One of them, Libo, had not made it back. All for her. *Licina*.

Balomar was staring intently at Albinus, an amused glint in his blood-shot eyes. 'My man Adalwin, though, he never forgets a name. He told me shortly after that he reckoned the men who had attacked us were definitely Roman and that a man named Albinus had commanded them. Something about rescuing a slave? Can't remember her name. Must be a coincidence, eh?' Balomar said, cuffing Albinus lightly on the arm.

'Yes,' Albinus said, remembering a battle in the darkness, a huge barrel of a man attacking him with a long sword. His body seemed to remember sidestepping a death stroke and lunging forward with his own sword, plunging the blade into flesh. 'What a strange coincidence. Albinus is, of course, a very common name,' he found himself saying.

'That so? I had no idea. So, about this break, I am *very* tired.'

'Yes. Yes, I feel a little jaded myself.'

Albinus ordered the column to stop at once. One of the scouts Albinus had out ahead had found a small clutch of trees which would offer at least the officers the pretence of shade for a while, and it was there Albinus was approached by Vettius Sabinianus.

Sabinianus had requested to travel with Albinus when legate Maximianus broke up the army, citing personal reasons for wanting to travel along the coast. Albinus had been frustrated, very much against the idea of an old enemy from Rome attaching himself to his convoy but had been left with little choice but to accept.

The senator had been investigated by the *frumentarii* after Albinus had uncovered vital intel from his home the night he had broken in, but it seemed the man had managed to wriggle free of the noose that had been closing around his neck. He had, though, been ordered north from Rome and then east with the advanced guard of the army. For Sabinianus, that in itself would have been punishment enough.

Albinus noticed with amusement that he still wore his white senator's toga, though it was now more yellow and brown, covered as it was in mud and dust. He had brought with him ten slaves and a cart to carry all his baggage, much to the collective annoyance of everyone in the column. The cart may have been fine on the streets of Rome, but out in the provinces, where the roads were not so maintained and the landscape full of hills and valleys, it had proved to be a nightmare.

'Centurion, I hope I find you well,' Sabinianus said, approaching Albinus.

'Fine, thank you, Senator. Yourself?' Albinus sat in the shade of a tree, sipping water from his canteen and lunching on hard bread and cheese.

'Quite well, yes, thank you,' the senator said, though Albinus could see his discomfort. His bulbous nose was redder than usual, and dry skin was peeling off in white clumps. His eyes were red-rimmed as always, and as he approached, Albinus thought he caught the vinegary scent of cheap wine.

'How are you finding the rigours of the march?' Albinus asked, knowing full well the senator had spent the majority of it in the back of his cart, lounging on layers of cushions and blankets.

'Oh, quite well, I think. You know, I used to be quite the military man in my youth.'

Albinus raised an eyebrow, looking in amusement at the thick layers of fat that rolled around the senator's belly with every step he took. 'That so?' he said.

'The years go by quicker than you realise when you are your age. Enjoy your youth whilst you can,' Sabinianus said with a sneer.

Nearby, some of the German warriors were practising archery. A wooden target had been fashioned from an old shield and nailed up against a tree. Balomar stood and watched as his men took turns to practise, cheering with gusto when one hit the target.

'Be good if one of us Romans could beat them at that, don't you think?' Sabinianus asked.

Albinus grinned, 'Be my guest, Senator, none of my men have any skill with a bow.'

'Maybe I shall,' Sabinianus said before moving off and summoning one of his slaves.

'What's that arsehole want?' Bucco asked, moving over and sitting next to Albinus. It had been a long time since Bucco had stopped the pretence that he was just another legionary in the century, subject to the same discipline as the rest. Wherever Albinus was, Bucco was. The other men in the unit had come to accept it and had even taken to planting ideas in Bucco's head, trying to get him to sell them to their centurion.

'Wants to have an archery competition with the auxiliaries,' Albinus said, thinking it was still strange to call the German warriors that.

'Ha! Well, good luck to him. Those lads would have been training with a bow since they were boys. Pretty lethal with them in battle, I seem to remember.'

'Aye, well, if he wants to make a fool of himself then that's up to him. Oh, here he comes.'

Sabinianus approached the party of warriors, a bow hooked over his right shoulder, a quiver of arrows over his left. 'Mind if I take a turn?'

'This should be good, come on, let's move in for a closer look.' Bucco nudged Albinus, encouraging him to his feet.

'Remember, no matter what we think of him, he *is* a senator of Rome and we, just lowly soldiers.'

'I know.'

'Mind your tongue, Bucco. That's an order.'

'Yes, *sir!*' Bucco said, snapping an ironic salute.

It seemed the rest of Albinus' century was as intrigued as Bucco, and before Sabinianus had even strung his bow, a crowd had gathered, Roman on one side, German the other.

'At what distance do you think your best man could hit the centre of the target, Lord King?' Sabinianus asked Balomar.

The old king mused a moment, rubbing his beard. 'Seventy paces,' he said, gesturing to one of his men. 'Show him, Adalwin.'

The man who had insulted Albinus earlier in the day stepped forward, eyeing Sabinianus with a sneer. He hefted and knocked his bow in one smooth motion, held it taught for five heartbeats before letting loose the arrow. It flew true, hitting just to the right of the shield's centre.

The onlooking Romans booed, and the Germans cheered. Then Sabinianus stepped up. He took longer than Adalwin had, steadying himself and taking a moment to check the fledge of his arrow. It was purple, Albinus noted.

He knocked the arrow and pulled the string back to his ear, visibly straining with the effort. His arms shook and his face went purple. Just as Albinus thought he was going to give up, he let the arrow fly, and it moved faster than his eye could see.

There was a collective gasp before slowly, the whole group burst into applause. Men moved forward, some towards Sabinianus, others to get a closer look at the target. Albinus pushed past his men, eager to see for himself where the arrow had hit.

It was dead centre of the target, the arrow's fledge quivering in the still air.

'Not bad for a fat old senator, eh?' Sabinianus said, standing at Albinus' shoulder.

'No, not bad at all.'

'May we speak in private, Centurion?'

Albinus was unwilling, but he nodded all the same, and the two men moved away from the crowd of soldiers.

'Where are we going?' Sabinianus asked when they were far enough away to not be overheard.

'Antioch.'

'Why?'

'Because that is where I have been ordered to go, with all haste.'

'Legate Maximianus gave you those orders?'

'He did.' Albinus knew this man was a traitor, knew him to be in the payroll of Avidius Cassius – at least he had been. He had been as furious as Commodus when Marcus Aurelius had pardoned the man and sent him east. He was determined not to tell the senator anything. But maybe he could plant an idea in the man's head? Slip him some false information and watch as he dug his own grave. He struggled to mask a smile.

'What are your orders in Antioch? Why is it so important you should go there?'

'I cannot tell you,' Albinus said, turning away to hide his amused expression.

'Lest you forget, Centurion, you are a lowly soldier, and I am a senator of Rome! I *order* you to tell me, this instant.'

Albinus nodded slowly, making a show of his reluctance. 'Fine. I am going there to meet an informer.'

'An informer from Cassius' camp?'

Albinus nodded. He marvelled at the power that knowledge gave him over the man. He knew Cassius was dead, Sabinianus did not.

'Where are you to meet this informer?'

'At the Circus. The northern end, where the Greens have their base.'

The Circus had been built as an almost direct replica of the Hippodrome in Rome. Each race day, thousands of spectators would cram onto the stalls to cheer on their favourite faction and charioteers.

'When are you to meet them?' Sabinianus asked.

'High noon, on the Ides. Hence the hurry.'

It was the seventh of September already. Albinus knew they would be hard-pressed to reach their destination by the middle of the month. But he was desperate to get there as soon as he possibly could.

'And how will you recognise them? Surely, it is a person you know? Or someone with a distinctive mark?'

Albinus paused. 'They will be wearing a hooded cloak, a green scarf wrapped around their neck.'

'Thank you, Centurion,' Sabinianus said, turning and walking away.

Albinus stood in solitude a moment, gazing out south towards the distant Mediterranean. Fullo approached, snapping a salute before speaking. 'You all right, brother?'

'Any of the men in particular pissed you off recently?' Albinus asked.

Fullo smiled in surprise. He rubbed the stubble on his chin, thinking. 'Not really. Tullo's on latrines for the shit state of his kit, Bronto always has something to mutter under his breath every time he's given a job. Actually, Pavo has been a right dick for a week or so now, moaning about his sore arse and thighs.'

'Pavo! Perfect! Go and grab him for me, will you? I've got a little task I need him to carry out.'

'I hope it's dangerous,' Fullo said through a smirk.

'Oh, deadly.'

# CHAPTER XXVI

**September, 175 AD**
**Antioch, Syria**

The heat in the press of the city was intense. The air was filled with the aroma of market day. Albinus pinched his nose as the stink of rotting fish wafted through his nostrils. He was glad to be out of his armour, though he felt naked without it.

They had arrived late the previous evening, and Albinus had managed to see his men billeted inside the city's barracks, as the legion that had been stationed there had marched south some months ago to meet up with the rest of Cassius' army.

He walked through the thronging streets of Antioch, half intrigued with the sights and smells, half dreading the encounter he was walking towards. It had been nearly three years since he had last seen Calvus and Habitus as they had set off on their journey from Carnuntum. Officially, Habitus had been going east to return to the country of his birth, Syria, and open a tavern in which he would finance his retirement, and Calvus had gone with him to help his friend set up his new life, but Albinus knew his old friend was also going on imperial business, working for the *frumentarii*.

Calvus had promised Albinus he would find Licina if he could. Albinus now dreaded his friend had succeeded. He thought of his wife always; it seemed there was no mundane task he could do throughout the day that did not bring back a memory of repeating the same task in her presence or watching her do it herself. When he buffered his boots, he thought of her chiding him, rubbing a dirty cloth over them so he had to start again. When he cooked, it brought back memories of the dinners she used to make them when they would eat alone together in their small apartment.

Grief was his constant companion. It had followed him south to Rome, back north again and now east. Each step he took, every building he saw, he wondered if she had been there, and if she had, what had she been doing? It was a torture he could not escape from.

'You okay?' Bucco asked, grasping his arm and steering him out of the path of a mule-led cart. 'You're in your own little world, there.'

'Sorry,' Albinus muttered, feeling more light-headed with every flutter of his heart. He was sweating buckets beneath his tunic, so much so, the wool stuck to his back and started to itch.

'Let's just get this over with, shall we?' Fullo said, looking uncomfortable himself. Albinus smiled at his friend. Like Albinus, he had grown up with Licina . He may not have loved her as Albinus did, but he was just as anxious to find out how she fared.

They crossed the bridge and entered the western side of the city. To the north of Antioch the river split in two, forming a small island in its centre, which is where the Circus had been constructed. There was a tavern along its western edge, the awning a deep shade of blue.

'That's the place,' Albinus said, wiping sweat from his forehead, where it was immediately replaced.

They entered, Albinus savouring the moment he was safely out of reach of the scorching sun. He wondered briefly if it was ever really winter here.

'There,' Fullo said quietly. Albinus followed his outstretched arm.

Two men sat in a dark corner. One was built like a bull, a bald head a dark shade of red from constant exposure to the sun. His eyes were dark and full of sorrow, and he filled his wine cup from the jug on the table, picking it up with his right hand, using his fingerless left to support the bottom of the jug.

His companion was smaller and thinner, an ageing man, his long, lank hair more white than grey. His beard was scraggly, the colour of old iron. He winced as he adjusted himself on the bench, one hand clutching his side.

'Thought I'd seen the last of you two bastards,' Bucco said, pushing past Albinus.

The two men sat up, feature-splitting grins spreading across their face. 'Gods, brother, how in Hades are you still alive?' Habitus said, wincing even as he walked to Bucco and threw his arms around him.

Calvus stood behind him, and Albinus noticed with horror that his old friend's grin slipped as their eyes met, the pained expression returning.

'It is good to see you, old friend,' Albinus said in greeting. Calvus could not meet his eye for long.

'And it is good to see you, Centurion. Gods, man, but you look like your father.'

'I have twice his hair, and I'm half his weight. I'd hardly say I have a likeness to him!'

'Oh, but you do. It's the eyes, lad, you have his eyes.'

'Nose too,' Bucco chipped in.

'Please, sit,' Calvus said. 'We have much to catch up on.'

The five men sat around the small table. Fullo ordered more wine, and for a time, they just sat and made small talk. Bucco spoke of the recent news from the northern front as well as telling – and exaggerating – the story of the miracle of rainfall in their battle against the Quadi and the fearsome battle fought against the Iazyges on the frozen Danube.

'So, you cracked the ice with axes and then just legged it?' Habitus asked.

'Pretty much. I had to do most of the work. Obviously, the centurion here is still lacking a little brawn,' Bucco said.

Albinus scowled. 'I have more than enough *brawn* to order my soldiers around, thank you very much,' he said.

'I hear you have been to Rome,' Calvus said suddenly.

Albinus nodded but said nothing.

'We were put in charge of keeping the caesar safe,' Fullo said proudly.

'Quite a responsibility,' Calvus said.

'Aye. And not one I much wanted. But I was asked by the emperor himself. Seems Taurus and Maximianus put me forward for it.'

'How is the old first spear?' Habitus asked, eager for news of his old comrades. 'And Rullus? Abas? Seen much of them?' Rullus was the standard bearer of the first cohort, Abas a centurion in the Fourteenth, previously their optio.

'No, not really. I saw them briefly when I returned to the north with Commodus. We spent an evening together, drinking wine and catching up. But I was sent east a couple of days later. Maximianus led the advance guard, Taurus stayed back with the rest of the legion.'

'Aye, we saw the legate,' Calvus said quietly. 'He says the advance guard is mostly made up of Germans? Seems hard to believe.'

'Much has changed since you came east. Most of the tribes are pacified now, though more seem to be coming off the eastern steppe to replace them. Sarmatians, they call them. Damn fine cavalrymen by all accounts. Why don't you tell us what you two have been getting up to for the last three years?'

Calvus and Habitus shared a look, both men clearly reluctant to speak. Albinus felt his dread grow in his belly, an unspeakable pain he could barely contain.

Habitus spoke first. He told them the story of the journey south from Pannonia, of the fight on board the *Neptune's Wings* and its sinking. He showed them the scar of his grievous wound on his leg. He told them everything, of Crassus and his rescuing of them, right up until they arrived at Alexandria.

'Albinus, may I speak to you outside?' Calvus said, putting a hand on Habitus to stop his friend speaking. 'I have some things to tell you, but they are for your ears only.'

'I should go anyway,' Fullo said. 'I have an appointment at the Circus.' He made his farewells and promised to see Calvus and Habitus again before they left the city. He and Albinus shared a look before Fullo departed. 'I'll report back as soon as I can,' was all he said before turning and leaving the tavern.

Calvus guided Albinus out into the sun. Judging by its position, Albinus supposed it was almost noon.

'We found Licina,' Calvus said. He blurted it out, as if the words could not be held in a moment longer.

Albinus didn't speak; he wanted to but found he couldn't. Tears welled in his eyes and his heart was thumping with the power of a galloping horse. He looked into Calvus' eyes and once more saw nothing but sorrow and despair. He knew there could be no good news, no happy ending to his protracted love story. But still, he hoped, still, he prayed.

'She is dead, Albinus,' Calvus said before breaking down.

It was a while before either man spoke. Calvus was sobbing, his shoulders bobbing up and down as he used his good hand to rub the tears from his eyes. Albinus found himself dry-eyed, staring at his friend in disbelief.

He recognised the moment his mind went from surprise to acceptance, skipping the expected anger and crushing grief. He realised he had been grieving for his wife ever since that December day in Carnuntum, when he had rushed back to their apartment – after the events of the parade had played out and Alexander of Abonoteichos had been arrested and taken away – to find her, only to find Meredith sitting on the wooden floor, cradling the baby Faustus.

He closed his eyes. In his mind, he pictured her beautiful face, her emerald-green eyes smiling at him. He saw her holding their son, singing to him softly, easing him off into a dreamless sleep. She had been perfect. She had been his, but she was gone now.

'Tell me everything,' Albinus said, putting a hand on Calvus' shoulder. 'From the beginning.'

For over an hour, they stood out in the heat and dust. Calvus spoke, Albinus listened. The Briton spoke of Alexandria and finding Licina a slave, Decanus her protector. Albinus was surprised to find, once again, his detachment from his emotions. Should he have raged at hearing Decanus had once more been his wife's lover? When Licina had told him of their affair when the two were together in Germania and the lands beyond, Albinus had been distraught, lost in his own melancholy. Soon, the sadness had turned to anger, and he had wanted nothing more than to find Decanus and run him through with his sword.

But Licina had calmed him. She had told him she would never love anyone else and that her feelings for Decanus had been more of friendship than love. She had just done what she felt she had to at the time, what she needed to do to survive.

On Calvus went. To their schemes for how they were going to rid the world of Avidius Cassius and save the empire from civil war. How Licina was determined to be the one to drive the blade into his heart.

'She was ready to die, Albinus. With God as my witness, I say she had seen enough life. I do not think you would have recognised the person she had become.'

'But it was Decanus that did it?'

Calvus nodded. 'He killed the senator, we tried to get to Licina, Habitus and me, but we couldn't cover the ground in ti—,' he broke off again, overcome with emotion.

'How did she die?'

'A blade,' Calvus paused, trying to catch his breath through flooding tears, 'a blade high to the chest. It was a quick death.'

Albinus nodded. He could feel the sadness coming now, creeping upon him like a predator in the shadows. He welcomed its embrace. 'She was the best person I ever met,' he said. 'So strong, so brave, so beautiful.'

'She was one of a kind, Albinus. But I'll say it again, the girl that died in Alexandria was not the girl you married. She had a hard life, and it showed at the end.'

'Thank you, Calvus,' Albinus said. 'Thank you for keeping your word and finding her. Thank you for helping her at the end. Thank you for trying to save her. You are a good man.'

'No, no, I'm not, not really. I've done a lot of bad things in my time, Albinus. Some of them for the right reasons, but they were still bad things. You should take some time for yourself. Grieve. I'm so sorry there isn't a body for you to bury or an urn with her ashes. I should have thought about—'

'No. No, you did all you could. Don't be hard on yourself, brother.' He moved forward and held the Briton in a crushing embrace. He truly was grateful, for the friends he had found, for the things he had experienced. None of it would have happened if his father had never been murdered.

'Why are you smiling?' Calvus asked. 'Oh, Jesu, you're not going mad with grief, are you?'

Albinus laughed. 'No, Calvus. I was just thinking. If the tribes had never united, if there had been no raid on the colony my father started, I would still be there, working on that farm, thinking there was nothing more to life than raising cattle and watching barley sway in the summer breeze.

'I think what I am trying to say is that even though my father's death crushed me, everything in life happens for a reason. You know, when someone says to you when one door closes another opens? Well, my father's death closed a door. But what it opened was a world of possibility. Look what I have done since he died. I have fought in a war, gained promotion and status in the army. I've been to Rome and served as the chief protector to the heir to the empire. And now, I'm here. Not once, when I was growing up on that farm, did I ever think I would be standing in Syria, speaking to a *frumentarii* agent, who just happens to be a close friend. My father never came here, did he?'

'Never left the north, far as I know,' Calvus said.

'Well, there you are. Nor did he ever babysit a petulant brat who will one day rule the world. You know, Calvus, for the first time, I truly believe I can see myself as my own man and not just the son of some famous old soldier. Gods know I loved Licina, and until the last day I draw breath I shall think of her as I wake and as I drift off to sleep and probably a hundred times in between, but for now, I am still here, and I shall endeavour to make the most of every day whilst I am.'

Tears sprung from Calvus' eyes once more. He hugged Albinus again, tighter this time. 'Your father would be so proud of the man you have become. Forget the achievements, though they are, of course, a feat in themselves; you are a fine man, Albinus. Never change.'

'I won't, old friend. Do you ever wonder how they're getting on, back north at the farm?'

'You know, Habitus and I were speaking of that just the other night. Is it still standing?'

'Aye. More and more veterans go there every year once they get their discharge papers. Hanno writes to me once a month, remember him?'

'I do. The African slave. He's just a boy though, surely?'

'A man now, he is of an age to me! He's still running the place but as a freedman. My father was going to free him when he died, he told me so. I freed him after I had joined the legion, and he promised to stay on and keep the place going. By what he says in his letters, the place is almost as big as Carnuntum now! Shame I shall never see it again.'

'Aye, you will, lad. You'll retire there one day and be glad to do so. Surely, it's a good thing, knowing you have a place you belong once your time under the eagle is done.'

'I have a nagging feeling I shall die in battle. I don't know why. Fortuna has been kind to me so far, but I do not think she will protect me forever.'

'Albinus, don't—'

'It's okay, Calvus. When my end comes, I shall meet it with my head held high. Though I would ask one more promise from you, if I may?'

'Anything.'

'If I die, go back north. Go to Meredith, Marcus and Faustus. Keep them safe. Your daughter is a fine woman, you know, you should be so proud of her.'

'I am. Is she well? I was reluctant to ask…' Calvus tailed off.

'She thrives, as does Marcus. He and Faustus are as thick as thieves, they keep her busy.'

'I'm glad to hear it. And I promise you, Albinus, if anything happens to you, I will be there for your son. He shall want for nothing.'

'With you and Meredith watching over him, he'll have all he needs.' Albinus looked back into the tavern. Bucco and Habitus were talking in the corner, and Albinus noticed Habitus still holding his side. 'What's wrong with Habitus? He looks in ill health.'

'He's not long left for this world. He has a growth on his side, gets bigger every day. He barely eats, doesn't sleep much. A dozen apothecaries have given him medicine for the pain, but nothing seems to work.'

'Can they not cut it out?'

Calvus shook his head. 'The growth is too big, connected to too many organs. There is nothing to be done. Trust me, we've been to every doctor in the east.'

'He does not deserve that,' Albinus said quietly.

'No. He is a good man, the best. I feel guilty. This was meant to be his retirement, and all we've done is get ourselves into trouble. He wanted nothing more than to find a nice place to open his tavern, see out his days in the sun. I feel as though I have taken that from him. He would have had a peaceful few years if it were not for me.'

'He'd have had longer if the army had actually discharged him in the right year,' Albinus said. Both men smiled, but they were sad smiles. 'Habitus has always been a warrior, not truly alive unless he was on the battlefield. And judging by the gleam in his eye as he spoke of what the two of you have been getting up to, I think he has enjoyed his retirement a lot more than he would have sitting around all day.'

'That's what he said! Still, if anyone deserved a break, it was him. God knows that man has seen enough death.'

Death.

With a start, Albinus looked up to the sun, seeing it was at least an hour past noon. 'Shit! Calvus, can you come with me? I've somewhere I need to be.'

'Will it be dangerous?' Calvus asked, a look of slight amusement on his face.

'Dangerous? Oh yes, probably.'

'I'm in.'

'Bucco! Bucco, we have to go, now!'

'What's going on?' Habitus asked, rising unsteadily to his feet.

'No time to explain. I've started something potentially foolish, and now, I have to go and finish it. You in?'

'I'll get my bow,' Habitus said, and Albinus noticed a spark of life behind those tired old eyes.

He nodded. 'Then let's go.'

They moved through the crowded streets at a run. Albinus had his sword drawn and used the flat of his blade as a baton, barging people from his path. A peddler, selling cheap knives from a wooden board joined to him by a rope around his neck, stood in Albinus' path. 'Finest iron in Antioch sir, yours for just three denarii.'

'Out of the way, old man,' Albinus shouted. The peddler didn't move, he was a thin, tall man, with lank grey hair and a long beard. His eyes were set too close together, and as Albinus got closer, he saw they were different colours.

'Finest iron in the land, sir, I've a *pugio* here that will serve you twice as well as the one at your waist.'

Albinus felt like drawing his military dagger and showing this old rogue just how good it was. 'I said, out of my way, in the name of the emperor!' He barged into the peddler, sending his wares sprawling over the dust-laden road.

'You owe me for them!' the peddler screamed, but Albinus and his companions were already gone.

They reached the north-east corner of the Circus, and Albinus could hear the distinctive sounds of combat. 'Come on, hurry!' he called to the men behind him, without turning his head to make sure they were still with him.

He rounded the bend, coming across a scene of chaos.

Fullo had twenty men from Albinus' century formed in a semi-circle, all with their shields held high. They seemed to be protecting a hooded man who lay lifeless on the cobbles. To their front was a howling mass of barbarians, hacking and slashing at the Roman shield wall, desperate to break through.

'It must be Balomar's men!' Bucco shouted from Albinus' rear. Albinus turned to see his old comrade straining to keep up. He slowed, Bucco arrived at his shoulder, followed by Calvus and Habitus, who still held his side. Albinus saw the old Syrian was deathly pale, but he had his bow in hand.

'What do we do, sir?' Bucco asked through shallow breaths.

'Charge them, we have to relieve the pressure from Fullo, give the boys a chance to fight back.'

'Oh well, never saw myself dying of old age anyway,' Bucco said, grinning savagely now.

'You have no part in this. Go if you want,' Albinus said to Calvus and Habitus. 'You two have been through enough.'

The two men shared a look, Habitus shook his head, Calvus shrugged.

'I'm already dead, young Albinus, and Calvus here never misses a chance to cleave through barbarians with that axe of his.'

'Well then,' Albinus said, taking a deep breath, 'let's go, shall we?'

They charged.

None of them wore armour, none had shields, but they hit the flank of the Germans, catching them unawares. Albinus thrust his sword into the side of the first man in his path, the blade biting, driving deep. He gave it a twist before heaving it free, blood spattering his face as he did.

A man came at him with a long sword. He wore a heavy woollen tunic above blue trousers. He lifted the blade above his head, aiming a two-handed chop at Albinus' unprotected head. Albinus raised his own sword, ready to block the blow, but it never came. The man fell back, an arrow through his chest.

'Just like old times!' Habitus called from somewhere behind him. 'Watch your right!'

Swivelling, Albinus saw a small man with two knives scampering up to him. Albinus lowered his stance, drew his own knife from his belt and held it in his left hand. His attacker feinted to Albinus' right, but the centurion ignored it, eyes never leaving his assailant's. Albinus then made his move, thrusting to his opponent's left, the attack blocked neatly with the two knives. But Albinus already had his other hand in motion, his knife slipping through the German's guard and burying itself high in his chest. The man screamed, staggered back, and Albinus finished him with a quick thrust to the throat.

Space around him now, Albinus panted as he surveyed the carnage. Fullo and the men from his century were pushing forward, keeping their formation tight. With the sounds of combat hot in his ears, Albinus moved to their rear, desperate to reach the hooded man, who still lay lifeless on the floor.

'Good to see you, sir!' Fullo said from the second rank of the Roman line, his face a mask of drying blood.

'Who the fuck are they?' Albinus said, motioning to the Germans still fighting to break through.

'No idea! We'll work that out later. Sabinianus is with them, though, I saw him a while back.'

'Where?'

'That way, somewhere,' Fullo said, pointing over the Roman shields. 'Whoever the Germans belong to, they're taking orders from him.'

Albinus rushed to the hooded figure on the ground. Gently, he turned the body. Lifeless eyes gazed up at him. 'Oh, Pavo,' he whispered gently. 'I am so sorry.' Albinus had commanded many men in battle, some of whom had inevitably fallen. But never before had he ordered a man to his death the way he had Pavo; the guilt engulfed him like a tidal wave.

His skin was milk-white, though still warm to the touch. Looking down, Albinus saw an arrow protruding from his chest, the fledge was purple.

'That traitorous cur!' he snarled, rising to his feet, sword gripped in a white-knuckled fist. He had to find Sabinianus and end this, now.

'Push, push them back!' he bellowed at his men, who huddled behind their shields. 'Come on, men, you are legionaries of Rome! Kill them!'

Albinus snatched a shield from one of the men in the second rank and forced himself into the Roman line. He slashed at the first man he saw, a young warrior with a shock of blond hair. The German fell back, a hand darting to rub a cut cheek. He was killed by an unseen blow.

'Forwards!' Albinus called, stepping out of the shield wall. He took a blow from a spear on his shield but turned the weapon aside and stabbed his sword into an unarmoured torso.

He saw Calvus to his right, using the haft of his axe to block a cut from a sword. Habitus was just behind him, bow discarded now, slashing with a blade and dancing away from his opponent.

Albinus kept moving forward. He noticed the German ranks were thinning now and guessed their numbers to be less than the Romans. They would not hold for much longer. Winning himself some space, he looked over the Germans' heads and saw Sabinianus standing next to a German with long, blond curls and a moustache to match, wearing a fine coat of fur despite the heat. Sabinianus had his bow to hand, and seeing Albinus, he let fly an arrow. Albinus moved his shield round to cover. The arrow hit with stunning impact, forcing Albinus back a step. The arrow itself had penetrated the shield, the tip exploding through the wood in a burst of splinters. It missed Albinus' hand by inches.

Losing sense of everything else around him, Albinus heaved through the remaining German warriors, killing one and wounding another without thought. Bursting clear, he looked up just in time to see Sabinianus readying another arrow. Albinus hefted his shield, and once more, the arrow struck with lightning force. This time, half the shaft penetrated the shield and the arrowhead grazed his arm.

'Traitor!' he snarled as he sprang into action, throwing aside the shield and charging Sabinianus. The senator did not stay to cross blades, instead ordering his German companion forward as he scurried off behind the nearest building.

'Out of my way,' Albinus said to the German, who had a long sword in hand. 'My quarrel is not with you.'

'Nor did I have one with you, Roman, but your men have brought death to my people. I shall not step aside.'

'So be it.' Albinus moved forward, sword ready, but before the two could engage in combat, a horn blasted off to the right, the ground rumbled and a cavalry squadron came around the corner at full gallop.

The German commander bellowed a quick command to his men, and they hastened away, leaving their dead where they lay. Albinus sheathed his blade, leant forward and put his hands on his knees, breathing hard. He hadn't realised how tired he was, but now the battle fury was leaving him, he just wanted to lie down.

'What in the name of the gods is going on here?' a decurion called, dismounting from a fine black horse.

Albinus stood straight and was about to introduce himself when he noticed the decurion was Flavius Bassus of the Ala Noricorum. 'Well met, brother. I have no time to explain fully, but the men escaping are traitors to the true emperor, in league with the usurper Avidius Cassius. I need a horse, now!'

Albinus watched the decurion, heart pounding, silently urging the man to come to the correct conclusion. The decurion was of equal rank to him, so he had no way of ordering him to obey his commands.

'We are loyal to the true emperor and have remained loyal. I place myself at your command once more, Centurion Silus.'

They rode. Bassus ordered five of his men to dismount and restore order on the street. Albinus, Fullo, Bucco and two legionaries mounted, and the pursuit began.

Their prey was lost to sight, hoofbeats on the dust and reins cut loose

267

with knives were all they left behind. Judging the enemy to be already across the bridge and back on the eastern side of the river, the cavalry squadron followed the carnage they had left in their wake. Tables and chairs lay strewn across the cobbles, citizens still lay where they had been knocked down, and every corner they turned, they found more destruction, more people yelling and pointing, telling them where to go.

Within a matter of heartbeats, they reached the eastern limits of the city. Clattering through the eastern gate, they did not see the ambush that lay in wait for them.

The Germans had dismounted and as soon as the Roman convoy was through the gate, they let loose a storm of spears. Albinus could do nothing but flinch as a spear tore past his face, burying itself in the man next to him. Fullo's horse was hit, and he fell screaming to the cobbles, his armour rattling as he bounced off the cut stone before lying in a heap at the side of the road. Bucco reacted first. Yanking the reins of his mount, he turned the beast and charged his nearest foe, leaning down to the right and swiping his sword at a man's head.

'Break! We need to break!' Albinus screamed at Bassus.

Bassus nodded and roared, 'At my command, split and ride them down!'

The men of the Ala Noricorum obeyed the command with glee. Horses charged left and right, ploughing through the Germani footmen as if they were made of mere straw.

Albinus kicked his mount into life, and the beast gave a snort as it leapt into action. It kicked out with a front leg, and Albinus heard the audible snap of bone, and a warrior fell screaming to the floor. He took the next one with a chopping blow to the top of the head before blocking a spear-thrust with his blade, forcing the spear wide and running the man through with his sword.

He was through them before he knew it, nothing to his front but open countryside. Turning back, he surveyed the last of the battle. Bucco was still engaged in combat but even as Albinus watched, Bassus trotted over and took Bucco's opponent in the back. Fullo was back on his feet, looking sore and sorry for himself, but it seemed he had survived his fall with nothing more than bumps and bruises.

'You never were a good rider,' Albinus said through a smile as he approached his friend, dismounting slowly now the aches of battle were starting to take their toll.

'You know I hate horses,' Fullo said. 'Where's Sabinianus then?'

'Gone,' Albinus said and spat in disgust. 'A coin for the man who finds me a survivor,' he said to the auxiliaries.

'Never a dull day when Centurion Silus is around, it seems,' Bassus said, approaching with a grin. 'Care to tell me what this is all about?'

Albinus smiled. 'A traitorous senator, a plot to overthrow the emperor, impending civil war, you been living in a ditch? Why are you here, anyway?'

'Legate Maximianus ordered us to replace the old garrison here. Had been a nice gig until you lot turned up and painted the town red. What's the plan then?'

Albinus slowed his breathing, composing his thoughts. He closed his eyes, but all he could see was Licina. *Focus.*

'Can you send riders out? These men were under the command of a senator, one of Cassius' men. I need to know where he went.'

'Consider it done.'

A commotion to their rear, turning, Albinus saw two auxiliaries lifting a half-dead German to his feet. He had a grievous wound to his left shoulder, blood pumped from it, bright in the sunlight. 'And keep that man alive. I have questions that need answering.'

# CHAPTER XXVII

**September, 175 AD**
**Antioch, Syria**

Habitus was dead.

Albinus and the men of the Ala Noricorum rode back through the streets of Antioch until they reached the Circus. The five men Bassus had left at the scene of the battle had done a decent job of clearing away the bodies. The Germani warriors lay heaped in a pile under an awning at the side of the road. Calvus sat in the shade of the Circus, cradling his dead friend.

'Oh Calvus,' Albinus said, slumping to his knees beside the Briton. 'I am so sorry.'

'It's ok, Albinus,' Calvus said gently. 'He was dead already. This has just saved him a lot of pain. It is, I think, what he would have wanted.'

Calvus was stroking Habitus' hair with a shaking hand. 'I am so sorry, my friend,' he whispered to the corpse, 'but what an adventure we had.'

Albinus cried. He cried not just for Habitus, but for Libo, lost in a pointless fight in the middle of Germania, dying for a cause not his own. For Longus, lost in battle against the tribes. For his father, who fought and died to protect a son he had never truly bonded with. For his mother, lost too soon to plague. For his wife, the shining jewel in a world of blood and dust.

'Come on, Albinus,' Fullo said gently at his shoulder. 'There's nothing you can do for him now. Let's question this prisoner whilst we can get some answers.'

Albinus nodded and rose unsteadily, feeling the weight of the world on his shoulders. *Everyone I love dies*, he thought despairingly. He felt the burden of command weigh heavier on his shoulders than it ever had before. Looking on the scene of carnage outside the Circus, the blood on the cobbles, Pavo's body still lying where he died, he thought how pointless it all was. What business of his was it who sat on the throne in Rome? He had no need of involving himself in the affairs of emperors and kings, he just wanted to go home. He wanted to hold his son, to shield him from this godless world and the greedy men who ruled it.

Fullo guided Albinus into a building, a butcher's by the look of it. Albinus slumped down on a wooden stool, taking an offered cup of wine. It was strong, unwatered. He thought it just what he needed, a way to help him forget, to wash away the guilt.

The German warrior was stripped naked, lying flat on the butcher's table. His hands were tied to the table legs with lengths of rope, and his wound had been treated with fire; the stench of burning skin filled the room.

'What do you want to know?' Bassus asked Albinus. He stood over the naked German, a red-hot knife gleaming orange in a gloved hand.

'I need to know who the German commander is. I need to know his links to senator Sabinianus and where the rogue has gone. Avidius Cassius is dead, but I don't think Sabinianus knows that yet. Surely, he would go south? Thinking to link up with his master.'

The questioning began. The German had some Latin, but it was halting, and twice he passed out from the blood loss and pain. Albinus sat on the stool, silent, waiting for the wine to dull his pain, waiting for his mind to sharpen. Neither happened.

The day slipped away, and Albinus was dimly aware of the sun sliding over the horizon, its light through the open doorway turning from gold to orange. Dusk approached, and they had achieved nothing.

'He doesn't know anything, does he?' Albinus said after a time. He stood, swayed, sat back down and poured himself more wine.

Bassus sat next to Albinus. He wore an old apron and was covered in blood. 'He serves Bandanasp of the Iazyges. They're one of the tribes that surrendered to us in the last year.'

'We fought them in the winter a couple of years ago, when the river had frozen over, you remember?'

'Aye, some battle that was. Seem to remember it was you that saved the day? Smashing the ice and causing havoc for their cavalry. Quite the hero, aren't you?'

'I'm no hero. So, what's the link between this Bandanasp and Sabinianus? Where did they meet? Why are they allies?'

'No idea. This lad's just a soldier, knows nothing. Though it would seem Bandanasp had taken Cassius' coin, but as to their motive or objective...' Bassus trailed off, making an evasive gesture with his hand.

'The men you sent out come back yet?'

'No, they've been too long. I've sent more men out to look for them, I hope they're all back before nightfall.'

'So, we know nothing. Great.'

'Sleep, Centurion. I have a feeling that come morning, you are going to be in need of your wits. Remember your responsibilities, you're no good to your men in your current state.'

'Aye, I know,' Albinus slurred. He slept.

He awoke the next morning to a pounding headache and an eager Bassus shaking him gently. 'We have news,' was all he said before handing him a skin of water.

Albinus sat up, smacking together dry lips before mumbling a curse. How much had he had to drink the day before? He drank from the skin, and putting it down, suddenly remembered that Licina was dead, as was Habitus. He was struck by melancholy once more.

'What news?' he said at last as he made his way out into the courtyard of the barracks. He realised he couldn't even remember coming here the previous night and made a mental note to stop drinking.

'My men finally came in some time after the third hour of the night. Your man went north, not south. Must be heading back west, surely? There's nowhere for him to run to if he stays north or turns east.'

'North? What help does he expect to find there? Doesn't make any sense.'

'I was thinking, just a thought, probably nothing...' Bassus trailed off.

'What?'

'Well, it's just… where's the emperor? He must be somewhere over the Bosporus now, right?'

'I'd guess. Why?' Albinus wondered where Bassus was going with this. It was true Marcus Aurelius and his entourage were making their way east, but their procession would be slow, their numbers huge. What could Sabinianus hope to achieve by going back to them?

'Well, I've never been much of a thinker, but I have been pondering this half the night. Say you were in league with Cassius, and you knew your master had been killed and that the rebellion was over. What would you do?'

'Hide, fall on my sword, maybe both? What's your point, Bassus? My head is sore and my attention span short, get to the point.'

'Well, what if you didn't want to hide or top yourself? You'd run back to the emperor, once again assuring of your absolute loyalty, and then cause some mischief.'

Albinus tried to kick the tired cogs of his mind into action. He knew Sabinianus, knew him to be a man with a wide span of connections and traitorous intentions. He also knew he was ambitious, greedy and clever.

His thoughts rolled back to a game of dice in Rome, a beaten-up legionary that led to a burglary. The Owl, The Mouse, The Fox.

'You ever heard of Claudius Dryantius?' Albinus said suddenly.

'Vaguely. Some senator isn't he?'

'Was he with the imperial procession?'

'How would I know?'

'He was in Pannonia when we left with Maximianus though, wasn't he?' Another shrug.

'Gods man, why don't you know!'

'I'm just a cavalry commander, you're the one that was in tight with Commodus. If anyone would know, I'd wager it was you.'

'Get your men mounted, Bassus, we need to go, now!'

They were away from Antioch before midday. Once more, Albinus drove the men on with unrelenting haste. Each man rode with a remount in tow, and at every *mansio* they passed, he ensured each man left with two fresh horses.

273

It was at the second one of these that Fullo pulled Albinus to one side. 'Brother, what exactly is going on here? Why is there such a need to get back to court?'

'I have a feeling in my gut.'

'Sure that's not just from the wine?' Bucco chipped in.

'No. Sabinianus is up to something. We have to find out what and stop him.'

'But what could he be doing? The emperor and Commodus have half the Praetorian Guard with them, plus three legions! And anyway, now that Cassius is dead, what good will it do him to kill the emperor?'

'If you were intent on hurting the emperor, what would you do?'

'I'd kill his heir,' Calvus said, walking up to the group. 'I'd set a trap, lure Commodus from the safety of the procession and kill him. Aurelius is an old man; anything could happen if he died without naming a successor. Plus, his son's death might just be enough to finish him off, he seems to have been in ill health for an age.'

'Exactly,' Albinus said. 'I refuse to believe Sabinianus isn't up to something, and I can see no other reason for him going north than to set some sort of trap. Fullo, how far behind us are Balomar and his men?'

'Half a day at least,' Fullo said. Albinus had ordered Balomar and his Germans to stay outside of Antioch when he had entered. They had marched around the city and set up camp on its south side, the side Albinus had expected to be leaving by. He cursed leaving them behind, five hundred men would come in very handy about now.

'We need to wait for them,' Albinus said. 'Calvus, would you go ahead for us? I need to know where the procession is and where they are going. I need to know where Commodus is.'

'Of course,' Calvus said, already saddling a horse. 'Can I take three men with me? I can use them as messengers between us.' Bassus nodded and ordered three of his men to join the Briton. 'Oh, one other thing,' Calvus said. 'You know who else is with the emperor, don't you? Avidius Maecianus.'

'Shit,' Albinus said. Once more, he thought back to Rome. 'Go, Calvus, report back as quick as you can.'

Back on the road and it was all Albinus could do to keep his mind from breaking into a thousand pieces. The same three men that had seemingly been conspiring in Rome were once more at large. Gaius Vettius Sabinianus had been known as The Owl. Claudius Dryantius had been The Mouse. Avidius Maecianus had been The Fox. Dryantius, Albinus knew, had kept very close to Commodus in the weeks since Cassius' rebellion had become public knowledge. He had been quick to denounce his father-in-law, reiterated his loyalty to Marcus Aurelius and made sure he was seen at court every day. Albinus thought it fitting they called him The Mouse: quiet, tiny, obscure. His role had been to nestle himself close to the imperial family, listen to their gossip, keep quiet about what he knew. He had played his part well.

Avidius Maecianus was another who had stayed close to the emperor as news of his father's treachery spread. Albinus remembered he had claimed to have had no contact with his father, and he was as surprised as everyone else at the news. He had been placed under guard, but not arrest, still free to come and go as he pleased. His properties had been searched as thoroughly as those owned by Sabinianus, but nothing of note had been found. But he was The Fox: cunning, slippery, clever. Albinus could picture the man whispering treason into listening ears, planting seeds that would one day grow into poisonous trees.

Albinus was missing something, he was sure of that, but try as he might, he could not place what it was, or *who* it was.

*Cleander.*

The freedman's name seemed to fix itself in his mind. He doubted himself though, unsure whether he was mixing his personal feelings for the man with something else. But still, there was something not right about him.

It was mid-morning the following day when they had news. One of Bassus' men found the convoy on the road, rounding the bend of the Mediterranean, turning west from their northern path. 'They're in Halala. The Caesar Commodus is not with them, he has been ordered back to Byzantium on imperial business, Calvus says to say he does not know what.'

'Shit,' Albinus said. His mind was already in action, piecing together a plan. 'How in Mars' name are we going to get to Byzantium quicker than Commodus? He's two days ahead of us at least.'

'There was one more thing, sir,' the auxiliary said, shifting nervously from one foot to another.

'Spit it out, man,' Bassus said in an impatient tone.

'It's the empress, sir, Faustina, she has been taken ill.'

'I do not see how that is relevant,' Balomar said. He still wore just a grubby tunic with a sword strapped to his waist. Keeping up with the fast pace of the ride north had visibly drained him, but Albinus respected him for keeping his silence about it.

'Faustina was supposedly in on the coup to get Cassius on the throne,' Albinus said. 'Calvus told me back in Antioch.'

No one spoke. It seemed as if everyone took an in-breath at the same time. 'The emperor's wife, Commodus' own mother, was in on a plot to put some senator on the throne? That doesn't make sense,' Fullo said. He rubbed the white scars on his forehead, as was his habit when thinking.

'It does if she and Cassius were lovers,' Albinus said through a huff of exasperation. 'And it does not matter to us now. We *have* to get to Commodus. The only thing I can think of is that Sabinianus and his cronies are involved in a plot to take out Commodus. You take him out, then it just leaves one old man in ill health on the throne with no heir. Come on, men, think!'

'You need a boat,' Balomar said. 'Only way to get there faster than a horse would be by sea, right?'

'Know anyone with a fleet of ships that can take five hundred men and their horses back west today, do you?' Bucco said with a snort.

'So, we steal one, obvious isn't it? Or are you Romans above such things?'

'We don't need five hundred men,' Albinus said, a wry grin fixing his face, 'and we don't even need the horses, not if we can sail into Byzantium itself.'

A day later, they were aboard a ship. *Poseidon's Doom* was a particularly poor name for a ship that braved the Mediterranean no matter the weather, but it seemed sturdy enough, and the captain came across as both humble and steadfast.

They battled the winds as they travelled westwards, Albinus insisting they stop for nothing. Three days sailing against an eastern wind brought

276

them to Byzantium. The ship had barely anchored at the docks as Albinus launched himself onto dry land and scurried off into the city.

It took them half an hour to reach the palace through thronging streets that reminded Albinus too much of Rome. Upon arrival, he was told swiftly that Commodus had not yet reached the city, but that he had been expected the previous day.

'What do we do?' Fullo asked, chewing loudly on a hard loaf.

'We need horses. Gods, I've been a fool! I should have thought through a proper plan, we should have brought the rest of our men and Balomar's.'

'But you said it yourself, we had to do something. So, what do we do?'

'I don't know, Fullo! I don't know.' Albinus walked off, shaking his head in disgust. He kicked an amphora that sat on the floor, then cursed at the sharp pain that slithered up his foot.

'You there,' Fullo said to the palace official Albinus had been speaking to. 'Why is Commodus coming here?'

The official looked confused. He was a eunuch, judging by his hairless face and squeak of a voice. 'Why, surely, you know?' He arched an eyebrow then settled it down as his face moved into a smug grin. Knowledge is power, and he was going to enjoy his moment of power over a group of soldiers.

'The Caesar Commodus is here to accept the formal surrender of King Bandanasp of the Iazyges tribe. There have been negotiations for quite some time, as I am sure you are aware, and Bandanasp has already offered one thousand men in service to his eminence Marcus Aurelius. But now, negotiations are finally at a conclusion, and Bandanasp is here in person to bend the knee and accept the rule of Rome.'

The eunuch's speech was greeted with stunned silence.

'King?!' Balomar roared, rousing himself from his surprise. 'That cock-sucking leech calls himself a king?'

'Friend, you are mistaken,' Calvus said, stepping forward and placing his good hand on the eunuch's arm. 'We saw Bandanasp ourselves, not three days ago. He was in Syria, he and his men attacked the emperor's soldiers in the streets.'

The eunuch stepped back, out of range of Calvus' touch. 'I think it is *you* that is mistaken, citizen. King Bandanasp is in this palace and has been for the last week.'

And just like that, the pieces of the puzzle clicked together. 'Who brought the news of Bandanasp's arrival to court?' Albinus asked in a quiet voice.

'Why, the senator Claudius Dryantius. He had been the one negotiating the surrender of the tribe. He stayed behind to complete the negotiations when the imperial procession continued east.'

'And what of Avidius Maecianus? Son of the newly dead pretender to the throne?'

'He is here, under guard. The emperor decreed this to be the best place for him, close enough to be able to attend the emperor if needed but far enough away to stay out of trouble. What do you mean by newly dead? Has something happened? Has there been a battle?'

'Take us to him, and Bandanasp, now, if you'd please.'

'Well, I'm not sure what legal right you think you—'

Fullo unsheathed his sword and held it to the eunuch's throat. Two palace guards immediately lowered their spears at Fullo. They soon raised them again, though, when they saw the ring of swords behind the *optio*. '*This* is our legal right, eunuch, take us to him, now.'

The palace was grander than anything Albinus had seen back in Rome: golden statues and the finest tapestries everywhere the eye could see, all above a floor of solid marble. He ignored it all.

They were shown into a vast chamber that could have held a chariot race and still left room for spectators to sit along the walls. The room was lit by huge iron braziers and smelt heavily of incense. At its centre was a ring of couches where two men dined on roasted boar whilst a handful of others stood around them, whispering and trying to look important.

Albinus recognised Avidius Maecianus the moment he saw him. He was a good-looking man with fine locks of dark hair, brown eyes and an easy smile that revealed two neat rows of gleaming white teeth. He stood as the soldiers approached, with the casual arrogance of all high-born young men.

Reclining on the couch opposite him was a heavy-set man with a long mane of blonde hair and beard to match. Even from a distance, it was evident he was uncomfortable in his surroundings and attire, as he kept shifting his toga whilst wearing a frown as if unsure where the garment should sit on his shoulder.

'Is that him?' Albinus spoke into the silence.

'No,' Balomar said.

'What is the meaning of this? In the name of Jupiter Maximus, I command you to tell me who you are and why you are here disturbing my lunch.' He spoke well, Maecianus, his voice hitting all the tones of an aristocrat.

'You must think well of yourself, sir, if you believe you speak for Jupiter,' Albinus said. He had slowed his pace now and tried to keep his face impassive, not wanting the malice to show. He thought of his father and how he would treat a merchant trying to overcharge him at market.

'I am the son of Avidius Cassius, the man you may, one day, bend the knee to. It would not be wise to cross me, Centurion... sorry, I did not catch your name?'

'Silus, Centurion Albinus Silus. Fourteenth Legion, sixth century, tenth cohort.'

'Ahh, a junior man. In that case, maybe I can forgive your insolence for ignorance. Not every day someone like yourself gets an audience with me.'

'Your father is dead, his rebellion at an end,' Albinus said, smiling coldly as Maecianus' face dropped. 'Killed by one of his own centurions, apparently. Seems your father should have been nicer to *men like me*.'

'You lie!'

'I do not. He was killed in Alexandria, my friend here saw it first-hand,' Albinus said, pointing to Calvus.

'He's right. Saw his head roll in the dust with my own eyes.'

'And as for men like you,' Albinus continued, moving within striking distance. 'I am the man that was charged with the care of our caesar when he first went north. I am the man who protected him throughout his stay in Rome, and I am the man who is going to save him from whatever trap you and your cronies think you are luring him into. What do you have planned?'

Maecianus sniffed and raised his head so he was looking down at Albinus through his nose. 'As if I would tell you.'

'Aye. Fair enough.'

In one smooth motion, Albinus whipped his sword free from his waist and plunged the tip into Maecianus' belly, the blade ripping free out of his back. 'This for my father. For the thousands of lives lost thanks to your cursed father and his ambition. This is for my wife.'

He ripped the blade clear in a shower of blood before hacking down into Maecianus' head, which split open like a ripe melon.

Wrenching his blade free once Maecianus had slumped, lifeless to the floor, he turned to Balomar. 'Find out who he is and what he knows,' he said, motioning to the German masquerading as Bandanasp.

Hands on his shoulders brought Albinus slowly back to his senses. They were surrounded by a ring of palace guards, each with shield and spear. Albinus circled, making sure to catch the eye of each one. 'This man was a traitor, the son of a traitor, and he has died a traitor's death, just as his father did. He was complicit in a plot to murder our caesar, the heir to the empire. What you have seen today is justice and nothing more. My name is Albinus Silus, I am the man that was charged with the caesar's life. I made a promise to our emperor, and I fully intend on keeping it. But now, I need your help to do so.'

There was a squeal in the following silence. Turning, Albinus saw Balomar with his hands around the German pretender's neck. He watched on absently as the life drained from the big blonde's eyes. 'Who was he?'

'Some cousin of Bandanasp, it seems. I have to say there is a likeness.' It was Adalwin who spoke while Balomar sat staring at the corpse he had just created.

'Did he know of their plans?'

'Commodus and his entourage are to be ambushed on the road, half a day's hard ride from here.'

'Dryantius?'

'Will lead the ambush. They have a man, he said he didn't know who, in on it, close to Commodus. He's going to be holding their convoy up, giving Bandanasp and Sabinianus time to catch them up.'

'They'll be surrounded, cut off east and west.'

'Sounds like that's the plan.'

'Can we get there in time?' Calvus asked as he rubbed his bald head with the stump of his left hand.

'We have to try, lad,' Bucco said, moving so he stood shoulder to shoulder with the centurion. 'We're with you, until the end.'

# CHAPTER XXVIII

**September, 175 AD**
**East Of Byzantium, Bithynia**

Two hundred armed men rode out of Byzantium and onto the eastern plains. Each had a remount; none had any provisions, save for a water skin. They were riding to war.

They hurtled through countryside that burst with life, a burning sun high in the clear, blue sky. They had no idea of where Commodus was, or his pursuers, or even where the ambush was to take place, though Albinus figured it must be on the main road that ran east from Byzantium.

Three hours' hard riding and the initial adrenalin of charging into battle had worn off, and they were just plain tired. Two centuries of the palace guard accompanied them, auxiliary troops, Thracian by birth. Each was a natural in the saddle. Albinus and his men still were not.

Albinus was just about to take out his frustrations on Bucco, who was moaning about his saddle-sores, when one of the auxiliaries let out a cry and pointed east.

'Dust cloud, sir! On the horizon.'

Albinus squinted, staring intently into the distance. The sun was high and to his right, its glare reflecting off the cobbled road, making visibility difficult. They were halfway up a gentle incline, and Albinus kicked his mount into a gallop, cresting the rise in a matter of heartbeats. Here, he slowed the mount to a stop, and shielding his eyes with his hand, he looked hard.

Ahead of him was a sweeping valley, lined on one side by a thick crop of trees and on the other, jagged rock. There was, indeed, a dust cloud on the horizon, the other side of the valley, but Albinus could not make out what, or more importantly who, was causing it.

'I need two volunteers,' he called to the column behind him, 'two men with sharp eyes.'

Two men came forward, both from the auxiliary rank, who had been posted at the palace. 'I served as a scout when we fought in the eastern wars,' a grizzled veteran said. 'Name's Thrax. This here is my little brother, Diomedes, he's the sharpest eyes of any man in our unit.'

Albinus smiled. 'Thrax and Diomedes, hey. Don't suppose you were given those names at birth, were you?'

Thrax chuckled. 'You know as well as I do you Romans can't understand a word of our language, let alone write it down. We were given new names when we signed up, happen to quite like mine, personally.'

'Well, Thrax and Diomedes, well met. I need you to go ahead to the next ridge, tell me what you can see. Also, check out those trees for me, would you? Wouldn't be difficult to hide a hundred men in there.'

Thrax and Diomedes saluted before riding off. Albinus ordered the men to dismount and water their horses, and he did the same.

'I've got a question, sir,' Bucco said, sliding up to Albinus and speaking quietly. 'This Claudius Dryantius left with another unit of auxiliary, right?'

Albinus nodded. 'I know what you're going to say, he left with more Thracians, so how can we trust this lot, yes?'

'Well, yes. Ain't you worried?'

'A bit. But Dryantius must have taken that specific unit with him for a reason; I'd guess they've been paid with some of Cassius' gold. This lot didn't put up a fight when we killed Maecianus and the German, so I'm assuming they're loyal? It's in the hands of the gods, brother.'

'You put too much faith in them if you ask me.'

'I didn't.'

Albinus walked off, not wanting to start an argument with his old friend. He watched intently as Thrax and Diomedes reached the base of the valley. Diomedes carried on up the other side whilst Thrax dismounted and moved towards the trees. Albinus held his breath. He had a nagging feeling in his gut, a worry he couldn't quite shake. It was the perfect spot for an ambush: enough cover to hide a unit of Thracians, far enough away from Byzantium to not be seen. He chewed his lip absently.

Thrax approached the trees and stopped. Albinus watched him enter cautiously, spear in hand. He counted his heartbeats, got to thirty, Thrax had still not reappeared.

'Something's wrong,' he said, more to himself than anyone else.

'What?' Fullo asked. The *optio* was rubbing a hand across his scarred forehead, betraying his anxiety.

'He's been in there too long.'

Diomedes crested the rise; he was there no more than the count of twenty before he turned his horse and galloped back down the slope. The dust cloud beyond the ridge was closer now, Albinus thought it almost looked like two separate clouds.

Diomedes reached the bottom of the hill and was passing the treeline. Albinus could hear him calling for Thrax as he rode. He was halfway along the treeline when a spear flew out and hit him high in the chest. Diomedes sagged in the saddle but managed to stay mounted. The horse, sensing its rider's fear, spurred once more into a gallop and Diomedes fell, lifeless, halfway up the rise to Albinus.

'Mount up!' Albinus roared. 'Spears and shields, helmets on, ready for battle!'

He grabbed his helmet from the hook on the side of his saddle and turned back to the dust cloud, growing ever closer. He was certain there were two. The first was about to crest the ridge ahead and the second must have been half a mile behind.

'Orders?' Fullo asked.

'Hold until we see what's coming. Every man to be mounted and awaiting the order to charge.'

*Jupiter Maximus, hear my prayers. Mars be with me. Watch over my men, see them safe.*

He prayed silently, eyes closed, face raised to the heavens.

In a burst of colour and noise, the first column crested the ridge ahead, and Albinus saw the imperial standard held high by a rider at the column's front. He could see immediately they were Praetorian Guard. They wore plain mail shirts over white tunics, their shields were black, a white scorpion painted on the front. Albinus made a rough estimate of their number and judged it to be roughly five hundred men. A single cohort then, charged with protecting Commodus as he journeyed back west.

At once, there was movement in the trees. Armed men streamed onto the road. Their armour was the same as the Thracians that accompanied Albinus. Each man had a short-sleeved mail shirt, the blue sleeves of their tunics showing from beneath. Each man carried a spear and circular shield.

'Make ready to charge!' Albinus bellowed. He turned back to his men. Bucco and Fullo were to his right, the older man checking the *optio's* helmet strap, not that Fullo needed it checking. He nodded to both men. 'This will be bloody,' he said.

'Good,' Bucco said through a wicked grin. 'Take it from me, lad, getting old sucks. You're not missing out on anything.' There was laughter from those in earshot. Nothing calms a soldier's nerves like a cheap joke.

On Albinus' other side were Calvus, Balomar and his three companions. 'None of you need to be here,' he said.

'I am sworn to serve my emperor,' Calvus said. 'Though God himself knows how I'm going to ride and fight.' He held up his stumped left hand to another chorus of laughter.

'I have unfinished business with that whoreson Bandanasp, we'll fight,' Balomar said, unsheathing his long sword and testing its edge on the air.

Albinus raised himself in the saddle, looking back on the men who had followed him. 'Those men down there are not your brothers,' he called. 'They are traitors! They have taken the pretender's coin and have turned their back on Rome, on you!'

There were growls of ascent, mumblings about missing out on coin and slurs on their countrymen's honour. 'I need you to ride now! To kill! For Rome! For the true emperor!'

Albinus hauled free his sword and held it high above his head, whirling the blade in the air. He kicked his mount into motion, the beast rearing before setting off at the gallop. Albinus lowered his blade, pointing it at the enemy.

He could see Commodus now, the caesar rode under a standard that bore an image of his father. He was surrounded by a ring of shields, his shock of dark hair plastered over his face. He could fight, Albinus knew, and worried he would not be content to sit back and let the soldiers fight for him. He was reckless and impulsive and would be eager to prove himself in battle.

They charged down the slope, Albinus watching on helplessly as the Praetorians smashed into the Thracian shield wall, horses falling in droves under the reach of the long spears. Heartbeats later, Albinus and his men hit the Thracian footmen, sealing them into a circle of flaying hoofbeats and spears. Whoever commanded them had not been idle – seeing Albinus and his men charge down the slope, he had their rear ranks form up two deep, the front rank kneeling and the second rank standing, so they presented a solid wall of spear tips and shields.

Albinus knocked aside the nearest spear with his sword and lunged down with the blade, but his short sword was not built for fighting on horseback, and he cut nothing but air. A moment later, he was defending for his life as two men reached out and grabbed his ankle and tried to heave him from the safety of his mount.

He lashed out with his foot, cut down with his sword and felt it bite deep into an unseen arm. Then he was free and once more he cut down with his blade, this time sending it bouncing off a helmet. He kicked his horse forward, deeper into enemy ranks. He wanted to look up and see how the Praetorians fared, but he dared not take his eyes off the enemy below. Another spear ripped past his face, and Albinus took his left hand off the reins and grabbed hold, pulling it towards him. Heaving it up past his body, he saw the soldier at the end being tugged helplessly along. He gave one more pull and watched with satisfaction as the soldier fell impotently onto the end of his sword.

'Men on the hilltop!' A voice shouted near Albinus. He glanced up, and sure enough, saw another line of horsemen on the ridge above. There were no standards, each man seemingly armed with a shield and long sword. They were the Iazyges. Sabinianus had arrived to put the cork on his trap.

'We have to break through to the Praetorians!' Albinus shouted. He hacked down once more, the blade digging through armour and burying itself in a shoulder. He tried to heave it free, but it was stuck. He let it go and moved on.

Another spear licked at his face, and this time, Albinus caught it two-handed and pulled it towards him. The Thracian at the other end had the sense to let go, and Albinus turned it in his hands, spear tip down, and sent it crashing down into a man's face. 'Forwards!' he bellowed.

The stench of battle filled his nostrils as he watched his mount toss two men from his path. Sweat and leather, blood and shit. Overhead, carrion birds were already circling, eager to begin their feasting at the fighting's end. A quick look up told Albinus he was only two ranks away from breaking through to Commodus. He called his name but heard no reply.

He was readying his spear for another strike when he felt his mount give beneath him, stagger and then start to fall slowly to the right. 'Shit,' he muttered, freeing his feet and leaping clear, heedless of the enemy below him. He fell hard to the cobbled road and rolled onto a corpse still spouting blood from a gash to the throat. He rose quickly, shuffling like a spider as he checked for imminent danger, though luckily there was none. He grabbed a discarded shield and sword from the ground, both unfamiliar to the touch. The shield was lighter than the one he used in the legions, it was small and round, offering him less protection. The sword, on the other hand, was longer and heavier, the blade curved at the end. It was a slashing sword, one that required much strength but little skill. It would serve.

He moved forward, feeling his men, still mounted, pushing towards him. He ducked under a thrown spear then lunged forward, striking out with the shield before cleaving the heavy sword through helmet and skull. He wrenched it free in a spray of blood and brains, screaming Commodus' name once more.

'Centurion!' came a reply from ahead of him, 'Fancy seeing you here!'

Commodus was blood-splattered, panting, but otherwise seemed unhurt. The two men grinned at each other, and feeling a renewed surge of energy, Albinus leapt once more into the fray.

Horses pushed past him as the loyal Thracians brought death to their brothers. Albinus let them move ahead, absently killing a wounded man who was reaching for a knife on the ground. 'What's your plan?' Balomar shouted, vaulting down from the saddle with the grace of a man half his age. He was enjoying himself, Albinus saw.

'Push through to Commodus and protect him. These men are finished, but the Germans will be much a much harder nut to crack.'

'Just you make sure that whoreson Bandanasp is left for me.'

They made it through to the Praetorians. Commodus embraced Albinus. 'I knew you'd come to my rescue. I don't know how, but I just knew.'

'It's Sabinianus up there with the horsemen,' Albinus said. 'It seems he was a traitor after all.'

'Tell me all about it later, let's just kill him first.'

They moved through the Praetorians. Half of the survivors had dismounted and locked their shields together across the road, the remaining stayed mounted on either flank.

'You should leave now, Caesar,' Albinus said, his eyes fixed on the ridge. He judged there to be over five hundred cavalrymen up there, readying to charge.

'And miss all the fun, I don't think so.'

'Caesar, these men are about to give their lives protecting you. It's all for nothing if you stay here and die with them.'

'Then you will come with me?'

Albinus shook his head. 'No. I shall stay and command the rear guard; you don't appear to have many officers left.'

It was true, looking at the surviving Praetorians, there was only one with the crested helmet of a centurion. 'Was there a tribune?'

'There was,' Commodus said. 'Gods, how has it come to this?' He kicked out at a corpse in despair. 'Fucking senators! I swear to all the gods, when I am emperor, I shall put all my trust in freedmen. What purpose does a senate serve, anyway?'

'Exactly as we have been discussing, Caesar,' a voice said, emerging through the ranks of Praetorians. It was Cleander, and all at once, Albinus realised his biggest fear. There must have been someone in Commodus' party that knew of the ambush, and now, Albinus was sure it must have been him.

Who, after all, would stand to gain the most from the emperor of Rome turning his back on the senate? Who would be risen to a position of power? A position in which he could exploit both the emperor and the senate.

Albinus grabbed Commodus by the arm and moved him away, out of earshot. 'We spoke once, in Rome, of Cleander,' he said.

Commodus nodded. 'You think he was part of this?'

'I do. I will send a man with you to Byzantium, he will explain everything. Be careful, Caesar. You have many enemies, and I worry for your future.'

'Do you know, Centurion, you really are the very best of men. Come with me, don't stay here and die.'

'These men need a leader. I need to buy you enough time to get away. Our horses are exhausted, you won't be able to move fast. Just go, please, live.'

'It would seem the gods have determined our fate, old friend, and we shall not get to be old men together, drinking wine by the sea, watching the ships sail by,' Commodus said, a single tear glistening in his eye.

'It was just a dream, Caesar.'

'Yes. But a nice one. I do not think either of us will live to be old men, but I make you one last promise, Albinus Silus. You and I shall drink wine together once more, either in this life or the fields of Elysium. I shall never forget you, Centurion, or the lessons you have tried to teach me. Goodbye, brother.'

They clasped arms, a warrior's embrace.

'Movement on the ridge!' Fullo called.

'You there,' Albinus said, turning to the one remaining centurion in the Praetorian cohort. 'Take your century, mount up and get Caesar to Byzantium, go!'

He turned to Calvus, who was trying to get the stump of his left hand into a shield strap. 'You won't be needing that, old friend. Go with Commodus, tell him everything. See him safely back to his father, and then go and find Meredith.'

'I'll not leave you,' he said.

'You promised you would look out for my son.'

'I can't just leave you here to die.'

'Yes, you can. You are *frumentarii*, men will listen when you speak, it has to be you. Go, make it known what happened here.'

With tears streaming down his face, Calvus took one last look at the young man he had come to love as a son. 'Your father would be so proud of the man you have become,' he said. Then he turned his back and went.

'Right, lads, prepare to repel cavalry!' Albinus shouted. He felt his mind clearing, all the stress and worry of the last years fading away. He had made his choice, there was nothing left to do now but fight.

'Fullo, Bucco, on me,' he said as he pushed his way through to the front rank of Praetorians, snatching a fallen shield from the cobbles. 'We hold here. Every moment we delay them gives Caesar a better chance of escape. You hear me? We hold them here!'

The German cavalry was in full charge now, streaming down from the ridge. Albinus adjusted the grip on his shield, sweaty palms sliding on the wood. He held still the heavy Thracian blade in his right hand; he thought it would suit this battle better than a short sword. 'Anyone have a spear left?' he called.

Fullo ordered the men with missiles to the front, and they held there, awaiting the order.

The ground rumbled, the German war cry filled the air, and still, the Roman line stood silent. 'On my command,' Albinus shouted into the roaring din. 'Loose!' he called as the cavalry charge were fifty paces away.

Up went the javelins in a silent arc of death. They crashed down with a crescendo of whinnying horses and screaming men as the spearheads plunged through flesh and armour and men fell in droves. 'Back behind the shields!' Albinus called, wishing he had the time and javelins to hit them one more time.

And then, all was chaos. The horsemen rode at the Roman shield wall and engulfed it like a wave on a rock. Albinus could not give any more orders, just fight for his life. A sword slashed down at his head and bit into his helmet. He jarred at the impact and at once felt blood flow down his face. Feeling dizzy he stumbled forward, his sword snaking out and cutting a gash on a horse's flank.

Hands on his shoulders pulled him back inside the protection of the shields, and Bucco stepped in front of him. Shield raised high, he slammed his blade home into a rider's leg, twisting it before pulling free.

Fullo was at Bucco's shoulder, grappling with a man who thought to stick him with a spear. Fullo had hold of the shaft and pulled down hard, taking the rider from his saddle. As the rider struggled to his feet, Fullo released his grip on the spear and with his free hand, drove his sword into his assailant's throat. But in doing so, he had turned his back on the enemy, and Albinus could do nothing but watch in horror as a rider galloped up behind Fullo and reared his mount, the horse flailing out with its front legs, thrashing Fullo on the back of the head with a hoof.

Fullo fell and never rose again.

Albinus rushed forward in a surge of emotion. 'Fullo!' he called, standing over his friend and slashing wildly with his sword.

'Come back, Albinus!' Bucco yelled, making a fighting retreat as he held off two mounted men attacking him with swords. 'Albinus, come back!'

But Albinus was lost to the frenzy now, the battle madness had descended, and he killed and killed without conscious thought. He danced aside from a sword blow before bringing his own blade up and slashing at a man's arm. Blood flew from the wound and plastered his face, he could smell it, taste it, he didn't care. A horse bit at him, and he hit it on the nose with his sword hilt before bringing the blade round and hacking at its face. The beast screamed and moved backwards, much to the annoyance of its rider.

Albinus continued forward, losing himself in a ring of horseflesh and mail. He turned and swivelled, ducked and dived as he battled just to stay alive. Glimpsing back through the mass of men and beasts, he saw his small force was surrounded and at the top of the western slope of the valley. The pursuit of Commodus had already begun.

He screamed impotently. There was nothing to do now but die.

Fighting his way back to the last of his men, he saw nearly all the Praetorians were dead, just the allied Thracians survived. Most fought on foot now, their horses either dead or spent, and they grouped together in a tight circle, their small round shields their only protection.

'Not looking good, is it,' Bucco said. He was a mask of blood and guts, heaving in great lungfuls of air as he battled fatigue.

'Fullo's dead.'

'I know, lad, I saw him fall. I am sorry it has come to this. Your father will be ashamed of me.'

'No man ever had a better friend than you, Bucco. You should have taken your retirement, seen out your years in peace. It is I that should be sorry. It was selfish of me to bring you here.'

Bucco threw down his shield and put an arm around Albinus, grasping him tight. 'It has been an honour to serve under you, a privilege to have known you. But I will keep my promise to your father until my last breath.'

An explosion of noise brought them back to the battle. Balomar grappled a giant Germani warrior with a mane of blonde hair. 'Now I've got you,' he spat as he ran the man through with his sword.

'Guess that was Bandanasp,' Bucco said. 'Come on, lad, let's see this thing done, shall we?'

He turned and ran. Sword held high, he launched himself at the nearest foe, toppling the man over with his bulk before finishing him with a quick strike to the throat. Albinus didn't move. It seemed to him the world had slowed, the noise fading.

Raising his head to the sky, he gazed at the setting sun, a brilliant orange haze against a backdrop of purple. In his mind, he pictured the friends he had made since becoming a man and joining the legions. Taurus, Abas, Rullus, Libo, Longus, Habitus and many more, most dead now.

His had been a hard life, one of blood and iron, but not a bad one. Breathing deep, he imagined he could smell the scent of a ripened crop at harvest time and for the first time in an age, allowed himself to feel homesick. Being a farmer wouldn't have been a bad life. Growing old, having a family and going to bed each night bone-tired but content. But the gods had carved him a different path, presented him with more challenges than he ever thought he could face. But he had met them head-on, embraced the bad times as well as the good.

He thought of his son, prayed he was safe and well. He was not journeying across the river with many regrets weighing him down, but the thought of not being there for Faustus tugged at his heart. He knew Meredith would raise him well, Calvus would teach him how to be a man and remind him daily that his father loved him.

To his front, the Thracians finally gave in, and the Iazyges burst through with a victorious cry.

Albinus kept his eyes on the sky, pictured Licina's face in his mind. He smiled; he would be with her once more, they would be happy, and at peace.

He held that image until the very end.

# EPILOGUE

**April, 197 AD**
**Veterans' Colony East Of Carnuntum, Pannonia**

The wind is soft, soothing on his skin. He stands ankle deep in the fast-flowing waters of the Danube, eyes closed, face raised to the rising sun.

Two weeks he has been here now, the place his grandfather built, the place his father had once called home.

He turns to the south and looks down the gentle rise that leads to the settlement itself. From his vantage point, he can see it all. Neat rows of timber-built homes, thatched roofs above smoking hearths. A stone aqueduct runs from the river down past the mill on the settlement's southwest corner, both recently rebuilt after they were destroyed in the wars. He is told his father used to marvel at them when he was a boy.

There is peace now, though. Some say the tribes simply ran out of warriors, so many have died in the last thirty years, fighting either against or for Rome in one of the many civil wars that have ravaged the empire. But across the Roman world, there is peace on every border.

Septimius Severus is the undisputed ruler of the Roman empire, having defeated Clodius Albinus in battle outside the city of Lugdunum two months prior.

Faustus was not there to see Severus claim the ultimate prize, though he has heard men say it was the bloodiest battle Rome has ever fought, the dead countless, the wounded lined up in carts on the road from Gaul to Italy, stretching for miles.

Faustus does not care that he missed it, he saw his small share of action, that was bloody enough for him.

He scratches absently at the stitches on his head, as he does when they become unbearable. Three surgeons all told him that he was mightily lucky to be alive; if the sword had bitten a fraction of an inch deeper into his skull, his brains would have been mush. It seems the gods are not quite done with him yet.

He's had good days and bad in the months since he was wounded. Some days, he wakes in a panic, unsure of where he is or even what his name is. Others are like today, he wakes peacefully, with a complete mind, and rises to watch the dawn, grateful that he is there to witness it.

'Morning, Faustus,' a rasp of a voice says off to his right. Faustus turns slowly, not fully able to twist his neck without pain.

'Salve, Uncle,' he says as Calvus limps up the last of the slope, his good hand resting on the walking stick he has become so reliant on. 'How are you today?'

Calvus caught a fever in the harsh winter in Gaul and has not recovered. He will die soon, he knows it. Faustus knows it too, and they each try to put a brave face on the day.

'My lungs are full of phlegm, my legs are numb and my back gives me nothing but agony. But I am here, and the sun is rising,' he says in a croak. With his stumped left hand, he rubs his throat as if that simple action alone could clear it.

'You have led a wondrous life, Uncle,' Faustus says. 'I am glad you persuaded me to come here.'

Calvus sits, heedless of the morning dew that still clings to the grass and reeds. 'Not sure wondrous is the right word, lad, but it sure ain't been boring. I, too, am glad you decided to accompany me here, you know, there's nowhere else I'd rather go to God.'

'I should hope your god can wait a little longer, I have need of your services today.'

'You finally ready, are you?'

'Yes. I want to do it today, whilst I have my wits. Who knows which Faustus will rise from his cot tomorrow?'

'You know it won't last forever, don't you? I've seen men get bangs on the head before. They always recover in the end. Why, I remember one summer, Libo – a big Numidian your father and I used to serve with – getting clubbed in the head by some German or other. Weeks he was in the hospital, not a clue who he was. He was all right though, after some time.'

'Did he too have rings of metal put into his skull?' Faustus asks with more than a hint of sarcasm. It had been a Greek surgeon who had operated on Faustus, he still does not know how anyone found him on that battlefield, let alone noticed he was still alive. But someone did, and he was. His skull had been broken, splintered, bits dropping down onto his brain. The surgeon had picked them all out, sealing the small hole he left with a metal disc. His reward, once Calvus had spread the word of his achievement, had been to accompany Severus back to Rome and serve as an imperial physician.

'Aye, you had a worse knock than most. But, by God, Faustus, you are on this earth for a reason, that I am sure. Another man would have died of that wound, or gently slipped away in his sleep in the dead of the night, left on that dreadful field. But you, you were found, you survived.'

'An act of God, hey?' Faustus says through a grin. 'Just like that rainstorm that saved the Fourteenth Legion in that battle you told me of. Or the ice breaking when my father fought the Iazyges on the Danube.'

'How can you say they were not?'

'Well, apparently, my father turned the battle against the Quadi and was already drinking their water stores when the rain began, and I'm pretty sure it was, once again, my father that broke the ice on the river, not your god.'

'But God was with him.'

'Gods, this is hopeless. Come, old man, I have a visit to make, and it is long overdue.'

Faustus helps the old Briton down the incline, and they walk through the settlement. As the sun rises, it begins to come to life around them; people throw open their doors, and the livestock are let from their pens. The smell of the farming life fills his nostrils, the rich aroma of an honest living, a peaceful life. The more time he spends here, the more he appreciates its virtue.

Faustus grew up a boy who never quite knew his place in the world. He was lost in Carnuntum, going from odd job to odd job, all the while conscious of the weight of his father's ghost on his shoulders. Here, he feels that shadow has been lifted, there is no pressure to try and emulate his father, he can just be himself.

A small crowd gathers around them as they reach the settlement's centre. At the front of the crowd is a man both tall and broad. His nose is flat and wide, crushed by twenty-five years' fighting under the eagle. His back is stooped with age, but his torso is still trim and his shoulders packed with muscle.

'Today is the day,' Faustus says to him.

The stooped man nods his head. He rubs at a squinting eye with a hand the size of a lion's paw, which bears more scratches than a training post. 'Good. About time, I'd say.'

'Will you come with me, Taurus? I know you and my father were close.'

The former first spear centurion of the Fourteenth Legion stands straighter, though Faustus can see it pains his back to do so. 'Would be my honour.'

They walk south out of the settlement and across fields that will soon sway with barley; Faustus is excited to see it. He is told his father loved the farming life when he was a boy, though all he remembers of him is armour and leather. He cannot remember as much as he used to; it is with considerable effort that he can picture his face, though maybe that is enough, or maybe more memories will come back to him in time.

At the southern end of the fields is a small graveyard. There are no fine mausoleums that line the roads out of Rome, in fact, only a few of the graves have stone headstones at all, but Faustus walks to one that does.

'*Here marks the passing of Centurion Albinus Silus,*' it reads. '*A man who fought for empire, a man who died for honour.*'

'*Here marks the passing of Licina,*' the one next to it reads. '*A more magnificent lady this world has never seen.*'

'We had them commissioned a few years ago,' a voice says. 'I hope you approve.'

'They are fitting tributes, Hanno,' Faustus says to the old freedman. Hanno had grown up a slave to his grandfather, he will die a grandfather himself, a free man who had honoured his former master's passing by pledging the rest of his life to maintain what Silus had built.

'My family is deeply indebted to you, the work you have done here is incredible,' Faustus says, gesturing to the thriving farm.

'It would have been nothing without your grandfather. All I have done is carry on his vision.'

Taurus steps up, hands Faustus a bundle of cloth. 'This was your grandfather's, given to him on his retirement. It passed to your father, and now, it comes to you.'

Faustus smiles. This, he can remember. He opens the cloth, his fingers tracing the hilt of an exquisite sword. The handguard is bone, carved into the image of an eagle. He draws the blade from its leather scabbard and marvels at the swirling patterns on the iron. 'My father told me off for trying to play with this once. We were in Rome, I think.'

'It's yours now, lad. Not sure your father ever actually used it.'

'No, I don't think he did.' He grips the sword by the pommel, and lowering himself to his knees, he sends the blade plunging home, deep into the earth in front of his father's headstone. 'I have no need for this,' he says. 'I have seen enough of war for a lifetime or more. I want peace, I want what he never had,' he says, motioning to his father's grave.

Faustus stands. The wind blows from the north, and he catches the fragrance of pine needles on the air. He smiles, looking to a clutch of trees that lie to the east. He knows if he walks beneath their canopy, he will see a small wooden fort, built at the base of a tree. Its timbers are rotting now, the woodland has begun to claim what once belonged to his father. Three days prior, when he had woken with his wits fully in check, he had walked within the palisade, entered the small covered room that had been his father's pride and joy and seen a rotting blanket, covered in moss, lying strewn on the floor. He wonders if that blanket has lain there since the day this settlement was raided by the tribes over thirty years ago. He pictures his father waking, finding his love gone and rushing out into the woods to search for her.

He never came back for it. He never came back here at all.

'He would be so proud of you,' Calvus says, staggering forward and putting an arm on Faustus' shoulder. 'I know I am.'

They embrace before walking away from the group. He looks back over the fields at a scene of tranquillity, a place his father was cruelly snatched from. Breathing in deep, he once more inhales the first perfumes of spring, welcome after a long and bitter winter. He smiles to himself.

Finally, he has found a place to belong.

# HISTORICAL NOTE

It's hard to know where to begin, this book has covered so much ground. The years 172 – 175 AD proved to be critical to the reign of Marcus Aurelius. His son and heir, Commodus, was maturing into a young man as war continued along the Danube border with tribes constantly raiding and trying to gain a foothold inside Roman territory. Plague still swept through the empire, though far less aggressively than in 161 AD (where *The Centurion's Son* began).

Aurelius' greatest problems were keeping the tribes subdued and his legions at full strength, all the while with a wary eye on the dwindling coffers back in Rome. Aurelius is often described as the last of the 'Five Good Emperors' who reigned throughout Rome's golden age. Aurelius, in my belief, was a truly brilliant leader. His reign may well have been turbulent if he had allowed the plague to ruin the empire or if he hadn't travelled north himself in support of the northern legions and their ongoing battle against the Germani tribes.

Yet, he triumphed. He seems to have been respected by both the senate and army alike, a feat not easy to match as the many emperors who followed him could attest to. First among them, his son, Commodus.

I have to admit I was at a crossroads when I began plotting out this novel. Do I leave Faustus alone for now and stick with Albinus? See him through to the truly turbulent reign of a man who would be condemned to *A de facto damnatio memoriae* – condemnation of memory? By order of the senate, all statues of Commodus were to be torn down, all monuments that bore his name were to be wiped clean. For Commodus, you would assume, that fate must have been even worse than death itself.

In the end, I decided to leave the reign of Commodus alone; that is a novel or two in itself, and initially, when I first sat down and wrote the opening lines of *The Centurion's Son,* I set out to tell the story of one remarkable young man: Albinus Silus. I decided to stay true to that vision and saw his story through to the bitter end. If you want to read more of Commodus and his reign of terror, I firmly suggest you look for Anthony Riches and Simon Turney in your local bookstores. Both have books based on his reign, both are excellent.

There are, however, certain facts I felt I had to get into the pages. Commodus really did order one of his slaves be killed for making his bath too cold, and he really did travel north with his father and then east when Avidius Cassius rose in rebellion.

Commodus' two slaves, Cleander and Saoterus, are real. Unsurprisingly, both were killed after they were caught up in separate plots to bring Commodus down. Perhaps that was Commodus' greatest flaw, turning his back on the senate and putting his trust in freedmen like Cleander, who abused the power and wealth bestowed upon them. Emperors were expected to treat the senators as equals, as if they were the first man among them, rather than the son of a god. Commodus, as with many other emperors, turned away from this path, distancing himself from men who he believed resented him. Ultimately, this paranoia would be his downfall.

Other great feats in this novel that are attested to have happened are firstly, the 'miracle of the rain' in the battle against the Quadi. The Roman army had been fighting uphill all day in the blistering heat, and out of water, they were beginning to give ground. Then suddenly, the sky darkened, and great bursts of rain fell forth. It is said men even removed their helmets to catch it. Also, the 'battle on the ice' is indeed said to have taken place, with the Roman legionaries standing on their shields to get a better purchase on the frozen bed of the Danube. Albinus' involvement in it and his smashing of the ice is, of course, my fiction.

Sources are not overly clear on how Avidius Cassius managed to mount such a serious rebellion, or why he did it. It was rumoured at the time he was the lover of empress Fausta, as I have attested to in this book, though, to my knowledge, there remains no proof to back up this theory.

His rebellion could well have succeeded. He had amassed a huge army and was in the process of mobilising his forces when he was executed by one of his own centurions in Alexandria. I have made that centurion Decanus in this novel, though again, that is purely my imagination. His correspondence with senator Herodes Atticus, who was retired in Athens at the time, is true. Cassius wrote, asking him to garner support for his rebellion in Greece. Atticus really did reply, 'You are mad.' I had to sneak that in there!

Licina, I feel, deserves a small mention here, though her part in this book is brief. She became my favourite character when writing *War in the Wilderness*. Her adventures in the far reaches of the known world were great fun, and I found I learnt so much more about her as I developed her story. For those who wanted to read more about her, I apologise, but this book would have been too long. She was a formidable woman, devoted to her family but so changed by the traumas she had endured, she felt all she could do for them was die for their future. Her character is based on the greatest person I have ever met, my wife.

Faustus' story in this novel takes place after the death of Commodus and a time which would be known as 'the year of the five emperors'. Two men really did have a bidding war for the throne, and the Praetorian Guard sold it to the victor gladly. In the end, it was Septimius Severus who won. An experienced military commander, he fought off both Clodius Albinus in the west and Pescennius Niger in the east. He would form a dynasty which, when compared to the reigns of emperors after him, formed a pretty stable head of state, for a while, at least.

So, that's that then. Many other interesting facts are hidden within these pages, but if I explain them all here you'll be reading this all day!

I have loved every word of the three novels based on Albinus. Each page has been a joy to write. Three books could easily have become six or seven, but, as with all things, best to leave them wanting more, as they say.

If, as I hope, you enjoyed this story, please leave a little review on Goodreads or Amazon – you would not believe how much they contribute to a book's success. I have my next project plotted out, and already, I can't wait to share it with you!

Until the next time,

Adam Lofthouse

February, 2020